WATER HAZARD

WATER HAZARD

SCOTT BORG

Delacorte  Press

Published by
Delacorte Press
Bantam Doubleday Dell Publishing Group, Inc.
1540 Broadway
New York, New York 10036

The trademark Delacorte Press® is registered in the
U.S. Patent and Trademark Office.

Library of Congress Cataloging in Publication Data
Borg, Scott.
Water hazard : a psychological thriller / by Scott Borg.
p.   cm.
ISBN 0-385-30606-7
I. Title.
PS3552.O735W38   1995
813'.54—dc20   94-19830
                                                                       CIP

Manufactured in the United States of America
Published simultaneously in Canada

April 1995

10   9   8   7   6   5   4   3   2   1

BVG

Dedicated to
PAUL GWYN ELLIS,
Scientist, Artist,
Futurologist, Friend

C H A P T E R   1

"**H**ey, old buddy!"

The loud voice cuts through the chatter of drinkers, bringing Anderson back to the present. It is a friendly bar, with lots of university students, but Anderson is sitting alone. In front of him stands a half empty glass, a few inches from a cocktail napkin. Rings of condensation decorate the bar top beside it. Anderson has been trying to remember how to meet people in bars, how to strike up conversations with strangers. If he ever knew how, he seems to have forgotten.

"How have you been?" the voice calls.

Anderson lifts his gaze, but sees no one near him. Across the darkened room, the video machines glow weirdly, as they play out demonstration games, ignored by the drinkers.

"Boy, was I surprised to see you." The sound is from somewhere over his shoulder. Not as loud as before, but nearer, speaking directly at him.

Anderson gradually realizes there is no one else nearby the voice could be addressing. His face comes to life with a tentative smile. He has chosen this place out of loneliness, and the prospect of seeing an old acquaintance fills him with warmth. He turns to greet this person who has so kindly remembered him.

But the man Anderson sees addressing him is completely unfamiliar.

The fellow stands beneath one of the recessed ceiling lights, a glass in his left hand. He is huge and muscular, but heavily hung with fat—like a bouncer in a tougher bar than this one. His face is coarse and fleshy, but not as battered as a boxer's. Although Anderson is tall, this fellow must be half a foot taller. He wears a gray, herringbone sports jacket, but with a red T-shirt under it. A damp patch on his chest darkens the upper part of the shirt.

"You've hardly changed at all," the big man booms. "Of course, you didn't have the beard when I knew you. But otherwise, it's remarkable."

Anderson stares at the face, wondering if anyone from his past life could have altered enough to look like this. He tries to imagine finer features or a thinner figure hidden within these mounds of flesh. But the more he considers it, the less likely it seems. Anderson has never known anyone with a frame this large.

His initial feeling of warmth is replaced immediately by suspicion. Automatically, he braces himself to repulse another drunk. It has been years since Anderson's picture was in the news, but every so often a stranger will still come forward to harass him.

"You know, it's been ages," the man says, as though reading Anderson's mind.

"Yes, a long time," Anderson replies. He is used to people giving him second looks, recognizing him vaguely, even if they can't quite place the memory. But they seldom do anything about it, unless they have been drinking. Coming to this bar was obviously a mistake.

"I can't get over meeting you this way," the big man says, laughing.

As he hears the laugh, Anderson realizes that he had actually noticed the man earlier in the evening—or at least noticed the two girls who were with him. The three of them had been sharing a table and laughing loudly. Anderson had wondered how so gross a fellow could attract such lovely women.

The man hadn't seemed drunk then. Perhaps the booze has just now caught up with him. He may have remembered Anderson from newspaper photos or television coverage and gotten up to create a little scene for the amusement of his girlfriends. He could be a real problem.

Anderson's perch on top of the bar stool suddenly feels precarious. He slides off onto his feet, trying to be unobtrusive about it.

The man's upper arms look as thick as most men's thighs. "Don't tell me you've forgotten your old drinking partner," he says, his grin now more menacing than friendly.

Anderson takes a step sideways, so that the bar stool is no longer directly behind him where he might stumble against it. "Sorry, I was just lost in thought."

The big man laughs again. "Yeah, that sounds like you. Lost in thought." The familiar manner has nothing reassuring about it.

Stepping back slightly, Anderson tries to size up this possible opponent. What if things really get ugly? Would Anderson's best punch have any effect on that heavy belly? Would a blow to that massive head even change the man's expression?

Suddenly, the man's smile is gone, and he looks more serious, but less aggressive. "Hey, listen, buddy," he says, lowering his voice to a whisper, "I've got to talk to you."

Oh, it's going to be money, Anderson thinks. Sometimes they just want money. He resolves to pay the man something, to humor him, to do whatever is necessary to avoid a fight. "What can I do for you?" Anderson asks, offering his hand.

The big man takes it gently between his fingers, as though Anderson's hand belonged to a child. As he does this, he rests three fingers of his other hand on Anderson's shoulder, still holding his drink in the remaining two.

"*You* want to know what *you* can do for *me*?" he asks, loud voiced again, as though the question amuses him. He is pressing forward now, invading Anderson's personal space, backing him along the bar.

Anderson looks around for possible allies, but no one is paying any attention. He tries to spot something he could use as a weapon. A whiskey bottle, perhaps. But the counter behind the bar is lined only with little bottles of beer and mineral water. Even those are out of reach.

"Listen, buddy," the man says, dropping his voice again. "I've seen you staring at the two broads I'm with."

"I'm sorry," Anderson says slowly, "I didn't mean to." He tries to keep any apology out of his voice. It will do him no good to seem weak.

The big man nods, once more giving Anderson his strange grin. His voice is intimate. "I bet you'd like to meet them. Go off with one alone. Have a little fun."

Backing away, Anderson raises his hand in a gesture of peace. "I'll just finish my drink and leave," he says.

"No, you don't understand me." The man is still smiling, but more earnest now, eager to make things clear. "Two of these college girls is one too many for me tonight. I thought you might want to share them with me."

Anderson is slow to take it in. "Well, that's nice of you, but—"

The man goes right on, talking faster now, but still confidentially. "I just met them a little while ago myself. Couldn't figure out how to get one of them alone. Until I saw you standing there. Told them you were my old friend from—well, I guess I implied —from college. But it could have been from somewhere else."

Anderson has got to say it now. "I'm sorry. I'm afraid I don't remember you."

But the big man doesn't miss a beat. "Of course you don't. We've never met before. My name is Brian. What's yours?"

"Anderson."

The man holds up his hands, palms forward. "Don't need a last name." He shrugs. "Hell, don't need a first name either. I'll just say you're 'Andy.' Did you ever go to college?"

"For a while."

"Okay, then I met you at college. What do you say? Ready for some action?"

"I don't think—"

"Tell you what I'll do, I'll let you take your pick. What could be fairer than that? You just pair up with the broad you like best." He pauses, eyes sparkling. "And leave the other one to me."

Anderson is relieved. At least this is better than having some drunk accusing him of murder. "Maybe another time," he says.

"Hey, what time's as good as the present?"

"I appreciate your offer, but not tonight, okay?" Anderson realizes there was a time, years before, when he would not have been so hesitant.

The big man gives him an impatient look. "I already *told* them you're an old buddy of mine."

"I'm sorry. Tell them it was a mistake. Tell them I just *look* like your old buddy."

"And have them think I'm too drunk to get it up? Come on! They might lose interest."

In the background, Anderson hears a country dance tune. Someone must have fed the electronic jukebox.

"You could try your idea on someone else," Anderson suggests. "I'm sure one of those guys over there would be happy to play your long lost pal." He gestures over his shoulder at the other Scandinavian and German types lining the bar.

But the man called Brian is not interested. "I already pointed you out to the girls. You don't want to disappoint them, do you?"

"It couldn't be *that* much of a disappointment."

"More than you might think." He grins again. "The girls were the ones who noticed you. They said you were cute. I said, 'What a coincidence! That's my old buddy!' I'm telling you, these girls are already wet for you!"

Anderson winces at the expression, but still feels flattered. He turns to give the girls a longer inspection. They are strikingly attractive, in a young, wholesome looking way. Both of them have light brown hair, turned blond by the summer sun. Their tank tops and cut-off jeans reveal wonderful bodies, which they are obviously displaying with pride. One of them has high, full breasts which seem to spread sideways, wider than her rib cage. The other has remarkable legs with a perfect satiny tan.

Anderson remembers noticing these two in the bar on a couple of previous visits, but never having the nerve to speak to them. Now they've turned to look at him. The one with the wide breasts flashes him a heart melting smile. Anderson feels his loneliness like a physical hunger.

"What have you got to lose?" the big man coaxes. "Just let me introduce you. If you don't like the way things are going, you can always make some excuse and leave."

Anderson shakes his head apologetically. "I'm afraid you've got the wrong fellow. I'm not good at this sort of thing."

"What's there to be good at? You sit down. You have a drink. You let me do the talking. It'll be easy!"

Anderson gazes across the barroom tables. "Those girls are awfully pretty," he admits.

"Even prettier up close," the man assures him. "Come on,

take a closer look. Let me buy you a drink while you make up your mind."

Anderson hesitates a moment longer, then smiles. "All right, I guess I can't refuse that much."

He picks up his half finished drink and lets the man usher him around the other drinkers and past a series of large square pillars covered with advertisements for beer. A mechanical wilderness scene with a constantly falling waterfall. An enormous plastic moose head. Beer logos spelled out in neon tubing or printed on mirrors.

Between the letters on one of the mirrors, Anderson catches a glimpse of his own reflection. His beard looks scruffy, but at least it's freshly washed. He pokes furtively at his tangled hair, trying to coax it into a more flattering shape. He hopes the girls will find him as acceptable up close as they did from a distance.

Turning back toward the girls, he sees them watching him and already feels embarrassed. The one with the remarkable bosom whispers something to her companion that makes them both laugh, but in a friendly, welcoming way. They really are gorgeous, Anderson decides. His heart is literally beating faster. God, just like a kid.

When they reach the table, he looks around helplessly. But the big man is ready to take charge of the situation.

"Here he is, girls—my old buddy—Andy!"

The awesome scale of the man makes the announcement seem dramatic. "Andy, this is Trudy," he continues, gesturing toward the girl with the long, satiny legs.

"Pleased to meet you," Anderson says, already feeling awkward.

"Hi," Trudy replies, extending her hand, as though bestowing a little gift. Anderson grasps it for a moment without quite shaking it.

"And this is Gretchen," the man says, indicating the girl with the large, wide breasts. "What a pair, huh?" Gretchen tilts her head, and Trudy giggles. "Hey, don't look at me that way! I meant what a pair of lovely ladies!"

"Hi," Gretchen says, cheerfully unruffled.

Anderson tells himself that if these girls aren't bothered by the man's lack of manners, then he shouldn't be. "How do you do," he says, as evenly as he can. Gretchen's hand is cold and wet from the drink she's been holding, but her grip is firm.

The big man beams at them. "Trudy and Gretchen are students at the university. Liberal arts types. Not jocks like you and me." He sits down at the small, square table, indicating that Anderson should take the chair opposite him. Beside the slender bodies of the college girls, the man looks even more immense.

"Were you a football player, too?" Trudy asks Anderson.

"Andy here is a swimming champion," the man called Brian answers. "He has a collection of trophies like you wouldn't believe."

Anderson is taken aback. This Brian is pretty sharp. He must have guessed Anderson was a swimmer from his broad shoulders and lean build. Of course, he doesn't have it exactly right. Anderson spent more time as a lifeguard than as a competitive swimmer. And when he did compete, he was never a star. But he does have a couple of trophies in a closet somewhere.

"Oh, wow, a swimmer!" says Gretchen.

"I've always wanted to meet a swimmer," says Trudy.

Anderson can't decide if they are making fun of him or not. He tries to look enigmatic, raising his eyebrows slightly.

"What do you all want for the next round?" the big man asks. "I want to raise a toast to old college days."

"Another light beer would be great," Gretchen answers.

"For me too," Trudy agrees.

But the man called Brian is shaking his head. "No, no. This occasion calls for something more than beer." Then he snaps his fingers. "Hey, I've just thought of the perfect drink." His broad grin makes him look like a jack-o'-lantern. "I bet Andy here knows what I've got in mind."

"Not really," Anderson says. Apart from his obvious designs on the girls, Anderson has no idea what the man is talking about.

"Sure you do," Brian insists.

"Uh-oh, dark secrets from the past," Trudy murmurs.

"Mysterious male lore," Gretchen adds.

"Hey, you know what I mean," he says, looking at Anderson. "That drink you invented. The one you called a 'Minnehaha.'"

"Oh, yeah, that," Anderson says, trying to play along.

"What did I tell you?" Gretchen says.

The big man turns to the girls. "I'm going to have the bartender mix us a 'Minnehaha.' Wait until you try it! Andy invented it for occasions like this. Isn't that right, Andy?"

"I guess that's right," Anderson says, trying to put some enthusiasm into his voice.

"You girls are going to love it," Brian assures them.

"How will the bartender know what you're talking about?" Gretchen asks.

"Is this drink that famous?" Trudy adds.

The man stands up with the swagger of a sailor. "I'm going to give the bartender the recipe and supervise the mixing myself." He glides off, humming a little tune.

With the big man gone, there's a moment of silence, while Anderson looks uncomfortable and the girls look amused.

"Before you joined us, we were discussing sexism," Trudy announces, her face straight, but a gleam of mischief in her eyes.

"Most men are irredeemably sexist," Gretchen says, sighing theatrically.

"Are you sexist, Andy?" Trudy asks.

"I don't think so," Anderson answers, struggling to find an appropriate reply. "I mean, not especially."

"He doesn't think he's sexist," Trudy says to Gretchen. "Do you think he's sexist, Gretchen?"

"Oh, he's sexist, all right. I saw him getting a look at your legs as he came up to the table. He was treating you as a regular sex object."

"It was *your* top he was trying to look down. If that isn't sexist, I don't know what is." Trudy puts her nose in the air. "Of course, girls like you just encourage these sexist types."

"*You* should talk!" Gretchen responds, with mock indignation. "You're the one who isn't wearing a bra!"

Trudy lifts her arms and stretches her shoulders. "Bras are just male inventions for restricting our freedom."

"What do you think of that, Andy? Do you think Trudy's freer, because she doesn't wear a bra?"

"I wouldn't know," Anderson says, still off balance.

"Now you've embarrassed him," Trudy says.

"Have I? Have I embarrassed you, Andy?" Gretchen asks, as though terribly concerned.

"Andy doesn't know where to look," Trudy says, all innocent sympathy.

"It's her top, though, isn't it?" Gretchen asks. "Not enough material to really be decent."

"It must be a such trial to have women dress this way," Trudy muses. "I'll have to remember to be more considerate."

Somewhere in the background, the music switches to a piece where the melody is carried by an acoustic bass.

"Do you find my clothes provocative, Andy? I've been worried I made my cut-offs too short. It's because my legs aren't as long as Trudy's, you see." Gretchen stands up beside the table and rises on tiptoe. The frayed edge of the denim is higher at the outsides of her legs than at her crotch. "What do you think?"

"That's okay, Andy. You don't have to answer." Trudy puts her hand consolingly on his thigh. "Gretchen just wants you to stare at her—"

"Tru-dy!" Gretchen sits down again. She puts her hand on Anderson's arm. "Don't pay any attention to her, Andy. She's been drinking."

"Is this stuff alcoholic? It doesn't taste alcoholic." Trudy looks at the glass of beer she is holding in her other hand.

"Trudy's got a point. If it were alcoholic, she wouldn't still have her clothes on."

"Gretchen, not so loud!" Trudy says in a loud whisper. "People are looking at us."

"That's never stopped you before," Gretchen comments. She looks sideways at Anderson, her eyes playful. "Trudy finds a crowd of people really turns her on. Sort of inspires her—you know—to take things off."

"She's just joking, Andy."

"What about that role you played in *Bus Stop*?" Gretchen accuses.

"I hardly took off anything!"

"You didn't have much on *to* take off." As Gretchen leans forward to make her point, she hunches her shoulders, revealing more of her own sizable bosom.

From this close, Anderson can see that Gretchen's tanned skin is covered with a fine down of pale blond hairs. It gives a golden sheen to the curves of her neck and breasts. Does she know what she is doing to him? He swallows and tries to act calm.

The two girls stare at each other for a moment with narrowed eyes, then laugh. Trudy leans confidentially toward him, adopting a British accent. "Gretchen's so envious, because I'm in the theater, while she has to spend her time with pots."

"Not just pots," Gretchen says with a smile.

"Well, *you* know what I mean. Pots, bowls, jars, the occasional kettle."

Grateful for a safer sounding subject, Anderson turns eagerly to Gretchen. "Are you a home economics major?"

"I'm an archaeologist," Gretchen replies. "I study ancient Mesoamerican peoples."

"Her pots are mostly old and broken," Trudy adds helpfully.

Anderson feels foolish. "You don't look like an archaeologist," he says, trying to recover.

"What do I look like, then?" Gretchen asks.

"I don't know. I guess you both look like actresses," Anderson says. "Or models, or something."

"I told you he's sexist," Gretchen says.

"Still," Trudy concedes, "he *is* kind of cute. Do you suppose that beard would tickle?"

"I don't know about the beard," Gretchen says, shaking her head, "but his shoulders look promising."

"Now, girls, control yourselves. You can peel his clothes off later." The voice comes from overhead.

It's 'Brian,' returning with the drinks. He displays them proudly on a little tray. "I bring you Andy's magic potion." The drinks are dark green in color and served in short glasses. One by one, he lifts them off the tray and puts them down at each place.

"They do look pretty wicked," Gretchen concedes.

"Are these things really strong?" Trudy asks.

"Why do you suppose Andy called it a 'Minnehaha'?" Brian asks in reply.

"Because it's a little laugh?" Trudy suggests.

"Because having to read Longfellow in freshman English drove him to drink," Gretchen says.

"Because drinking one is like going over a waterfall!" Trudy exclaims.

"Hey, you two are pretty smart," Brian acknowledges. "Those are the very reasons Andy once told me. Isn't that right, Andy?"

"Absolutely," Anderson says.

The big man holds his glass up to the light. The liquid is so cloudy, it's almost opaque. "Here's to old college friends," he says, "and to new college friends!"

"Hear, hear," the others chorus, "I'll drink to that! Right on!"

The girls taste their drinks and make faces. After one sip, Anderson, too, has all he can do to avoid puckering his mouth. The 'Minnehaha' seems to combine crème de menthe, lime juice, bitters, crème de café, and God knows what else, with a base of pure ethyl alcohol. The glass has been chilled, but the drink has no ice in it. The girls look at Anderson as though he is crazy. Anderson looks at Brian, wondering if this is supposed to be a joke. But the big man smiles calmly, still holding his glass aloft.

"Tastes terrible, if you just sip it," he explains. "You've got to knock it back. Otherwise it won't get to the right parts of the palate."

"*Now* he tells us," Gretchen complains.

"Here, I'll demonstrate the proper way to drink it." Brian places the drink directly in front of him, carefully centering it. He pulls back his jacket sleeves, revealing the beginnings of over-sized forearms. He takes a deep breath, lifts the glass to his lips, and, tossing his head back, downs the drink in one draught.

The girls clap, and they all turn expectantly to Anderson. It's a challenge Anderson realizes he cannot, at this point, refuse.

He centers his glass on the table, just as the big man had done. If he is actually going to drink this concoction, he may as well go through the whole ritual. He slides back his sleeves, pats at his beard, and finally picks up the glass. Taking a deep breath, Anderson tosses it back.

The big man is right: the drink doesn't taste so awful this way. But Anderson can't imagine drinking one for pleasure.

As he puts down the glass, the girls provide another round of applause. Anderson and the man called Brian now look expectantly at them.

"You've *got* to be kidding," says Trudy.

"Oh, no," says Gretchen, "I can't drink anything that fast."

"I hope you won't be offended, Andy," Trudy says apologetically. "I'm sure it's a really great drink. It's just"—she begins to break up with laughter—"it's just"—she is convulsed—"that these are my own teeth—and I'm not ready to dissolve them yet."

"Don't get us wrong, fellas," Gretchen says between giggles. "We're genuinely impressed. That was really macho. Downing those the way you did."

It's a moment before the girls can get themselves under control.

"I guess there are some things only men can do," Trudy says, more flirtatiously than sarcastically. "We could never do anything like that, could we, Gretchen?"

"Oh, I'm still considering it," Gretchen replies. "Maybe I just need another drink first. To get my courage up."

"I could use a chaser myself," Anderson says. "How about if I get another round of beers?"

"Light beers," Trudy specifies. "Some of us have got to watch our figures."

"Hey, I'll help you watch your figure," the big man offers. He leans to the side, so he can run his eyes down the whole length of Trudy's body. Then he looks over at Anderson, as though appraising his condition. "Sure, light beer, why not?"

Anderson scans the room for a waiter, wondering if he should get up and go over to the bar. The scene around him is no busier than it was earlier, but it seems more confused. Anderson has difficulty focusing on the people playing pool or working the self-serve popcorn machine. In particular, he has trouble distinguishing the waiters from the customers. The 'Minnehaha' must be affecting him more than he'd expected.

Finally, someone with a tray and towel looks his way. "Light beers," Anderson mouths silently, moving his finger in a circle to indicate a round. The waiter nods.

His immediate task accomplished, Anderson turns his attention back to the conversation. But now he has difficulty separating the words from the background noise. Gradually, he becomes aware that Brian is telling the girls about some prank Anderson had supposedly pulled while working as a lifeguard.

"And then," the big man is saying, "when everybody's expecting the swim meet official to make his announcement, out walks this penguin."

The girls laugh and give Anderson admiring looks. Despite their aggressive teasing, he decides they really are terribly nice. He smiles and shakes his head at Brian's story, trying to look modest, without committing himself to the story's veracity.

Odd, Anderson thinks, that the story should make him out to be a lifeguard. He can't remember telling Brian anything about that. Of course, identifying Anderson as a former lifeguard is just a step beyond identifying him as a swimmer. But the big man still seems surprisingly perceptive.

"Do you play lots of practical jokes?" Trudy asks. There is something very sexy in the way she asks a question, lifting her chin, parting her lips, showing her front teeth.

Anderson realizes he is the one Trudy is staring at so expectantly. What was the question? Oh, yes, does he play practical jokes? "Only occasionally, when things get too dull," Anderson answers. He is relieved to hear his tongue doesn't sound as thick as it feels.

"That trick with the penguin was awfully ingenious," Gretchen says.

"If you think that was ingenious," the big man tells her, "you should hear about the stunt he pulled with a fire hydrant."

Anderson is aware that both girls are looking at him, expecting another story. He tries to change the subject. "I'm a little embarrassed about that one, Brian." Anderson hopes the man will take the hint and lay off.

"Hey, it was one of your greatest triumphs!" the man insists. "I'm sure Gretchen and Trudy would love to hear about it."

Anderson doesn't know what to say. He has never played a practical joke. Why is this Brian suddenly making things so difficult?

"Come on, Andy, tell us," Gretchen urges, putting her hand on his leg the way Trudy had done earlier.

"Yes, Andy, I want to hear all about it," Trudy adds. She reaches for his other leg, as though not to be outdone by her friend.

Between the effects of the drink and the physical contacts,

Anderson is losing the thread of the conversation. The confusion he had felt earlier as he looked around the room is now encroaching on their little group. Anderson feels he needs someone to help him. Someone who would understand. Yes, someone like Gretchen.

"Andy's just modest," the big man explains. "He's pulled some really amazing stunts. Things hardly anyone would dare try."

"Not really," Anderson says, hearing the first signs of slurring in his own voice.

"See, what did I tell you?!" Brian exclaims. "Such a modest guy."

"It sounds as though Andy's led a pretty interesting life," Trudy says.

"Oh, he has, he has!" the big man exclaims. "Of course, he has more time for it than the rest of us. Andy doesn't have to work for a living."

"Don't tell me he's rich too," Gretchen remarks. She looks wryly at Anderson, as though this were the best joke yet. "Are you rich, Andy?"

"Well, not exactly rich," the man answers for him. "But he does have this little inheritance from his grandfather that sort of takes care of things."

Anderson is startled. This is something he would never have talked about. How does Brian know about his grandfather? Something is very wrong here.

"That's not right," Anderson says, his words now noticeably slurred.

"Are you feeling okay, Andy?" Gretchen asks gently, putting the back of her cool fingers to his forehead.

"What's the matter, Andy?" the big man asks.

His confusion growing, Anderson struggles to puzzle it out. "What's the matter, Andy?" Anderson repeats. Oh, yes, the inheritance from Grandfather. The big man has just mentioned it. He shouldn't be mentioning it. But why not? Oh, yes, a delicate subject. We must keep quiet about it. But why keep quiet? Hell, why do anything?! Oh, yes. Gretchen. That's it. Gretchen might not understand. Trudy is awfully sexy, but Gretchen is even sexier. Gretchen is his one true love.

The man called Brian reaches over to steady him. "Looks as though he's had a bit too much to drink." With one hand still on Anderson's arm, the big man stands up. "I better get him outside for some fresh air."

"Thanks," Anderson manages to say. His whole mouth is now entirely numb. "I could use some air." Can anyone understand what he's saying?

"Come on, old buddy," the man says, helping Anderson to his feet.

As he tries to stand, Anderson loses his sense of balance. His head is swimming. He grabs the table's edge for support. For a moment, he stands there, slightly swaying. Then, taking a deep breath, he manages to revive. With Brian's hand guiding him, he turns toward the exit. His first two steps are so wobbly, he seems in danger of falling. But the big man catches him and holds him upright.

Once more, Anderson feels grateful for the unexpected kindness of this man. He seems to be the old friend he was pretending to be. Anderson feels lucky to have met him. Especially on a night like this, when walking is so difficult! The idea strikes Anderson as funny, and he chuckles to himself. Does the big man understand how funny it is that Anderson can hardly walk? 'Probably,' Anderson decides. After all, the man is awfully understanding.

But how does Brian know these things about Anderson that Anderson hasn't told him? Anderson is still troubled by this. He resolves to ask him about it as soon as he can talk better.

Meanwhile, with a hefty arm around Anderson's torso, the big man is ushering him toward the door. Anderson is surprised to notice that Brian smells more of good cologne than of sweat and beer. The man's hip pushes against Anderson's side, levering him upward. Anderson remembers this sensation from his childhood when a grown-up danced with him. His feet touch the floor and go through the motions of walking, but they carry no weight.

He marvels at the ease with which Brian manages to avoid the tables. People can see that Anderson is being helped along and stand aside, most of them looking amused or sympathetic, a few looking disgusted. Brian keeps murmuring little explanations about his friend having had one drink too many.

Finally, the big man pushes open the front door of the bar and maneuvers Anderson out into the open air. It is a humid night, unusually warm for late September, but Anderson finds it reviving. "I feel better now," he says, but realizes his words are still too slurred to be intelligible. Brian continues moving them along the sidewalk in front of the bar.

Anderson tries to halt their progress by stretching out his legs and gently freeing himself from the big man's grasp. But this only causes the man to tighten his hold. Believing his movements are simply being misunderstood, Anderson makes a firmer effort to separate himself from his protector. This time he meets with stronger resistance.

Suddenly, Anderson realizes he is being forcibly constrained. The man's grip, just below Anderson's rib cage, is rough and painful. His other hand twists Anderson's wrist until it hurts, even through the numbness. Anderson tries to struggle free, but his muscles won't respond. This feels nothing like previous occasions when he had drunk too much. It is more like trying to awaken from a deep sleep.

Then the explanation hits him. He has been drugged. Some narcotic is doing this to him, not alcohol. This Brian must have put something in his drink.

Anderson feels shocked, then bewildered. How could Brian do this?! Why would he want Anderson drugged?!

By this time, the two of them are in the parking lot alongside the bar. There are some other people back near the bar's entrance, but no one here among the parked cars. Brian is trying to push Anderson toward a nearby station wagon.

Anderson tries to shout that he doesn't want to go, but the words come out all garbled.

The big man makes a noise imitating Anderson's. "Oh, Andy, Andy," he says mockingly, "how many times do I have to tell you? If you can't hold your liquor, you shouldn't drink."

To the bystanders, they must look like drunken pals.

As they approach the station wagon, Brian begins singing "Waltzing Matilda," but with nonsense syllables substituted for the words. He is now dragging Anderson along, with no further pretense of helping him.

They stop near the back of the vehicle, and Anderson crumples to the ground. Brian holds him down with one hand, while he uses the other to unlatch the station wagon's rear door.

Pressed against the blacktop, Anderson realizes one of his legs is bent beneath him. While the man is pulling the door open, Anderson gets the leg firmly planted under his body. Then, just as Brian is changing his grip, Anderson makes a mighty effort to push himself free. He comes off the ground with surprising force. The back of his head knocks Brian's jaw.

For a few seconds, Anderson is loose and running free. But his struggle is now with the drug. His legs feel stiff, heavy, and too short for the steps he needs to take. His whole body feels muffled by upholstery. The few moments of renewed clarity Anderson had gained when he had hit the fresh air are now leaving him.

Anderson begins to stumble forward just as Brian catches up to him, pushing him hard from behind. Anderson goes down, protecting his face with his arms, but hitting the ground with his chest. The air goes out of him, and he almost blacks out. Brian stands over him, breathing heavily, then kicks him in the side.

With no resistance left in him, Anderson is dimly aware of being picked up, carried back across the parking lot, and thrown into the back of the station wagon. His shin bangs against the side of the car as he is pushed in, but he feels little pain. Anderson tries to maintain a coherent picture of what's going on. But the back section of the vehicle, the inside of the door, the long glass windows—it all seems wavy. As though everything were painted on water.

And then someone begins to stir the water. The colored surfaces and textures are pulled apart, distorting and twisting as they swirl in different directions. Only Anderson's sense of being trapped remains. Nothing around him seems solid, yet he cannot seem to break free.

As he loses consciousness, Anderson's last realization is that he has been kidnapped.

Anderson is aware of being unconscious. It is like a dream in which he knows he is dreaming. He has some control over his mind, but cannot rouse himself. Things drift by hazily. He makes an effort to move, but his body remains immobile. He concentrates on his eyelids, trying to open them. But nothing happens. He cannot tell if it's because his body is paralyzed, or because his mind is not giving his eyelids the proper signal.

Somewhere there is a sliding, clicking sound. Anderson cannot tell where it's coming from. He feels curiously detached, not just from outside reality, but from the different parts of his own body. It's as though the connections within his nervous system were themselves partly dissolved. He must make an effort merely to communicate with himself. He keeps losing the thread of his own thoughts. Yet he can still think, can still receive a few sensations from the outside world.

Anderson tries to grab hold of these. He is like a drowning man groping for something to cling to. The sliding, clicking sounds are like objects floating on the surface of water. Anderson needs to use them to pull himself back into consciousness. But as he reaches for the sensations, they keep breaking up. He tries to hold them together, to concentrate on them, to memorize them. They are his lifeline. But each time he is about to capture them, they slip away.

Stretching, reaching, unwilling to give up, Anderson finally manages to get ahold of something. It's a tenuous hold, liable to dissolve at any moment. But there is definitely a connection there to something real. Slowly, carefully, he draws on the connection, holding it tightly, as though swimming upward along it.

For a moment, his face breaks the surface of consciousness.

His eyes are still closed, but he can hear something in the air. As he presses forward, that last bit, he can even feel something brushing his face.

The sound he hears is strangely mundane. Anderson struggles to put a label to it. Then it comes to him. It is the noise of a scissors. There is also a gentle tugging at his beard, but Anderson is still unable to open his eyes. The sensations seem thin, delicate, weblike.

Then there is a whushing noise and the lime smell of shaving cream. Anderson feels the cool, astringent foam being spread across his cheeks. A few moments later, he feels the sensation of a razor being drawn across his whiskers. Anderson has an overwhelming sense of nostalgia. He remembers the time when he used to shave, the time, in fact, when he had first begun to shave. He senses that what is happening to him now is somehow connected to what had happened to him then.

There had always been something makeshift about Anderson's childhood. His parents had separated shortly after his birth, and his mother had moved back in with Anderson's grandfather. She had intended to start a career and move on, but never seemed to get around to it. With a child to raise, she had plenty to keep her busy. It was easy for her to postpone doing anything else, because there was always enough money for the things they really needed. Her one way of clinging to her ambitions was to refuse ever entirely to unpack. For years, half their possessions were stored in cardboard boxes, stacked in the corners of their rooms.

Although Anderson had never really known his father, he had dreamed frequently of his father coming back and taking them off to some warmer place. Somewhere far from the bitter cold of the Minnesota winters. Somewhere where his parents and he could be a family again. Although he knew it was silly, he couldn't help thinking it was his fault his father had left. He thought that if he were very good, if he did everything right, his father would return.

Then one day his mother told him his father had died of a liver disease. It had actually happened several weeks earlier, but the news had only just reached them. As Anderson watched the tears running down his mother's face, he realized that they would probably never leave his grandfather.

Later, when Anderson's mother had fallen ill and been moved to a hospital, it had seemed natural for Anderson to stay on with the old man. The two of them went to the hospital together five or six times a week. Sometimes they would stop on the way to pick out flowers or paperback books. But they never became close. At most, they seemed to reach a kind of implicit agreement not to expect too much of each other.

Even this understanding soon became strained. As Anderson's mother faded, the boy wanted to buy her presents that were more and more expensive. It was as if the very extravagance of the gifts would show her how much he loved her and help keep her with him awhile longer. But his grandfather said the gifts would be wasted. Anderson's mother could no longer recognize her own son or father, let alone what they brought her. Anderson knew his grandfather was right, but found it hard not to hate him for it.

When Anderson's mother finally died, his grandfather became his legal guardian. The old man was always conscientious in caring for Anderson's material needs, but he never treated the boy with much warmth. This was hard on Anderson, who would sometimes weep in the night for the parents he was already beginning to forget. There were compensations, however. While other teenagers were struggling to claim their own identities, Anderson was allowed a great deal of independence. His grandfather only required that he do his chores and 'stay out of trouble.'

The high school swim team gradually came to serve as a second family for Anderson. It provided personal relationships he could take for granted. More than that, it became a forum for proving his manhood. Anderson especially enjoyed the trips out of town, when the swimmers got to compete with schools farther away. Those were the first times he got to stay in motels and explore strange places, the first times he met girls who were not somebody's sisters or classmates. In a sense, the trips were his coming of age. It was on the swim team trips that Anderson learned to shave.

As Anderson teeters on the edge of these adolescent memories, the sensation of the razor stops. Anderson feels his cheeks being wiped with a warm, damp cloth. He feels the air, now icy cold on his beardless face. After a few moments, he feels his body being shifted. He realizes he is lying on a blanket or large cloth and that the cloth is being tugged this way and that. Then he hears a car door slam and the engine starting up.

Soon, Anderson feels the muffled vibrations of a car cruising along at high speed. There is little jostling from side to side and little variety in the sounds. The highway is evidently straight and flat, with no large bridges, no river valleys, and no rolling hills. Anderson is vaguely aware that, since they started in the Twin Cities, they must be heading north. It is roughly the route he used to take to his grandfather's cottage in northern Minnesota.

At first the cottage had been merely a summer home. Then, when Anderson's grandfather had retired, the old man had sold his house in the Twin Cities and begun living year round at the lake. Anderson had no alternative but to go with him. For a while, the north woods had seemed a lonely place for a teenager. But gradually, Anderson had begun to enjoy the outdoor work and the water sports. As long as he checked in with his grandfather first, he could do pretty much what he pleased.

"I'm taking the boat across to Stauffer's Landing, okay?"

"Have you done all your chores?" the old man would ask. "I don't want you fooling around on the lake with your chores unfinished."

"Everything is done, Grandpa."

"What about the dock? It should have been put in weeks ago."

"It's all finished. I laid the last section of planking this morning."

"Well, it's about time! Now what we need is to get more sand dumped on the beach."

"I'll ask Stauffer about it, when I'm over there."

There was a certain satisfaction in handling the practical jobs his grandfather expected of him. In the years since, Anderson has often wished the other problems he has faced were as easy.

The car stops, the engine is switched off, and a door is opened. Once again, Anderson has the sensation of cold air blowing gently across his clean-shaven face. He smells the sharp fragrance of pine trees and hears the gentle crunching of needles underfoot. Like the smell and sounds of the forest around his grandfather's lake home.

Then he hears a woman's voice, calling out, quietly. Eager, but cautious. After a few moments, a male voice replies. Not the voice of the big man from the bar, but another one, new to Anderson. The woman laughs nervously. Then she quiets as the man reassures her, goes to her, embraces her. Anderson seems to be eavesdropping on a nighttime rendezvous. He recognizes the sounds from years earlier when he had been a participant.

With great fondness, Anderson remembers the girls he used to meet at his grandfather's place in the summertime. They were mostly teenagers who came up to the lake resorts on vacation with their families. After a few days of squabbling with siblings, sharing in family picnics, and riding boats around the lake, they would be going crazy with boredom. Anderson would see them in the game room at the big lodge or near the gas pumps dockside, where the motorboats came to refuel. The girls would wear two-piece swimsuits, but with loose shirts modestly covering them. Since he was still a teenager himself, every detail was part of the adventure. With elaborate casualness, he would ask the girls if they wanted to meet him later in the evening.

On nights when the mosquitoes weren't too bad, they would go walking along the shore and out on the docks. On other nights, they would roam the big screen porches that ran along the lake side of the resort buildings. Anderson would stop with his arm around the girls and gaze out across the lake. His fingertips would reach under their cut-off jeans.

"What are you doing?" the girls would ask, as though it had never happened before.

"Feeling you up," he would whisper with a smile, so that they knew it was definitely happening.

"Ooh, you have wicked fingers," one particularly forward girl said. She had pretty wicked fingers herself, so she must have known what she was talking about. At the time, it had seemed daring, but now, looking back, it was a period of blissful innocence.

Again, Anderson hears a woman laughing, this time with a kind of hysterical gaiety. Anderson hears the man's voice saying to "stop that." It sounds startlingly loud after what has come before, a voice rebuking all frivolity, a voice implying business must be attended to.

The tone of the voice reminds him of the time his grandfather had caught him with a girl and scolded him for it. The force of the old man's wrath had shaken them both.

"If you don't mend your ways," his grandfather had threatened, "you'll end up exactly like your father. You'll get some girl pregnant before you're ready to handle it, then run off and leave her. You'll carry so much guilt, you'll probably drink yourself to death. Is that what you want to do with your life?"

"No, Grandpa."

"Ruin yourself and some poor girl? Before you've even grown up? Because you can't control yourself?"

"I won't do that, Grandpa."

"That's what your father did. You look enough like him. You want to act like him too? Well, you just go right on doing what you're doing. You'll see." His grandfather had stormed off toward the cottage, his words ringing in Anderson's ears.

Somewhere, a door slams. The man's voice fades away. Footsteps approach. Anderson feels the cloth beneath him stretch tight and begin to move. For a moment or two, he is swung over space, as though in a hammock. Then he is lowered to the ground and dragged along it. He feels his body bumping over small obstructions—rocks and sticks, small bushes, protruding roots. He is cushioned slightly by the cloth, but feels the blows all the same.

He begins to struggle with the memories, trying to stop them from coming. But each time he relaxes, they start seeping through. He remembers snatches of conversations with his grandfather, misunderstandings that were never cleared up, bits of unfinished business from a relationship broken off unexpectedly. Most of these memories are too fleeting to trouble him. But they are like a reservoir, threatening to overwhelm him if the dam should ever break.

Finally, the cloth transporting Anderson comes to rest. But he feels himself rocking in the stillness, as though the sensations of the last few minutes were still hitting him. He sprawls there, dizzy from the movement, tilting inside, to and fro, as though swept by waves. He hears the quieter sound of lapping water. He must be near the shore of a lake. The small waves are not breaking, but simply slapping a little water over the stones and wooden dock supports. It would normally be a gentle, soothing sound, but Anderson feels more anxious than reassured. He remembers how his grandfather insisted on swimming every morning, beginning early in the spring, regardless of the weather.

After Anderson was in college, he had challenged his grandfather about this practice. It seemed crazy to subject an aging body to the rigors of icy water.

"Are you sure you should still be doing that?" he asked.

"Doing what?"

"Going swimming so early in the morning. You know, when the water's still so cold."

"Why shouldn't I?" his grandfather asked, belligerently. "Been doing it all my life."

"Yeah, but what about your heart condition?" Anderson asked gently.

"What about it?"

"I just thought the shock of the freezing water might put a strain on your circulatory system."

"Nonsense. These swims are what keep me fit. Anyway, the water's not freezing. It only seems that way to you, because you've been spoiled by all those heated pools."

"You're not as young as you used to be. You should take it easier."

"I'll take it easier when I'm good and ready."

The old man's tone seemed to allow no further argument. For years afterward, Anderson wondered if he could have handled the conversation differently, if he should have been more persistent, if anything he could have said would have changed the way things turned out.

Still struggling with the burden of the past, Anderson hears a low voice issuing instructions. He strains to make out the meaning, trying to get it right. He feels as though someone's life depends on it. Perhaps his own. But the words are muffled, and Anderson is unsure whether he could trust their meaning anyway.

He remembers how his grandfather had given him instructions on what to do in case he *did* have a heart attack.

"You've got to give me one of these pills," the old man said. "See what they look like? Big gelatin capsules."

"The ones you keep in your pillbox?"

"That's right. There are always a couple in the left-hand pocket of my sports coat. And there's a whole bottle on the middle shelf of the refrigerator. Just give me one."

"Then call Doctor Barrett," Anderson added.

"Yes, but don't do anything else until you've given me a pill. If I'm already in bad shape, just push one into my mouth. Get it down somehow. That will hold me until the doctor gets here."

"Okay," Anderson said.

"That's why your mother died, you know. The people taking care of her didn't bring her the right medicine."

"Don't worry, Grandpa," Anderson assured him. "If anything happens, I'll do exactly what you've told me."

They were instructions Anderson never thought to question. If he hadn't been so obedient, perhaps things would have been different. His mind tugs at the past, trying to pull it into some other shape, but these are memories coming back, not imaginings. Nothing he can do could change them now.

Then Anderson hears a sudden silence, the disturbing sound of no sound. He realizes his kidnappers have left him alone. But he experiences no relief—only a sense of abandonment. He feels deserted, even by his enemies. He remembers the horrible silence that morning at the lake shore.

Anderson had been out the previous night with one of the summertime girls—out with her until dawn. When he got back to the cottage, his grandfather had already left for his swim. Anderson had grabbed a towel and followed, hoping the camaraderie of cold water would prevent the old man from giving him too much grief for staying out all night.

But no sound of splashing came from the lake as Anderson approached. The old man wasn't even in the water. He was crouched on the dock, back where the boards began to extend out over the lake itself. One arm was around a dock post, the other pushed against his chest. His breathing was labored, and he couldn't speak.

"I'll get your pills!" Anderson shouted, hoping to reassure him.

But the old man only sat there, gasping for air. It was what Anderson had long dreaded, what he had warned his grandfather about.

As the image comes back now, Anderson tries vainly to rouse himself from this bad dream. Then he is in motion again. Too much motion. Jolting along, faster than before. The blows this time are even rougher, buffeting him from beneath. The cloth offers little protection.

Pine boughs whip against his face. He remembers how he had raced back to the cottage for his grandfather's heart medicine, putting everything he had into that frantic dash. His heart pounded with the exertion of climbing the steep hill, taking the steps partway, three in a stride, then cutting across the pine covered hillside. Before he had even reached the top, his thigh muscles were quivering with the strain.

He grabbed the bottle of pills from the refrigerator. As he bounded down the hillside, dropping several feet with each step, the bottle shook in his hand like a rattle. Anderson had all he could do to avoid sliding or somersaulting forward. Somehow, he managed to stay upright, hurtling toward the lake, on the edge of losing control.

But he got there too late.

His grandfather had fallen off the dock onto the sandy beach. He lay on his side, soaking wet, half in the water. His legs were drawn up into a sitting position, as though he'd been tilted sideways off a chair. His face rested on the sand the two of them had hauled in and dumped there. When Anderson knelt beside the body and touched it, the flesh had already gone cold. There was no way to make the dead man swallow the pills Anderson was clutching.

Anderson feels himself being rolled off the large cloth. For a while, he lies crumpled like his grandfather on the sandy ground. Then he's turned over, his limbs and clothing straightened, his pockets searched. He feels a hot light shining on him and has a sense of being inspected. Hands tug at him, rearranging his clothing. A wallet is put back in his pocket.

When the physical inspection is over, Anderson hears voices raised in irritation. He remembers how the police had questioned him about his grandfather's death. Hour after hour, they had gone over the same points, until Anderson thought he would go crazy.

"Why do you keep asking me this?" Anderson finally demanded. "I did everything I could to save him."

"We don't think you did," the officer said coldly.

"Look, some people with bad hearts *die* of heart attacks," Anderson said. "It's a fact of life."

"But your grandfather *didn't* die of a heart attack," the policeman told him.

"What are you talking about?" Anderson asked.

"The autopsy shows he died of drowning."

Anderson could hear the blood rushing in his ears. It is a sound that has come back to him many times since—a sound that comes back to him now.

Then Anderson hears more hostile words he can't quite make out. He remembers how the police kept implying that he was concealing something, asking him accusing questions, almost jeering at him.

"Why didn't you try mouth-to-mouth resuscitation?" one officer asked.

"What we don't understand is how your grandfather could have drowned in the first place," another officer added. "Got any ideas about that?"

"You claim to be a qualified lifeguard, don't you?" the first officer said, before Anderson had even had time to reply.

The barrage of questions went on for hours. When one set of policemen became tired, they were replaced by another. Eventually, when Anderson himself was too exhausted to continue, they would let him go home. Then they would bring him back in a day or two later. They questioned him down in Minneapolis as well as at the county sheriff's office near his grandfather's cabin. Again and again, they made Anderson tell his story, as he has told it to himself a thousand times since.

Finally, the police asked Anderson if he would agree to a lie detector test. They said that if the machine showed he was telling the truth, they would not have to bother him any longer. They assured him that whatever the results were, they couldn't be used against him.

During the questioning by the technician, Anderson was

overcome with grief. He remembers realizing, for the first time, that he had lost his whole family. When the technician asked him about his grandfather, Anderson kept thinking about his mother and about the father he had only known in his imaginings. He felt terribly alone and horribly responsible.

The memory makes Anderson moan aloud, and he finally manages to move slightly. Someone curses in response. Anderson's hands are lifted up and cold metal slapped against them. Hard edges pinch his wrists, but he is still too numb to feel pain. What he feels is the weight of handcuffs. It's a sensation he knows all too well.

He remembers how the police had informed him of the lie detector results, how he had listened to the news without surprise, how the police had finally accused him, in so many words, of murder.

"You did it for the money, didn't you?"

"What money?" Anderson had asked, confused by this most of all.

"The money your grandfather left you in his will."

"I didn't know he was going to leave me any money. I didn't know he *had* any money."

"How do you suppose he paid the bills?" the policeman asked.

"I never thought about it," Anderson said.

"There's a lot you never thought about, isn't there?" The question was left hanging in the air.

His actual arrest was almost a relief. It gave him something to do, almost a sense of purpose. From another prisoner, Anderson got the name of a good criminal lawyer. This man, Arnie Freilinger, was said to be very expensive, but highly competent. The police were generous in letting Anderson use the phone. It took several tries, but Anderson finally got through to him. An appointment was scheduled for the next day.

Freilinger had curly, gray hair and wore an elegant silk suit. Anderson's first meeting with him lasted only a few minutes and was mostly concerned with how Anderson was going to pay. Even now, as Anderson remembers him, he marvels at how relaxed the man could be when dealing with criminal proceedings.

Anderson is left once again in silence. After a long wait, the

handcuffs are removed from his wrists. He remembers how Freilinger had gotten the charges dropped, only a couple of days after
their first meeting.

"Come on, you're being released," the lawyer had told him.

"What's happened?" Anderson asked.

"I have persuaded the District Attorney's office that there is
insufficient evidence to justify holding you further. You just have
to sign these papers."

"What are they?"

"Routine stuff," Freilinger explained. "The more important
ones have the effect of protecting the agencies involved from
being sued for false arrest. You sign them and you're out of
here."

"It's as easy as that?"

"It is now. That's what you pay me for."

For a few hours, perhaps even for a few days, Anderson had
thought that would be the end of it. But the ordeal never ended.
The authorities had stopped tormenting him, but the public kept
it up.

Lying helpless on the ground, Anderson hears people talking
about him. He cannot make out the exact words, but he knows he
is the one being discussed. He remembers, after he had been
released, gradually discovering how many people had seen the
newspaper and television accounts.

There had been little else in the news at the time, so the
media had made his case their feature story for several days.
They called it "The Mystery of Stauffer's Landing." One reporter
had somehow gotten hold of a family photo album, with pictures
of Anderson and his grandfather. Each night, when the story was
at its peak, the news broadcasts were illustrated with snapshots
from his childhood. The anchorwoman on one local station liked
to accompany each image with little exclamations. How sweet the
old man looked with his soft white hair! Wasn't he the sort of
'All-American Grandpa' everyone wished they had? How happy
the boy and his grandfather seemed as they played with their
dog! Then, each night, she reminded the viewers how strangely
the old man had died. The public apparently got a thrill wondering whether so idyllic a relationship could have resulted in
murder.

It took Anderson a while to realize how readily everyone believed the worst. At first, he thought the expressions of sympathy were genuine. When people described the broadcasts to him, he thought it was because they were truly horrified at the way the television news teams had covered his case.

Then ruder people set him straight. A few, feeling sentimental about his grandfather's pictures, had actually taken punches at him. After that, whenever people recognized him, Anderson could imagine the contents of their hushed conversations. It wasn't paranoia. Like the muffled talk he was hearing now, the tone would be clear, even if the words weren't.

"That fellow who was in the paper. You know. The one who murdered his grandfather."

"What about him?"

"He's sitting over there."

"Doesn't *look* like a monster."

"Looks guilty, though, doesn't he?"

"Yeah. Guilty as sin."

"They should have taken him out and shot him."

After that, Anderson had practically stopped going out. He dropped out of the university and bought a house in a neighborhood where nobody knew him. He grew a beard that hid much of his face. His small inheritance paid for the groceries he bought late at night from convenience stores. He hardly ever spent an evening with friends or went out with a girl. He never became a total recluse, but since the weekend of his grandfather's death his own nightmares were usually all the company he could stand.

As he tries to shake loose from these memories, Anderson feels himself being dragged through wet grass. He remembers his own previous nightmares, dragging him back to the spot, pulling him inexorably along to the place where his grandfather had died.

He tries to become calm by telling himself these things are all *past.* Just memories and nightmares. But the nightmares turn real, as the cold, wet sensation of the grass and of the lake water restores him to consciousness.

This time, there is no escape in wakefulness. Anderson's heart races with the realization, even though the rest of his body remains inert. Yes, he is really back on a northern lake. He is being dragged through the reeds at the water's edge.

He feels the pull on his feet, feels his shirt slide up and the wet grass on his bare back. He hears the sound of his own legs dropping in the water. Then comes the sudden wetness. He feels his arms lifted, swung around, and the rest of his body dumped in as well.

Experiencing everything as though in slow motion, Anderson gradually becomes aware that someone is trying to drown him. Hands push on his shoulders, holding him under. He cannot breathe. His lungs ache for air. His diaphragm begins to quiver as his breathing reflex battles his instinct to keep out the water. Soon the reflex will be too strong. His diaphragm will jerk downward convulsively, drawing in water. He will die of suffocation.

At first, Anderson simply accepts this. After all, he is surely guilty, even if he cannot figure out how. Drowning is appropriate for him. Drowning is, in fact, what he has been doing for a long time.

But then, as he's on the verge of losing consciousness, something inside him screams out, 'No!' No, he is not *that* guilty. No, he cannot just accept this. No, he will not give up and die. Anger surges through him. And he begins to fight.

His body is slow to respond. But the cold water soaking his clothes and the adrenaline released by his anger bring his limbs back to life. He manages to plant a foot on the muddy lake bottom and to push his body sideways. As he does this, he shrugs his shoulders, trying to slip out of the attacker's grip. For a moment, the attacker is caught unprepared. The man's hands fumble for a better hold. Anderson's other foot connects with the bottom, and he pushes upward. His head breaks the surface, and he draws in air.

For a second or two, Anderson sees the lake in the dawn light. The shores are covered with birch trees and pines. There are no cabins or other signs of human life nearby. The early morning calm gives everything a dreamlike quality. Only the weight of his wet clothes makes Anderson certain he is awake.

Then the attacker is on him again. Anderson's effort to escape has turned his shoulders perpendicular to the attacker's, so that the attacker is now grabbing Anderson's head from the side.

He gets Anderson's head between his forearms and again forces it under. Anderson tucks his shoulder, puts his hand against the attacker's chest, and pushes away as hard as he can. As Anderson does this, he tips his head sideways, toward the attacker. The man tries to tighten his grip, but his hands only slide across the side of Anderson's head, raking his ear, but leaving Anderson free.

Gasping for air, Anderson digs in one foot and reaches forward with the other, as if running in slow motion. The attacker is behind him now, and Anderson wants to put distance between them. But Anderson is moving away from shore, and his next stride fails to connect with the bottom.

The attacker launches himself at Anderson's back, getting his arms around Anderson's neck and pulling Anderson's head against his own lower chest. Then he leans forward, getting the weight of his shoulders above Anderson's head, forcing Anderson's head once more under the water. Anderson's neck is now clamped firmly from behind by the attacker's forearms. In front of him, there is little but greenish water. The silvery gray surface of the lake is only a foot or so above his head, but there is no way Anderson can reach it.

Still dizzy from the drug, Anderson is slow to make a further effort. He realizes there is something vaguely familiar about his present position. The situation is like one he has experienced before. For a moment, Anderson doesn't see how this could be. When has anyone in the past actually tried to drown him?

Then he remembers. It was part of the exercise in 'rear head-hold releases' from senior lifesaving. Anderson has even taught the class himself. There is a standard maneuver any lifesaver is supposed to make, if a drowning person grabs him from behind. Anderson struggles to concentrate, to think about what he is doing.

Slowly, the old skills return. Anderson reaches up and finds the lower of the two arms folded around his neck. He grasps the attacker's wrist firmly with one hand. Then he puts the palm of the other hand under the man's elbow. Turning his head sideways and tucking his chin, Anderson pulls down on the wrist, while pushing up on the elbow. This breaks the head hold, just as it's supposed to do.

Anderson slides down and backward, under the man's arm, remembering to hang on to the wrist. When Anderson breaks the surface again, gasping for breath, he is behind the man, twisting the man's outstretched arm. If the man were actually a drowning person, this would subdue him, allowing Anderson to tow him to shore. For a moment, Anderson feels he has his attacker under control.

Then the man does something unexpected. He turns a forward somersault. This releases the pressure on the man's arm and turns his body around, so that he is facing toward Anderson, but off to one side. Before breaking surface, he bends his outstretched arm and pivots behind Anderson, where he can get the fingers of his other hand on Anderson's face.

Anderson feels the man levering himself upward, using Anderson's head as a fulcrum and forcing Anderson's face downward. Anderson realizes that there is no way he can simply escape. His attacker won't quit. Not for a moment has the man wavered in his efforts to drown Anderson. Not for a moment has the man offered Anderson any chance of getting away. In order to survive, Anderson will have to hurt him, disable him, put him out of action.

As Anderson dangles there under water, other swimming techniques of his youth come back to him. The maneuver of 'taking the ball under' from water polo. And his long dormant ability to hold his breath.

If he could only get more air! He tries downward-directed frog kicks to propel himself out of the water. At first, the resulting surge of power suggests this tactic is going to work. But the man hanging on to his head is positioned too much above him. No matter how hard Anderson kicks, he cannot get his face above the surface. His exertions only serve to make him more desperate for air.

Then Anderson reverses tactics. He draws his arms and knees upward, as though trying to lift the water itself. This accelerates the rate at which he is sinking. His attacker is unprepared for this maneuver. As Anderson drops toward the bottom, the man is forced to readjust his hold, giving Anderson a chance to twist loose. Slipping from the man's grasp, Anderson continues pushing downward. His chest is now in pain and his vision is going. His feet and hips hit bottom at the same time. He folds his body forward, struggling to get his legs under him, convulsively expelling air. As he starts to lose control, he feels his heels digging into the bottom. He pushes off.

This time, as he breaks surface, Anderson is several feet away from his assailant. Panting for air, he is surprised to see the man's legs disappearing into the lake, as the man does a surface dive. Although the man is wearing a shirt, Anderson notices that his legs are bare. There is a moment of silence as Anderson wonders what is going on. Then the man plows into Anderson under water, tackling him around the waist, and levering him backward. Anderson, too, is forced under, but this time manages to reach down and get hold of the man's neck. As Anderson tightens his grip around the man's throat, the man tightens his grip around Anderson's middle, squeezing the air out of him.

They are now once more in shallower water. Anderson manages to break surface for a moment, grabbing another breath. Then the man's hands are around Anderson's neck. The man tries to tilt Anderson backward, so that he is again forced under, allowing the attacker to breathe. Anderson counters by reaching back with his leg and bracing himself against the bottom. This keeps the man's head under water. Low on air, the attacker begins to twist rapidly from side to side, like an animal trying to shake himself dry. For the first time in their fight, Anderson feels he has an advantage. But the man is still choking him, refusing to let up. Anderson chokes him back, strangles him as he has been strangled. Drowns him as he has felt drowned.

Finally, the attacker goes limp.

Still filled with the adrenaline of anger, ready to drown him again, if necessary, Anderson pulls his attacker's head to the surface and looks into his face.

At first, it doesn't register. His nervous system seems to freeze. His mind rejects what his eyes are telling him. But the sight in front of him is too plain to be denied. It is utterly strange, but also utterly familiar.

Anderson is staring at *his own face.* The drowned man is not merely someone *like* Anderson himself. It actually seems to *be* Anderson himself. It is not his own face in a metaphorical sense. It is his own face in a literal sense. Only inches in front of him. Unmistakable in the early morning light. Without a beard, without as many circles under the eyes, perhaps, but *his* face, nevertheless.

The expression on this face is vacant, as though his mind were elsewhere. His eyes stare upward and out into the distance. A string of green-brown weed hangs from one of his ears and dangles across the cheek below. His mouth is slightly open, and water gurgles out of it. But there is no voluntary motion, no sign of life.

Anderson loosens his hold, and the head begins to sink again into the lake. Its hair floats upward, giving the face a startled look, as the water begins to obscure it. Then Anderson grabs the collar of the man's shirt with one hand and twists it toward him. Tucking his elbow down under the water and pushing his forearm against the man's body, Anderson hoists the head once again into the air. The string of weed has now been washed away. With his free hand, Anderson touches the cheek and mouth of the dead face. He needs to be sure that it is real, that it feels the way it looks. But there can be no doubt. The face is just as much like his as it appears to be. And just as dead.

Anderson's perceptions seem utterly clear. In the cool air of the morning, he can see every detail. In the silence on the lake, he can hear every sound. Yet his mind is filled with confusion. Has he drowned himself? Then whom does he hear breathing? If he is dead, then who has survived? Terror jerks his body, like an electric current jolting through him. Hysterical laughter interrupts the silence. Then terror again. A shaking, sweating terror.

Anderson drops the dead body, pushing it away, unable to bear touching it for even a moment longer. He staggers backward, splashing loudly in his efforts to remain upright. The body drifts under the water, its pale face still visible, eyes staring, arms reaching. Anderson can see it in front of him, as he continues to back away. Yes, he knows exactly how it looks.

Then Anderson turns and runs.

CHAPTER 3

Anderson flees. He flees from his attacker and from his victim. He flees from his would-be murderer and from the man he has killed. He flees from himself.

As he runs from the lake, he is more aware of the noises he is making than anything else. The sloshing sound of his own feet in soaking tennis shoes. The impact of their rubber soles on the changing ground. The way they are slapping the pine needles, crunching the twigs, whipping the grass. The soft, squeaking noise, as each stride pulls at his wet clothes, stretching them tight. The rasp of his own breathing as he tries to keep up the pace.

His path lurches first one way, then another, as he struggles to keep his balance in his headlong dash over the uneven terrain. His knees lift almost to his chin as he strains to propel his body up the steeply rising ground. His only direction is upward, away.

As he reaches a ridge overlooking the lake, Anderson pauses and looks back. His heart is beating so loudly, he can hear it through his rushing breath. Frantically, he scans the horizon. He does not recognize any landmarks. It could be any lake among thousands. There are pine trees, some birch, granite boulders, and, far off down the shore, a few docks.

He rubs the moisture from his eyes to see better. Near the docks, where some of the trees have been cleared away, he can make out the distant roofs and gables of three or four buildings. Others must be hidden in the trees. It looks like a small resort. Then Anderson's gaze travels along the shoreline, and he identifies the area where he had been fighting in the water. He thinks he can even see something floating beneath the surface.

As he registers this, Anderson's body is swept by a wave of

nausea. He turns and bends over, gagging on his own saliva. Retching, heaving sounds emerge from his chest, but his throat only emits a thin string of brown mucus. Wiping his mouth with the back of his hand, he straightens up. His face and ears go hot and cold at the same time. Then his head becomes steadier, and he staggers forward, once more managing something like a run.

On the crest of the ridge, Anderson finds himself clambering over big trees, blown down by windstorms. He is desperate to put these natural barriers between himself and the scene he has just left. At first, he tries to jump from one trunk to another. Then he steps on a log that has lost its bark, and his wet shoe slips. He tries to catch the next trunk with his arms, misses, and lands on his stomach. For several minutes, he is pawing and scrambling, propelling himself over the logs as much with his hands as with his feet. His knees become slick from the wet moss. His fingernails catch in the damp wood.

Putting the last fallen tree behind him, he moves forward again on his feet. The land dips a little and levels off. The high trees become farther apart, and the brush thicker. Anderson tries to keep up his pace, despite the heavier going. His cheeks and forehead are scratched by branches. He struggles to wave away the mosquitoes as they catch in his eyes and nostrils. The softer leaves that slap against his face are almost a relief, because they brush the insects away. But the stiffer branches stab him and trip him. In the increasingly dense foliage, Anderson finds himself running whichever direction presents the most openings. He follows paths he is dimly aware were made by animals.

Gradually the land begins to climb again. The brush thins. The ground becomes rockier. In the clearer landscape, Anderson can see the trees swaying slowly, as though under water. He feels a chill, but cannot tell whether it is from the cold or from the associations the sight has for him. He tries to warm himself through his exertions, to lose himself in the effort of running.

The rising land comes to a kind of summit. There is now a firm breeze that blows away the mosquitoes. Despite the boulders in the ground, it becomes possible once more to run in a relatively straight line.

But which way is he going? Is he still moving away from the thing he wants to avoid? Anderson tries to choose his direction without thinking too much about why he is choosing it. He cannot see far enough through the forest to pick out a reference point, but he can detect a general direction in the leaves, the moss, and the more barren branches.

He reassures himself that he is actually covering distance by noticing that the terrain is changing. The pine trees give way to maples and occasional birches. The ground is less rocky now, and there is pale green grass between the tree trunks.

Anderson runs on through the forest, settling into a regular rhythm. At one point, he hears something off to his left. He cannot tell if it is a man, a deer, or even a moose, but it sounds large. He swerves away from it and jogs along without self-consciousness, oblivious to his own appearance, afraid, perhaps, to become self-conscious.

He has no idea where he is, except that it seems to be northern Minnesota. He has memories of places like this from his past, places near his grandfather's lake home. It is a kind of landscape he has not visited since his grandfather's death. Once he would have felt at home here. Now his memories make him all the more determined to move on, to escape.

After a while, the ground slopes steeply downward. In the distance below him, the blue surface of another lake glistens between the trees as it catches the morning sun.

Trying to keep up his pace on the sloping ground, Anderson starts to fall forward, catches himself, and then slides. Under patches of leaves, the slope is muddy, and he stops just short of a small stream. Getting to his feet, he pauses long enough to rinse his muddy hands in the cold, running water. Then, rather than tackle the other muddy bank, he heads along the ravine, pushing himself to go as fast as he can. The stream bed brings him almost to the shore of the lake.

As he emerges from the ravine, Anderson can see a boathouse and, farther away, a long stack of neatly split logs. He smells the smoke of a wood fire. But he does not want to meet any people yet. Turning back into the woods, he begins jogging again. His side aches constantly now, and he struggles to control the regular waves of nausea.

Without thinking much about it, he veers away from the occasional cabins. The forest is now mostly pine trees again, with sparse undergrowth. Anderson tries to avoid passing where people might see him, partly because if no one sees him, he will not have to see himself.

He wishes he could disappear, merge with the trees and lakes, disintegrate into the scenery. But most of all, he wishes to escape what he has seen that morning, what has happened to him in the last few hours, what he has done. All his exertions are a kind of reaching for oblivion.

But his efforts are self-defeating. As fatigue slows him down, his mind grows paradoxically clearer. He notices the morning sun is to his left and has been for some time. The wind is blowing gently from his right. He has been instinctively heading south and eastward. Exhausted, and vaguely aware of the need to conserve his energy, Anderson slows to a walk. His clothes are still wet, and he feels increasingly chilled. The weather here is much cooler than down in the Cities. The trees have more the colors of fall. As he hikes along, Anderson folds his arms across his chest and hunches his shoulders for warmth.

Because he is making less noise himself, Anderson begins to hear things he had not noticed before. Bird calls, including the gentle cooing of mourning doves and the insane, laughing melodies of a loon. Dragonflies buzzing in the clearings. Then a high, whishing noise, almost a whistle—the sound of wind blowing through the pine needles. Mixed in with it is the noise of birch leaves rippling in the moving air.

Somewhere behind these other sounds is a periodic rumble he cannot place. At first it sounds like an effect of the wind, but with more of a hum. Then he notices that it seems louder when the wind dies down. Gradually, he recognizes it as the sound of traffic.

With great caution, he heads toward it. Almost due east. But the sound is much farther away than he had expected. The noise grows as he moves along, but so slowly, he is not always sure he is heading in the right direction.

Just as he begins to think he has wandered off course, he is startled by the rush of a truck, passing him abruptly only a few yards away. He seems to have arrived at the place he was aiming for. The brush comes to a sudden end, and Anderson finds himself at the edge of a wide, treeless swath, cutting through the forest. Half its width is occupied by a two-lane blacktop road, the other half by a power line with knee-high grass beneath.

Afraid of walking in a circle and returning to the place he has left, Anderson begins following the cleared swath. When cars or trucks pass, he ducks back to avoid being seen, but there are few vehicles on this road. Because he is walking along the sunny edge of the treeless swath, he begins to feel less chilled.

A burst of noise, only inches in front of him, makes him jump sideways, his heart hammering. But as the beating of wings passes over his head, he realizes he has startled a nesting grouse.

The road and power line rise and fall over low hills, but Anderson realizes they would make a nearly straight line on a map. The sun has climbed high in the sky, making it sometime around midday. Although the slopes of the hills are not steep, they are long and tiring to hike across.

Trudging over the top of one, Anderson sees a white painted building several hundred yards ahead and slightly below him. A small grocery store with a gas pump in front. Beside it, a gravel road intersects the blacktop he has been following. As Anderson draws closer, he sees the store is open for business. He is hesitant to approach, but feels hungry and tired. He can't stay in the woods forever.

As Anderson is approaching this isolated store, a bus comes over the hill he is hiking down. This time Anderson makes no effort to hide. The bus roars past him, enormously tall and loud. It is white on top and dirty silver below. In between is a band of dark tinted windows with a set of red and blue stripes underneath. A thin, white dog is stenciled clearly on the back window.

As the bus approaches the grocery store, it slows to a stop. A man in overalls, carrying a huge cardboard box, comes out of the store. Desperate still to get as far away as possible, Anderson sprints for the bus.

Arriving panting beside it, Anderson discovers he needn't have run so hard. The driver has gotten out and opened one of the outside luggage compartments for the man's carton. He and the man in overalls are discussing whether it will "be okay there."

While he stands by the front of the bus, catching his breath, Anderson is unusually aware of even the most commonplace details. The sign over the front window of the vehicle says TWIN

CITIES. Lower down, at roughly chest height, there are big, metal, cut-out letters on a black panel, spelling out GREYHOUND. The bus has two sets of large tires on each side in back, one set in front. The tinted windows make it impossible to see inside. For Anderson, the vehicle has an ominous look, but it represents a way out.

The driver finally swings down the door to the luggage compartment and gets back in the bus. The man in overalls follows, nodding at Anderson as he goes by. An older woman in a flowered dress climbs aboard as soon as the steps are clear. The man and the woman both seem to be headed for nearby towns. Anderson has never heard of the places.

When it is his turn to get on, Anderson tries to act calm and to make his voice sound normal. "I'd like a ticket to the Twin Cities, please."

"Which one?" the driver asks.

For a second, Anderson is confused. "I'm sorry, I don't understand."

"Which 'Twin City,' Minneapolis or Saint Paul?"

"Minneapolis, please."

The driver tears off a ticket. "That'll be twenty-four dollars and ninety cents."

Anderson reaches for his wallet. But the one he pulls from his pocket isn't his.

Anderson is momentarily frozen in surprise. Not knowing what else to do, he pays the driver with the money he finds inside. There is more than enough for the ticket. The bills are still damp, but the driver doesn't seem to notice. Anderson receives a dime in change.

Moving down the aisle of the bus, Anderson feels as though the other passengers are all staring at him. His legs are now so shaky, he can hardly walk. He must look very muddy, even if his clothes have dried. Does he look like a fugitive? Does he look like someone who is carrying a wallet that isn't his?

He tries to pick the most anonymous seat he can, one halfway back, with no one sitting beside or across the aisle. Lowering himself onto the cushions, he studies the area around him in the bus. He tries not to turn his head too much or to do anything to attract attention. He is relieved to discover the seat backs are very high, offering considerable privacy. They make the bus seem dark, because they are upholstered in a dark, patterned fabric and have dark, imitation leather covers over their headrests. The green light filtering through the tinted windows makes everything look as though it is under water. Anderson tries not to think of this.

Scanning the seats from behind, it is difficult for Anderson to tell which ones are occupied. In the armrests are buttons allowing them to tilt back slightly, but the empty seats seem tilted as often as the occupied ones. Overhead is a metal rack for hand luggage, but there is too little in it to provide clues to where people might be sitting underneath.

Gradually, Anderson convinces himself no one is watching. He takes the strange wallet out of his pocket and examines it. It holds only a modest amount of cash, but is full of credit cards. There is also a driver's license. The leather used for the pockets inside the wallet is very thin and expensive looking. There are no see-through plastic card-holders. The inside leather is a light tan, the outside a darker brown. Just another lost wallet, classier than most, but otherwise unremarkable. Anderson is only puzzled about how it came to be in his pocket. Then he notices the picture on the driver's license. He begins to shake again. The picture seems to be his. But the address is one at which he has never lived. And the name beside the picture is 'Peterson.'

Anderson feels as though he is going to faint. He puts his head between his knees and takes deep breaths. He tells himself to take everything one step at a time. His faintness might be as much a physical symptom, due to fatigue and hunger, as it is a psychological one. He will have to do something about it, even if it means drawing a little attention to himself. After all, if he were to collapse completely, he would be even more conspicuous.

When his head clears, he goes forward to speak to the driver.

"Excuse me. Is there a rest stop coming up where I could get some food?"

"There's none scheduled," the driver says matter-of-factly.

Anderson feels a moment of despair, but knows he can't afford to give up so easily. "Gee, that's gonna be hard. I didn't have time to eat anything this morning."

"Well, I'll tell ya," the driver says, softening a little. "We're making good time today. You should be able to buy sandwiches, pop, and candy bars at the next passenger stop, if you're quick about it."

"Thanks. I'll be as quick as I can."

"When I blast the horn, you'll have about one minute left to get on board. Then I'll have to be pulling out. The next bus is the same time tomorrow."

"Thanks. I get the message."

Anderson returns to his seat, for a time thinking of little more than the food he hopes to pick up en route.

When the bus makes its next stop, Anderson hops off as soon as the door opens. The rough timbered building looks like a bar from the outside, but inside it is only a bar at one end. In the middle of the room are shelves stacked with groceries and fishing supplies. At the opposite end are four tables set like a restaurant.

Anderson glances quickly over the odd conglomeration of products—the pancake mix and fishing lures, the dehydrated meat and lighter fluid. "What kind of sandwiches do you have?" he asks.

"Egg salad, tuna salad, and meat loaf."

"I'd like two meat loaf, please."

The woman opens an old, white enamel refrigerator, behind the bar. She takes out the sandwiches and hands them to Anderson. They are made with white bread, unlabeled, and wrapped in thin, clingy plastic.

"Those are a dollar eighty-nine apiece."

"I'd also like two of those Nut Goodies. A bag of potato chips. And two cans of orange pop, please."

"Fanta?"

"Fanta is fine."

She punches the keys on an old, mechanical cash register. "That'll be six sixty-eight, altogether."

Anderson hands her seven dollars from the wallet he found in his pocket. He takes the change she scoops from the cash register drawer, gathers up his purchases, and runs for the bus.

"Have a nice day," the woman calls after him.

"You too," Anderson shouts over his shoulder.

The driver hasn't used the horn, but he pulls out as soon as Anderson climbs on board.

Back in his seat, Anderson tears into the food, ripping through the plastic and paper. He has to remind himself to chew, so that he will be able to digest what he is eating. Despite his thirst, he finishes most of the solid food before opening the first can. Then he guzzles the pop.

Feeling better, Anderson tries to make himself relax. He is not up to dealing with anything more at the moment. He needs to collect himself, to digest his meal, to gather his energies. He leans back, resting his lower legs on the back of the seat in front of him, and stares out the window, his face blank, registering little of the passing scenery. As he rides toward Minneapolis, his mind keeps returning to the girl called Gretchen.

Anderson visualizes her sitting and talking with Trudy and Brian. Did she help them plan how best to trap him? He remembers her giving him that remarkable smile. How could she do that and still be setting him up? He visualizes her displaying her legs in the cut-off jeans. Was she consciously using her body as bait? He pictures the contours of her body, including the portions he hasn't seen. He imagines her trim belly curving downward to the mound between her legs.

He recognizes the direction his thoughts are taking and is momentarily appalled. What is he doing having sexual fantasies about this girl? Could there be anything more ridiculously inappropriate? Is he so sexually obsessed that he can only think of an attractive woman in sexual terms? Is he, in fact, as 'irredeemably sexist' as Gretchen had claimed?

Then he has an hysterical impulse to start laughing at his own absurdity. Here he is—someone who has recently been drugged, kidnapped, and nearly murdered, who has just committed a murder himself, who is even now fleeing the scene of his crime—here he is, after all this, worrying about whether he is sexist!

Perhaps, Anderson thinks, almost giggling, he really *is* mad. Perhaps he has been hallucinating everything. Perhaps all he needs to do is switch his more upsetting delusions for pleasanter ones. Delusions, for instance, involving Gretchen. Yes, that's it: Gretchen laughing, Gretchen dancing, Gretchen as hysterical as he is. His body shakes, this time, perhaps, with sobs. Is he, Anderson wonders, finally coming apart? Will he go to pieces right here on the Greyhound?

The lurching and jolting of the bus's movement in city traffic causes Anderson to wake up. He realizes he must have been sleeping for some time. It's now early evening. The bus wends its way through back streets and around construction sites. Finally, it pulls into the big garage of the Minneapolis bus depot, sliding into an angled berth between the other buses and coming to a stop.

The driver climbs out to open up the outside luggage compartments. Still trying to be inconspicuous, Anderson slips into the line of disembarking passengers near the middle. He climbs down from the bus and pushes his way through the glass doors leading to the waiting room. Inside, Anderson tenses. He half expects a squad of policemen to appear and handcuff him. But no one takes any notice.

Temporarily reassured, Anderson pauses to survey the setting. In the middle of the large room is a kind of corral, surrounded by a carpeted fence and filled with connected rows of plastic bucket seats. Little, coin-operated television sets are mounted on metal arms between many of the seats. Old ladies and children gaze blankly at the screens, unaware that Anderson is looking at them. He imagines them all glancing furtively his way, murmuring about what he has done and about who should call the police.

Around the sides of the room are coin-operated luggage lockers. A sign warns that nothing may be left in them for more than twenty-four hours. To Anderson's right is a ticket counter, to his left, the entrance to a small cafeteria. Realizing that he is again almost weak from hunger, Anderson heads for the cafeteria.

There is no one in the serving line. Behind the counter, Anderson sees wieners cooking on a rack of rotating pipes. Anderson walks through, picking up a hot dog and two cartons of milk. He intends to have something more as soon as he gets home. The young, black cashier takes Anderson's money in silence, but looks him up and down while returning the change. Anderson finds his inspection unnerving.

Taking a seat near a window, Anderson squirts ketchup on the hot dog and quickly wolfs it down. It tastes good to him. He drinks the milk more slowly, giving the food time to settle. As he drinks, he takes out the strange wallet and once more inspects its contents. What is he doing with this phony driver's license and all these credit cards? Or is it a real license, issued to someone who just looks like him? The picture is, after all, very small and badly printed. Anderson stares at the laminated plastic, trying to see his own face in the stamp-sized photograph. Suddenly, for a moment, he sees the face of the dead man. He chokes on his milk and reaches for a napkin.

Putting the wallet back in his pocket, Anderson gets up and goes out to the taxi stand. Three taxis stand empty, while their drivers argue about the latest fluctuations in wheat and soybean prices. After a few moments, one of them notices Anderson and opens the rear door to the first vehicle in the line. It has the usual dome light on the roof reading TAXI. Otherwise, it looks like an ordinary compact car.

Anderson climbs in. The driver shuts the door for him, strides around the car, and climbs into the driver's seat.

"Where to?" he asks, without looking back.

Anderson gives the driver his home address in northeast Minneapolis. "Do you know where that is?" Anderson asks.

"You bet," says the driver, turning the ignition.

Anderson feels a wave of relief. After the trauma of the last twenty-four hours, his one instinct is to hide, to go for cover, to withdraw, just as he has done so often in the past.

As he revs the engine, the driver reaches over and pushes a button on an electronic meter mounted over the dashboard. Then he pulls out into the traffic. Below the meter, Anderson notices the microphone of a two way radio, swaying on its hook. Beside it is a clip holding the driver's picture and a taxi license. To Anderson, these things represent a threatening world of regulations and officials he would just as soon forget. He closes his eyes and tells himself he will soon be home.

The driver hums for a while to himself, then breaks in on Anderson's thoughts. "Ever play the futures market?"

Anderson opens his eyes to see the driver observing him in the mirror. "No, I never have," Anderson says.

"You should try it sometime," the driver says. "It's more fun than the ponies!"

Anderson closes his eyes again, and the driver resumes his

humming. It is only when the taxi enters his own neighborhood in North Minneapolis that Anderson begins looking out the window. He wants to be able to point out the last couple of turns and to tell the driver the exact house where he should stop.

The driver finds Anderson's street without further instructions. He heads down the block past the familiar buildings. Suddenly Anderson's routine arrival home becomes less routine.

Parked directly in front his house, Anderson sees a police car. At first, he thinks it might be a coincidence. Then he spots another one around the corner. A light is on in his living room. Two uniformed patrolmen are standing around the back, beside his car.

All Anderson's fears and hostilities involving the police come flooding back. Before, when he was innocent, they had been convinced of his guilt. What chance would he have with them now when he has actually killed a man? The idea of stepping out of the taxi into that swarm of officials is terrifying.

The taxi, meanwhile, is slowing down, as the driver tries to read the house numbers.

"Drive on, will you?" Anderson tells him.

"Drive on where?" the driver asks.

"I've gotten the address wrong," Anderson explains. "Just a minute and I'll think of the right one."

The taxi slides by Anderson's house, but continues to slow down. The driver peers at Anderson in the mirror.

"Keep driving," Anderson says. "I'm sure the place I'm going is farther along."

But the taxi pulls over and comes to a complete stop.

"What are you doing?" Anderson asks.

"We're not allowed to take fares cruising," the driver says, turning around to give Anderson a skeptical look.

"I don't want you to go cruising," Anderson exclaims. "I just want you to drive on."

"I can't drive anywhere unless I'm given a proper address."

Remaining there, only a couple dozen yards past his house, is the last thing Anderson wants to do. At any moment, the patrolmen might see them and become suspicious.

Unable to think of anything else, Anderson pulls the unfamiliar driver's license from his pocket and reads the driver the address printed on it. It is on North East Main, by the northeast bank of the Mississippi, near Nicollet Island.

It is the only address he can think of at the moment. As he says it aloud, Anderson realizes it is also his only real clue to what has been happening.

The taxi driver gives him a disgusted look. "That's way the hell back by where we crossed the river."

"I'm sorry," Anderson says. "I'd forgotten I had it written down."

The driver shifts back into gear and accelerates off. He expresses his impatience with Anderson by driving noticeably faster, braking sharply at stop signs, and taking the corners at high speed. Anderson, for his part, is simply relieved to be out of there.

It only takes them a few minutes to reach a major thoroughfare and to follow it back to the river. There the driver turns onto old Main and continues along the northeast bank.

Anderson studies the neighborhood, trying to get an idea of where they are headed. He has been there before, although not in several years. It is St. Anthony-on-Main, the oldest part of the city. After decades of neglect, the area was renovated in the 1970s with trendy shops and yuppie restaurants. But now the converted warehouses are out of fashion once more. Hooks for hanging plants jut naked from the overhangs, and broken 'Art Nouveau' windows stand partially boarded over. The taxi has to slow for the expensive cobbled streets, but speeds up over the cheap asphalt repairs.

When they arrive at the address, Anderson finds it is a huge apartment building, perhaps twenty stories tall at its highest point. The complicated design incorporates various wings and levels to add interest and increase the window area. Like the other buildings on the street, its walls are finished with brown brick. Small trees and other ornamental shrubbery decorate the terraces and balconies. It looks expensive.

Anderson intends merely to look the place over from outside and then leave. But, as the taxi pulls up in front, Anderson is spotted by the doorman, who runs out to greet them. Before Anderson has figured out what he is up to, the man has opened the taxi door.

"Welcome back, Mr. Peterson," the doorman says in a hearty voice. "I didn't know you were coming back tonight."

Startled and confused by this, Anderson lets the doorman help him out of the taxi. "Hello," he says, nodding noncommittally.

"Can I get your luggage, sir?" the doorman asks.

"There's no luggage," the taxi driver volunteers and looks at Anderson expectantly. "Seven dollars and eighty cents," he says.

Anderson fumbles for the wallet in his pocket, wondering what to do next. How can he get away from here, without making things even more awkward?

The doorman sees his hesitation. "I'll take care of it, sir," he says, quickly pulling out a roll of small-denomination bills. He peels off two fives for the driver and gives the man a little salute, indicating he expects no change.

"Thanks," the driver says. "Have a good evening." He drives off.

The doorman turns back to Anderson. "I almost didn't recognize you without your beard." He gives Anderson a broad grin. Then he turns and opens the door to the building, gesturing for Anderson to go ahead.

For a moment, Anderson is tempted to turn and run. But he knows any unexpected action might only get him into further trouble. He can even imagine how the doorman might start shouting and chase him up the street, if he were to bolt. He forces himself to act calm. To speak as little as possible. To do nothing abrupt.

Realizing the door is still being held for him, Anderson enters the lobby. The floor is of polished stone and the furniture of satin and fine wood. Pictures decorate the rose-patterned walls, and lush green plants surround the furnishings. The light fixtures look like French street lamps from the nineteenth century. In this setting, Anderson feels even more out of place.

"It makes you look younger," the doorman says, catching up with him. "Not having a beard, I mean."

Anderson tries to smile, as though pleased at the remark, hoping this will be a sufficient response.

"There's been a lot of mail in the last couple days," the doorman says, stepping behind the reception desk. "I'll carry it up to your apartment with you."

"That's okay," Anderson says, forced to speak. "I can get it later."

The doorman is pulling mail out from somewhere below and stacking it on the counter. As he hears Anderson's words, he stops and looks at him for a moment, apparently puzzled. Then he resumes his task. "I've already put most of it inside," he says. "If I bring this batch up now, you'll have all of it."

"Here, I can take it," Anderson says, desperate to avoid an escort.

"No, I'll bring it," the doorman says. Before Anderson can protest further, he scoops it up in his arms and heads for the marble stairway. At the bottom, he stops and waits for Anderson to go ahead.

Anderson feels he has no choice but to go along. At the top of the stairs, there is a blank wall. It has a wide corridor running in front of it, perpendicular to the stairway. The floor is covered with a dark blue carpet, stretching in each direction. Anderson hesitates. Right or left? Then he looks back and sees the doorman veering to the right, so he goes in that direction. The doorman follows without comment.

As they reach the first apartment doors, Anderson begins to slow down. How will he know which one to stop at? What will he do when it's time to unlock the door? They pass the first couple of doors without incident, but Anderson is painfully aware each apartment they approach could be the one he is expected to enter.

When the corridor takes a turn to the left, the steady sound of the doorman's footsteps seem to push Anderson around the corner. Then, with a long, straight stretch ahead, Anderson hangs back, hoping the doorman will take the lead. Anderson wants to be behind him, not just so the doorman will show the way, but so that no one will be between Anderson and the exit, if he has to make a run for it.

For a moment, as Anderson slows down, the doorman almost stops. But finally, as Anderson stands aside, the doorman walks past him and on down the hallway. To Anderson, the dark blue carpeted floor looks like a river or a canal. He feels himself being swept down it, as though by a strong current.

A few seconds later, their destination becomes clear. It is the apartment door in the wall across the far end of the corridor. Its heavy wooden panels look imposing. As they approach it, Anderson tries frantically to think of an excuse that will allow him to get out of there. Could he say he has left his key somewhere and must go to get it?

But before Anderson can speak, the doorman takes a key chain from his pocket, fumbles with it until he finds the key he wants, and then unlocks the apartment door. Pushing the door open with his knee, the doorman steps inside, sets down the mail, and switches on the lights. Then he returns to the hallway and begins removing the key from his key chain.

"I guess if you're going to be here awhile, you won't need me to water your plants," the doorman says, holding the key out to Anderson.

Anderson takes it, wondering what else is expected of him. "Thank you for everything," he says.

The doorman pushes the apartment door until it is open wide and holds it for Anderson. Anderson steps through it, then turns back toward the doorman, wondering if he should be giving him some money.

But the doorman is already closing the door and turning to walk away. The soft thud of the door against its frame seems to echo in both directions. Before he has even realized what has happened, Anderson has been left alone in the stranger's apartment.

With the doorman somewhere outside, Anderson doesn't feel that he can just turn around and leave. Not for a few minutes, anyway. Nor is he sure he wants to. He leans against the door frame, his forehead touching the molding. He makes himself breathe more deeply and slowly. What is his next move? What will allow him to escape this nightmare once and for all?

Somewhere in this apartment should be the answers he needs. He must force himself to find them.

C H A P T E R 4

What Anderson sees, when he looks around, amazes him. It is an enormous, ceremonial entry hall, running across the front of the apartment. The room is perhaps fifteen feet deep and three times as wide. Facing him, on the wall opposite, are carved stone panels and pillars. It is like something out of a medieval church or abbey. There are niches that seem to be designed for statues, but there is nothing in them.

The Gothic stonework draws his eye upward. Although the corridor outside is of normal height, this entry hall seems to be nearly two stories. High in front of him, thrusting out from the wall, are deeper pedestals protected by stone canopies. But these, too, are empty. Below, and beneath Anderson's feet, is a polished marble floor. The overall effect is very grand and vaguely French.

For a moment, Anderson stands there, almost too awed to move. Then he turns his attention to the more practical aspects of the situation. His pulse is too fast, his breathing too rapid. He tells himself to slow down, to take things as methodically as possible.

In the middle of the entry hall, between Anderson and the carved stone wall, is a long, wooden table with two chairs. It is piled high with mail, including the stack the doorman has just carried up. Beyond it, some distance on either side, are two wide doorways, opening into darkness.

Listening for any sound of human presence, Anderson tiptoes forward to look more closely at the mail. The name and address on each item are the same as on the driver's license in Anderson's pocket. Most of the envelopes appear to be advertisements and business correspondence. There are none that look like personal letters. Anderson checks a couple of post-marks from the bottom of the pile and sees that they are from several weeks earlier. The fact that no one appears to have opened the mail in so long causes him to relax slightly.

He runs the knuckle of his forefinger over the top of the hall table and finds it leaves a track on the dusty surface. This, too, reassures him. It seems no one has been here recently, except to drop off the mail.

With considerable nervousness, Anderson realizes he needs to explore the rooms beyond. Somewhere here, there should be at least a hint of what has led to his kidnapping and near murder. He will just have to be careful not to disturb anything.

Looking right and left, he notices narrower doors at the ends of the room. Through one, he sees a towel rack and the corner of a sink. Through the other, some coats, a tennis racket, and a bag of golf clubs. They make the Gothic setting seem more like someone's home.

Turning back to the front door, he sees it has dead bolts, top and bottom. He reaches out to slide one home, then hesitates. Anyone who arrived and found the door bolted from inside would know someone was in the apartment. That could make escape more difficult.

His hand drops. He notices ornamental benches to each side and, above them, broad wooden cupboards, set into the paneled wall. He pulls one open. Inside are shelves filled with scarves, gloves, and hats. The sight of the gloves gives him an idea. He picks out a pair and puts them on. His hands are shaking. But the gloves fit perfectly. He uses them to wipe the cupboard knob and the table he has just touched.

Feeling that the gloves are somehow protecting him, he moves around the table toward the left hand door that pene-trates the stonework. He is no longer on tiptoe, but he is acutely aware of each sound. Cautiously, he gropes for a light switch.

As the table lamps go on in front of him, he finds himself entering a 'gentlemen's lounge.' The decor is very masculine, but stunningly luxurious, full of rich wood paneling. High-backed, leather chairs are arranged beside elegant, wooden end-tables. Expensive lampshades give off a golden light. It reminds Ander-son of photographs he has seen of fashionable London men's clubs. Moving deeper into the room, he recognizes the distinctive odors of saddle soap and unburned pipe tobacco.

His attention is caught by some hunting pictures on the walls. One shows men with shotguns and dogs walking through a field. Another shows a group of hunters gathered around a kill. A third shows a table piled high with game. They are the sort of scenes normally regarded as reassuringly traditional, but the details are slightly gruesome. The hunting dogs are drooling madly. The freshly killed animal is bleeding profusely. The game has staring, lifeless eyes.

Anderson turns away with a shudder. Between and below the pictures he notices bookcases, built into the walls. The ones extending to the ceiling hold old, finely bound volumes of ancient classics and philosophy. The ones lower down hold volumes on law, politics, and economics. It occurs to Anderson that these books might be an important clue to the owner's identity. They are very decorative, but they seem to have been chosen for more than their bindings.

Taking the decor as a whole, Anderson decides it is the sort of lounge that might belong to a rich attorney or stockbroker. He wonders if the next rooms will confirm his guess. Another door stands open in the opposite wall, but he chooses one to his right, turning off the lights as he leaves the room.

For a few seconds, he is left mostly in the dark. Groping along the wall, he notices this new room smells of furniture polish and wool carpeting. Several yards farther to his right, he can see the brightly lit doorway leading back to the entry hall. But it doesn't illuminate the area where he now stands.

Then his hand stumbles on the light switch. More than a dozen lamps of assorted sizes and varieties go on in front of him. Anderson finds himself standing in a huge living room. If the lounge had seemed comfortably large, this space is immense. There are several clusters of chairs and sofas, creating a series of areas for intimate conversations. Straight ahead, some distance away, the floor descends through four levels, forming an arena like conversation pit. Each level is strewn with cushions and pillows. In the middle of this arena is a large circular fireplace with a free standing chimney rising above it to the ceiling.

As he moves farther into the room, the sheer size of it makes

Anderson feel almost overwhelmed. There is simply too much to take in at once. Anderson is struck by the richness and softness of the carpet, the many upholstered surfaces, including walls and cabinets, the use of fur, suede, and silk. On the main level, nearer to him, on his left, stands a baby grand piano. Two giant, white statues of Greek or Roman heads are placed asymmetrically in the other quadrants, helping to provide a balance for the fireplace and piano. Despite a considerable quantity of furniture, there are still large areas of open space.

Anderson can see at once that the layout would be perfect for large cocktail parties. In fact, as Anderson thinks of this, he notices a complete bar built into the far, left hand wall. Like the entry hall, the whole living room is rather theatrical in decor. But otherwise it is consistent with Anderson's guess that the apartment belongs to a wealthy attorney or broker. The colors are a conservative mixture of pale blues, pinks, and grays. Looking from one area to another, Anderson finds it easy to imagine dozens of clients being entertained here at the same time. The silence, in a room so obviously designed for conversation, is slightly disturbing.

Across the living room, in the far wall, are high windows. Conscious that he might be visible from the street, Anderson walks over to close the draperies. As he moves between the furnishings, he notices that every part of the room is dotted with original art works. They come from a variety of periods, although very few of them are abstract or aggressively contemporary.

Pulling on the drapery cords, Anderson looks for some significance in these art works. At first, he doesn't see why they were selected. Then he notices they all have something in common. Each painting or sculpture appears innocent at first, but on closer examination, coyly erotic. There are flowers suggestive of sexual organs, figures who seem to be groping each other in the places hidden from view, faces with expressions a little too ecstatic. Only the two classical heads seem free of innuendo, and even they are made voyeurs by the presence of the other objects.

As he surveys the art works, Anderson notices an enormous aquarium between two of the conversation areas. He approaches it and sees it is teeming with exotic tropical fish. The tank is without decorations, but the fish are the most brilliantly colored

Anderson has ever seen. They are swimming vigorously around, darting at the surface, competing for the white flakes of food floating on the water.

Anderson freezes. The fish have just been fed. At the rate they are eating, the food couldn't last for more than a few minutes. He looks around for further signs of human life, listening intently. Has someone just left the room? Is someone still in the apartment?

Then he hears a whirring sound coming from the top of the fish tank. More flakes of food hit the surface of the water. He realizes there is some kind of electric feeding mechanism built into the top of the tank. He relaxes slightly and begins moving around again.

Gradually, Anderson notices features that make the room useful for more than cocktail parties. Behind some of the furniture and here and there against the walls are bookcases holding coffee table sized volumes on art and travel. The built-in shelves beside the elaborate sound system hold thousands of classical and jazz CDs. There are also bound volumes of music, again mostly classical. A man with a taste for the arts could spend many pleasant evenings here, alone or with a single companion.

Anderson has seen enough of this room. But he has a nagging feeling he is missing the significance of something. He senses some peculiarity in the furnishings, but can't say what it is. Perhaps, as he moves on, he will think of it.

He passes an open door in the wall opposite the entry hall. It leads to a dining room. A few yards beyond it is a door to a hallway. Anderson reaches through it and pushes a switch. It lights a corridor that seems to run from the living room, down the middle of the apartment, to the far end. Set into the walls of the hallway are bookcases, interrupted at regular intervals by doors. To Anderson, it seems a tunnel into the inner recesses of the apartment owner's personality.

But Anderson doesn't enter this hallway right away. Instead, he turns back toward where he has come from and enters the room adjoining the gentlemen's lounge. Standing inside the door, Anderson is not sure, at first, what he is looking at. It appears to be an excessively large pool table with excessively small pockets. Then he realizes it must be a snooker table.

The surroundings are once again like an elite men's club. But this time the walls hold no pictures. Instead, there is only a rack for cues and a set of velvet panels displaying military decorations. The awards are far too numerous and diverse for one man to have received them all. They include both a Congressional Medal of Honor and a Victoria Cross. Yet despite the number and variety of the medals, the collection does not seem to be historical. The ribbons and medallions show no signs of age.

Anderson tries to imagine the kind of personality that would assemble such trophies. Could his hypothetical lawyer or stockbroker have had an earlier career in the military? Do these medals suggest a continuing involvement with the military? And why would a man want to display other men's medals anyway?

Glancing upward, Anderson notices rows of bookshelves near the ceiling. They hold English and European fiction. He wonders how these books fit in with the medal collection.

Then a telephone begins ringing, a few feet away.

It takes Anderson only a moment to locate it. The phone is just inside the door to the next room. Automatically, Anderson reaches for the light switch and turns it on.

Stepping cautiously through the door, Anderson stares at the phone, but doesn't answer it. The ringing seems to go on interminably. Then, finally, it stops.

The phone sits on the corner of a huge, leather topped desk. The desk sits toward one end of what appears to be a large private office.

The most striking feature of the office, as Anderson glances around it, is a collection of antique scientific instruments. There is a brass microscope, a large metal syringe, a metal and glass device for distilling liquids, an apothecary scale, an air pump connected to a bell jar, and a set of surgical tools in a velvet lined case. On the desk itself is an antique scalpel with a dull blade, apparently now used as a letter opener.

Apart from the instruments themselves, the furnishings are in a late nineteenth century, American style. The chairs are of wood, but with padded arms and backs. Around the sides of the room are tall bookcases holding volumes on medicine and biology.

Across the room, Anderson spots a large, glass topped case,

standing on its own legs. He walks over to it and, for a moment, holds his breath. The case contains a carefully mounted display of bones. They are skeletons of paws, feet, flippers, and hands, all laid out side by side, like an exhibit of comparative anatomy. There are no labels, but the analogies between the skeletal structures are easy to spot. The human bones are treated no differently than the others.

Anderson realizes these furnishings are not consistent with his idea of an attorney or stockbroker as the apartment's owner. They are more like those that might have been chosen by a distinguished physician.

He bends over to get a closer look at the one picture on the wall. It is an eighteenth century print, actually showing a visit to a physician. With some surprise, Anderson finds he can recognize the artist's style. It is Hogarth or someone imitating him. To a modern eye, the picture looks quaint, but it is still disconcertingly satirical. The physician is engaged in bloodletting. As he holds a little cup near the patient's neck, the dark liquid can be seen spurting out.

Is this the sort of print a modern physician would choose for his private office? Anderson can't decide if it confirms his guess or makes it less likely.

Returning to the desk, Anderson begins pulling open the drawers. The top ones are shallow and nearly empty. They contain pens, a ruler, a box of paper clips, some credit cards for local stores, and some plastic sealed identification cards for video rental shops. All the cards are in Peterson's name.

The next drawer on the left is deeper and holds bills addressed to Peterson. They are mostly for household expenses, such as electricity and gas. The only 'personal' ones are for tailored clothing and for dental work. Each bill is marked "paid," with the amount written in longhand. The recent utility payments were all four times the amount owed. Evidently, Peterson had covered this quarter in advance.

The other drawers merely contain office supplies and phone books. No jottings or letters. No address book or appointment calendar.

Disappointed at finding nothing more revealing, Anderson moves on to the next room. As he turns on the lights, he is startled by movement on all sides. He jumps back, banging his shoulder on the door frame. When he stops moving, the movement around him stops as well. Anderson is in an elaborately mirrored bathroom. He is surrounded by images of himself. But it is not himself as he thinks he looks now. It is more himself as he had looked a few years earlier.

Only after close examination does Anderson realize this is indeed his face, his figure. His beard is gone, and he looks surprisingly healthy. He stops to examine his features up close. Then he realizes that this is the face of the dead man. The dead man had also been clean shaven. The dead man had also looked the way Anderson had looked a few years before, the way, in fact, Anderson looks now. Staring at the mirror, Anderson feels seasick. The blood drains from his head. It is all he can do to keep from vomiting.

He staggers through the door on the far side of the bathroom, back into the central hallway. Still reeling from what he has seen, he stumbles against the bookcases in the far wall. He notices he has pushed in some of the books and pauses to straighten them. In his present frame of mind, he finds even the most innocuous histories and biographies seem ominous. He tries to push from his consciousness the things too disturbing to deal with now. He tells himself to calm down, to breathe deeply.

Across the hallway, a little farther along, is another door. Stepping through it, Anderson realizes he is in the dining room. Its decor is Scandinavian Modern—austere, but pleasant. The ubiquitous bookcases hold atlases and folio volumes of natural history. The one unsettling element is an enormous sheet of fossil rock, mounted on one wall. Embedded in the stone are the remains of a prehistoric fish, several feet long. Its most distinctive features are a large eye, with a ring of bone around it, and a long snout, with numerous small, sharp teeth. Dead for millions of years, it still looks menacing.

Anderson withdraws, heading back across the hallway, into what appears to be a 'high tech' study. On a series of separate stands, he finds a computer, a document scanner, a printer, the largest visual display unit he has ever seen, and a number of electronic devices he cannot identify. It is only the numerous green plants, luxuriant under their 'grow lights,' that prevent the place from looking excessively sterile.

Near the main computer keyboard, Anderson spots a small plastic filing cabinet. He opens it eagerly. Inside, he finds numerous floppy disks. But they all have printed labels, identifying them as holding commercial software. None of the disks looks as though it contains any personal documents. Nor is there any larger, hard disk in evidence.

Despite the numerous eccentricities of the apartment, Anderson is struck by the fact that it contains very little of a really personal nature. There are occasional signs that the apartment has actually been lived in. But the lifestyle of the occupant seems too perfect, too uncluttered. Anderson feels more perplexed than ever.

He takes a closer look at one of the unfamiliar electronic devices. It is a glass globe nearly a foot across. As he watches, it springs to life with a dancing, treelike 'sculpture' of electron beams. It must have been turned on with the lights, but only now warmed up. Anderson brushes his hand against it and finds that the beams rearrange themselves to flow toward his fingertips. The beams are mesmerizing, but Anderson forces himself to turn away.

He scans the room for any clues he might have missed. Once more, he notices bookcases set into the walls. There have been so many already, he is in danger of taking them for granted. This set holds works on computer programming, mathematics, and the physical sciences.

When he considers these books, along with the computing equipment, Anderson is once again forced to revise his guess about the apartment's owner. No physician, whom Anderson has ever heard of, would be at home with so much mathematics and electronics. This study is more what Anderson would expect of a high tech entrepreneur or inventor.

Moving on to the next room on the same side of the apartment, Anderson at first thinks his new deduction is confirmed. It is a workout room or gym, gleaming with the latest technology. The room's centerpiece is an elaborate exercise machine. It is a complicated assembly of chrome bars, hydraulic pistons, thick black pads, and molded leather grips. There are electronic gauges and counters on each side, devices for measuring pulse rate and blood pressure, controls for setting tension curves. It is the kind of thing that has an instruction book as thick as a programming manual.

Anderson thinks of the exercise equipment that stands gathering cobwebs in his own basement. The shaky wooden frame, which he had built for himself as a weight bench. The plastic disks filled with concrete, which he would clamp on a pipe as weights. The rusty, jangling springs, which would pinch his flesh, when he used them as a chest expander. It all seems pretty pathetic, compared to the machine standing in front of him now.

Circling around it, Anderson sees it is not the only piece of high tech training equipment. Toward one end of the room is a padded leather massage table with electronic controls for activating various combinations of rollers and vibrators. A cross country skiing simulator stands beside it, facing a machine for playing video recordings. But no videotapes are in evidence.

Then Anderson spies something far more interesting. Spread across the far wall is a collection of framed photographs. They catch Anderson's attention, because they promise to be more personal than most of what he has seen so far. He hurries over for a closer look.

Viewed from only a few inches away, the photographs seem so ordinary, so familiar, that it takes Anderson a moment to see what is so odd about them. Then, almost like a physical blow, the significance of the images hits him.

The photographs are pictures of Anderson himself. They show him with people he has never met. He is bearded in most of the pictures, clean shaven in a few of them, but unmistakable in nearly all. Some of the surroundings in the photographs are vaguely familiar, but the situations are ones he is sure he has never been in.

In one photo, he sees himself sitting in a park with a local television anchorwoman. He gazes off at the horizon, while she looks adoringly up at him. Her face is one he knows well, and he can almost hear her voice, but he is sure he has never met her.

In another photo, he is arm in arm with a United States senator. He looks calm and self-possessed, while the senator turns nervously toward him, as though desperate to gain his approval. Anderson remembers once hearing this senator speak at a public rally, but he is sure he has never been within a hundred feet of him.

None of the other photos shows Anderson with people he recognizes. But the figures pictured beside him all look glamorous and important. Most of all, they look eager to please him.

Anderson turns away in a daze. Drifting absent-mindedly across the hall, he finds himself in the apartment's kitchen. His mind continues to take in data, but he can't process it immediately. He opens a door to his right and is vaguely aware of a pantry leading to the dining room. He turns back to the kitchen itself and is dazzled by its profusion of equipment. The counters and recesses seem to contain every kind of culinary appliance imaginable. He opens a cupboard and finds the most complete spice rack he has ever seen. Between the cupboards are shelves of cookery books. In the middle of the work space is an enormous, butcher block table with pans of all sizes suspended above.

Turning toward the other end of the room, Anderson sees a breakfast area resembling an outdoor patio. Amid enormous planters filled with flowers, there are four chairs, a small table, and a large chaise longue. Beyond are tall windows, curtained in yellow and white.

Anderson tries another door, near the one to the pantry. It leads to a large storage room stocked with cans, packaged foods, and cleaning supplies. Then he notices a curious door in the opposite wall with a rubber seal around its edge and a lever for a handle. Pulling it open, Anderson finds himself looking into a climatically controlled wine cellar. It is like a cavern beneath a French or German castle, complete with cobwebs. The whole space is chilled, damp, and musty smelling. From floor to ceiling, it is stacked with wine bottles, including large quantities of champagne.

With the cold air on his face, Anderson suddenly feels less dazed. He decides he needs another look at the photographs in the workout room. Did he really see what he thinks he saw? Could there be some simple explanation he has missed? Closing the wine cellar door, he heads back across the hall.

This time, as he stares at them, the photographs make Anderson feel literally unreal. Their presence is consistent with the surroundings. His presence is not. They will remain solidly framed and fixed to the wall. He will finish his explorations and then disappear. Instead of the images in the pictures haunting him, he feels as though he is haunting them.

Anderson shivers and turns away. He hurries through a sliding door to the adjoining room and feels as though he has stepped into summer. It is a private 'spa' in the most sybaritic Californian style. In the middle is a small plunge pool, with a floating cover of bubbled plastic. Toward one end is a large Jacuzzi, tightly covered with plasticized canvas. The floor itself is carpeted with a green, waterproof material, like artificial grass, only softer. If he were a genuine guest, he would be tempted to take off his shoes.

All around the Jacuzzi, Anderson finds the accoutrements of luxurious living. Within easy reach is an electrically chilled champagne bucket. Nearby are a telephone and a set of electronic controls, waterproofed by a flexible plastic casing. On a low table about two feet away is a huge candelabrum, full of white candles, all half-burned. Set into the wall opposite is a video screen.

Anderson kneels and pulls back the corner of the Jacuzzi cover. Despite the fact that no one seems to have been here for weeks, the water is warm enough to make steam rise from the surface. Anderson hears a faint whir as a fan starts up, apparently triggered by the humidity. He removes one of the gloves he is wearing and puts his fingertips in the water. It feels very hot indeed. Is the Jacuzzi always this temperature or does it operate on a timer? The electronic controls might be capable of specifying the time the water is heated. In which case, was someone expected back here tonight? Or does the apartment's owner have the Jacuzzi ready every evening?

Surveying the total effect, Anderson can no longer match up his impressions of the apartment with his idea of a high tech entrepreneur. It is not that this room is out of character for an entrepreneur, but that it tips the balance too much toward self-indulgence. Throughout the apartment, there are simply too many facilities for partying, too many distractions, too many aspects of every room devoted entirely to pleasure. Whoever lives here must be someone who never has to worry about getting any work done. Anderson now finds himself imagining the apartment's owner as a playboy dilettante with inherited wealth.

Walking around the plunge pool, Anderson heads toward a door at the end of the room. It seems to lead to another bathroom. Before entering, Anderson braces himself for another view of his own reflection. But after the photographs on the workout room wall, he finds his own image, and the image of the dead man, much less disturbing.

Compared to the luxury of the Jacuzzi room, the bathroom seems relatively ordinary. It contains twin washbowls and a bathtub, with a toilet and bidet in a separate little room. There is a huge medicine cabinet behind one of the mirrors, but when Anderson looks inside he sees only standard drugstore remedies. The makeup table is slightly unusual, because it has lamps that can be adjusted to simulate several kinds of lighting. And there is an unusually large shower, separated from the rest of the room by a tiled wall. But the basic bathroom fixtures are like those in any expensive modern home.

Leaving the bathroom by the door through which he entered, Anderson circles back past the plunge pool, and opens a sliding door opposite the one from the workout room. The air on the other side of this door is noticeably drier and tinged with incense. Pressing the light switch, Anderson finds himself looking in on a kind of fantasy bedroom, obviously designed for 'play,' rather than sleep. There are scores of cushions and pillows of varying sizes, piled and strewn about, so that the low bed is only the largest cushion among many. The pillows are covered with a medley of hues, but dominated by reds, pinks, purples, and lavenders.

As he moves farther into the room, Anderson discovers the carpeted floor is so soft, it is difficult to walk upright across it. He imagines a female guest with a few drinks in her, giggling and falling to her knees as she is shown inside.

From a few feet into the room, the effect is like being in a tent. Draperies or curtains stretch from the ceiling back toward the walls. At one end of the room are Moorish windows, with pointed arches and intricately carved traceries. Everywhere else, the walls are upholstered in deep dyed silks. The ceiling is lower than in the other rooms, but there is a feeling of spaciousness, because nothing but cushions and pillows interrupts the sweep of the space. It is like the setting for an Arabian harem.

Anderson perches on the edge of the bed. Around the sides of the room are more bookcases, set low into the wall. He bends over for a closer look. The finely bound volumes seem to be works of theology and pornography, some so ancient or exotic, it is hard to tell the difference.

His eye is caught by a set of electric switches above the upper end of the bed. He shifts to a kneeling position, reaches across, and pushes the first button. Almost at once, he hears a low rumble coming from somewhere overhead. He ducks and rolls aside, landing on his hip and shoulder, then scrambling to his feet.

But nothing crashes down from above. Instead, he looks up to see a sliding panel slowly uncovering a mirror directly over the bed. Leaning across for a better view, he sees his own face peering back at him. He reaches out and presses the second switch. Another panel slides open with a similar low rumble. It reveals an angled mirror set in the wall at the head of the bed. A third switch uncovers a large video screen in the wall opposite.

As he thinks about the way everything is laid out, Anderson realizes he is feeling more than curiosity and apprehension. He is feeling envy. Envy for someone rich and uninhibited enough to create an apartment like this. Envy for someone who has obviously been leading a life far preferable to his own.

The odd thing is that throughout this realm, otherwise designed for pleasure, there are such vast numbers of technical and academic books, on such an incredible range of subjects. It is this that puzzles him most as he prepares to move on.

Stepping through the door on the far side of the bedroom, he feels as though he has entered a very expensive clothing store. Racks of clothes surround him, covering the greater portion of every wall. Between them are tiers of shelves holding folded shirts, underwear, and socks. The racks themselves contain long rows of trousers, sports coats, and suits, all grouped by color.

When he walks farther into the room, he is ambushed by moving figures. But this time he is ready for them. He rapidly realizes they are confined to floor length mirrors, grouped in sets of three and five. In front of the larger set is an elevated platform with spotlights and footlights, forming a little stage. Facing it are a chaise longue and two chairs, providing seating for a tiny audience.

Anderson wonders about the nature of the performances. Then he notices some further racks of clothes, shielded by screens to the sides of the platform. Stepping up for a closer look, he discovers they hold women's lingerie in a variety of sizes and styles. Most of the pieces are small and very revealing.

Looking over the rest of the room, Anderson spots the sort of idiosyncratic items he is beginning to expect. Mounted high in the walls are primitive masks, apparently from Africa, New Guinea, and Central America. Lower down, alternating with the clothes, are more bookcases, mostly devoted to the social sciences.

In one of the bookcases, Anderson notices some photograph albums. He takes one out and opens it. Inside are candid pictures of people relaxing, drinking, partying. At first Anderson thinks they are all people he doesn't recognize. Then he sees his own face, his own body. He is laughing beside a swimming pool. He is driving some kind of speedboat.

He has no memory of any occasions like those shown in the photos.

Turning the pages, he comes upon other photos of a more private nature. Women posing provocatively in various stages of undress. Amateur fashion parades of sexy lingerie, like the kind he has just seen. Men fondling women or being fondled by them. Naked couples engaged in a variety of sexual acts.

These photos look very different from the kind taken in a studio. Most are over- or underexposed, so that the bodies look unnaturally pale or unnaturally tanned. The figures are often caught at unflattering angles, so that even the trimmer bellies have folds in them and even the firmer breasts appear to sag. In the backgrounds are untidy bedrooms and bathrooms. Discarded clothing lies on the floors and furniture.

But the pictures are not, for the most part, candid shots that have caught their subjects unawares. Most of the faces look coyly or brazenly at the camera. A woman pulls down the neckline of her white summer dress to display a plump breast with a large brown nipple. A man stands proudly displaying himself, his hands on his hips. Another woman beckons the camera to come closer to the area between her widely spread legs. Even the more energetic couples strike self-conscious poses.

Anderson is in some of these pictures too.

One of them shows the television anchorwoman Anderson had recognized earlier in the wall photo. She is naked on all fours, her breasts curving out and downward, while Anderson crouches kneeling behind her. The open mouthed expression on her face leaves no doubt as to what he is doing to her.

As Anderson stares at the woman's photo, he suddenly realizes why her face had seemed so familiar, why he could so easily remember her voice. It was *her* news program which had led the others in the coverage of his grandfather's death. It was her voice which had provided the commentaries on the photos from his family's album. If he has never seen her in person, he has nonetheless thought of her often. Not recently perhaps, but with an anger he can still feel.

Anderson breaks into a sweat. He closes the album without going through the rest of the pictures. His hands are shaking. He puts the album back on the shelf and turns to leave the room.

The far door opens into a laundry room. It is very long, relatively narrow, and starkly practical. Strung out along the sides are the washing machine, two laundry tubs, a dryer, a clothes press, and drying racks. There is a door in the middle of the opposite wall, festooned with extra locks. Anderson decides this must be the back door to the apartment. He tries to open it, but finds he cannot undo the locks.

Eager now to get out of there, he tries the remaining door. It leads back to the kitchen. Anderson walks rapidly past the cooking facilities, down the central hallway, and through the living room. Along the way, he switches off the few lights he had left on earlier. The darkness closes in behind him. Arriving back in the entry hall, Anderson pauses, trying to think of any signs he may have left of his visit. But he is fairly certain he has disturbed nothing.

He opens the front door of the apartment, still wearing the gloves he has worn throughout his explorations. Then he removes the gloves and puts them back where he had found them, closing the cupboard with his sleeve. With a final glance at the Gothic stonework, he steps to the other side of the door and begins pulling the door shut with his forearm, so as not to leave fingerprints.

As he is doing this, Anderson hears the sound of fabric rustling down the corridor. He straightens up, self-consciously. The woman who is coming into view looks as though she is returning from some fashionable social event. She is a very leggy, sophisticated looking brunette. Her outfit is entirely black, except for long, dramatically white gloves. Her thighs push enticingly against her skirt, as she moves along the hallway in her high-heeled shoes.

She sees Anderson balanced there, halfway out the door. She smiles and looks directly into his eyes. For a moment, Anderson stands frozen, staring at her. Then he tries to give her the sort of smile and nod used for acknowledging neighbors. With a little luck, she will enter one of the other apartments, forgetting she ever saw him.

But the woman doesn't turn aside, nod back, or look away. She continues to hold his eyes with hers, walking straight toward him. One of her hands clutches the lapels of a short, brocaded jacket, draped lightly over her shoulders. The other holds a small purse. Her smile turns into a grin as she draws closer.

"Well, don't *you* look dashing," she says in a quiet, musical voice. She stops a few feet away and stands looking at him, her eyes sparkling.

"Hi," he says lamely. A friendly neighbor is the last thing he needs right now.

"Why you ever wanted to cover up that darling chin, I can't imagine."

Anderson realizes the woman must be mistaking him for Peterson, just as the doorman had earlier.

"How have you been?" he asks, hoping her answer will give him some clue to who she is.

But she is too interested in *him*. "I wasn't sure you were back. How was your vacation?"

"Fine," he answers. The terse reply sounds awkward, but he is afraid if he says more, he will get something wrong.

"I'm so glad I've found you in," she says.

Anderson can see she expects a specific response, but doesn't know what kind.

The woman seems amused at his confusion. "Don't tell me you've forgotten me already!"

She is classically beautiful, with high cheekbones, delicately sculpted features, and large brown eyes. Anderson is sure he has never seen her before. How well did Peterson know her?

"There's no way I could forget anyone who looks like you," he says truthfully.

But she's already shaking her head. "And after such an encouraging invitation too!"

Anderson is stymied.

She leans forward, raising her eyebrows. "I'm Dotty's friend, remember?"

"Oh, yes," he says, trying to sound convincing, but sure he isn't succeeding.

"You know you *did* tell me to drop by any time." There is a note of rebuke in her voice, but her tone is still playful.

Anderson raises his hands in a vague gesture of apology.

"I phoned a little while ago, but you didn't answer," she explains. "Then I was driving by and saw your lights. I thought I'd see if you were receiving callers."

"I am pleased to see you," he says, somewhat belatedly.

"Then aren't you going to invite me in?" She makes the suggestion lightheartedly, but pauses, waiting for his reply.

Anderson doesn't see how to avoid it. He realizes her arrival will have the effect of trapping him in the apartment awhile longer. But he still intends to escape as soon as he can.

He pushes the door open, switches on the lights, and ushers her into the entry hall.

Her head tilts slowly back as she takes in the Gothic stonework. "Oh, my. I *am* impressed. What did you do, ship it all over from Europe?"

Anderson is relieved. It sounds as though she has never been in the apartment before. She must know Peterson, but not very well. It occurs to Anderson he might actually be successful in passing himself off as Peterson, at least long enough to get rid of her.

She turns her back to him and lifts her jacket. Anderson takes it off her shoulders.

"Thank you," she murmurs.

He carries the jacket over to the closet at the end of the room.

"I was at the most boring party," she says, as he is walking back. She sets her purse on one of the ornamental benches and begins removing her gloves.

Now that her jacket is off, Anderson is very aware of the way she looks in her black dress. The straps in front cross over each other and go around her neck. They leave her shoulders and upper back completely bare.

"You know what I mean," she continues, "the kind of party that makes you want to say or do something outrageous. Just to make things more interesting."

Anderson nods, distracted by the way she is slowly peeling off her gloves.

"Anyway, it made me think of you." She pauses and smiles, as though to herself. "It made me think of that little invitation you gave me."

"I'm flattered."

She drops her gloves on the bench beside her purse. "Isn't it lucky I saw your lights?"

"Yes, I guess so."

"Have I come at a bad time?" She sounds genuinely concerned. "Oh, my God, you don't have another woman here right now do you?"

"No. There's no one here but me." Anderson wonders if he has understood her correctly. She seems to be implying she is one of a series of women, constantly visiting the apartment.

"Well, then," she says, "what are you going to do to make me feel welcome?"

"Can I offer you a drink?"

"I had more than enough to drink at the last party."

"What would you like, then?"

There's mischief in her eyes. "Come on, make me another offer."

"Something to eat?"

"You can do better than that." She cocks her hip, resting her hand on it.

Anderson tries to remember how to be a proper host.

"Would you like to come into the living room? Put on some music or something?"

"Let's stay in here a minute. It's like a monastery, isn't it?"

"I guess so."

"But it must be a very decadent monastery."

"Perhaps." Anderson swallows. As he struggles to give the appropriate responses, he finds himself responding almost too well.

"What takes place in a very decadent monastery?"

"What do you mean?"

"Do the monks succumb to temptation?" Her eyes open wide as she asks the question, and a smile plays at the corners of her mouth.

Anderson knows he is being manipulated, but can't bring himself to stop it. "What sort of temptation?" he asks.

She steps forward, stretching her body upward. "How about this?" She kisses him lightly on the mouth. "Is this what the monks like?"

Anderson notices she is trembling, but if she is nervous or cold, there is no other sign of it.

She kisses him again, at first just nibbling his lips, then pressing her mouth more firmly against his, finally probing him lightly with her tongue.

Anderson can't help but respond. He feels a hunger he can't control. As he pushes his tongue into her mouth, she opens it cavernously around him, so that, no matter how far he reaches, he can barely graze her with his tongue's tip.

"Ooh, that's nice," she murmurs, as she stops to catch her breath.

Anderson starts to speak, but she puts her fingers to his lips and shakes her head. He realizes he is losing control of the situation, but doesn't know how to regain it.

She smiles as though she is aware of this. "Here," she says, "let me show you what else might interest the monks."

She steps back, undoes the strap around her neck, and lets the top of her dress drop forward. Then she stands there a moment, so he can admire her. Under her dress, she is wearing a strapless garment that supports her breasts from beneath. It holds them up and out, as though presenting them for inspection, not quite covering her nipples. Her nipples are very pink, a little larger than half dollars, her breasts surprisingly full, given her slender figure. Below her breasts, the garment extends downward past her waist.

Anderson has some memory of such items of clothing being called 'merrywidows.' This one is deep purple in color, so dark it seems almost black. Above it, the woman's breasts look startlingly white. They jiggle slightly, as she reaches her arms above her head and removes a clip from her hair. Pleased with the effect she is having on him, she poses for a moment with her arms in the air, moving them to move her breasts. Then she opens her mouth and slowly licks her upper lip with the tip of her tongue, her eyes dancing. It is a parody of a sexual come-on, but no less sexy for being ironic.

She steps toward him again, putting her arms around him and tilting her face up for another kiss. Anderson realizes that by catering to him, she is increasingly controlling him. As he kisses her, she arches her body slightly away from him and begins undoing his shirt buttons. Reaching the lower ones, she pulls his shirt tail out of his trousers. When she has undone the last button, she pushes the shirt back off his shoulders, so that it falls part way down his arms.

Smiling in appreciation of his swimmer's muscles, she steps away again. She reaches her arms behind her and struggles for a moment with the back of her dress, her slender arms and elbows pointing outward, like wings. The dress falls to the floor, forming a kind of drapery around her feet. She steps out of it, shaking it gently off her foot.

The garment beneath ends just above her hips. From the bottom of it extend garter straps that connect to her sheer, black stockings. There are little ribbons tied in bows over the snaps at each end. Crossing the garter straps is a pair of delicate lace panties with a dark silk triangle in the middle. Between the stockings and the undergarment is a wide expanse of pale thigh.

Still in her high-heeled shoes, she takes a further step back, so that she is six feet or so away from him. She holds her left leg out for him to admire it, smoothing the stocking tantalizingly upward with her hands. Her legs look endlessly long in the high heels and dark stockings. Then, with a mischievous look, she turns around to face away from him, spreads her legs, and bends over. She smiles at him from under her arm, her face upside down, her hair hanging away from her head.

Anderson stares at the way her dark silk panties stretch tightly across her firm bottom. He has a sudden feeling that he is witnessing a performance. He knows she is toying with him, but has no will to resist. He swallows, his throat getting thick.

The woman puts her hands between her legs and caresses the backs of her thighs with her fingertips, watching him all the while. Each move she makes seems to have something deliberate about it, as though every detail has been choreographed in advance. "I wouldn't do this for anyone else," she murmurs, slipping one finger inside the edge of her panties. Her eyes are now half closed, but they watch for his response.

As he wonders exactly what is expected of him, Anderson is intensely aware that this has all been planned for someone else. The woman is shaping her performance to the specific desires of the man watching her. But these desires, although ones he can share, are not precisely his. He knows he is the only man present, the sole object of the woman's attentions. Yet he feels as though he is looking in on someone else's love scene. Her provocative posture as she runs her fingers over her shapely thighs is not one he himself would have encouraged. Yet for this very reason it excites him all the more.

The woman straightens up and turns back toward him. She eases off her shoes and approaches him in stocking feet, holding out her arms to softly push him backward. Anderson is drawn irrevocably into the performance. He feels a fear akin to stage fright. The role in which he is being cast seems a long way from any he has played in the past. He knows he should be doing something different, that the way things are going is not a good idea. But he doesn't know what else to say or do.

With the woman guiding him, he backs into the living room until he feels the nudge of a high backed chair against his shoulder blades. The light from the doorway makes her appear as a curvaceous silhouette, edged with golden highlights. Still keeping him for a moment at arm's length, her fingers find his nipples and lightly brush against them. Then, at last, she moves in closer, pressing her body against his.

This time, it is silk and lace his fingers reach under. He feels the material stretching against the back of his hands. It is very different from the cut-off jeans and cotton he has known before. The woman's body, too, is very different. There is nothing girlish about it. Her figure is long and lean, without a trace of puppy fat. Yet her flesh seems softer and more delicate than any other he has felt. Touching her makes him forget all other concerns.

As he finds the delicate, moist spot inside her panties, he feels her reaching for his zipper and hears her pulling it down. He eases the tip of his finger into her. Her hand gropes inside his fly. They stand for many moments, each making the other shudder and quiver, poised on the edge of something more. Then she gently frees herself.

She slides downward until she is on her knees, her face and hand burrowing in his lap. He feels her taking him in her mouth. He looks down and sees the top of her head rocking slightly from side to side, her thick, dark hair falling against his trousers. He feels the flat of her tongue, the rim of her lips. Slowly at first, then gradually faster, her head moves up and down. Her mouth moves with it.

For the time being, at least, Anderson's nightmare becomes a dream.

C H A P T E R 5

The telephone is ringing. Anderson wakes with a sense of emerging from some dark, turbulent realm. He lifts his head and looks around. He is alone and, for a moment, uncertain where he is. Then, gradually, he recognizes the setting. He is lying on a couch at the end of a huge living room. The one he was exploring the night before. The seductive woman is gone. There is a knit blanket spread over him and a cushion under his head. The bright light of day gilds the edges of the drapes along the far side of the room. The classical heads loom in profile.

The telephone continues to ring. Anderson stands up and finds he is naked. He looks around for his clothes, but sees only a paisley robe draped across the couch he was lying on. He feels disoriented and struggles to get his bearings. The memories coming back to him do not seem to have any obvious gaps. But it is as though everything during the last couple of days has taken place in a haze or in some strange light. Even the things around him, that he remembers from the night before, all look slightly different.

On a nearby coffee table, Anderson sees a note, anchored by a ceramic dish and protruding over the table's edge. It is written in dark blue ink on pale blue note paper. The handwriting has large round loops with little hearts dotting the *i*'s and periods, like the penmanship of a little girl, showing off. The message is short:

My Darling Genius,
*   You were perfect last night. Let's do it again soon! Had to leave early for an important business meeting. Will phone later.*

*   Love,*
*   Shannon*

At first, the salutation makes Anderson feel even more disoriented. Only after he has stared at the words for several seconds does he realize the note must have been left for him. Its author must have been the seductive woman of the night before. Apparently, her name was Shannon. Apparently, the note is just to explain why she has gone. But who was she, apart from being a woman named Shannon? And why would she call him a genius?

It occurs to Anderson that she could be the one trying to phone him that very moment. But he doesn't dare pick up the phone. After a few more rings, it finally stops.

In the silence that follows, Anderson becomes aware that he is still naked. What has happened to his clothes? He pulls on the paisley robe and sets off to find them. He doesn't remember doing anything with them. Maybe there are gaps in his memory after all. He walks back through the living room, then on through the adjoining rooms, crisscrossing the central hallway. Scanning each room for the missing clothing, Anderson is relieved to notice the apartment is roughly as he remembers it. But his memories from the day before are very disturbing.

Reaching the kitchen, Anderson realizes he is starved. He opens the refrigerator, but finds no milk, eggs, fruit, or bread. Nothing fresh or suitable for breakfast. Only fancy preserves, brandy butter, green mustard, and caviar. Things that have been pickled or candied. Little jars that look like toy food.

Anderson closes the refrigerator and opens the nearby storage room. The containers there are equally exotic, but more promising. He takes out a tall, red can with square corners and a paper seal over the lid, like a whiskey bottle. It is labeled "Amaretti." Prying it open, Anderson finds little, individually wrapped cookies. He begins gulping them down, almost as fast as he can strip off the papers.

On another shelf, Anderson finds cans containing tropical juices. Mango, lychee, papaya, kiwi, loquat, guava, and others he has never even heard of before. He can't find a can punch, so he removes the tops with the electric can opener. Drinking directly from the cans, he finds the juices sweet, pulpy, and surprisingly mild in flavor. With these nectars to quench his thirst, he eats most of the can of cookies.

Still carrying an open juice can, he moves on into the laundry room. There he finds his clothes soaking in one of the large tubs. Shannon must have put them there, when she was tidying up. The wallet he had found in his pocket the day before is sitting on the counter. Beside it is the apartment key the doorman had given him. Forming a ring around them both is his belt. Anderson doesn't touch them. Instead, he reaches into the tub and lifts his trousers from the water. The movement stirs the dirt, turning the water almost black.

He can hardly wear his clothes in this condition. They are now dripping wet as well as filthy. After a moment's hesitation, Anderson pulls the plug in the laundry tub and transfers his clothes to the washing machine. As the dirty water drains from the tub, he finds his tennis shoes in the bottom and puts them in the washer as well. Then he adds some liquid detergent and starts the wash cycle.

While the machine is filling with water, Anderson leaves the laundry room. He wanders back through the kitchen and walks slowly down the central corridor. He wonders what to do next.

In the light of morning, with some food inside him, he realizes his predicament is more than he can cope with alone. He needs advice, help, support. He goes into the office, sits down at the desk, and takes out the Minneapolis phone book. He finds the number of a couple he had once regarded as his best friends.

It has been a long time since he has seen them, but he has known them since college days. He and Jack had lived in the same dorm. He nursed Jack through several migraines, and Jack, in turn, nursed him through several hangovers. When Jack started dating June, the three of them would often go out to a movie together. The couple always made him feel welcome, even after the scandal.

Anderson dials their number, hears June answer, and gives his name. There is a long silence on the other end. Anderson imagines her beaming with surprise. "How have you been?" he asks.

"What is this?" June asks in reply. "Some kind of joke?" She sounds angry, but Anderson can't think why.

"I just wanted to talk to you," he says meekly.

"You're sick, you know that?"

"What do you mean?" Anderson asks, completely taken aback.

"You *knew* I'd see the story on the morning news." Her voice is trembling, barely under control.

"What story?" he asks.

"Are you trying to spook me?" She sounds furious, but on the verge of tears.

Anderson tries to imagine the expression on her face, but finds he can't. He has never seen her like this. "I don't know what you're talking about," he says.

"Who *are* you?" she asks, now clearly crying.

For a moment, Anderson has no idea how to respond. Something is terribly wrong. "You *know* who I am," he says finally, in desperation.

There is another pause, then she speaks with more deliberation. "Your imitation of his voice isn't that good."

"It's not—" he begins, but she cuts him off.

"If you bother me again," she says in an icy rage, "I'm calling the police."

The line goes dead.

Anderson sits there a minute staring at the phone. He feels like crying himself. What kind of misunderstanding could have made June react this way? He will have to see her and Jack as soon as possible to clear it up.

Right now, however, he needs someone who can offer immediate, practical help.

He looks up the number of his former lawyer. He dials it and reaches the receptionist. Again he gives his name.

"I'm a client of your firm," he explains. "I'm trying to reach Mr. Freilinger."

"Just a minute, please," the receptionist answers.

There is a long wait. Then the receptionist comes back on the line. "I'm sorry, sir. We have no client by that name."

Anderson makes an effort to be patient. "I'm not involved in any legal proceedings right now," he says, speaking slowly and deliberately. "I have been represented by Mr. Freilinger in the past. I need to consult him now on another matter."

Her voice is cold and factual. "Mr. Freilinger is no longer

accepting clients except by referral. I suggest you try elsewhere." She hangs up.

Anderson dials the same number again.

"Listen," he says, when the receptionist has finished reciting the firm's name, "just tell Mr. Freilinger I'm on the phone. I'm sure he'll want to speak to me."

"Mr. Freilinger is not available for consultation except by appointment."

Anderson's patience is going fast. "I just need—" he says slowly through clenched teeth, "to have a few words—with my lawyer."

"Mr. Freilinger is not available for consultation *by phone* except by appointment."

"Tell Mr. Freilinger it's an emergency. If he's not there, give me one of the other partners."

"Just a minute, sir."

This time there is an even longer wait. Finally, the receptionist comes back on the line.

"I'm sorry, sir. This firm does not represent you. I'm sure you will able to find suitable representation elsewhere." Once again, she hangs up.

Anderson puts down the phone, his hand shaking. His anger is being rapidly supplanted by a kind of panic. He looks around the office with its scientific exhibits. In the morning light, they look less like charming antiques and more like instruments of torture. Staring at them, Anderson finds himself gasping for breath. He feels like an animal that has been placed under the bell jar, while the air is slowly pumped away. He has to get out of there.

He is sure he will be able to straighten things out, if he can just see his old lawyer personally. The receptionist must have confused him with someone else. Evidently, he will have to go down to Freilinger's office himself.

Anderson looks down at the elegant robe he had pulled on earlier. Apart from this robe, he is still without clothes. He pulls up the hem and sees his ankles are still dark with mud. He draws back the sleeves and sees that his forearms are scratched as well as dirty. Before he can leave, he will have to get cleaned up and dressed.

He heads back to the master bathroom. Passing the mirrors, he catches sight of himself again. Without his beard, he looks almost like a stranger. Perhaps even like this stranger people keep taking him for. His reflection still unnerves him, but not the way it did the day before. He notices his hair is matted at strange angles, like the hair of someone who has been 'sleeping rough.' It seems odd the woman named Shannon hadn't mentioned his bedraggled appearance the night before. Or did Peterson often look that way?

Anderson is aware of so many questions that need answers! But he is not ready to tackle them yet. He feels himself trembling uncontrollably each time he starts to think of his larger predicament. It will be all he can do to take things one at a time.

He hangs the paisley robe on a ceramic hook, uses the toilet, then walks around the tiled partition into the large shower room. Inside, he sees that the shower is more unusual than he had realized. In the middle of the space is a webbed plastic chaise longue. Surrounding it, up and down the walls, are multiple shower heads, all aimed at roughly the same area.

Anderson spots a control knob set for 'medium hot' and cautiously pulls it out. First there is a moment's delay. Then Anderson is hit by jets of water, coming from all directions. The bulk of the spray strikes him a little above the waist and bombards his legs. He looks for a way to turn off the superfluous shower heads, but finds only a single lever mounted on the wall. Moving it around, he discovers it shifts the focal point of the streams from one part of the shower room to another. With a little experimentation, he is able to direct most of the spray toward a spot near his chest. By stepping a yard or two away, he can lather on the liquid soap without having it instantly washed away. But the effect is still like showering in a hurricane.

Emerging from the shower a few minutes later, Anderson is surprised to discover the mirrors are already being cleared of mist by little air vents around their edges. He looks more closely at his beardless face and sees it now looks shadowed and stubbly. This is not something he has needed to worry about for several years. But now that he has been shaved, he will have to keep it up daily, if he wants to look respectable.

After drying himself with one of the huge towels, he begins

rummaging through the drawers beneath the bathroom counters. In one near the makeup mirror, he finds an electric beard trimmer and three different types of electric shavers. He takes one out, plugs it in, and cautiously sets about shaving. The air vents dry his skin, making the job easy. But Anderson finds it hard to get used to his beardless face.

When he is through, he goes to get his clothes, passing through the dressing room on the way. The washing machine is finished, so Anderson transfers his clothes to the dryer and pushes the start button. He hears the regular thump of his tennis shoes, as they begin tumbling around in the revolving drum.

He walks back into the dressing room, wondering what to do while his clothes are drying. The sight of his body in the mirrors reminds him how naked he is. Even a pair of underpants would make him feel less vulnerable.

He goes over to the shelves holding underwear. The underpants are in an ordinary Jockey style, but made of silk. Anderson runs his fingers across them. With so many on hand, surely no one would notice if there were one pair less. He takes some off the shelf and pulls them on. They feel amazingly smooth, cool, and light. To Anderson, they also feel slightly effeminate.

He realizes it will be some time before his own clothes are ready. The prospect of staying in the apartment that long makes him feel increasingly apprehensive. If he borrowed some of Peterson's clothes, at least he'd have the option of leaving sooner.

He chooses a shirt from a nearby shelf. It's pale gray with little flecks of color. As he takes out the pins, he sees that the label says "Turnbull and Asser." It is not a brand he recognizes. He drops the pins and cardboard in a nearby wastebasket. Stepping in front of a mirror, he puts the shirt on and begins to button it. It feels a little tight across the shoulders, but tapers nicely at the waist. Anderson is not sure whether the shirt is too small for him or whether it is supposed to fit this way.

Standing around in a shirt and underpants seems silly without trousers, so Anderson quickly picks a suitable pair. They are gray, but much darker than the shirt. When he gets them on, Anderson finds the trousers are slightly large for him, but no more so than they would be if he had recently been losing weight.

Now nearly dressed, Anderson sees he is still barefoot. He

takes a pair of socks from one of the shelves and looks around for shoes. There are over forty pairs arranged on a special rack. They come in every shape and style, from heavy hiking shoes to lightweight loafers. The first two pairs he tries on are too big for him. But the third pair runs a bit smaller. He exchanges the first socks he had chosen for thicker ones. With these on, he is able wear the slightly smaller shoes without too much trouble. As long as he doesn't have to run, he should be fine.

Looking with some trepidation in the mirror, Anderson is surprised to see how good he looks. The colors he has chosen suit him. The clothes look as though they could be his own. The only thing at all wrong is the trousers, which bag at the top without a jacket.

Turning to the racks of sports coats, Anderson has trouble finding one he would be comfortable even trying on. Most of them seem excessively elegant. Then he spots a rack of jackets in corduroy. He chooses one in a subdued green. The label says "Yves Saint Laurent," a designer even Anderson has heard of, but the styling seems unobtrusive. Shrugging the jacket into place on his shoulders, Anderson is startled by how comfortable it feels.

Once more, he looks at his reflection in the multiple mirrors. His appearance, this time, is almost too perfect. He fluffs his hair with his hand and pats it back into place. He could be a photo model for *Gentlemen's Quarterly.* He turns and moves his hands as though gesturing in conversation. He is handsome, graceful, poised. He looks like a man who would be at ease in any social situation. He looks, in fact, like the sort of person he once dreamed of being, but never was.

Anderson tries to connect this image with the way he used to look. But it seems very remote from his scruffy reflection in the beer sign, the night he met Trudy and Gretchen. His present appearance is closer to the image of the drowned man. But, in many ways, it is entirely new, disconnected from the past—an image with possibilities still unknown.

As Anderson thinks about what to do next, it occurs to him he should remove the more obvious signs of his visit. In the kitchen storage room, he finds a plastic-coated shopping bag from Dayton's Department Store. Into it, he drops the empty juice cans and cookie wrappings. Taking a dish towel off the rack, he wipes the doorknobs, cupboard handles, and can opener. He goes into the laundry room, gets his hot, damp clothes, and stuffs them into the shopping bag as well. He sees the 'Peterson' wallet sitting on the counter with the apartment key. After a moment's hesitation, he puts them in his trouser pocket. But he adds his belt to the shopping bag. Then he heads back toward the front of the apartment, carrying the bag with him and wiping his finger-prints off everything he remembers touching.

Passing through the living room, Anderson spots the note from Shannon. He picks it up and slips it in his pocket with the wallet and key. He takes the shopping bag into the entry hall and sets it down just inside the front door. Then he turns and looks back at the apartment, trying to think of what he might have forgotten.

His attention is caught by Peterson's mail, still piled high on the entry hall table. It was this mail, after all, that was responsi-ble for his being ushered into the apartment by the doorman. Anderson decides to have a quick look at it before he leaves. He opens the cabinet next to the door and takes out the gloves. It bothers him that he keeps thinking of such precautions, because it seems like the way a criminal would think. But he puts on the gloves anyway.

This time, as he sorts through the mail, he is struck by the fact that many of the envelopes have no return addresses, even though they look like business correspondence. Some are also much thicker than they would be if they contained ordinary let-ters. When Anderson weighs them in his hand, they feel as though they have stacks of paper forms in them.

Anderson finds an envelope that is splitting along the edge and carefully squeezes the opening apart to see inside. The 'pa-per forms' have the same sort of sharp, greenish edges as money. Anderson takes off one glove and eases the tip of his little finger into the opening to feel the edges. They are stiff to his touch. By increasing the size of the opening, Anderson is able to see that the stack inside is composed of crisp hundred dollar bills.

He puts the glove back on. His heart is pounding again. He goes back to the office and gets the scalpel that seems to be used as a letter opener. With this, he makes small slits in the edges of several similar envelopes. Each one contains money.

Anderson's hands are shaking now. He cuts into more envelopes. He finds more money. Not in all of them, but in the majority.

In his excitement, Anderson worries less about leaving traces of his search. He slits the end of one envelope entirely open and tilts the contents onto his hand. There is a handwritten slip reading *II—J.S.* Aside from that, there is nothing in the envelope but a stack of hundred dollar bills. Anderson counts them. There are forty-eight in the pile.

He slits open several more of the thicker business envelopes. Each contains a similar sum. The smallest amount in any one envelope is $4,650, the largest $12,300. The bills all seem to be hundreds and fifties. In most of the packets, they are new, but the serial numbers are not consecutive.

No covering letters accompany the money, just slips of paper, each with a numeral or date and a set of initials. The numerals are all twos, except for a couple of threes. The dates are mostly from July, but several are more recent.

Anderson begins cutting open anything that looks important. Some of the mail, of course, consists of advertisements and other junk mailings. Some of it consists of invitations to parties, gallery openings, and benefits. A few items are company reports, tables of projected earnings, and related business documents. But much of the mail is money, sometimes in the form of checks, more often in cash.

Anderson examines the checks. All are handwritten, made out to Peterson, and drawn from the personal accounts of people Anderson doesn't know. Several of the checks have little pictures of Minnesota scenery printed on them. Most of their envelopes have return addresses matching the ones on the checks themselves. Except for three in California, the addresses are all in the wealthier neighborhoods and suburbs around the Twin Cities.

Although there are far fewer checks than packets of cash, the checks tend to be for much larger amounts. Anderson does some counting. He estimates that the pile of mail contains over $140,000 in cash and nearly $100,000 in checks.

To Anderson, this money is just as frightening as the photos he had found the previous evening. It seems obvious that Peterson was involved in something highly unconventional and probably illegal. Whatever it was, having this much cash pouring in would have to be risky. If nothing else, it would tempt lots of otherwise moderate people into doing things that would be extreme and ruthless. Peterson himself probably had to do something extreme and ruthless to set it up.

Anderson has a sudden feeling of being out of his depth, of having nothing beneath him but unfathomed darkness. Even though he doesn't know what is going on, he suspects it involves things entirely outside his experience, things he wouldn't know how to handle.

This realization makes his need to get out of there all the more urgent.

But as he looks at the packets of cash, he recognizes that this money could also solve one of his immediate problems. He can't use his own resources, if he wants to avoid the police. The money in the wallet he found in his pocket is now almost gone. He needs a loan from somewhere, just to get this mess he is in straightened out. If he borrowed some of the money in this mail, he would be better able to cope.

He tells himself he would be more than justified. After all, the normal rules of behavior hardly fit these circumstances. The money was probably obtained illegally anyway. And the amount he needs for his immediate use would barely make a dent in the total.

He stares at the pile for a few moments more, an emptiness somewhere in his stomach. It is a feeling he has had several times before, when looking down from a diving board that turned out to be unexpectedly high. Like a diver, he deals with it by trying to clear his mind of all thought. His hand simply reaches out and takes two of the more anonymous looking envelopes. He tears them completely open and shakes out their contents. He puts a small stack of bills in the wallet he is carrying and a larger bundle in the pocket of the jacket. Then he crumples the empty envelopes and the initialed slips, adding them to the contents of the shopping bag.

He picks up the bag, twists the open end shut, and turns to leave the apartment. He intends to get rid of the gloves after he has used them to get through the door. He glances around, taking one last look, then reaches for the doorknob. The doorbell rings.

Anderson's feet remain fixed to the floor, but his body seems to jump. He curses himself for having delayed so long over the mail.

The doorbell rings again, more persistently. With the button held down, the repeating chime sounds like an alarm.

Anderson decides to wait it out. Perhaps the visitor will conclude that no one is home and simply go away. Taking care to hold the shopping bag away from his body, so it doesn't rustle, Anderson tiptoes back toward the living room.

Then someone starts pounding on the apartment door. A low thudding noise, hard enough to shake the whole door in its frame. The person must be using the bottom of his fist for a hammer.

After a few seconds the pounding stops. Anderson hopes the person has given up. But he soon hears voices, conferring outside in the hall. There must be more than one visitor.

"Mr. Peterson?" a voice says, louder now and speaking through the door. "This is the Minneapolis Police Department."

Anderson freezes, his heart racing. What could he say to them? How could he ever explain what he is doing here?

"Mr. Peterson," another voice says, "open the door please." The pounding resumes. Then the doorbell.

Anderson is filled with panic. He looks around for a way to escape, but can think of none. He doesn't know how to open the door in the laundry room. Even if he found a way out of the apartment itself, he would still be easy to spot leaving the building.

There is another pause in the pounding and ringing. "We spoke with the doorman," the first voice says loudly. "We know you're home."

"Mr. Peterson, we just need to talk with you for a minute. We're from the police department."

Anderson can think of no alternative, but to let the police in. He reaches inside the living room and sets the shopping bag against the wall, where it cannot be seen from the front door. He notices he is still wearing the gloves and hastily pulls them off, dropping them on top of the bag. Then he turns and walks back to the entrance, this time letting his leather soles rap loudly on the marble floor. He takes a quick look at the mail piled on the table, to make sure no money is spilling out. The stacked envelopes look completely innocent. Taking a deep breath, he unlatches the door.

The police are in ordinary business suits. They hold up little wallets with their left hands, displaying their badges and photo identifications.

"Hello, I'm Lieutenant Berglund," one says, extending his other hand.

Anderson shakes it awkwardly, hoping the man doesn't notice his sweaty fingers.

"This is my partner Detective Holmquist," the officer adds, making a gesture of presentation. Anderson shakes Holmquist's hand as well.

Now that the door is open, the detectives are polite to the point of being deferential. Berglund is the most Scandinavian looking black man Anderson has ever seen. Holmquist looks like another Swede or, judging by his name, another Norwegian.

"We're sorry to bother you so early in the morning," Holmquist says.

Anderson realizes he must look startled and tries to control his face.

Berglund inspects him without blinking, but offers an apologetic smile. "We wanted to talk to you before you left for the day."

Anderson can see their eyes straying to the entry hall behind him. It is clear some of their deference is due to the impressive surroundings and their feeling that whoever lives here must be a person of influence.

"There are some questions we need to ask you," Berglund says.

"Mostly routine inquiries," Holmquist adds. They look at Anderson expectantly.

He realizes they assume he is Peterson. They obviously expect him to invite them in. Much as he dreads the idea, Anderson doesn't see what else he can do. After a moment's hesitation, he opens the door and steps aside. "Come in, by all means," he says. His one thought is to placate them somehow, so that they will go away, allowing him to disappear.

The police enter the front hall, but Berglund notices Anderson's reluctance. "You have the right to have a lawyer present when you're talking to us, of course."

"Although we don't see why you would need one," Holmquist adds quickly.

"It's not as though we've come to arrest you or anything," Berglund explains, smiling wryly.

Anderson is still trying to find a way out of the situation. "I'm afraid you've caught me at an inconvenient moment," he says. But as soon as he says it, he sees their faces hardening. "That's all right," he hastens to add, "I'm sure I can spare a few minutes." As long as they eventually leave without him, Anderson figures he will still be able to escape.

"If you'd like to call your lawyer to make this a more formal interview . . ." Berglund lets his voice trail off.

"I don't need a lawyer to answer a few questions," Anderson concedes. The only chance he can see of getting rid of them is to play along with their assumption that he is Peterson. "Would you like to sit down?" he asks, pulling one of the chairs from under the hall table.

"Thank you," Berglund says, promptly sitting down. He reaches into his jacket and takes out a small notebook with a spiral binding at the top.

Holmquist, meanwhile, is inspecting the carved stonework. "It looks like the Reformation came through here," he says, pointing to the empty niches. "Those were probably full of nice statues until some Puritan types smashed them." He steals a glance at Anderson, enjoying the effect of this unexpected learning. Then he rests his rear end on the edge of the table.

Anderson sits down on the other chair, not knowing what to say.

Berglund chuckles, his teeth very white against his dark skin. Then he opens his notebook and sits up straighter, indicating it is time to get down to business. "Our information," he says, "is that you are still registered at a resort in northern Minnesota."

"The Running Deer Hunter Lake Lodge," Holmquist recites from memory.

"The manager there says you have not checked out and have not paid your bill." Berglund makes this statement matter-of-factly, but obviously thinks it requires a response.

If this is the sort of thing the police are concerned with, Anderson decides he can readily deal with it. "There's nothing to worry about there," he tells them. "Of *course* I will pay my bill."

"May we ask why you left the resort without checking out?" Berglund continues.

"Because I intended to return. I saw no reason to check out, if I were coming back almost at once."

"You said you 'intended' to return. Is that still your intention?"

"No, I realize now I won't be able to get back there this season," Anderson says, thinking fast. "But don't worry about the bill. I'll phone the resort and arrange to pay by credit card."

"I understand you left some personal possessions in the room," Berglund says. "Some clothes, toiletries, things like that."

"I'll have the resort send them down to me."

"We've also been informed that you left your car up there," Holmquist says, his voice harder this time.

Anderson's heart races, while he tries to come up with a plausible explanation.

Berglund, meanwhile, is ruffling through his notebook. "You apparently returned to the Twin Cities by bus yesterday afternoon." He lifts his gaze and looks Anderson in the eye. "Could you tell us why you did that?"

Anderson swallows. Then, as he opens his mouth to speak, he finds he has an answer. "I discovered I had to get back here for urgent business reasons. But I'd been having trouble with migraine headaches, so I didn't want to drive."

"I see," Berglund says, thinking it over. "Yes, I guess that explains it."

Anderson is relieved they find this answer acceptable. He has never had a migraine himself, but knows about them from his friend Jack, who used to get them often.

"Did you spend last night here in this apartment?" Holmquist asks, taking the initiative.

"Yes."

"And the previous night?"

"Up at the resort."

"What about yesterday morning?" Berglund interjects.

"I was up at the resort, getting ready to leave."

"But you didn't pack anything," Holmquist says.

"I don't function very well when I have a migraine. It was all I could do to get dressed and get out of there." Anderson hopes they can't see how much he is sweating.

Berglund consults his notebook. "The waiters didn't see you at breakfast."

"I get very nauseated when I have a migraine." From what he remembers of Jack's symptoms, he is sure this is right.

"How did you leave exactly?" Holmquist asks.

"Someone offered me a ride to the bus. I don't know who. A man. I'm afraid I didn't pay much attention to what he looked like."

"Do you remember what kind of vehicle he was driving?"

"Not really. Some kind of pickup truck, I guess,"

"Does a migraine interfere with your memory?"

"As a matter of fact, it does."

There's a moment's pause. Anderson relaxes slightly, surprised at how easily the answers are coming to him. Berglund writes something in his notebook.

"What do you take for your migraines?" Holmquist asks.

Anderson hesitates. "I don't remember exactly. Whatever my doctor prescribed for them."

"How are you feeling now?"

"Oh, I'm over the headache. But they leave me rather exhausted."

Berglund has stopped writing. "Did you notice anything unusual before you left the resort, any strangers or anybody doing anything out of the ordinary?"

"No, nothing at all."

"You're sure?"

Anderson nods slowly two or three times. He notices it is far easier to lie when he is being 'Peterson' than it would be if he were being himself.

There is a momentary pause. "Well, that's about it," Berglund says, getting to his feet. "There's just one thing . . ."

"Yes?" Anderson says, half out of his chair.

"Could you show us your migraine medicine? We need to make a note of it for our report."

Anderson's pulse races. He feels an urge to turn and run. "I'll go and get it for you," he says. His own voice sounds distant to him. He feels the policemen's eyes upon him. Forcing himself to move slowly, he turns and walks through the door to the living room.

He has some vague idea of climbing out a back window or breaking his way through the laundry room door. But then he hears one of the policemen coming with him. Glancing over his shoulder, Anderson sees that it is Holmquist.

With shaky, but deliberate steps, Anderson leads him across the living room and down the central corridor. They have to go through the workout room and the Jacuzzi room to reach the large bathroom near the back of the apartment. "Quite a place you have here," Holmquist murmurs, as they pass the plunge pool.

Inside the bathroom, Anderson goes directly to the medicine chest and pulls open the huge mirrored door. Thank God, he at least knew where it was. He stands there frantically scanning the shelves, trying to spot something that would seem plausible as a treatment for migraine. There is a faint odor of rubbing alcohol and bandage adhesive. For a moment, Anderson has hopes of salvaging the situation by picking some suitable painkiller. But his hopes sink as he sees nothing but cold remedies and stomach medicines. He is strongly aware of Holmquist standing close behind him. But he begins thinking once more of how to make a break for it.

"Is this what you're looking for?" Holmquist asks. His arm reaches past Anderson to pluck a plastic vial from one of the lower shelves.

Anderson takes the amber container. The prescription says RX 790501. DR. SWENSON. FOR: PETERSON. NEMBUTAL. 100 MG. #30. ONE OR TWO CAPSULES AS NEEDED FOR MIGRAINE.

"Yes, that's it," he says. Anderson feels like jumping in the air at this stroke of luck. Or is he underestimating himself? It occurs to him he may have noticed the medicine earlier in a subliminal way. Perhaps that's why he mentioned migraines in the first place. For a moment, his near panic is replaced by exhilaration. He feels as though he possesses unexpected powers. Then he brings himself under control, so he won't make the detective any more suspicious. "Is there anything else you need?" Anderson asks in a casual voice.

"No, that will do," Holmquist says, once more taking the vial. The detective leads the way back to the front of the apartment.

Anderson has another bad moment when he sees Berglund staring at the stacks of mail. But the detective doesn't seem to have touched anything, and there is no sign that he suspects the envelopes of containing money. Holmquist shows his partner the medicine vial, and Berglund makes another note.

"You'd better keep those where you can find them," Holmquist says, handing the pills back to Anderson.

Anderson decides it's his turn to ask some questions. "May I ask what all this fuss is about?"

"You may," Berglund says, suddenly very serious. The two detectives look thoughtfully at Anderson. There is a long moment of utter silence.

"A man was killed yesterday," Holmquist says finally, "near the resort where you were staying."

"A man," Berglund adds, "named Anderson."

Anderson feels as though he has once more been dropped into cold water. He struggles to stay calm in manner, but is sure the detectives will have seen something of his reaction.

"Do you think you might have known him?" Holmquist asks.

"No, I don't think so," Anderson replies.

"The county sheriff's office for the resort area has been on the phone to us," Holmquist explains. "Asking for our help."

"We'll be handling the Minneapolis phase of the investigation," Berglund says, digging into the side pocket of his jacket. "In fact, here's my card. If you remember anything that might help us, please get in touch."

"Here's mine too," Holmquist says, removing one of his own cards from his wallet. "The phone number's actually the same."

Anderson accepts the cards without comment.

"And please notify me or Detective Holmquist," Berglund says, "if you intend to travel outside the metropolitan area at any time during the next few weeks."

"I guess that's it," Holmquist says, reaching forward again to shake Anderson's hand.

"Thank you for your cooperation," Berglund says, doing the same.

"You're welcome," Anderson says.

He feels the two policemen looking him up and down, as though trying to guess his weight. Then they turn to leave, with Holmquist opening the door.

"Be seeing you," Berglund says.

"Watch out for those iconoclasts," Holmquist adds, tilting his head briefly toward the empty stone niches. He gives Anderson a wink and pulls the door closed behind them.

As the latch clicks into place, Anderson realizes that he is being investigated for his own murder.

CHAPTER 6

The minute he is convinced the detectives have gone, Anderson leaves the apartment. His eyes dart nervously up the corridor, scanning every doorway. He feels self-conscious, not just to be there, but to be dressed in such expensive, borrowed clothes. Under his arm, he carries the shopping bag containing the evidence of his visit. There does not seem to be anyone around, but Anderson has the feeling someone might emerge from an apartment at any moment. Trying to move as quietly as possible, while still looking 'normal,' he follows the blue carpet back toward the building's entrance.

As he approaches the marble stairway leading down into the lobby, Anderson hears guitar music. The composition is so simple and the sound so clear, he realizes it must be live. He braces himself for a possible greeting and turns the corner.

It is the doorman who is bent over the instrument. He sees Anderson coming down the stairs and puts the guitar aside. "Good morning, Mr. Peterson," he says, and steps out from behind the desk.

"Good morning," Anderson says, without breaking stride, heading directly for the front door.

"I've got a new one for you," the doorman says, moving into the space where Anderson is headed. The man smiles expectantly.

Anderson slows to a stop, holding back a little, so as not to stand too close. After all, this is someone who must have seen Peterson daily. It would be pointless to let the doorman recognize him as an impostor when he is this close to escaping.

"Is everything okay?" the doorman asks, looking at him uncertainly.

Anderson is nervously aware his features are now in a far brighter light than they were the night before. Will the doorman see he is someone different?

"I'm fine," he says, his voice a little too forceful.

"How was your vacation?"

"Just great, thanks." Anderson wonders if he should say something about returning unexpectedly the previous evening. Should he be repaying the doorman for taking care of his cab fare? Or do Peterson and the doorman have a regular arrangement for handling such things? As he hesitates, Anderson is acutely conscious of being inspected.

"I can't get over how different you seem without your beard."

Anderson tries to think of something to divert the doorman's attention. "Quite a day out there," he says, gesturing toward the glass door.

The doorman continues to stare at him.

As he hears his own words, Anderson realizes the weather outside is perfectly ordinary. He tries to smile. "Well, I've got to be going," he says, moving forward in an arc that will take him around the doorman.

"Wait a minute," the man calls.

Anderson has another moment of near panic.

"I've written a new one," the doorman says. He reaches enthusiastically for his guitar. "I think you'll really like it. I'm just having my usual trouble with the bridge."

Anderson does not feel up to any more tests. He needs to get out of there. "Sorry," he says, "I've got an appointment. I'll have to listen to it later."

"It's called 'Our Love Makes It Right'!" the doorman announces, putting the guitar strap over his head.

"I'm sure it's great—" Anderson begins, trying to make his apology more emphatic.

But the doorman holds up a hand as though physically fending off Anderson's objection. "Okay, okay, you're right. The title sounds derivative. But you'll be able to tell me how to make it more original."

"I really have to rush."

"It'll only take a minute," he says, adjusting his guitar strap. "Wait till you hear the way I set up the hook!"

"I'm already late—"

"This could be my breakthrough song, the one that puts me at the top of the charts! I'm gonna make Bobby Dylan sound like an amateur!"

Anderson lifts his hands in a gesture of helplessness.

"Oh, all right," the doorman says, making a face of comic disappointment. "I'll just keep working on it. Maybe I can think of a bridge without your help. I've done it before, you know."

Anderson moves toward the door, but the doorman calls out again. "Uh, Mr. Peterson, there's one other thing."

Anderson pauses, turning back with an inquiring look.

The man still has the guitar hanging from his neck, but he seems to have forgotten it. The instrument tilts oddly. "I've got a lot of maintenance work at the moment. So if you need anything and find me away from the front desk, just leave a note. Okay?"

"Okay."

"You'll be sure to do that?"

Anderson nods, edging through the door as he speaks. "If I need anything, I'll definitely leave a note."

Escaping at last the doorman's relentless helpfulness, Anderson emerges into the fresh air. The sidewalks are still damp from rain during the night. The sun is shining brightly, but clouds cover much of the sky.

Anderson moves off down the street. With each step away from the apartment building, he knows he should be feeling safer. But he experiences no relief. The familiar streets look strange to him, full of undefined menace.

He makes an effort to be more level headed. Across the river, he can see the downtown skyline. He knows roughly where he is and recalls a bus route nearby. He used to take it occasionally during his student years, when his car had broken down. But nothing looks quite as he remembers.

Suddenly, without knowing why, Anderson has the distinct impression someone is watching him. He looks over his shoulder. Near where he is standing, an old woman walks her dog. Back by the apartment building, a motorcyclist bends down, trying to fix something on his machine. Neither seems aware of him. But Anderson still feels watched. It occurs to him this may be due to his own fear and guilt. But it's also possible the police have him under surveillance. Perhaps they are inside one of the other apartments overlooking the street.

Trying to contain his anxieties, Anderson crosses the street, walks another block, and sits down at the bus stop near the corner of First Avenue and North East Main. The traffic at this time of day is light. Anderson can't stop himself from looking nervously around, but no one seems to notice him. After a few minutes, a bus pulls up. The yellowish green letters over the windshield say 27 DOWNTOWN. When the door opens with a hydraulic hiss, Anderson climbs aboard.

Beside the driver is a machine for digesting the change people pay for their fares. Anderson takes out a dollar bill, but the driver holds up his hand and shakes his head.

For a moment, Anderson can't figure out what to do. The period in his life when he had ridden these buses seems more than a lifetime away.

"You need eighty-five cents, exact change," the driver tells him.

Anderson wonders if he'll have to get off. Then he hears the jingle of coins beside him. An elderly woman is counting out the change for a dollar from her coin purse. She holds it out to him, and he hands her the bill. "Thank you," he says. "That's a real help."

The bus lurches as he drops the money into the machine. Looking out the window, he sees high, tan arches, supporting blue-green cables. They are on a suspension bridge that crosses the Mississippi. Grabbing the hand bars for balance, Anderson staggers to the rear and takes a seat in the back row, so no one will be able to watch him without his being aware of it.

He feels cut off from everyone around him. But he is heartened by the thought that at least, with Arnie Freilinger, he will have a first rate lawyer on his side. Among the poems and public service announcements mounted over the bus windows, Anderson notices an advertisement for a legal aid center. Thank God he won't have to explain his situation to a group of lawyers like that, ones he has never met.

The bus heads down Hennepin Avenue, for decades a center

for bars and movie theaters. Anderson is vaguely aware that in recent years it has also been a center for drug dealers, but he has heard that the current wave of urban renewal has been pushing them out.

When the bus makes a stop between Seventh and Eighth Streets, across from the Skyway Theaters, Anderson gets out. He crosses Hennepin and walks up Eighth Street, past Shinder's News and Dayton's Department Store, under the skyways, past the IDS tower, then right on Marquette Avenue. It's a route that takes him through the middle of the business district. Anderson no longer has any specific sense of being followed. But with so much activity about, there's no way to tell.

He realizes he is still carrying the shopping bag and deposits it in a sidewalk waste receptacle. No one seems to notice.

A short walk down Marquette brings him to the Foshay Tower, where Freilinger's law firm has its offices. Anderson has never been there before. During his previous dealings with Freilinger, he met the attorney only in the conference rooms and hallways of the city jail.

The Foshay Tower is the oldest 'skyscraper' in Minneapolis. It looks like a dirty Washington Monument with windows. Years ago, it dominated the skyline. Now it seems almost lost among the many taller buildings. Up close, however, it retains a certain grandeur. It stands in the middle of a block still occupied mostly by lower level buildings. Only the Twin City Federal Savings and Loan impinges on its air space.

Anderson enters from the Marquette side, walking through the long, wide corridor that leads from the sidewalk to the tower itself. The interior is gleaming marble and granite, with Art Deco fixtures. Pale pink and azure are the predominant colors. A security guard stands by the elevators, behind a three sided marble counter, but he pays no attention to people coming and going. Beside the counter is a gray metal letter-box fed by a glass chute from the higher floors. A letter comes fluttering down as Anderson watches.

Anderson finds the number of Freilinger's firm on the building directory and pushes the button for the elevator. There are four of them, with ornately sculpted metal doors, portraying the building haloed in clouds and sunbeams. When the elevator doors open, Anderson sees a mirror on the back of the car with a frosted pattern that repeats the image of the building 'wreathed in glory.' Anderson gets in, along with a secretary bringing back a takeout lunch from a nearby restaurant. She gets off at the four-teenth floor, leaving Anderson to ride higher alone.

When the elevator stops, the doors open onto a wood paneled wall with a brass plate announcing the law firm's name. Apparently, the firm occupies the whole floor. Anderson notices that the hallway makes a reversed 'L,' with the longer side running in front of the elevators and the other side running around the corner to the stairway serving as a fire exit. For a few moments, he drifts up and down the hallway, sizing up the place. There are several doors, but only one that looks like an entrance. Taking a deep breath, Anderson opens it and goes in.

The large blond receptionist greets him with a warm smile, until he gives his name and announces his desire to see Freilinger. "Excuse me," she says and gets to her feet. She is not fat, but has big bones and a heavy way of moving. She disappears through the door behind her desk.

Anderson looks around the waiting room. It is paneled in dark wood with no windows. There are four leather chairs, a large green plant, and a table covered with sporting magazines. Oddly enough, they all look new and unread. In the far wall is another door. The plant looks plastic. On impulse, Anderson steps over and touches it. He is surprised to discover it is real.

After a few moments, the receptionist returns. "I'm sorry, sir. I have to ask you to leave."

Because of the response to his phone call that morning, Anderson is prepared for this. "I really need to speak to Mr. Freilinger," he says. "I won't take up much of his time, but I do need to see him personally."

The woman gives him an odd look. "You're the one who called earlier, aren't you?"

"The name is Anderson. Yes, I phoned earlier."

She shakes her head. "We know you're not Mr. Anderson."

"What do you mean?" He is suddenly very conscious that the clothes he is wearing are not his own. The woman continues to look at him. "I *am* Anderson," he says, a little too loud.

"Sir, the police have already been here. They have informed us that Mr. Anderson was murdered early yesterday."

Anderson struggles to speak slowly and simply. "There's been a mistake. I'm Anderson. I'm not murdered. I *need* to see Mr. Freilinger."

"Mr. Freilinger is not available." She crosses her arms.

"Then I need to see someone else. Someone capable of recognizing I'm still alive."

"Excuse me a minute." Once more, she disappears through the door, but this time she is gone longer. When she returns, she looks distinctly apprehensive.

Anderson notices that despite her large frame, she is actually very young, probably still in her teens.

She fiddles with a jar of pencils on her desk, reluctant to speak. She crosses her arms and looks up at him.

"Yes?" he asks.

She swallows and takes a deep breath. "I've been instructed to tell you that no one here wants anything to do with you, dead *or* alive."

Anderson feels as though he has had his face slapped. For a moment, he just stands there, wondering what to do next. Then he moves toward the door behind the receptionist.

"You can't go in there," she says, reaching for her phone. "That's private."

But Anderson opens the door and walks through. He finds himself moving down a corridor lined with law books. To his right are two offices with doors standing wide. Inside them, he sees expansive desks and large windows that actually open. The lawyers behind the desks are not ones he recognizes. To his left is a work area with computers and copiers. A young man in a pale blue suit is rummaging through some files. Otherwise, there is no one around. As Anderson surveys the layout, he realizes the whole floor is quite small in area, due to the building's tapering shape.

Where the corridor makes a turn to the left, one of the office doors is closed. Anderson grabs the knob and swings it open. The large corner office is filled with light. Three narrow windows wrap around the corner itself, with a wider one on each side. Behind the huge desk, talking on the phone, is Freilinger. He looks just as Anderson remembers him. His curly, gray hair is almost the same shade as his elegant silver gray suit. His crimson tie adds a touch of warmth.

Anderson feels a flood of relief. This is the person who had saved him before when he was in trouble, the person he is counting on to straighten things out now. "Boy, am I glad to see you," Anderson says. "Your receptionist didn't seem to understand I'm one of your clients."

Freilinger looks at him, as imperturbable as ever. He puts down the phone and sits up straighter. "I don't know you," he says.

For a moment, Anderson hears a rushing noise, like water going over a falls. Then the sound subsides. "You defended me—" he begins. But the words are difficult to pronounce. "Several years ago. Anderson. You know, the murder charge. When my grandfather drowned." He can hear his own voice, but the sounds seem to have no effect. "Don't you remember?"

"Of course, I remember."

"Then what's the problem?"

"The problem is you're not Anderson."

Anderson starts to interrupt, but Freilinger holds up his hand to stop him.

"I admit you bear a striking resemblance to Anderson. In different circumstances, you might even have been able to pass yourself off as Anderson. But we happen to know Anderson is dead. The body has been conclusively identified."

"But I'm still alive. I'm here. I'm Anderson."

"It won't wash. The police have already been in touch with us, asking for our assistance. They have briefed us on all the salient facts."

"The police have got the facts wrong!"

"Now, how would they have done that?"

"You know better than I do how the police get things wrong!"

"The county sheriff's office seemed to have the case well in hand."

"A county sheriff's office in that part of the state isn't up to dealing with anything out of the ordinary."

"They're getting assistance from the state agencies and from the metropolitan police."

"They won't want to spend their budget on services from outside agencies. *You* told me that. And the communications between agencies is always a mess. Look how they bungled things when my grandfather died!"

"They'll get it all sorted out eventually."

"I'm directly involved. I need to come forward now."

"So, come forward. What's the problem?"

"It's all very complicated. I need serious legal help."

"That may well be, but not mine. My client was Anderson. Anderson is dead."

"Listen. There's been some kind of mix-up. I was drugged and kidnapped. Then someone tried to drown me. But I came to. And the other person was drowned instead. Only someone's mistaken that other person's body for mine. Then, when I got back to the Cities, people started mistaking—" His voice breaks off. Even as he speaks, Anderson realizes how crazy he must sound. It occurs to him he was more convincing yesterday and this morning in the role of Peterson than he is right now in the role of Anderson.

Freilinger is shaking his head. "I think it's time you were on your way." He picks up the phone and presses one of the buttons. "If you leave now, I won't need to inform the police of this intrusion."

"I don't understand why you're so reluctant to represent me. I did everything you told me last time. The case was a success. I paid you promptly."

Freilinger turns away and speaks into the phone. "Joanna, would you please call the police. I need to have an intruder removed from my office." He pauses, apparently listening. "That's right," Freilinger continues, "the Minneapolis Police Department. He looks as though he might be too much of a handful for the building security."

Hanging up the receiver, Freilinger turns blandly back to Anderson. He interlaces his fingers and rests his hands on his desk. He seems ready to wait in silence until Anderson leaves or the police appear.

Anderson decides Freilinger is bluffing. While the lawyer was on the phone, Anderson couldn't hear the slightest sound to indicate there was anyone else on the line. Anyway, Freilinger would hardly be in the habit of calling the police to have them remove potential clients. But why is he so reluctant to admit that Anderson is Anderson?

Anderson makes a conscious decision to provoke the lawyer into speaking further. "All right," Anderson says, "let's look at it from your standpoint. If I'm not Anderson, who in the hell do you think I am?"

Freilinger gazes calmly back, his face a blank. "Probably some associate of Anderson's, trying to complete a business deal."

"An 'associate'?" Anderson asks, puzzled by the word.

"Yes, a business associate."

"What 'business' could you possibly be talking about?"

Freilinger raises his eyebrows. "Why, drugs, of course."

Anderson is bewildered. "What makes you think that I—that Anderson—was involved in drugs?"

"Because the police found large sums of cash in briefcases in Anderson's house."

"That doesn't make sense. I didn't keep any cash."

"The police are holding an awful lot of it as evidence."

"I have no idea how that money could have gotten there." As soon as he says it, Anderson realizes how lame it sounds.

Without unclasping his hands, Freilinger places them behind his head, leans back, and rests his feet on the corner of his desk. "No individual leaves that much cash behind, unless something drastic happens to him, preventing him from returning for it. Getting killed, for instance." Freilinger pauses for effect, as though in a courtroom. "Furthermore, no private individual has a need for such large cash sums, unless he is involved in something illegal."

Anderson feels the guilty weight of the money packet in his pocket. He shifts uncomfortably from one foot to the other.

"Since drugs," Freilinger continues, "are the largest illegal business at the moment, it seems highly likely that Anderson was involved in it. His death was probably the result of a drug deal that went wrong."

For a moment, Anderson is too flabbergasted to speak.

"Could you actually believe that?" he finally asks. "Are you telling me that Anderson seemed the kind of person who would deal in drugs?"

"Oh, quite possibly." Freilinger smiles. "I don't think his inheritance was nearly as much as he was expecting."

Anderson feels stung. This was the sort of thing the police had said all those years ago, when they had questioned him about his grandfather's death. "I wasn't expecting any inheritance."

Freilinger seems oblivious to his discomfort. "Yes, Anderson *said* the same thing. It was a very good position to take from a legal standpoint."

"What are you talking about? It wasn't a 'position to take' for legal purposes. It was the truth."

"Fortunately, I'm not required to decide what might be truth. I'm only required to decide what is good legal strategy."

"Wait a minute. Did I—did Anderson—seem like someone who would be capable of murder?"

"My late client seemed like the nicest person in the world."

"So why do you doubt what he told you?"

"Oh, come now! Wouldn't *you* make an effort to appear 'nice'—a very *sustained* effort—if *you* wanted to get away with *murder*?"

Anderson is almost too stunned to speak. "What are you saying? That Anderson was just playing a part?"

"Many people I encounter in my practice are like that: manipulative, goal-oriented personalities, who act charming, but who don't care much about other people. They are very interesting to deal with professionally. But they are not the sort of people one would knowingly befriend."

Anderson feels angry, but also hurt. Tears come to his eyes. He waves his hand vaguely through the air in front of him. "I'm sorry. I thought that's what you'd done. Befriended me, I mean."

Freilinger registers no emotion beyond mild interest. "A member of my profession has to maintain a certain professional distance."

"It's just that you've got Anderson all wrong. He was never uncaring. If anything, he was always *too* worried about others. That's why he failed the lie detector test. He was too prone to feel guilty over nothing."

"Do you think what Anderson did to his grandfather was 'nothing'?" The lawyer's voice has a cold edge to it.

Somewhere in the background Anderson hears sirens. His eyes lock with Freilinger's. The man's gaze is hard and unwavering. For a moment, Anderson has a sense of personal connection.

"You *know* I'm Anderson, don't you?"

Freilinger maintains the stare, but tilts his head back, so that Anderson is presented with more of the lawyer's nose and chin. "I really don't care."

Anderson looks down, then leans forward, placing his hands on the desk. He looks up at Freilinger from under his lowered brow, his voice soft, but intense. "Why won't you represent me?"

The lawyer leans forward in response, raising his eyebrows. "I think you're involved in drugs. It doesn't matter to me who you are. I don't represent drug dealers."

"And if I swear I'm *not* involved in drugs?"

"Then whatever you're involved with is something I want no part of."

There is a moment of total silence. The sirens must have stopped in front of the building. Evidently, Freilinger hadn't been bluffing about calling the police. If the officers catch an elevator right away, they could be up to that floor in a minute or two.

Anderson turns and leaves the office, kicking the door closed behind him. Near a water cooler across the corridor, he sees another door that must lead to the hallway in front of the elevators. He eases it open and looks through the crack. The elevators are less than a dozen yards away. There is no one in sight.

Anderson slips out and hurries down the hallway, past the elevators. He turns the corner and heads for the fire exit he had spotted earlier. As he pulls on the heavy steel door, he hesitates. He is on too high a floor to take the stairway all the way to the ground. The police might well have a description of him. If he tries to catch an elevator right now from a lower floor, they might spot him on their way up. If he hides for a while, they might spot him later leaving the building. Thinking about it makes Anderson feel increasingly trapped. Then he sees what he must do.

Stepping into the stairwell, Anderson closes the steel door carefully, so that it doesn't bang. Then he runs *up* the stairs to the floor above. He eases open the fire door and sees no one in the hallway. Darting down it, he peers cautiously around the corner, then, seeing that it's clear, sprints to the elevators, and hits the down button.

After a few seconds, he hears an elevator stopping at the floor below. When it arrives at his floor moments later, it is empty. Anderson gets in and pushes the button for the lobby. As he passes the floor below, he holds his breath.

The elevator doesn't stop until it reaches the ninth floor. By this time, Anderson is happy to have additional passengers, because they will make him less conspicuous when the doors open below.

On the ground floor, he gets off the elevator without incident and heads down an Art Deco corridor, narrower than the one he had taken earlier. It leads to Ninth Street and is lined with a barber shop, a tailor shop, and a French restaurant. Each has a handful of customers, but otherwise things are fairly quiet.

Just as Anderson is about to step through the glass doors into daylight, a pair of uniformed policemen appear in front of him. They are moving toward him so quickly, there is nothing he can do to avoid them. His body goes rigid. He is aware of guns and radios, blue shirts and badges. Then, suddenly, they are past.

Either they didn't have his description or they failed to recognize him. His muscles move again. He emerges from the doors of the building feeling lighter.

But the relief is short-lived. As he walks down the street, Anderson again feels shadowed. He looks around in all directions, but sees no one who looks suspicious. He blames it on the tension he is under and decides he needs a drink. But first he must get out of this part of town.

He sees a taxi stand up the street and hurries toward it.

CHAPTER 7

Anderson pushes the doorbell below the name plate for Jack and June. He hears it chiming inside. The building is an old frame house in south Minneapolis. It had been a duplex when Jack and June had first moved in, but they have bought the other half and are in the process of turning it back into a single dwelling. The wood siding is painted white. In the light of the setting sun, it has a warm glow. The grass in the front yard hasn't been cut lately. But the flower beds are perfectly weeded and have well tended clusters of blue asters and pink mums.

Anderson realizes, as he waits, that it's been quite a while since he has seen his friends. He hopes they are all right. June must have heard of his supposed death sometime before he phoned. That's the only thing Anderson can think of that would account for her strange reaction.

He pushes the bell again. After a moment, the door swings slowly open, and Anderson sees his old friend Jack looking out at him.

Jack stares. "It *is* you, isn't it?"

"Yes, it's me. I've lost my beard, but otherwise I'm intact."

"That was you on the phone, then. This morning."

Anderson nods.

Jack's face gradually breaks into a grin, but his eyes remain worried. "June's been so upset."

"There's been a big misunderstanding."

Jack stares at him a moment longer, then steps forward and gives Anderson a long hug. When he finally breaks the embrace, Anderson's old friend is blinking tears away. "Come on in," he says, holding the door.

The front hallway is piled with paint cans, tarps, and a folding stepladder. But beyond, through the right hand doorway, is a perfect, informal living room in a comfortably rustic style. Thick, dimpled cushions in flowered chintz are fastened by ties to sturdy wood furniture. Kerosene lamps with glass dome shades have been wired for bulbs and electricity. A jigsaw puzzle lies unfinished on the front table. Anderson feels as though he is returning to the home he never had.

"I'm so glad to see you," Anderson says.

"What's going on? The news stories all said you'd been drowned. They said the local police suspected murder."

For a moment, it seems almost a sacrilege to begin telling his story in this cozy setting. Then Anderson realizes there is no way to avoid it. He stops amid the decorating paraphernalia, where a workman might pause to wipe his feet. He wants to get it out in as few words as possible. "Someone else was drowned. But the police think it was me. When they find out I'm still alive, they're going to assume I'm responsible."

Jack remains where he had first paused, a couple feet of inside the front door. He gives Anderson an openly appraising look. "Are you sure you're not just being paranoid? After your other experience, I mean."

"No, they're definitely going to accuse me of murder. All over again."

"Hey, take it easy. It'll all get straightened out."

"I'm not so sure. You see, this time I *did* kill someone."

"What do you mean?" Jack asks, more puzzled than ever. "You wouldn't murder anybody."

"It was self-defense. This guy was trying to drown me. I don't know who he was or why he was doing it. I just know he was trying to kill me."

"Jees-us. You've got to explain this—"

"Wait, there's more. People keep mistaking me for someone else. I'm not sure, but I think they've been mistaking me for the man I killed. He looked so much like me, I was afraid I was going crazy."

The corners of Jack's mouth twitch as though he is trying to keep from smiling. "This does *sound* pretty crazy." He looks at Anderson as though waiting for the punch line. But in the silence that follows, the expression of amusement fades from Jack's face.

Anderson's jaw muscles remain tense. "It gets even crazier," he says. "I tried to see my lawyer, but he wouldn't acknowledge who I am. And there seems to be all this money—" But before he can explain further, Anderson starts to shake.

Jack grips Anderson's shoulders. "Relax, we'll handle it together. Let me get you a drink. You look like you need one." He drops his hands and takes a few steps into the house, then stops and turns to make sure Anderson is all right.

Anderson leans on the cold hallway radiator to steady himself and tries to breathe more deeply. "Where's June?"

"She's upstairs resting. By the way, I think it would be better if we didn't talk about this with her right now. The doctor said she needs—"

"Jack?" a voice interrupts.

Anderson recognizes it as June's voice. She is calling down from upstairs. He starts to walk toward the stairway, but Jack catches his arm.

"Listen," Jack says, "you and I will take care of this without worrying her about it, okay?"

"Sure, whatever you say."

"Jack?" June calls again. "Who was at the door?" Her voice this time is closer.

Anderson looks up to see her halfway down the stairs. He meets her stare with an embarrassed smile. He doesn't know what to say. "See?" he finally says. "I'm still alive."

For a moment, June seems afraid to believe what her eyes are telling her. She stands there open-mouthed. "The newspapers and the radio said—"

"A mistaken identification," Anderson explains.

"Oh, thank God." She hurries down the remaining stairs and throws her arms around him. "Thank God," she says again.

As he hugs her, Anderson notices she feels different. She seems to have put on a lot of weight. But it's not soft flab. It seems to be almost hard and all near her waist. Anderson steps back to look at her, holding the tips of her fingers in his outstretched hands. She is wearing a loose smock, but her shape has certainly changed.

"You're . . ." He hesitates, afraid of getting something like this wrong.

She nods, her face dimpling with a goofy, sheepish smile. "Yes. I'm pregnant."

"Oh, my," Anderson says, thoroughly delighted at the idea. "Congratulations. How far along are you?"

"Approaching the end of my sixth month. The baby should be due the first of January."

Jack puts his arm around her, beaming with pride. "Do you think they'll give us a new car or something, if we have the first baby of the new year?

Anderson shakes his head, hardly able to believe it. "I didn't realize it had been so long since I last talked to you."

"It's been *twice* that long, you old hermit!" June scolds.

"We haven't heard from you in nearly a year," Jack reminds him.

"And with those darn earphones you always wear, you *never* hear your phone."

Jack looks Anderson over, from head to toe. "You look great, by the way."

"Thanks."

"Actually, you look awful," June says, "but the clothes look great."

"Well, that's not surprising. *You* certainly look good."

"Not fat and blotchy?" June asks.

Anderson smiles and shakes his head. "Radiant."

"Ha," June barks at Jack. "I *told* you I looked radiant."

"Is it going to be a boy or a girl?" Anderson asks.

June gives him a disgusted look. "Do we look like the sort who'd peek in our present before the big day?"

"We asked the doctors not to tell us," Jack explains.

"What if you get things in pink and have a boy? Or get things in blue and have a girl?"

"Yellow," June says abruptly. "We're getting everything in yellow."

"Don't worry," Jack says, "we're all prepared."

"If it's a boy, we're putting him down for Eton," June announces, her nose in the air. "Or was it the Bozo School?" she asks, making a face like a lunatic clown.

Anderson laughs.

Jack suddenly becomes more serious. "Actually, we have an

important question to ask you regarding the arrangements for this baby. We were wondering if you'd be interested—"

"Of *course,* he'd be interested!" June interjects.

"—when the baby's born—" Jack continues.

"The responsibility will be good for him!" June says to Jack.

"—in being the baby's godfather," Jack finishes.

Anderson is profoundly touched. "Gosh, I hardly know what to say."

June beams at him. "We figure any kid who has to put up with *you* as a godfather will appreciate *us* a lot more."

"I'd be delighted," Anderson says.

Despite her smile, June's eyes are once more overflowing. "Want to see the room we've been redecorating as a nursery?" she asks.

"I'd love to. Do you need another carpenter or painter?"

"Not for the nursery," Jack says. "But maybe you'd like to start on one of the other rooms." The gesture he makes over his shoulder seems to take in the whole house.

Anderson notices that there are more paint cans stacked along the hallway running toward the back of the house. Most of them are decorated with pastel drips.

June reaches out to each of the men, giving them an affectionate squeeze. "You boys go on up. I need to make a little trip to the bathroom, and then I'll join you." She shuffles off down the hall.

"She's really high from you showing up this way," Jack explains, lowering his voice. "But she's been suffering from some periods of depression and anxiety lately. I think it would be best if we didn't give her anything else to worry about right now."

"I understand."

"I just finished a big programming job, so I don't have to work tomorrow. We can start sorting things out then. In the meantime, you look like you need to relax."

"Thanks, Jack. But there is one thing I have to ask you right away. Can I spend the night here? I don't really have anyplace else to go."

"Of course," Jack says. "No problem. The guest room upstairs is piled with stuff from the redecorating. But that couch over there folds out into a bed. You can sleep down here."

"Thanks."

"It's getting a bit cool this evening, isn't it? Why don't you build a fire, while I get you that drink I promised. What'll it be?"

"I still mostly drink beer. I had a couple this afternoon. They didn't do much good, though."

"Let me mix you something a little stronger. Bourbon and soda?"

"Sounds great." Anderson takes off his jacket and drapes it over a chair. He pats the pocket to verify that the bundle of money is still there. Then he sets to work, crumpling old newspapers. He piles them together in the cast iron fire grate, weighing them down with sticks of kindling.

After a few moments, June returns. "Don't you want to see the nursery?"

"We'll go up in a minute," Jack calls from the kitchen. "I'm just mixing some drinks."

June makes a face of comic frustration. "Now that I can't have any, Jack's *always* mixing drinks."

"I thought pregnancy was supposed to give you a natural high," Anderson says.

"Well, it comes and goes."

As Anderson places the logs on his pile of kindling and paper, he becomes aware that June is looking at him strangely. "What is it?" he asks.

"You seem different this evening," she says, studying him.

"What do you mean?"

"I don't know. It's not just that you've shaved your beard. It's your voice, I guess."

"I'm a little hoarse," Anderson says, realizing that it's true. "I didn't dry off soon enough after swimming."

He checks to be sure the flue is open, then lights the newspapers in several places. The chimney begins to draw almost at once.

Jack returns, squeezing the large glasses into a triangle between his hands. There is an orange juice in the front for June. She takes it at once to make Jack's burden less precarious, giving Jack a little bite on the neck as she does so. Jack blushes slightly and hands Anderson his drink.

Anderson tastes it immediately. "You're right," he says,

"that's exactly what I needed." Anderson puts a folding fire screen in front of the fireplace. "Now I'm ready for the grand tour," he announces.

They head on up the stairs, June leading the way, Anderson in the middle. For the rest of the evening, they talk of babies and home improvements, computers and fishing. Despite Jack's warning, June seems in great form, funny and resourceful, ready to handle anything.

They eat a beef stew that June has had simmering all afternoon in a large Crockpot. She was planning to freeze half, so there is plenty to go around. Jack tells self-mocking stories about how excessively 'domestic' they've become since June got pregnant. There is lots of laughter. Anderson and Jack both drink more than usual. But it's June who seems most merry.

When June decides it's time to retire, Jack helps Anderson open the foldout bed and finds him some clean towels. The bed is already made up and only needs to be supplemented with pillows from an antique chest. June kisses Anderson good-night and heads on up to bed. Jack pours Anderson another brandy. Then he gives Anderson another bear hug and follows June up the stairs.

Anderson can't remember when he has had a nicer evening. He has temporarily put all his worries aside. The breeze coming through the open window has gradually grown chilly, but Anderson likes the feel of it. He puts more logs on the fire. They roll forward in the grate, so Anderson uses the fire poker to prop them at the back where he wants them. He turns off the lamps, so the fireplace is lighting the room. Then he sits down on the foldout bed. The 'rustic' furnishings look beautiful to him.

Still sipping his brandy, Anderson shifts to a more comfortable position. He lies back at an angle, making sure his shoes are extending over the edge of the bed. He doesn't want to smudge the blanket. His head rests on the pillows. Without moving anything but his arm, he can reach over and set his glass on the floor.

This is the peace he needs. He puts his hands behind his neck and gazes into the fire. He knows he should get up, clean his teeth, and get undressed. But for the moment, he is too comfortable to move. He stares at the small yellow flames that dart back and forth over the glowing logs. Slowly, almost imperceptibly, his eyelids slide shut.

Then he finds himself running. Pine needles brush his face and cover the ground beneath his feet. He is back among the trees of northern Minnesota. But mostly he is back among pine needles. They are prickly and slippery at the same time. And they keep getting wetter.

Anderson knows he must go faster. There is somewhere he must get to, but he doesn't know where. He hears his grandfather's voice shouting instructions at him. But he can't make out the words. He only knows that his grandfather is angry, that he has done something wrong.

He strains to run faster, but the pine needles keep getting in the way. As the needles get wetter and wetter, they keep gaining weight. Anderson tries to push them aside, but the quantities are too much for him. They seem to be everywhere. There are pine needles in his arms, pine needles in his legs.

Freilinger's voice has joined his grandfather's. Each echoes the other. Their instructions grow more urgent, more angry. But Anderson can't hear what they're saying. Masses of wet needles blot out the sound.

Now he is swimming. The billows of pine needles are like clouds of water. But heavy, oh, so heavy. And he needs to go faster.

Hands reach out to help him. Tender, feminine hands. Not one pair, but two. Stroking and urging. But pulling him in different directions.

He realizes he is sinking. But he doesn't know the way to the surface. The masses of wet needles are turning and pivoting. He is caught in a kind of slow motion turbulence.

Somewhere in the swirling masses, he can feel a woman trying to keep him from drowning. Her hands are the right ones, the ones pulling him toward air. But he can't see who she is, and she soon gets pushed aside.

Other nightmare hands force him under. They seem stronger than the hands of the woman trying to save him. Stronger, even, than his own hands. It seems an eternity since he last drew a breath. A large weight is squeezing his chest, holding down his shoulders. He is almost out of air. Even in his dream, he feels the adrenaline rush of fear.

Then Anderson's nightmare again turns real. He is no longer asleep, no longer dreaming. There *is* a large mass pushing into his face. But it's not wet, no, not wet at all. It is plugging his nose, covering his mouth. It is a large, feather pillow.

For a moment, Anderson has an impulse to laugh. The object of his fears has turned out to be something soft and comforting, familiar and welcome. Then he discovers he still can't breathe.

He tries to turn his head, but the pillow is clamped too hard against his ears. He feels large, rounded weights, pressing into his shoulders. His arms have only limited movement. Someone is trying to smother him, pinning his head with the pillow, kneeling on his chest.

He recognizes the weights on his shoulders and upper arms as his attacker's knees and shins. As he starts to struggle, they press painfully into him. His efforts to draw in air only cause the cotton cloth to cling more tightly to his nostrils and mouth.

Frantically, Anderson battles with his arms. But he can only brush the back of his attacker's thighs. There is no way to get a grip, no way to reach anything vulnerable. He kicks his legs in the air, trying to connect with something. But there is nothing there. He tries to push against the bed. But the mattress is too soft under him. There is nothing to lever against, no way to change position. It is like floating in water, but without the freedom of movement.

Desperate now, Anderson begins swinging his legs from side to side, twisting his hips with each swing. This time, the softness of the mattress works in his favor. He is able to tilt his shoulders more each time. He can feel his attacker leaning more and more from side to side. The attacker's knees slip off Anderson's shoulders. But the pillow is still pressed tightly over his face.

All this struggle has used up the little air left in Anderson's lungs. His heart races as he begins to lose consciousness. His muscles begin to quiver uncontrollably. Yet still he tilts and twists from side to side.

Suddenly, Anderson feels the weight go off his left arm. Then there is a crash over to his right, as his attacker collides with a lamp. Anderson turns his head to the left as the pillow flops free. His face is still covered, but he can drawn in air.

Breathing almost convulsively, Anderson folds his knees to his chest and rolls onto his left side. He is almost unconscious, but he manages to grab the bed's edge with his right hand and to pull himself into a kneeling position. His lungs strain for air.

Then a blow to his left side sends him falling from the bed. Anderson realizes he has been hit with the lamp base he had heard crashing to the floor a moment earlier. He lands sideways on the floor with his hip taking most of the force.

His lower ribs throb with pain, as he struggles to his hands and knees. He is now beside the bed, facing away from the fireplace. The last attack had come from the other side of the bed and from somewhere behind him. Anderson crawls forward to avoid another blow. He wants to get away from the source of the violence. But the next sound is from somewhere in front of him. His attacker has apparently circled around the bed.

Anderson tries to get to his feet. But just as he gets halfway up, his attacker aims a kick at Anderson's groin.

In the flickering firelight, Anderson sees it coming. He lunges forward, grabbing the attacker's leg. The attacker's shoe misses its target and goes between Anderson's legs. But the force of the leg itself leaves Anderson winded.

For a moment, they are locked together. Anderson clings to the attacker's leg, while the attacker tries to shake him off.

Then the attacker pitches himself forward. Anderson is flipped onto his back. He hits the floor hard, and his head snaps back against it with a force that jars his brains. Only the braided rug keeps him from being knocked out.

Anderson's head is now near the fireplace. His has lost his grip on his attacker's leg. He lies with his face, throat, and stomach unprotected, but is almost too dazed to move. Looking back, past the top of his head, he sees the fire poker sticking out of the fireplace. He reaches back over his head to grab it. The brass handle is barely within the range of his fingers. For a moment, the poker seems to be stuck.

Anderson squirms backward with his shoulders to get a better grip. He gets his hand around the handle and pulls again. He seems to have no strength.

Then the poker comes loose in a shower of sparks. Glowing coals fall across Anderson's face and scatter across the area around him. He shakes his head and brushes at his chest to avoid being burned.

Before he is free of the fiery debris, he hears something coming at him. He swings the poker in the direction of the sound. As he shifts his gaze, Anderson sees the shadowy figure of his attacker bending toward him. He realizes he is going to connect with his attacker's head. He flexes his shoulders to put as much thrust as possible into the blow.

There is a metallic clang. The impact sends a jolt back through Anderson' s arms. He seems to have stunned his adversary, but not enough to make the figure fall back. For a moment, Anderson cannot fathom what has happened.

Then, in the glow of the scattered fire, Anderson sees that the figure standing above him is wearing some kind of helmet. It is colored black, like the rest of the attacker's clothes, but its glossy surface produces faint highlights. In the dim light, it's hard to see any details. But there seems to be no face.

The blank figure comes at him again. This time, Anderson swings the poker at the attacker's body. He hears a dull thud when the poker connects, as though it were striking leather upholstery. The attacker grunts in pain. But the shaft of the poker is caught in the attacker's hands. Anderson struggles to wrench it free. But his adversary's leverage from a standing position is much better. The brass handle slips from Anderson's hands. His own weapon comes swinging back toward him.

Anderson rolls to the side. He hears the poker strike the floor. Hot cinders sear his arm and hands, burning into his knees. He paws at the brickwork of the fireplace, scrambling to get himself upright. The shoes, still on his feet, are his only protection against the live coals littering the floor.

A blow from the poker lands across his back. It sends him sprawling against the log bin at the side of the hearth. Grabbing for balance, his hands encounter the logs. He gets his fingers around one of the longer and thinner ones. He yanks it from the bin and pivots, holding the log in front of him with both hands. It is just in time to block a savage blow. The poker is deflected against the bricks. Anderson swings out with his log. He connects only with a glancing hit, but it serves to hold off the assault.

As the light of the fire glows brighter, Anderson gets a better view of the figure in front of him. His first thought is that he is looking at some sort of diving suit. He still has a feeling of being submerged. He has trouble separating what is happening from the events in his dream.

Then he sees that the diving helmet is really a motorcycle helmet. His attacker's clothes are motorcycle leathers. There is no face, because the tinted visor on the motorcycle helmet is down.

The attacker seems enraged at being seen, even if hidden in motorcycle gear. Blow after blow comes pounding at Anderson. He fends them off with his piece of wood, returning hits as much as he can. The log holds up against the poker, but its blows have nothing like the poker's force.

Anderson finds himself being driven backward. He tries to circle toward the door to the hallway. As he continues to parry the blows, he feels the wood start to splinter. He gropes with his foot for the doorway behind him. Finally, his shoe hits the molding. As he backs through the doorway, he makes a stabbing motion with the log, thrusting upward, beneath the helmet's chin guard. He seems to connect. His adversary makes a hoarse, gurgling sound and falls back.

Then Anderson steps on something thick and soft. He tips backward, landing hard on his tailbone. In the dim light, he realizes he has stumbled over Jack. His friend is breathing loudly, but apparently unconscious. Anderson reaches out. The hair on his friend's head is wet with something dark. Feeling the slight stickiness where it has begun to dry, Anderson realizes it is blood.

He is now leaning on the base of the stairway. There are sounds of footsteps in the upstairs hallway.

"Jack?" a voice calls. "What are you guys *doing* down there?" It is June at the top of the stairs.

Anderson struggles to his feet. Looking back through the doorway, he sees that the bed is now on fire. He wonders vaguely how to put it out.

Then the figure in black rises up in front of him. A growl of anger, deep and involuntary, comes from Anderson. He lunges for the attacker, arms extended, going for the throat.

But the faceless figure lowers its head, and the helmet crashes into Anderson's jaw.

Once more, Anderson goes down. His fall is broken by Jack's body, but his head feels full of sparks. Anderson turns it slowly from side to side, trying to clear his vision. Above him on the stairway, he hears June. As she reaches the lower stairs, she begins to scream Jack's name.

Anderson feels the leather clad figure stepping across him. There's the sound of a blow, then two further thuds, as June hits the wall and topples forward off the steps. The screaming stops.

For a moment, the only sound is the soft crackling of the spreading fire. Then Anderson manages to get himself moving again. Fumbling awkwardly in the dim light, he gets his arms around the attacker's leg. He brings his shoulder against the shinbone and begins levering the leg backward. The attacker falls, knocking over a pile of empty paint cans. The cans go clattering down the hallway.

Anderson begins working his way up the attacker's body, crawling with one hand, pounding with his other fist at the legs and stomach. But it is hard to tell whether his punches are having any effect through the thick leather padding.

Then Anderson feels a foot planted against his shoulder. He struggles to push it away, but the heel digs into his chest, and he feels himself being pushed off into the air. The thrust of the leg sends him flying backward. He lands hard on the hall floor.

The helmeted figure is up first. Anderson sees the dark silhouette heading back through the doorway, now bright from the fire. He tries to follow, but the air, when he stands, is dense with smoke.

Coughing and squinting, Anderson sees the figure near the bed, doing something that seems to be spreading the flames. Anderson moves forward to stop it. The attacker yanks at the flaming bedding with a snapping movement that makes the flames flare brighter. Then the whole fiery mass comes flying at Anderson's face.

Anderson ducks backward, but the bedding hits his chest. He beats at his clothes with his hands trying to stop them from catching fire. The smoke is now so thick, he can hardly breathe. Across the room he sees the faceless figure heading for the kitchen. Anderson starts to follow, but before he has taken more than a couple of steps, he begins coughing uncontrollably. He bends down toward the floor, trying to find more oxygen. For a moment, this seems to work, since the air is clearer there.

Then there is heavy jolt as a log slams into his head. Anderson's face hits the floor. The log bounces off his shoulders. Anderson is not completely unconscious. But he is too stunned to move.

For a while, he lies there, merely trying to breathe. Then he begins inching forward toward the kitchen. His progress is slow. He can't open his eyes to see, because they sting too much. His chest and stomach drag against the floor. He moves his body along by pulling himself forward with his hands and pushing with the inside edges of his shoes. There is fire all around him. He is not sure where he is, but he crosses onto linoleum tile.

The smoke gets slightly thinner, and he gets up on his hands and knees. More by chance than design, he blunders against the back door. He twists the knob and pulls the door inward. It opens easily. He pitches forward against the screen door beyond. It tears open with a splintering sound, and Anderson falls down the outdoor steps.

As he draws the clear air into his lungs, his coughing at first gets worse. Then the spasmodic movements subside, and he begins breathing more normally. It takes a few moments longer for his head to clear. He is vaguely aware the attacker must have long since escaped. Then Anderson realizes that Jack and June must still be in the building.

He gets to his feet and lurches desperately back toward the door where he just came out. But the smoke is so thick, he cannot even see inside. Then he remembers that Jack and June were lying only a few feet from the front door.

Anderson climbs back down the steps and hurries around the side of the house. Despite the flames he had seen inside, from the outside he mostly sees smoke. If he can just drag Jack and June out the front door, they should at least escape the fire.

Anderson scrambles up the front steps and tries the doorknob. He is horrified to find it locked. He jumps down from the

steps and darts over to the front windows. But the curtains are
burning and the front room looks impassable. Returning to the
front door, he begins kicking it hard near the doorjamb. The
wood splinters, but holds. Anderson feels increasingly frantic.
Bracing himself against the handrail, he puts every bit of strength
he has into his kicks. The railing bends outward. The door finally
begins to crumple inward. At first, it doesn't swing completely
free. But there is a crack of an inch or so at the edge. Smoke
pours out.

Then the paint cans begin to explode. At first, there is a low
thud. Then another. Then still others. Following these comes a
low rumbling sound, soft, but deep pitched. For a second or two,
Anderson doesn't realize what has happened. Then he notices
the light from inside the house has suddenly grown much
brighter. Waves of flame begin rolling through the crack around
the door, driving Anderson backward. Then larger waves come
rolling toward the front windows.

In a few minutes, the entire inside of the ground floor seems
to be a balloon of flames. A loud, steady roar drowns out further
detonations. The heat makes it impossible to remain even in the
front yard.

From back on the sidewalk, Anderson can only stare. No one
could survive such heat. His only friends are being burned before
his eyes. The baby they'd expected him to protect is burning with
them.

After a few minutes, he becomes aware of other people on
the sidewalk beside him. Then he hears the fire sirens approaching. Someone asks him to step back, but Anderson can't move.
He stands there, gazing blankly. The tears in his eyes are evapo-
rated by the heat.

A fireman in a rubber raincoat shoves him to the side. Then
the hoses come on and shoot water at the blaze.

The crowd grows, and Anderson watches with the rest. He
tries to tell himself that what has happened is not his fault. Yet it
was he who spilled the coals, starting the fire. And it was he who
must have drawn the attacker to the house. He tries to tell himself he did all he could to save his friends. Yet he knows if he had
thought of them sooner, if he had headed out the front door
rather than the back, things might have ended differently.

His right arm throbs with pain. Anderson looks down at it with some surprise. His shirtsleeve is black and crumbling. He pulls it back to look at the skin beneath. The inside of his arm, from his wrist to well past his elbow, is bright red and already blistering. He realizes he has a serious burn. But it's not the sort of injury that will take long to heal.

It's not like being incinerated alive.

The thought makes him feel he deserved to die. If his guilt had limits before, it has none now. No punishment could be too great for bringing this on his friends. No death could be too painful or soon enough in coming.

But even as he thinks this, he realizes he is not sure whom he means. Who is it, exactly, who deserves to die? And who actually provoked the attack? Anderson? Or Peterson? Anderson is filled with rage at himself. But his rage is also rage at Peterson, and the two blur together.

"It's quite a little fire, isn't it?"

Anderson hears the words, but they don't register.

"I said, quite a little fire. . . ."

Gradually, Anderson realizes that the man standing next to him is trying to make polite conversation.

"I'm going to kill the person who caused it," Anderson says in a normal voice. "I'm going to find out who it was—and kill him."

The man looks at Anderson's face, apparently uncertain if he has heard him correctly. For a moment their eyes meet. Then Anderson turns and plunges into the darkness.

CHAPTER 8

Pain wakes him. Anderson's arm feels as though someone is heating it slowly with a blowtorch. It throbs and burns. He tries to change its position, only to discover that every other part of his body aches as well. His head is a mass of soft, tender swellings. His joints feel bruised on the inside, where the bones come together.

He smells flowers. And something else—perhaps, alcohol. For a moment, Anderson thinks he is in a hospital. Then he opens his eyes. A few inches in front of them, on a low bedside chest, a piece of chocolate candy rests on a small, white doily. Beside it, in front of a white ceramic lamp base, a snifter holds a shot of cognac. The fragrance of flowers comes from a bouquet a little farther away.

Despite the stiffness in his neck, Anderson lifts his head to see more of the room. In one of the far corners is a brass stand for holding a suit. Then nearer, facing the foot of the bed, is a high chest made of dark wood. One of its doors stands open, revealing a television inside.

Turning his head the other way, Anderson sees a black railing supported by vertical spokes. In the wall, a few feet beyond the railing, there is a window extending downward. It looks out on a riverside vista from a height of seven or eight stories. A circular iron stairway descends to the floor below.

This is not a place Anderson, at first, recognizes. But, as he comes more fully awake, he recalls what he is doing there. He is in a two story suite at the Whitney, a luxury hotel occupying a building that was once a nineteenth century flour mill. It stands a few blocks north of the Minneapolis business district, overlooking the Mississippi.

Anderson remembers thinking the night before that this hotel would be a safe refuge from which to launch a response to his tormentors. He also remembers reasoning that a truly classy hotel would be less likely to make trouble about his disheveled appearance and lack of luggage.

The night clerk had lived up to his expectations, checking him in without question or comment. As soon as he was shown to the room, Anderson had bandaged his arm and collapsed into bed. He had slept deeply and apparently without dreams.

But surveying the room in the morning light, Anderson feels less comfortable. It is not the sort of place he would ever think of staying in ordinary circumstances. The individual furnishings are almost austere in design, but the total effect is one of luxurious indulgence. Looking around the room, Anderson asks himself, 'Who *would* stay here?' And almost at once he knows the answer. The sort of person whose apartment he'd been exploring two nights earlier. Peterson.

On the floor beside the bed is a bag of things Anderson had picked up the night before from an all-night pharmacy. Wincing from his injuries, Anderson bends over and rummages through it. He finds a bottle of ibuprofen, takes two of the tablets, and washes them down with the cognac.

Then he climbs out of bed and descends the iron stairway for a closer look out the window. Pulling back the long, gauze curtains, he has a sweeping view of the Mississippi River. The Whitney Hotel is only a few blocks downstream from Nicollet Island and not much farther from where Peterson's apartment is located on the opposite bank.

Out in the river, opposite the hotel, is an enormous complex of dams, locks, and hydraulic works, much of it visibly under repair. This is today all that remains of the mighty St. Anthony Falls, the original source of water power that had caused the city to be built on this site. Although the rocky ledge across the river has long since been replaced by concrete barricades, the drop is still considerable. Even today, the water turns into a roaring rush of white where it goes pouring through the chutes.

A couple of miles to the east is the bar where this nightmare began. Anderson realizes he could get there from this hotel in less than twenty minutes.

The thought galvanizes him into action. But as he starts up the stairway, he finds he is still groggy. Glancing around the lower sitting room, he spies a telephone and reaches toward it.

There is no wait. "Good morning," says the cheerful, feminine voice. "May we help you?"

"I'd like room service, please."

"What can we bring you, sir?"

"A pot of coffee. And I guess some breakfast. Orange juice. Maybe a Danish roll?"

"Will there be anything else?"

"No, that's all. —Wait. Is there a shop in the hotel where someone could get me a shirt?"

"We don't have a men's boutique. But we'd be happy to get you a shirt, sir."

"It would be a tremendous help."

"What type and size, sir?"

"Any standard dress shirt. A sixteen collar, thirty-four sleeve. Pale blue or white."

"It should be there within the half hour. Could you give me your room number, please."

"Gee, I'm afraid I don't remember. The name is"—Anderson hesitates, trying to recall what he said when he checked in—"the name is Peterson."

"Thank you, sir."

Anderson hangs up, looking toward the door to the room. A heavy chair is wedged under the doorknob. He remembers setting it there as an extra barricade when he went to sleep. The sight of it brings back memories of the night before.

For a moment, Anderson has trouble breathing. His chest grows tight, and the air feels thick with water or smoke. His vision blurs. Somewhere in the haze before him, he sees wavy images of Jack and June. His diaphragm jerks convulsively as it did when he was being drowned. But this time he hears himself sobbing.

It is several minutes before Anderson can get a grip on himself. Even when he does, he remains shaky. He can keep himself under control only by concentrating on the most mundane tasks. He pulls the chair away from the door and puts it back where it belongs. Then he climbs the circular stairway to the level above. Grabbing the bag of drugstore items, he heads for the bathroom.

He uses the toilet and steps into the shower. The powerful spray makes his bruises hurt more, but the pain seems entirely appropriate. For a few seconds, he wishes his suffering were more intense. Then he realizes that further pain now would accomplish nothing. The bandage covering his burn comes loose. He pulls it off completely. He squeezes some of the water from the soaking gauze, then opens the shower door and throws the soggy mass into one of the two sinks. The burned area on his arm feels hot, even when he adjusts the water to room temperature.

Finished with the shower, he blots his burn lightly with a clean towel, then dries the rest of his body. He takes the tube of burn ointment from his drugstore bag and squeezes rows of the clear jelly across the red and blistered area. After spreading the ointment with his finger, he takes four of the large gauze pads out of their wrappers and lays them across his arm. The ointment holds them in place as he tapes them down.

By this time, the mirrors are beginning to clear. Anderson inspects his other wounds. The blow from the poker that caught him across his back seems the worst. It has left a purple welt nearly two inches wide, with the skin split in the middle. His shoulders, tailbone, hip, and elbows are all somewhat discolored. His jaw is swollen. There are tender, lumpy spots on his head, beneath his hair.

His face remains unmarked, but he has not gotten used to the way he looks without his beard. He still seems to himself like a stranger. He reaches into the drugstore bag and pulls out a packet of disposable shavers. He feels brilliant for having had the foresight to think of these the night before. He makes a lather in his hands with the hotel soap. It is very thin compared to shaving cream, but it seems to do the job. It is a long time since Anderson has shaved with a safety razor, but he gradually manages, nicking himself four or five times. The lather is stained pink, but the bleeding stops almost at once. After rinsing his face, he splashes his hair and combs his fingers through it, so it won't dry at odd angles.

When he emerges from the bathroom, he still feels sore almost everywhere, but he knows he is moving more smoothly. He puts on one of the thick terry cloth robes the hotel provides for guests, taking care not to snag his bandage. Then he gathers up his clothes, grabs his bottle of ibuprofen, and goes downstairs.

Room service has arrived while he was in the bathroom, leaving a cart with more food than he ordered. The coffee is in a large silver pot. Other heated items are under heavy silver covers. A rose petal decorates the butter dish. Beside the plates of food is a new white shirt in its plastic wrapping.

Anderson dresses while he eats. He puts on the clothes he was wearing the day before, but substitutes the new shirt for the old, charred one. The sleeves cover the bandage on his arm. He stuffs the damaged shirt in the wastebasket. Checking his appearance in the mirror, Anderson realizes the sports coat he was wearing the day before was lost in the fire. And with it, the packet of cash. He puts his hand in his trouser pocket. Peterson's wallet is still there, along with Peterson's key—and the note from Shannon. Looking inside the wallet, Anderson sees there is still a considerable amount of money left, as well as the numerous credit cards.

He slides a card out of the wallet and turns it over. The signature beneath the magnetic strip looks exactly like the examples in the handwriting book Anderson had used as a child. It occurs to Anderson that this is itself a clue to something, but he is not sure what. It also occurs to him that Peterson's signature would be easy for him to imitate.

Glancing around the room, Anderson spots the hotel key lying on a counter over a small refrigerator. He reaches over and scoops it up. Then he turns and opens the door to the public corridor. Outside, where someone might expect to find a doormat, is the morning newspaper. Almost without thinking, Anderson picks it up and turns it over. Toward the bottom of the front page, he sees the headline: FIRE KILLS SOUTH MINNEAPOLIS COUPLE.

With shaking hands, he reads the article. It was obviously inserted just before the paper went to press. The account is brief and clearly written, but the words barely register. Their meaning is too horrible to contemplate. Anderson feels blank, vacant, numb. Only the last sentence remains in his mind: "The cause of the blaze is unknown."

Anderson sets the paper back inside the room, pulls the door shut, and heads off down the corridor. Something about the surroundings makes him uneasy, but he cannot, at first, decide what it is. The decor seems pleasant enough. The walls are lined with a herringbone fabric in an off-white color. Little pairs of brass lamps are mounted at regular intervals between framed prints of natural history specimens: sea shells, flowers, nuts, birds, fruit, butterflies. Then Anderson recognizes what is bothering him: these pictures remind him of the specimens on display back at Peterson's apartment.

As he walks farther along the corridor, Anderson begins to feel once again as though he is under water. But this time, it is less like a lake and more like a brackish sea.

He reaches the landing near the elevators and hurriedly pushes the button. Around him are elegant furnishings, obviously designed to be soothing. But to Anderson they are images from an undersea nightmare. The white upholstered chairs and sofa, with their hints of pink and blue, loom like coral reefs. The brass chandelier, with its many curved arms, hovers like a giant octopus. A fine, old clock, mounted on the wall, seems spilled from the wreck of a ship.

Anderson closes his eyes for a moment, trying to clear these images from his brain. But this only makes him think of the helmeted attacker, whose costume had resembled a diving suit.

The sound of the elevator arriving on his floor wakes him, as though from a dream. With a feeling of momentary relief, Anderson steps into the dark, wood paneled interior.

Arriving in the hotel lobby, Anderson sees that it is even more imposing than he had realized the night before. He walks past the tall white pillars, the huge potted plants, and the ivory colored piano. Behind, to his left, he notices a monumental stairway descending to the glassy, stone floor. He stops at the main desk, where a slender, freckled woman with reddish brown hair wishes him good morning. He hands her the room key.

"I'd like to check out," he says.

She types the room number into a computer. "Did you enjoy your stay, Mr. Peterson?" She asks as though she really wanted to know.

"The room and service were excellent," he assures her. He hears a high speed printer whirring behind the counter.

She hands him the printed bill. "How would you like to pay?" she asks.

Anderson sees that the total cost of his overnight stay with room service, a new shirt, and taxes comes to $264. He realizes that counting out that much cash and waiting for change might make him rather conspicuous. He takes out Peterson's wallet, extracts the credit card he had examined earlier, and hands it over.

The woman takes it, flashing him a further smile. "Just a moment, please" she says, inserting the card into a machine.

Anderson wonders if he has made a mistake. He has a sudden vision of the police descending and arresting him right there. To cover his fears, he forces himself to study the bill. It includes the price of his shirt, but no charge for fetching it. "Can I add a tip to this?" he asks. "For the person who found me a shirt."

"Of course, sir. On that line there." She points to the appropriate spot on the bill.

Anderson scribbles in a sum, exercising his generosity at Peterson's expense. After all, it is Peterson who is somehow responsible for what has happened to him. Peterson should pay. Or does he mean Peterson's estate? That thought is too disturbing to consider right now.

The woman behind the counter takes the bill and inserts it once again into the printer. There is another whirring sound. Then she hands it to him for his signature.

Anderson takes a deep breath, then writes Peterson's name in the handwriting he was taught in grade school. It is a very good approximation of the signature on the credit card, but there is no sign the woman is comparing it. She hands Anderson a copy of the bill, along with the card itself.

"Have a nice day, Mr. Peterson," she says.

"You too," Anderson replies. As he is putting the credit card back in the wallet, he has another thought. "Could you give me some change?" he asks, taking out a twenty dollar bill, the lowest he has left. "With three quarters and a dime."

"Certainly, sir." She drops his twenty on the counter and

counts out the bills and coins from a drawer below. "Will that be all?"

"Yes, thank you." He turns and leaves the hotel.

"Taxi, sir?" the doorman asks.

But Anderson shakes his head and crosses the street, heading into the parking lot beyond. The bare streets in that end of town seem blindingly bright in the late morning sun. A few blocks away, the mirrored buildings of downtown Minneapolis reflect a pale blue sky. The open spaces make Anderson feel very exposed. He looks around for anyone who might be watching him, but sees nothing out of place. Hurrying on to Washington Avenue, he catches a bus heading toward the university area. This time he has the exact change.

A few minutes' ride takes him east over the river, near the place where it bends. Once in the vicinity of the university, the bus begins making frequent stops. Anderson gets off a few blocks from the old campus, about a mile and a half from his house. From the bus stop, it is only a short walk to the bar where he was kidnapped.

Arriving outside, Anderson is amazed at how different the bar looks in daylight. The concrete block walls, enameled window fittings, and dark wood siding are all well maintained. But the construction is cheap, and the various building materials have not weathered into any kind of harmony. Evidently, the congenial atmosphere Anderson associates with the place requires darkness and artificial lighting.

Anderson is uneasy walking past the parking lot, where he had been knocked to the ground and hustled into the station wagon. But the pavement and cars look so ordinary, he feels foolish. He squares his shoulders and heads for the entrance.

When he steps inside, he is at first unable to see. Windows look out on the sunny street in front, but, seeing them from the inside at this time of day, Anderson realizes they are heavily tinted. As his eyes grow accustomed to the dark, he sees that this dimly lit interior is much the way he remembers it. The video games and beer signs look just as they did before. The pool tables present the same expanse of green felt.

Yet even in the back corners, the daylight intrudes through a series of high side-windows, giving the main room a bleaker look than it had at night.

Anderson heads for the main bar, picking his way between the scattered tables. At this time of day, the place is almost deserted. His stomach tenses as he spots the table where he had sat three days earlier with the trio who had called themselves Brian, Trudy, and Gretchen. But Anderson tries not to let it show. He pulls back a bar stool and sits down.

The bartender sets a cocktail napkin on the polished bar top. "Well, hello there," he says, as though Anderson were someone he was looking forward to seeing. "A little early for you, isn't it?"

Anderson is startled by the familiarity. "Are we supposed to be friends?" he asks.

"I try to think of all my regular customers as friends," the bartender replies with an easy confidence. He is short, young, and prematurely bald, but extremely muscular.

"Am I a regular customer?" Anderson asks.

The bartender looks him over, wary, but good humored. "What is this? A sociological interview?"

"No, I was just a little surprised at your greeting me that way."

"Oh, I get it," the bartender says, smiling. "You didn't expect me to recognize you without your beard. That's it, isn't it?"

"I'm just trying to figure something out," Anderson says.

The bartender's smile turns back into a look of wariness. "Do you want a drink?"

"Do you have coffee?"

The bartender waves his forefinger in the air, as though pushing an imaginary button. "Smart choice."

Anderson wonders if the bartender thinks he has already been drinking. He takes a deep breath and tries to look as steady and sober as possible.

The bartender sets a cup and saucer on the bar, along with some paper packets containing sweeteners and creamers. Then he gets a glass coffeepot from a stand on the counter behind him and fills the cup. "Let me know if that's too strong," he says. "I could add some more hot water."

Anderson sips the coffee, without adding anything to it or thinking about how it tastes. "So humor me a minute, okay?"

"Okay. I got nothing better to do."

"Why *did* you give me such a friendly greeting?"

The bartender shrugs. "I've seen you here several times. I thought maybe you were making this your local hangout."

The explanation makes sense. Anderson had been to this bar a few times before the night of the kidnapping. But he still feels the fellow's greeting was excessively enthusiastic. "Is that all?"

"Sure."

Anderson holds his gaze, waiting for something more.

After a moment, the bartender looks away and smiles. "Of course, a big tip always makes a customer more memorable."

"Did I give you a big tip?"

The bartender turns back to him, his eyebrows raised in amusement. "No. But your friend sure did."

"What friend?"

"The big guy. The one with you three or four nights ago. When you had a little too much to drink."

Anderson's heart beats faster. He has to make an effort to speak casually. "That big guy—is he a regular customer?"

"Why? Isn't he a friend of yours?"

"I just met him for the first time that night. I'm afraid I owe him an apology for not holding my liquor better." As he hears his own voice, Anderson is surprised at the ease with which he is stretching the truth. But he knows he will get no answers without a plausible explanation. He chooses his next words with special care. "I also wanted to repay him for my share of the bill. Do you know who he is?"

"No," the bartender says. "Never saw him before that night." He sounds as though he is telling the truth.

Anderson's hopes begin to sink. If the man called Brian was only in this bar that one time, there might be no way to trace him. "Have you got any idea how I might find him?" Anderson asks.

The bartender shakes his head. "Can't help you there."

Anderson tries to conceal the intensity of his frustration. He takes another sip of the coffee, wondering where to go from here.

The bartender looks at the paper packets and pokes them with his finger. "Don't Gretchen and Trudy know him?"

Anderson's heart begins to pound again. "You know Gretchen and Trudy?"

"Sure. They live in the neighborhood. They usually stop in a couple nights a week."

"Do you know their address?"

"No. And if I did, I wouldn't give it to you."

"Why not?"

"Come on. When a pair of attractive women want you to know their address, they'll tell you. In the meantime, you can find them by hanging around here."

Anderson nods. "I might do that. I really want to pay those folks back."

"Just drink a little more slowly next time, okay?"

For a moment, Anderson is irritated by the bartender telling him what to do. But then he has to smile. The fellow's assertive manner, like his bulging muscles, is such an obvious compensation for being short and bald.

"Okay," Anderson says. "Sorry about last time."

"No problem. You didn't throw up or get obnoxious."

"By the way, what was in that drink the big fellow had you mix?"

The bartender chuckles. "Everything but lighter fluid. Actually, I'm not sure. I just named a price for filling the glasses. He did most of the pouring himself."

Anderson nods. "I figured he might have."

The bartender grins again at the very thought of the concoction. He shakes his head in disbelief.

Anderson nods. Without finishing the coffee or asking how much it costs, he takes a five dollar bill from Peterson's wallet, places it on the counter, and leaves the bar.

CHAPTER 9

Out on the street, Anderson sees a row of academic books in a bookstore window. He remembers he is still near the main campus of the University of Minnesota. The books look unusually familiar, but Anderson can't think why. Then he realizes they remind him of the academic books filling most of the shelves in Peterson's apartment.

Recognizing that this could be an important clue to Peterson's activities, Anderson decides to find out if Peterson had some connection with the university. The obvious place to start is the registrar.

Anderson walks a few blocks down the street and crosses onto the campus. At first, he is struck by the amount of activity, the lively voices, the sheer energy of the students. This is not the way he remembers it. Then he realizes that the fall term has just begun. Everybody is new to the school or just back from summer vacation. Students are still attending all of their classes. No one is disillusioned or worn out yet.

He cuts across the lawns, heading for the older buildings behind the huge auditorium at the end of the Mall. Somewhere among these buildings, he remembers, is the new underground complex that houses the big university bookstore and the registrar's office.

The surroundings are familiar to Anderson from his student days. But they give him a creepy feeling, because he has not been back since his grandfather's death. The crowds of students on their way to class look ridiculously young. As Anderson passes between the buildings, a policeman seems to be staring directly at him, but Anderson attributes this to his own anxiety.

Near the place where he expected to find it is a large descending ramp lined with vines. Anderson walks down it, through two sets of swinging glass doors. Everything inside is finished in rough concrete, but made less austere by wood fixtures and green plants.

On the first level below ground, he comes to a triangular booth with large windows labeled "Information." Anchored to the ceiling of the corridor beyond is a sign showing the way to the different facilities. Anderson sees a listing for "Registration and Student Records." The arrow beside it points downward to the "Lower Concourse." A little way along the corridor, Anderson spots a pair of yellow and stainless steel escalators. As he watches, an enormously fat girl rises into view, eating a glazed doughnut.

Anderson rides the other escalator down to the next level. To his left are windows looking out across the maze of bookcases that cover the large floor of the university bookstore. The 'lower concourse' itself is two stories high, with skylights opening onto it. Small trees grow from huge fiberglass planters, and large tan pipes jut up through the floor, ending abruptly in air vents.

The registrar's offices are opposite the bookstore, separated from the corridor by a glass wall with sliding glass doors. Little monograms dot the wall at chest level to prevent people from walking into the glass, but the dust and occasional handprints make the markings superfluous.

Wondering how he should phrase his inquiries, Anderson steps cautiously inside. He finds himself in a public waiting area. Apart from some large plants, everything is beige and gray, but further skylights and illuminated ceiling panels make the space seem pleasantly airy. Directly ahead is a high counter with two women perched behind it on tall stools. The older of the two is explaining something about the mailing of transcripts to an exasperated student. The younger is watching the people pass by outside the glass wall.

Anderson walks over to the younger woman. Up close, he sees that one of her arms, extending from her short sleeved blouse, is a stump, ending at the elbow. She stares vaguely ahead, saying nothing. For a second, Anderson wonders if she is also mute.

"Would it be possible," he asks, "to find out if a certain person attended this university or was employed here?"

It is a moment before she seems to notice him. Then she answers rapidly, her voice like a recorded announcement: "All degrees and dates of attendance are public information, as are the names and titles of academic faculty, past and present. Those requesting this information are not required to give reason or to disclose their identities. For information on nonacademic personnel, you need to consult the Personnel Office. I do not know their policy regarding disclosure of information."

"So what do I do?" Anderson asks.

The woman reaches for a pen and clipboard with her normal arm. Then, retaining the pen in her hand, she rests the clipboard on the edge of the counter and holds it in place with her abbreviated arm. "Your first name or nickname—?" she asks, her pen ready.

Anderson hesitates, then says "Andy."

The woman enters this name on her clipboard, along with the time.

"The name of the person in question and any known address—?"

He tells her. She writes this information down on a green slip of paper, along with the note "Date of Att., Degree."

"Please take a seat. I will be back shortly." She slides off her stool and walks around to the other side of a high partition. Stretching his neck to see where she is going, Anderson glimpses filing cabinets, computer terminals, and steel desks. As he watches her walk away, he notices that despite her truncated arm and strange way of talking, she moves with unusual grace.

After a couple of minutes, when she doesn't return, he takes her advice and sits down. He notices there is nothing to read, except the *Minnesota Daily,* the campus newspaper, but this doesn't bother him, since he is too nervous to read anyway. He leans forward, resting his forehead on his hand, partly to hide his face. It is unlikely that anyone would recognize him here, but he does not want to attract any further attention until he has a better idea of what is going on.

As his thoughts begin to wander, he hears someone calling, "Andy." Since he is not used to this nickname, he doesn't respond at first. Then he remembers and returns hurriedly to the counter.

The woman is back on her stool, but puzzling over her own notes, jotted on the back of the green slip. "This is very strange," she says, a more human voice replacing the 'recorded' one. "The fellow you were asking about received a bachelor's degree in mathematics after only three years and a Ph.D. two years later. But there is a note in the computer, saying his Ph.D. was 're-voked.'"

"What does that mean?" Anderson asks.

"I don't know," the woman says. "I've never seen anything like it. Here are the dates of his enrollment, if you want them." She hands Anderson the green slip.

He turns it over in his hands. "Let me make sure I've got this straight. The University of Minnesota gave Peterson a Ph.D. in mathematics."

"That's right."

"Then they took it away again."

"You got it."

"I don't understand. What did they do? Find a mistake in his calculations? An equation that turned out to be wrong?"

She shakes her head sympathetically. "Beats me."

"Is there any more information there that might explain this?"

"If there were, I wouldn't be allowed to tell you." She smiles. "But there isn't."

"So how do I find out what this means? Where do I go from here?"

"You might try Wilson Library, across the river. That's where all the dissertations are kept."

Anderson nods. "Thanks for your help." He hesitates, then speaks on impulse: "You move like a dancer."

The woman beams. "I *am* a dancer."

"Well, it shows," Anderson says, leaving her smiling. He is sure she has given him a valuable lead, but hasn't a clue what it means.

He makes his way out of the underground building, circles the east side of Northrop Auditorium, and climbs the steps to the plaza in front of it. The auditorium is an enormous brick building with ten massive, Ionic columns on its front side. It overlooks the grass- and tree-covered Mall that forms the core of the old campus.

For a moment, Anderson pauses to gaze at the buildings where he had once gone to class. Eight of them line the Mall. The nearer ones all have three-story, Ionic columns providing grand entryways. Carved in stone above the columns are the buildings' names. Anderson recalls how magnificent this had all seemed to him when he was beginning his studies. What high ambitions he had once had!

At the far end of the Mall is the student union, separated from the rest by a highway. It holds snack bars, ballrooms, and movie theaters. Remembering the times he had spent there with classmates, Anderson feels a wave of nostalgia.

He walks down the dozen or so steps to the Mall, then cuts diagonally across the shady lawns. Students sit on the grass, talking and eating their lunches, enjoying the pleasant weather. Many have books with them, but no one seems to be studying. The atmosphere is relaxed and friendly. Anderson remembers a time when people would have nodded greetings at him as he walked this route.

Then he has a chilling thought. His time as an undergraduate at the university overlapped the period when Peterson was a graduate student. Did Anderson look enough like Peterson then, so that people who didn't know them very well could have mistaken one for the other? When people he barely knew in those days were nodding greetings at him, did they think they were greeting Peterson?

The implications make Anderson feel queasy. He suddenly realizes that the existence of someone who looked like him may have been affecting his life for years, without his ever being aware of it. The main campus had something like 46,000 students in those years. If Peterson had been studying mathematics, he would have been going to different buildings than Anderson, who had majored in sociology. But even the huge Minneapolis campus is not that vast. The two of them must have been in the same vicinity a number of times. Even though they never met, they must have encountered at least some of the same people.

Anderson realizes he is physically shaking. He stops at one of the stone benches along the Mall and sits down. He makes a conscious effort to put the things he has discovered into a reasonable perspective. After all, *lots* of people look alike. Apart from a few neighborhoods in Minneapolis and St. Paul, the state of Minnesota is one of the most ethnically homogeneous areas in the country. Anderson himself is a typical Minnesota mix of Scandinavian and German stock. When he was attending the university, there must have been hundreds of young men on campus who looked at least approximately like him. Unless people had encountered Anderson in the exact circumstances where they were expecting to find Peterson, or vice versa, they would not have been likely to make the wrong identification.

The logic of this argument makes Anderson feel better. He is forced to admit his resemblance to Peterson might have created some small confusions on a few occasions. But these confusions would not have had any significant effect on his life. If anyone had mistaken him for Peterson in any important context or for more than a few moments, he would have been aware of it. Wouldn't he? Yes, of course, he would.

Anderson looks around at the students lounging on the grass. The whole scene appears so totally normal that his anxious thoughts seem like a wild aberration. He feels foolish, having let himself get so upset. Terrible things have been done to him and to his friends. But it will do him no good to get carried away with speculations.

Anderson gets up and continues along the Mall. Toward the far end, he cuts between the buildings on the west side and heads for the Washington Avenue Bridge, the same one he crossed earlier on the bus. He takes a wooden boardwalk up to the top level, reserved for pedestrians and bicycles. A glass passageway runs down the middle for use in bad weather, but on a day like this, most of the students walk outside it, enjoying the sunshine. Many still wear shorts. A few have Walkmans. A couple are even gliding along on Rollerblades, the local invention for making roller skates more like ice skates.

As he walks along the railing that guards the edge, Anderson tilts his head to peer almost straight down. Far below, at a dizzying drop, he sees the river rushing beneath him. Swirls of white foam make topological patterns that seem to move more slowly than the current. But from this height, it's hard to tell which effects are real and which are optical illusions.

When he reaches the West Bank of the river, Anderson finds himself on a sprawling terrace of little pebbles set in cement. Jutting into it at regular intervals are modern buildings of light brown brick, some as high as fourteen stories. They house the history, social science, and business faculties. Anderson recalls having classes in more than one of them. It's the part of the campus he knows best.

At the far end of the terrace is a three story bridge of glass corridors, connecting two of the buildings at their upper levels. Anderson passes beneath it to arrive at the front of Wilson Library, the largest and most comprehensive of the university collections. He enters through an automatic door and pushes through one of the mechanical turnstiles inside. At first, it seems nothing in the library has changed. The main catalogue is still straight ahead, with the information desk in front of it.

Then Anderson notices the computer terminals. Their number has been greatly increased, so that they now nearly fill the area in front of the card files. Anderson goes up to one and sees it is already displaying the program called "LUMINA." He pauses a moment, trying to remember how to work one of these things. Then he types in "A=," adds Peterson's name, and hits the "Enter" button.

A list of authors with the same name fills the screen. Each name is followed by one or more dates and abbreviated book titles. Anderson uses an 'arrow' key to move the cursor down to the name with the most likely birth date and the most technical sounding title. Once again, he hits "Enter."

Almost immediately, the screen refills with the entry for Peterson's doctoral dissertation. The full title is *Investigations into the Consequences of Quantified Modal Logics for Decision Theory, with Special Reference to Nonalethic Operators*. Below the title are data on the copyright date, length, format, and subject headings. The latter indicate that the dissertation could be classified as "Logic (Philosophy)" and "Game Theory," as well as "Mathematics."

Apparently, Anderson was on the right track when he guessed that the inhabitant of Peterson's apartment had a technical background. There might also be a connection between the philosophical aspects of the dissertation and the broader interests reflected in Peterson's bookshelves.

As far as Anderson can tell, the catalogue entry is a completely normal one up until the last two lines, where the location and call number are listed. There the entry reads:

LOCATION: MATHEMATICS
Call Number: QA9 Pe

This is not what Anderson was expecting. Dissertations are supposed to be filed together in a special section of the stacks. The woman in the registrar's office had been referring to this policy when she suggested he try Wilson Library.

Anderson goes over to one of the librarians. The fellow stands bent over behind the information desk, consulting a cardboard chart. "Excuse me," Anderson says. "Could you explain one of the catalogue entries to me?"

The librarian looks up at him, without straightening his back. "Of course." He is thin and dark, with a slightly furtive manner.

"It's this one over here." Anderson gestures to the screen he was using, drawing the librarian over toward it. "I'm trying to figure out where it's stored."

The librarian barely glances at the screen. "That's in the Mathematics Library."

"But it's a U. of M. dissertation."

The librarian takes a second look. "Oh, I see what you mean. How odd. Let me check the card file."

He leads Anderson back to the brown, wooden card files and pulls out one of the long, narrow drawers. With amazing speed, he ruffles through the little cards. "Yes, here it is." For a moment, he studies the entry. Then he looks up at Anderson with a puzzled expression. "This is very strange. The thesis was apparently registered with the library as a regular dissertation. Then, sometime later, it was reclassified."

"Reclassified?"

"Evidently." The librarian stands aside, while still holding his fingers between the parted file cards. "Look. You can see where the old classification was crossed out. It used to say 'Location:

142 ■ SCOTT BORG

Wilson Thesis,' with an MNU-D call number listed below. But someone has drawn a line through it and written in the same call number that's listed in Lumina."

"What does that mean?"

"It means that instead of being shelved among the dissertations, it is now shelved among the other books on its general subject, namely, mathematical logic."

"Isn't that rather unusual?"

The librarian nods cheerfully. This cataloging anomaly has clearly brightened his day. "The really peculiar thing is that it wasn't just a matter of reshelving the book right here in the Wilson Library. The Mathematics Library is in Vincent Hall, way over on the other bank. It has its own head librarian and its own acquisitions policy."

"It sounds as though somebody went to a lot of trouble to get this book removed from the register of dissertations."

"They certainly did." The librarian's tone of voice suggests he admires their diligence.

"And then they went to a lot more trouble to make sure a copy was still retained in the library system?"

"That's right."

"So the dissertation itself probably wasn't defective or inadequate?"

"Oh, no, probably not. In fact, I would guess that it made an important contribution to its subject."

"So why did someone decide it wasn't valid as a dissertation?"

"Quite a puzzle, isn't it?" The librarian smiles contentedly. Apparently, his job, as he sees it, is to identify such problems, not to solve them.

"Is there some way I could find out more about what was going on when this dissertation was reclassified?"

"Perhaps someone over in the Mathematics Library will be able to assist you."

"Okay. Thank you for your help."

The librarian bobs his head and shoulders in a gesture halfway between a nod of agreement and a bow for applause. "Have a nice day," he says.

Anderson leaves the library and retraces his earlier route,

across the terraces of the West Bank campus and over the Washington Avenue Bridge.

Arriving at the end of the Mall, he pauses for a moment, trying to remember which building is Vincent Hall. He is fairly sure it is the one on the far side of the Mall between the physics building and the one housing anthropology, but he never had any classes there. The only time he remembers passing through Vincent was on his way to Murphy Hall, directly behind it.

This thought fills him with a terrible sadness. In those days, his friend Jack had occasionally written articles on sports for the university newspaper. The newspaper offices were located in the basement of Murphy Hall. Anderson would meet Jack there, and the two of them would walk down to Stub and Herb's for a beer. Sometimes June would join them.

Anderson's eyes overflow with tears. He can't get used to the idea that Jack and June are now dead. He has a terrible need to call them on the phone, to tell them what he's doing, to ask them for advice. The fact that this is no longer possible only makes his need more intense. He knows he is being irrational. He tries to make his thoughts more realistic, to plan actions he can actually carry out.

Then he gets a new idea. Maybe the events that caused Peterson's degree to be revoked were public enough to make the university newspaper. After all, if the bureaucracy went to so much trouble, they must have been motivated by an event of some magnitude, one that would be difficult to keep secret. The *Minnesota Daily* might well have covered it.

Drying his eyes with the sides of his hands, Anderson walks across the Mall toward Vincent Hall, then detours around it to reach Murphy. The side door he tries doesn't open from the outside, so he strides around to the front of the building on the next street. Climbing up one of the outside stairways, he enters beneath huge stone letters spelling JOURNALISM.

The newspaper offices are down more stairs, half a story below street level. Stepping into the reception area, Anderson hears a hum of activity, but sees no people. A paper strewn desk and battered couch stand deserted. On the wall straight ahead, he sees the painted logo of the *Minnesota Daily,* with open-ended, wood mailboxes covering most of the space below it.

A wave of laughter comes from around the corner to the right, and the sound of arguing voices from around the corner to the left. But no one actually appears. Anderson looks for a bell to ring, but finds none. He takes a deep breath, squares his shoulders, and walks on in.

A warren of chin-high partitions fills the large office area to the left. They are upholstered to absorb sound and have plastic counters along each side for computer terminals and telephones. Where the counters end, there are bright yellow filing cabinets, badly dented from heavy use. Grimy notebooks and empty Styrofoam cups are scattered everywhere. But there is still no one in sight.

Only in the farthest section of the room does Anderson finally encounter some of the staff. Three women and four men sit on the counters, talking loudly. The argument in progress seems to be about whether a photo of an attractive female cheerleader should have been used to illustrate an article about the fall athletic season. A male photographer is arguing that the picture celebrates female athleticism, since the cheerleader is vaulting through the air. A female reporter is arguing that the photo 'marginalizes' female athleticism, since the cheerleader will be assumed to be leading cheers for a male team. The other staff members groan and laugh at both sides.

One of the ones laughing loudest notices Anderson and ambles over to him. "Steve Iverson," he says, extending his hand. "What can I do for you?" He looks more like a football player than like Anderson's idea of a journalist.

Anderson reaches out and shakes his hand. "Anderson," he says. "Pleased to meet you." For a moment, he is uncertain how to continue. "I'm doing some historical research," he explains finally. "I thought the *Daily* might have some files that would help."

"Historical research?" Iverson repeats.

"It's relatively recent history," Anderson hastens to add. "I was wondering, for example, if you have a subject index that would allow me to see how you've covered certain news stories."

"Are you writing a critique of our work?"

"No, nothing like that. It's the news events themselves I'm interested in."

"What's this for, a research paper?"

"I don't know yet. I guess you could say I'm still scouting for leads."

"Do you think what you're investigating might produce a story for us? We're always interested in unusual angles, you know."

"I'm afraid the things I'm looking into are more old news than new news."

"Well, tip me off, if you come up with anything interesting you could let us have. My name is Iverson. I-V-E-R-S-O-N."

"I'll remember."

"Our 'library' is over here." He leads Anderson back toward the reception area, but takes a jog to the left, so that they end up behind the wall covered with mailboxes. "You're welcome to use it as long as you don't remove anything."

"I wouldn't think of it."

"The bad news is that the guy who's supposed to run this department is off drinking beer with his fraternity. The good news is that you can use his desk."

"Thanks. I shouldn't need much space."

"We don't have a 'morgue' as such. In other words, we don't clip stories and file them by subject. We just have one big index on file cards. That's in these drawers here." He pulls one open. It resembles a library card catalog. "If you want to look at the actual story, you'll have to use the big, bound volumes of back issues. Those are in the cabinets over there. You see how it works?"

"Yes, it all seems clear enough."

"If you want to photocopy something, talk to Marci. She's the Jewish princess in the shamelessly tight, purple dress, with the ridiculous, neo-Afro hairdo." There is a squeal of indignation from somewhere behind Anderson. A Styrofoam cup bounces off Iverson's head. "She's also my girlfriend."

Anderson turns around in time to see a short, dark haired girl sticking out her tongue at Iverson. She puts her chin in the air, turns, and flounces away. Anderson smiles. "You're a lucky man."

"Yeah, she thinks so too." He gazes fondly down the corridor where the girl has disappeared, then turns back to Anderson. "If you have any questions, just ask. We won't know the answers, but we'll commiserate with you."

Iverson nods at him, then walks back toward his friends, leaving Anderson alone.

Anderson looks over the index cases and spots a drawer near the floor labeled "O-Po." He crouches down and pulls it open. Each three by five card has a name or subject typed in the upper left hand corner. The headlines for the relevant stories are listed below, with the dates and page numbers for each story noted underneath. Here and there, among the cards, are file tabs identifying the 'big subjects.' The ones in this drawer are "PARKS," "PERPICH, RUDY," and "PHOTOGRAPHY."

It takes Anderson only a few seconds to find the card for Peterson. Beneath Peterson's name are the headlines for three stories: "Disciplinary Committee Considers 'Exams for Friends' Case," "Degrees Revoked by Disciplinary Committee," and "Central Figure in 'Exams for Friends' Case Speaks Out."

Anderson memorizes the date and page number of the first story. Then, using a scrap of paper from the nearby desk to mark his place in the drawer, he turns to the area where the back issues are stored. It is actually a small adjoining room. The doors to the dark gray, metal cabinets stand open. Inside are large volumes bound in simulated leather, with gold lettering giving the academic quarter, volume number, and year. Larger letters, near the top of each spine, read *Minnesota Daily*. To make the filing easier, each volume also has a white paper sticker with a felt pen number.

Anderson pries out the volume he is seeking and pages through it until he finds the story. It is on an inside page of a weekday issue and not very long. Anderson scans it eagerly, but doesn't know what to make of it. At first, he thinks he must have the wrong entry, because he sees no mention of Peterson. But the title—"Disciplinary Committee Considers 'Exams for Friends' Case"—is definitely the one listed on Peterson's file card.

Returning to the beginning of the story, Anderson reads it through more carefully. Apparently, some students had cheated on their exams by having another student take the tests for them. During the week when the news story was published, the disciplinary committee was calling the students in to testify, one by one, before acting on the case. Because no disciplinary action had been taken at that point, the story did not reveal the names of the students who were accused. It did comment, however, that no money seemed to have been involved. The student who actually wrote the exams had apparently just been doing it as a favor for his friends. Amazingly enough, the exams were in a number of apparently unrelated subjects: biochemistry, musicology, astronomy, linguistics, and classical archaeology.

This sounds to Anderson like the range of subjects he had found among Peterson's books. Anderson's breathing and heartbeat quicken. Was Peterson the unnamed student who had taken the other students' exams? That would explain why the article was listed under Peterson's name in the card file.

Anderson sets the volume on the corner of the desk and returns to the open file drawer. He checks the reference for the second story: "Degrees Revoked by Disciplinary Committee." It came out nearly four months later. This puts it in the volume next in sequence. Anderson is, by now, very excited. He picks up the volume he has just been consulting, carries it over to the metal cabinet, and trades it for the one that follows.

The second story identifies Peterson by name in the first paragraph. It describes him as a Minneapolis resident and as the only son of "a prominent surgeon, now deceased." According to this story, Peterson was indeed the one who had taken the exams for his friends. There were five college students he had helped in this way. All six of the students, including Peterson, had been given degrees by the university in the intervening period. Because five of these degrees were awarded, in part, for courses in which the students had cheated, these degrees were declared invalid. Because Peterson "had shown wanton disregard for the academic code of ethics and for the procedures of academic accreditation," his degree was revoked as well. The degrees the five college students had lost were B.A.'s and B.S.'s. The degree Peterson had lost was a Ph.D.

Turning breathlessly back to the file drawer, Anderson finds the date and page number for the remaining story. It was published only a few days after the second story, and Anderson only has to turn a few pages to find it. This time, Peterson's picture is printed beside an "exclusive interview." Anderson studies it for a few seconds before reading the article. Even in those earlier days, Peterson was wearing a beard. This made him look somewhat different from Anderson, who didn't grow one until after the publicity surrounding his grandfather's death. But the resemblance between the two of them was still striking.

In the interview, Peterson attacks the university testing procedures as "a ludicrous sham." He asserts that "most of the exams employ multiple choice questions in which *all* of the proposed answers are fallacious or inadequate." Students should not be required to take such exams, Peterson says, because "success in choosing the currently fashionable fallacies does not demonstrate that the student grasps the subject, but often the reverse." Furthermore, Peterson claims, "most of the essay questions are marked by graduate teaching assistants who are not qualified to assess any genuinely informed answers." In order to get high scores on the tests, Peterson claimed, he himself had to put aside his real understanding of the subjects and "write down the silly, predictable nonsense" the people marking the exams were looking for. The fact that some of his friends were less able to do this, he said, did not mean they were ignorant of the relevant subjects. "It only means they were unable to treat the university examination system with the contempt it deserves."

To Anderson, the arrogance displayed in the interview is breathtaking. Yet he also feels a twinge of sympathy for this man Peterson. Here was someone whose obviously brilliant academic career was ended by a scandal, just as Anderson's own, more modest academic career was ended by a scandal. The whole series of events recounted in the newspapers seems incredibly stupid. Peterson was undoubtedly guilty of violating the rules. But his guilt had nothing to do with the quality of his work. Cutting a man like that off from the institutions of research and higher education seems a terrible waste. Peterson was clearly some kind of genius.

As this thought occurs to him, Anderson finds himself caught by the word 'genius.' He repeats it aloud to himself. 'Genius.' Anderson knows he has encountered this word only days or hours before. But for a moment, he can't think where. Then the rest of the phrase comes back to him: *"My Darling Genius."* It was the salutation on Shannon's note. He puts his hand into his trouser pocket. The note is still there. He pulls it out and smoothes the folds. It is exactly as he remembers it.

Suddenly the personal implications of the old news stories come home to him. The black and white photo stares out at him like his own reflection in a mirror. As each successive thought strikes him, the face seems to pulse in intensity. This 'genius' in the picture was the man who had tried to drown him. This 'genius' was the man he, in fact, has drowned. This 'genius' was the man Shannon had been trying to seduce, when she had presented him with her body. This 'genius' was the man whose clothes he is wearing as he thinks these very thoughts.

Anderson's strangely intimate relationship with the dead man makes him feel dizzy. He can't decide if he has been horribly violated or if he has been the violator. Peterson may have had the worst of intentions, yet Peterson only succeeded in getting himself killed. Anderson may have had relatively innocent intentions, yet he has killed someone of extraordinary talents.

Without entirely realizing what he is doing, Anderson closes the volume of back issues and returns it to its place in the cabinet. Then he puts the scrap of paper he was using to mark his place back where he had found it. As he closes the drawer of file cards, he notices that the girl named Marci is watching him. "Thank you," he says. "You people run a great newspaper."

"You're welcome," she says, beaming at him, as though he has paid her a personal compliment.

Moving like an automaton, Anderson finds his way out of the newspaper offices. A sign points him down a corridor to the right, where an emergency exit takes him directly outdoors. Outside, in the fresh air, he climbs a concrete stairway to ground level. This brings him to the side of the physics building, with the Mall off to his left.

As he strolls back toward the Mall, Anderson tries to imagine what Peterson's reactions were when the scandal broke. The first newspaper story had implied it was Peterson's 'friends' who had identified him to the disciplinary committee. How would this have made Peterson regard those he had tried to help? And how would he have felt about an academic system that took his doctorate away for something he had regarded as an act of friendship? The more he thinks about it, the more Anderson appreciates how bitter Peterson must have been.

Reaching the Mall itself, Anderson glances both ways before starting across it. What he sees to his left makes him freeze in mid-step.

Gretchen is roughly thirty yards away. The sight of her jolts Anderson back into the present. She is looking over her shoulder, laughing and shouting, apparently calling out a greeting to someone. As she does this, she is walking away from the place where Anderson is standing. Between her and Anderson, all along the sidewalk, are crowds of students changing classes. Gretchen doesn't seem to have seen him.

Anderson turns to follow her, trying to close the gap between them as quickly as possible, while remaining inconspicuous. From the way Gretchen is behaving, it appears she really is a student. Evidently, a few parts of her story were indeed the truth. But what about the rest of it, the other things she said and did? Once more, Anderson finds himself wondering how she could look and act so sweet, while setting him up to be kidnapped. He feels a wave of anger at the thought. But even as he tenses with rage, he gets a better view of her and is struck again by how appealing she looks.

Still some yards ahead of him, she turns and heads for the entrance of Ford Hall. As she walks with long strides toward the pillared building, Anderson sees her clearly from the side. This time, she is wearing a modest skirt, but it still shows off her shapely legs. The afternoon sun brings out the gold in her hair. A tight sweater molds her blouse to her body, and her breasts bounce fetchingly with each step. Watching her moving along the sidewalk, Anderson feels a catch in his throat.

Then she disappears through the doors of Ford Hall.

Anderson hurries after her. But for a few seconds, he is prevented from following by a crowd of students emerging from the building. He pushes impatiently through the mob. Then, inside, he finds he has lost sight of her.

Immediately ahead are stairways going both up and down. Anderson has no way of knowing which way Gretchen has gone. More students seem to be heading up, so Anderson runs that way, taking the steps three at a time. The floor above is a bustle of activity, but there is still no sign of Gretchen. Anderson walks up one side of the wide central corridor, then down the other, peering into the lecture halls. The chairs with their tablet arms are filling up quickly. But he sees no one he recognizes.

At the end of the hall, a man in a brown suit stands staring in Anderson's direction. Anderson isn't surprised to have attracted the man's attention. After all, Anderson is older than most of the students, and his frantic search must look odd. But he can't worry about it now, if he is going to find Gretchen.

Deciding she must have gone the other way, Anderson runs down the steps to the floor below. Here again, he finds a central corridor, surrounded by lecture halls. The students by this time are settling down, and the corridor is less crowded. Anderson makes a quick circuit of the lecture halls, as he did on the floor above. But some of the professors have already begun lecturing, so it is harder to check inside.

When he fails to spot Gretchen on this floor as well, Anderson concludes she must have gone farther up the stairway. The building, he recalls, has four or five stories. He returns to the front stairs and begins running up them, taking as many as he can in each stride. As he glances back, he notices the man in the brown suit starting up the stairway at the other end of the building. This seems strange, but Anderson puts the thought aside. His whole focus is on finding Gretchen.

Bursting through the doors one flight above where he had searched before, Anderson finds himself looking into huge, nightmare faces. Their nostrils are enormous, their eyes protuberant. He gasps, then sees they are only masks, mounted in a glass display case. A sign beside them says "Papua New Guinea." He is in the anthropology department.

He pauses for a moment to get his bearings. The plan of this floor is very different from that of the other two. Instead of one central hallway, there are two narrow corridors, one on each side of the building. These corridors are connected by shorter hallways, crossing the building at each end. Anderson is standing in one of them now.

At the intersections, in each corner, are large lecture halls. Anderson hurries over to one, then across to the other. But Gretchen doesn't seem to be in either. The rest of the floor seems to consist of faculty offices with closed blue doors. There is no way to tell if Gretchen is inside one.

As Anderson stands there, debating what to do next, he suddenly sees the man in the brown suit watching him from the far end of the building. Slowly, without taking his eyes off Anderson, the man starts toward him, down the long corridor.

Anderson's first thought is that this is a professor or perhaps even a university security person, checking to see that he belongs there. Anderson smiles and takes a step forward, trying to think of something innocuous that will explain what he is doing in Ford Hall.

But the man in brown does not return Anderson's smile. Instead, he continues to advance on Anderson, staring blankly. It is as though Anderson has done nothing to acknowledge his presence.

Hesitantly, Anderson begins to back up.

The man's slow pace begins to quicken.

Anderson backs around the corner. With measured, but deliberately loud steps, he walks past the anthropological display to the other corridor, parallel to the first one. Then, running on tiptoe, making as little noise as possible, Anderson dashes down this corridor along the other side of the building.

When Anderson reaches the end, he slows down and looks back. The man is still coming after him, faster now, but not bothering to run. His eyes seem to take in Anderson, but give almost as much attention to the rest of the physical setting. It's as though Anderson were an animal, being slowly stalked.

Anderson turns down the cross corridor, pushes through the doors midway along it, and heads down the stairway at the back of Ford Hall. This is the stairway the man in the brown suit had come up a couple of minutes earlier. Anderson's first impulse is to run down the steps as fast as he can. But the slow pace of the man following him makes Anderson hesitate. A man stalking game moves that slowly only when his prey has not yet seen him or when he is trying to drive his prey into a trap.

What is going on here? Was the girl named Gretchen once again serving as bait? Had she been aware of Anderson after all? Was it her job to lure Anderson into this building?

Suspecting an ambush, Anderson pauses at each landing and

peers around the corner, before descending. He has a powerful impression he is being threatened, but has no clear idea what form the threat will take next.

Who is this man in the brown suit? Could he have been the person in the motorcycle helmet? The person who almost killed him? The person whose attack resulted in his friends' death?

Anderson hears sounds on the stairway above him. He is now one flight up from the building's rear entrance. He looks down at the area inside the doors that lead outside. There is no one there. Except for Anderson's own breathing and the footsteps above him, the building seems silent. It occurs to Anderson he may have been reacting to nothing, putting a sinister interpretation on innocent events. But it still seems a good idea to avoid the man in brown.

Anderson hurries down the stairway toward the doors. He is eager now to get out of the building, to reach the larger spaces open to the sky. He raises his hands to push through the doors.

Then he sees a second man waiting outside. There is nothing special about this one's appearance. He is wearing a blue blazer and light tan trousers. He could almost be another professor. But something in his blank expression and the way he is standing reminds Anderson of the man in the brown suit.

Anderson stops short. He backs away from the door. But it is too late. The man outside has already seen him and is starting toward him.

There is no longer any doubt in Anderson's mind that these men are after him. What's more, they are making no effort to conceal what they are up to. They are systematically surrounding him, closing in.

Anderson dashes back into the building, taking the steps to the next floor down. This is one of the floors filled with lecture halls, which Anderson had been exploring earlier. Under the staircase that had led from the entryway to the floor above is a heavy steel door. Anderson pulls it open and darts through. Inside the door are more steps. As the door swings shut behind him, Anderson hears two sets of footsteps coming down the stairs above.

Anderson is running now, dropping down the steps with the aid of a handrail, three, four at a time. He hits the bottom and dashes forward. He is in the basement of the building. It seems to hold archaeology labs and storerooms. The first door he tries is locked, but the next opens readily. Anderson looks inside. He sees a workbench for photographing artifacts. Around it, lining the walls, are shelves holding archaeological specimens. There is no place to hide and no way out but the door where he is standing.

Pushing on frantically, Anderson reaches the front of the building. Just ahead are stairs leading up to the entrance. But Anderson is reluctant to take them. If his pursuers had the back entrance covered, they will probably have the front covered too.

To Anderson's left is another storeroom, its door slightly ajar. Anderson hears footsteps on the stairs behind him. Seeing no alternative, he pulls at the door and steps through. As he eases it shut behind him, he sees he is not alone. A few steps into the room is a woman, facing away from him. She is pulling her sweater off over her head. As it comes free, she drops it on her book bag, shakes her hair loose, and begins retucking her blouse. Then, suddenly, she freezes, realizing she is not alone. She turns. It is Gretchen.

Anderson stares, fascinated, but accusing. Up close, she looks even better than he remembered. "Did you lead me here on purpose?" he asks, still out of breath.

Her face is tense, but relaxes as she sees who it is. "You've shaved off your beard."

"I guess I have," he manages.

"You're the swimmer," she says, apparently pleased to remember. "I like your face better this way."

Anderson raises his hand impatiently. "Where can I hide?"

His question seems to throw her. "What are you talking about?" she asks.

Does she really have no idea? "Some men out there are after me."

She frowns, then seems to accept it and starts from there. "There's a steam tunnel connecting the buildings. You could take it over to Chemistry—"

"Where's the entrance?" he asks, cutting her off.

"In the maintenance room." She points toward the door behind him.

Anderson turns and peers through the crack at the door's edge. Directly across the hallway, he sees the maintenance room door. It is closed, but not tightly enough to have latched. He feels suddenly hopeful. Then, off to his right, he sees the man in brown, moving methodically down the hallway, searching each room as he reaches it.

"Why are they after you?" Gretchen asks.

"You tell me," he replies, wishing she would.

He waits until the man has gone into the archaeology lab, then steps quickly across the hallway. There's no time for a backward glance. He slips through the maintenance room door, taking care to make as little noise as possible.

The room is full of equipment for the electricity and heating: panels of circuit breakers, transformers, holding tanks, and steam pipes. But in the wall directly across from him, he sees the exit Gretchen had said was there. It is a tunnel-like corridor leading to the next building.

He hurries across the room and heads down the tunnel. It has steam pipes along the right hand side, lining the wall from floor to ceiling. A loud roar of fans and steam drowns out all other sound. The air is stiflingly hot. Bare filament bulbs hang from the ceiling at regular intervals, but in between, the corridor is almost dark.

A short way down the tunnel, on the left hand side, is another tunnel leading off at a right angle. It is marked with a sign reading "Chemistry Bldg." with an arrow below the lettering, pointing left. This is the route Gretchen had suggested.

Anderson hesitates, wondering if it's a trap. The side tunnel seems to extend indefinitely without branchings, whereas the main tunnel ahead seems to offer a number of intersections. Even if Gretchen can be trusted, Anderson figures he will have more chances of losing his pursuers on a route with more turnings. Each intersection he passes should make it harder to tell which way he went.

He runs forward in a crouch, trying to avoid hitting his head on the obstructions above. He hunches his shoulders and tucks his elbows in front of his chest, so as not to brush the hot pipes beside him. Up ahead, he sees that the tunnel opens into a larger space. He rushes toward it.

Ducking beneath the last of the low hanging pipes, Anderson finds himself in a large, high-ceilinged room. There is a big steam tank, more electrical equipment, and a caged area with a stairway beside it leading upward. To the right is another tunnel, leading off. This one is marked with a yellow sign pointing to "Murphy Hall," where Anderson had visited the newspaper offices. It seems like a route backward. He takes the stairway instead. At least this will take him out of there.

He dashes up the steps, sweating heavily from the heat. At the top is a steel door. Grasping the knob with damp fingers, he finds it won't turn. He has a moment of panic. He feels trapped. Desperately, he takes hold with both hands, bracing himself to twist with all his might. But this time, the knob turns easily. He realizes he had made it stick the first time by leaning on the door before turning the knob. 'Take it easy!' he tells himself.

He pushes the door gently. It opens onto a milk machine in a corridor lined with green lockers. Anderson realizes he is in Vincent Hall, the one next to Ford, the one behind Murphy. He steps out into the corridor.

Someone grabs him from behind. Arms slip under his. Hands lock behind his head. Anderson tries to turn, but finds himself pinned in space, his head forced forward.

"Now, just you relax," a voice says. "Put your legs apart and stand nice and calm. When I release you, I want you to lean forward and put your hands against the wall. Otherwise, you're going to be hurt. I have a gun, but I don't want to use it."

As the man speaks, Anderson feels himself being shoved forward. He tries to step out, to keep from falling, but the man's leg catches his foot. As he falls, Anderson realizes his arms are now free. He reaches out to catch himself before his head strikes the locker in front of him. His hands make a booming noise as they hit the metal lockers. Almost at once, he feels his foot kicked sideways. A hand pats him under the arm and along his body and leg, first one side, then the other.

"Okay, that'll do it." The man's voice is now farther away.

Anderson turns his head. The man is smiling at him sympathetically. It is a uniformed policeman. The same one Anderson had noticed watching him, when he had first arrived on campus. The officer takes a two way radio from his belt. One hand rests on his gun. He squeezes a button on the radio and talks into it. "Eckert here. I've got Peterson over in Vincent Hall." While he speaks, he keeps his eyes fixed on Anderson. There's an unintelligible roar from the radio when the officer is finished. Then he spins a knob with his thumb, and the sound dwindles to a low crackle.

"You're not under arrest," the policeman tells Anderson. "Detective Berglund just wants to talk to you. It's apparently pretty urgent."

Anderson feels dazed. He holds up his palms in a questioning gesture, but does not otherwise move or say anything.

The policeman relaxes slightly. "Sorry about patting you down that way. Its just that they make us take certain precautions. I realize in your case it's not very appropriate. But you know what regulations are like."

The door Anderson came through swings open. The man in the brown suit steps out. He looks impatiently at Anderson. "What were you playing at?" he asks.

"I didn't know you were a police officer," Anderson says.

"Yeah, well, you're coming with us voluntarily, okay?"

"Okay."

The man in brown takes Anderson by the arm and escorts him down the hallway, with the uniformed policeman walking behind. It is only a short distance to a door leading outside. Beyond it, a short flight of stairs takes them up to ground level. Looking around, Anderson sees they are waiting beside a large loading dock. After a few seconds, a plain blue car rolls up the driveway between Vincent Hall and Ford. The man in brown steps forward and opens a rear door, keeping a hand on Anderson's arm. "Get in."

Anderson climbs into the back seat. The car door slams shut behind him. Inside, Anderson sees that a metal grid separates him from the front seat. The interior of the car smells of Lysol disinfectant. At the wheel is the man in the blue blazer, whom Anderson had seen guarding the back entry of Ford Hall. The man in the brown suit climbs into the front seat from the other side.

Anderson notices that there are no door handles or window cranks in his part of the car, just metal plates covering the places where the handles would normally be located. He has not actually been locked in, but there is no way to get out. He struggles to control a wave of panic. He feels claustrophobic as well as intensely apprehensive about having to deal again with the police.

The car accelerates off, heading for downtown.

CHAPTER 10

The unmarked police car pulls up at the Minneapolis Courthouse. The building looks like a gray stone fortress. As the braking car tilts him forward, Anderson sees they are at the Fourth Street entrance. It is in the middle of the block, directly beneath the building's imposing clock tower. Across the street, the flashy signs over the storefronts advertise bail bondsmen and twenty-four-hour lawyers. Above these signs rises a parking ramp shielded by all-weather panels in swimming-pool blue.

The policeman in the brown suit gets out and opens the rear door. Sliding sideways, across the seat, Anderson emerges. He feels extremely self-conscious, standing there on the sidewalk. The car door slams. This time, the officers do not take him by the arm, but merely walk on each side. When they need to go through a narrower space, one officer moves in front, the other behind.

They march Anderson through the doors of the building, past the information desk, and into the central atrium. It is square in shape, several stories high, and finished in gray marble. The far wall is covered with stained glass windows, most of them lit from behind, but some dark. Below the windows is a monumental staircase. Arched balconies look down on the space from the other three sides. To the right and left below are six elevators.

"We have to go up a floor," the officer in the blue blazer tells Anderson. They stop in front of the elevators on the right, rather than heading for the stairs. The man in brown greets a friend, and the two exchange remarks about fishing.

Anderson looks around the atrium. It has painful associations. Although his grandfather had drowned in one of the northern counties, Anderson had been here in Minneapolis the last two times the police had called him in for questioning. The day-long sessions had taken place in one of the upstairs interrogation rooms, perhaps the very one where they are headed now. It was in this building that Anderson had failed the lie detector test. Then, after his arrest, it was in this courthouse jail that they had locked him up, until Freilinger had arranged his release.

The feature of the atrium that has haunted Anderson ever since is a huge statue of a river god. It stands in the middle of the floor, facing the entrance. Anderson remembers it is called the 'Father of Waters.' The powerful, bearded figure sits on an alligator and a turtle, on top of a low pedestal. One leg is drawn up, and his arm rests on his knee. In the river god's hand, he holds a stalk of corn. A fishnet is draped across his genitals. The god's eyes stare slightly downward and into the distance, seeing everyone that passes to his right, but not quite focusing on them.

The officer in the blue blazer nudges Anderson. A light has gone on over the middle elevator. Anderson and his escorts take it up a floor. They step out onto the lowest of the atrium's balconies and move clockwise around the marble balustrade. Below them, to their right, the river god sits watching.

On the far side, they take a corridor leading away from the atrium. Recalling the route, Anderson tenses. Their destination is through a set of glass doors directly ahead. The lettering on them reads "Room 108: Criminal Investigations Division," then in smaller print below, "Assault Unit, Forgery Fraud Unit, Homicide Unit, Robbery Unit." It is 'Homicide' they are heading for.

This is the very place where Anderson had been brought for questioning several years earlier. Will the same detectives still be working there? Will they recognize him as Anderson? The detectives must have questioned tens of thousands of people since Anderson was last being investigated. But if several of them are investigating his 'murder' right now, this must have refreshed their memories.

Stepping through the doors, Anderson bows his head. Without being too conspicuous about it, he tries to keep his face turned away from anyone who might remember him. The last thing he wants to do right now is to try explaining how he came to kill Peterson in self-defense. He feels sweat running down his back and hopes the police do not notice.

The rooms housing the Criminal Investigations Department look deceptively innocuous. Inside the double doors is a small reception area with a salmon pink couch flanked by black and brown chairs. A large office space lies ahead and to the left. Behind the counter, a woman is extracting crumpled sheets from an electronic printer that seems to be jammed.

"Hey, Sally," the officer in the brown suit calls out. "When are you going to get yourself a typewriter?"

She groans at him, without looking up, then waves her crumpled papers at the wall behind him, as though urging him to get lost.

The policemen lead Anderson down a corridor to the right. But before they have gone very far along it, the officer in the blue blazer opens a door on the left and ushers Anderson through it.

"Lieutenant Berglund will be with you in a minute," he says. Then he closes the door, leaving Anderson unexpectedly alone.

As far as Anderson can recall, this interrogation room is not the one he was taken to before. But it is very similar. The ceiling is high, and the floor space limited. There is a small metal table topped with green plastic. Around it are arranged three metal chairs, their arms and seats upholstered in another green plastic, darker or perhaps dirtier. The walls are a pale peach and the floor carpeted in gray. Anderson wonders what would happen if he got up and tried to walk out.

After a few moments, the door opens and Detective Holmquist enters. "Good to see you," he says, extending a hand.

Anderson reaches over and shakes it. Holmquist gestures toward one of the chairs, and Anderson sits down.

"I hope those fellows who brought you down here treated you right," Holmquist says. "They're so used to dealing with scum-bags, they probably don't know how to treat a man of culture."

Anderson can't decide how much irony there is in Holmquist's remark. "They were fine," Anderson says. "I just didn't realize they were police officers at first, so I tried to avoid them."

Holmquist laughs. "I don't blame you. I'd do the same thing." He takes a seat near Anderson at the end of the table, rather than across from him. Despite Holmquist's friendly manner, Anderson feels the man is infringing slightly upon his personal space.

Berglund enters a moment later, carrying a large folder stuffed with documents. He pulls the door shut behind him, nods hello to Anderson, and puts out his hand. Anderson rises partway to shake it, then sits down again. With both Holmquist and Berglund now in the room, the space seems smaller than ever.

Berglund sits down at the table across from Anderson. He sets the folder on the edge of the table, but at an angle, so he can consult it without revealing its contents to Anderson. He is very businesslike.

"You are not under arrest. But you are being questioned as part of a criminal investigation. Hence, anything you say might be taken down and later used against you in a court of law. If you think you might be in danger of incriminating yourself, you should remember that you have the right to remain silent and the right to have an attorney present. Are those rights clear to you?"

"Yes, they are."

Berglund takes out his notebook and sets it on the table in front of him. Then he opens the folder and takes out five photographs. All five show the same objects, but at different angles and distances.

"Do you recognize the items in these pictures?" Berglund asks.

"That's a fishing rod, and that's a box of fishing tackle."

"Do you recognize that particular rod and tackle?"

"No, I don't think so."

"The sheriff up there has evidence you rented them from the Running Deer Hunter Lake Lodge. Do you recognize them now?"

"They look familiar, but I couldn't identify them for certain."

"When did you last see them?"

"I suppose I saw them the last time I went fishing."

"When was that?"

"I don't remember. I guess it was the day before I left the resort."

"You had those items in your possession then?"

"I guess so."

"Where did you last put those items?"

"I think I left them in my cabin."

"That rod and tackle were found on the shore of the lake, near where this fellow Anderson was drowned. Can you tell us how they might have gotten there?"

"No, I'm afraid I can't."

"Something else that's still puzzling the county sheriff is your bus trip back here." As he speaks, Berglund extracts a legal sized sheet from the folder. It is photocopied from a map. He sets it beside them, where they can both see it. "The resort you stayed at is over here." He points to a mark by a lake. "And you caught the bus down here." He consults his notes, then points to another mark. "Now, why didn't you catch the bus at the closer stop, up here?" He points to a third mark.

"I don't know. I just got the bus where the fellow who gave me a ride dropped me off."

"Ah, the fellow who gave you a ride. What did you say he looked like again?"

"I don't remember."

There is a long pause while the detectives wait to see if Anderson will say something more. Then Berglund looks again in his notebook.

"This county sheriff is also worried about your diet." Berglund smiles at this statement, as though he has made a clever joke. Then he turns serious again. "You told us you were too nauseated to have breakfast. But the sheriff says"—Berglund consults his notes—"that you later bought two meat loaf sandwiches, two Nut Goodies, two cans of Fanta, and a large bag of potato chips. Were you able to eat all that without getting sick?"

"I was feeling better then. That was later in the day."

"When, exactly, did you start to feel better?"

"Sometime during the bus trip, I guess."

"I want you to look carefully at these pictures." Berglund puts three photographs on the table.

Anderson has all he can do not to gasp. Two of the pictures show Jack and June individually. Their graduation photos. The third is a wedding portrait. This is not a development Anderson was expecting. He is too startled even to feel saddened by the touching images. How could the police have connected 'Peterson' with Jack and June? How could the police, in so short a time, have connected even 'Anderson' with Jack and June?

"Do you know either of those people?" Berglund asks.

"No, I don't."

"Do you think you might have seen them around somewhere?"

"No, I don't think so."

"Where were you yesterday evening?" Holmquist interjects.

"At home."

"What were you doing there?" he continues.

Anderson becomes conscious again of the burn on his forearm. He hopes the bandage is not noticeable beneath his shirt. "Nothing special," he says finally, in answer to Holmquist's question. "I had a quiet supper, then read for a while." He puts his forearms under the table, where they will be less visible.

"Did you have any visitors or speak to anyone?"

"No."

Again, there is a pause. Holmquist and Berglund exchange looks. Anderson senses the next question will be an important one.

"Do you ever," Berglund asks, "carry large sums of cash in your pockets?"

Anderson makes a special effort to appear calm. "No. Why would I do that?" He holds his body as steady as possible, while his thoughts go racing ahead. He remembers the jacket he had borrowed from Peterson's wardrobe. He remembers the large packet of bills he had stuffed in its pocket. He remembers that the jacket had been hanging on a chair in Jack and June's house when the fire had started.

It seems obvious from Berglund's question that the burned remnants of the jacket and money must have been found in the ruins of Jack and June's house. That would explain why the police were looking for a connection between Jack and June's death and Anderson's death. Both investigations would have turned up similar bundles of cash.

Once they were looking for a connection, Anderson reasons, the police would be able to discover that Anderson had been one of Jack and June's friends. But, as far as the police were concerned, the only connection to Peterson would be Peterson's presence near the lake where 'Anderson' was drowned. Unless, of course, they were able to trace Peterson's jacket—

Anderson becomes aware that Berglund is speaking. "I'm sorry," Anderson says, "what did you just say?"

"I said, have you ever known anyone you thought might be involved in the drug business?"

Anderson relaxes slightly. This is the same conclusion Freilinger had drawn. If the police pursue it, they are unlikely to come up with anything immediately threatening. "Not really," he replies. Then he feels he should explain his hesitation. "Some of the people I know might use them occasionally. But they're not what you'd call 'involved in the drug business.' "

"Have you actually seen these people you mention using drugs?"

"No, I haven't." Anderson pauses, then feels he should add something more. "I'm well aware that it's against the law."

"Don't worry," Berglund assures him. "We're not interested in drugs. That's another department."

"Unless the drugs provide a motive for murder," Holmquist adds.

"We have one more picture for you to look at," Berglund says. "I'm afraid it's a little unpleasant, but I want you to take a careful look at it anyway." He takes a modest sized glossy from the folder and places it on the table in front of Anderson.

For a few moments, Anderson stops breathing. The picture shows Anderson's head and shoulders. But the way he would look if he were drowned. His face is bloated and white. His flesh sagging. His eyes staring, but glazed, as though they were lightly frosted over. Black, ugly bruises mark his neck and shoulders. His skin looks as though it were on the verge of peeling off. He is barely recognizable. But recognizable enough.

Anderson wonders what the policemen are up to. Surely they can see how much this picture looks like him. He shivers at the sight, but can't bring himself to turn away. This must be the man he killed. This must be the way he looked when he was pulled from the water. This must be Peterson.

"Did you know that man?" Berglund prompts.

"No, I didn't know him."

"Are you sure?" Berglund leans sideways, so that he can see

the picture better himself. "He looks almost as though he could be a relative of yours, doesn't he?"

Anderson feels his head go cold and his vision fade. "I don't think he was a relative." He sways slightly in his chair.

"Are you okay?" Holmquist asks.

"Some people find it hard to look at the dead ones," Berglund comments. "When they're not used to it, I mean."

Anderson grasps the table to steady himself. "I guess I haven't had much to eat today. I got so caught up in research at the U."

"Would you like a can of juice?" Holmquist stands up. "I'll get you a can of juice." He goes out of the interrogation room, leaving the door slightly ajar.

"Holmquist thinks fruit juice is the cure for everything," Berglund explains. He gathers up the various photographs and sets them in a neat stack on top of his folder. "I'm sorry I made the crack about that corpse looking like a relative. It's easy for us to forget how gross this stuff can be for people who don't deal with it every day."

Anderson can't think of anything to say. He sits there for a moment staring at the table. The photo he sees on the top of Berglund's pile shows the rod and tackle. What was it doing at the scene of the drowning? Peterson had certainly not been fishing. But he obviously wanted people to *think* he'd been fishing. That means Peterson's plan was to make his death look like an accident.

But Peterson's plan went wrong because a *real* accident took place: Anderson came to. So instead of a quiet drowning, there was a vigorous fight. That meant that the body showed signs of violence. Hence, the death wasn't taken for an accident. And, of course, the 'wrong' man died.

The irony is that the central part of Peterson's plan still worked: Peterson was left with Anderson's identity, and Anderson was left with Peterson's.

But neither man was prepared for the other's identity.

"Do you think you might have had some business dealings with this Anderson?" Berglund asks. "You know, encountered him in some context that you might not immediately recall?"

"No," Anderson says, shaking his head, "I think I'd remember." For a moment, he has an hysterical impulse to laugh. The police seem to sense there is some kind of relationship between Anderson and Peterson, but they can't figure out what it is. Struggling to get a grip on himself, Anderson wonders if it is only a matter of time before they find out. And if they do find out, what will happen to Anderson then?

Holmquist returns carrying two cans. "Cranberry-apple or tropical blend?"

"A tropical blend would be nice," Anderson says.

Holmquist opens it and hands it to Anderson. Then he opens the cranberry-apple can for himself.

"Thank you," Anderson says, taking several swallows.

Berglund stands up. "I'll go see if I can find you a ride," he says, leaving the room.

Anderson concludes they are finished with him for the time being. He gets to his feet and begins walking back toward the department's reception area. Evidently, this is the appropriate thing to do, because Holmquist walks cheerfully at his side. They finish their drinks near the front counter, and Holmquist retrieves Anderson's empty.

"This is Patrolman Gorman," Berglund says, reappearing.

Anderson turns to see a uniformed policeman looking him over. "Hello," Anderson says, extending his hand.

The patrolman seems surprised by this gesture, but shakes hands automatically. Then he turns and opens the glass door, gesturing for Anderson to go first. Not knowing what else to do, Anderson walks where he's directed. The patrolman falls in beside him. He escorts Anderson down to the Fourth Street entrance, then along the street to a black and white patrol car.

A second patrolman stops leaning on the trunk as they approach and opens the rear door. Climbing inside, Anderson notices that the back seat is far larger than the one in the unmarked car, but otherwise very similar. A metal grid walls off the front seat, the doors have no inside handles, and everything reeks of Lysol. Anderson feels another wave of claustrophobia as the door slams, locking him in. But he tells himself this immediate ordeal will soon be over.

The patrolmen climb in and drive off. Anderson wonders

where they're going, but decides it doesn't matter—as long as they turn him loose when they get there.

"How was Lieutenant Birdland?" the second patrolman asks Gorman.

"Well, you know those guys in homicide," Gorman says. "Always acting superior."

"Yeah. God's gift to corpses."

Gorman laughs. "That about says it."

The patrol car turns left and heads for the Third Avenue Bridge. This crosses the river just upstream from the old St. Anthony Falls, three blocks northwest of the Whitney Hotel. As they move onto the bridge, Anderson can see the maze of dams and locks off to the right.

"Man, look at *that* view," Gorman exclaims.

Anderson turns and sees that Gorman is nodding toward a woman in silk jogging shorts. She is fast-walking away from them on the other side of the bridge, about halfway across. A classic Minnesota blonde, tall and large shouldered, but still shapely.

"Do you think she's seen any crimes committed lately?" the second patrolman asks. "Maybe we could interview her for a while."

Gorman shakes his head wistfully. "I'm really going to miss that kind of sight when the weather turns cold."

Farther upstream, on the left, Anderson can see Nicollet Island. Peterson's apartment is on the river bank just beyond it.

With a slight start, Anderson realizes that this is where they are taking him. He should have expected it, of course. Everything at the university would be closed by this time, so the obvious place to bring him would be the apartment where they think he lives.

A few minutes after crossing the bridge, the patrol car pulls up in front of Peterson's building. Gorman gets out and opens the rear door for Anderson. Looking across at the entrance, Anderson sees that the doorman has already spotted them. The fellow stands directly outside the front door, holding it open for Anderson's arrival.

Anderson climbs out of the patrol car, trying to figure out the best way to handle the situation. "Thank you for the ride," he says. He hopes the police will drive off right away. That will enable him to make some excuse to the doorman and to get away from there himself.

But the police seem in no hurry to leave. With the patrol car stopped in front, Anderson has no choice but to enter the building.

"Good evening," the doorman says, as Anderson walks past him.

"Good evening," Anderson repeats, forcing himself to maintain a pleasant expression.

"You've got some more mail," the doorman announces cheerfully. He follows Anderson into the lobby and hurries over toward his post behind the counter. As he sorts through the piles of envelopes, he hums something to himself.

Anderson feels that he should say something friendly. "How is the songwriting coming?"

The doorman looks up at him with a big grin. "I've had a brilliant idea, but I haven't gotten it all worked out yet." He hands Anderson the mail. "If it goes the way I hope, I'm going to be able to start right at the top."

"That's good," Anderson says lamely.

"You better believe it! All my years of 'toil and tears' are finally going to pay off in a big way."

"I'll look forward to hearing about it," Anderson says. He expects the doorman to start telling him the idea that very moment.

But the doorman seems to sense, for once, this is *not* a good time. He nods at Anderson without speaking further.

Acutely aware that both the police and the doorman are now watching him, Anderson walks up the marble stairway and down the corridor to Peterson's apartment. Reaching the locked door, he gropes in his pocket for Peterson's key, finds that it is still there, and lets himself in.

The light switch inside the door makes the Gothic entry hall reappear. For a moment, Anderson is dazzled all over again. Then he sets the new mail down on the long wooden table and goes through the right hand door into the living room.

The draperies are still drawn, but Anderson finds his way by the early evening light filtering in around them. He walks over to the windows and pulls the heavy fabric aside, to look out. The street directly below seems deserted. Anderson leans forward until the side of his head touches the window, in order to see as far along the street as possible.

Up at the corner is a car with someone sitting in the front seat. It is parked where the street makes a 'T' with North East Main. A person in that spot would be able to watch the front entrance of the apartment building as well as its side. Anderson tries to get a look at the person's face, but the car's roof and doorpost make this impossible. He decides it doesn't matter. If the person in the car is a plainclothes policeman, Anderson wouldn't recognize him anyway.

Letting the drapes fall back across the window, Anderson wonders what to do next. He is not surprised to see he is under surveillance. But it makes him feel even more trapped than before. Once again, his impulse is to flee, to somehow elude the watchers outside. But at this moment, he feels too exhausted and hungry to try.

Uncertain what else to do, he heads for the kitchen. He opens the refrigerator, looking for a beer, but can't find any. The closest thing is a bottle of champagne. Pulling it out, Anderson sees that the label reads "Veuve Clicquot La Grande 1979." It is not one of the two or three brands he has heard of. He peels the foil off the top, unfastens the wire, and twists the cork until it pops in his hand. The liquid foams down the sides, but Anderson gets the bottle over the sink before it soaks the carpet. The first glass he finds in a nearby cupboard is a straight sided tumbler, so that's what he fills with the fizzing liquid. As a substitute for beer, it's not bad.

Sipping champagne from the tumbler, he looks around for something more substantial to eat. What he really wants is a hamburger, but he knows he isn't likely to find one in this kitchen. The foods in the refrigerator look more like garnishes and hors d'oeuvres than things that would make a proper meal. The provisions in the cupboards and storage room look as though they would need the skills of an accomplished cook.

Fortunately, the foods in the freezer look more manageable. There are dozens of gourmet dishes in single serving packets. According to the directions printed on the backs, most of them only need to be heated in an oven. Anderson picks out a "Lobster Cardinal with Perigord Truffles," a "Leek Pie," a "Lamb Argenteuil," and an "Aubergine and Wild Rice Casserole." The controls on the microwave look bewildering, so he sets the regular oven. Then he unwraps the frozen dishes and places all four on a cookie sheet. When the 'preheat' light goes off a few seconds later, he slides them in to bake.

Noticing he has forty-five minutes before the food will be ready, Anderson refills his tumbler with champagne and wanders across the hall to the exercise room. It is the photographs on the wall that continue to fascinate him. He stares at them from several feet away, trying to find relationships between them. He steps forward until his nose is almost touching the panes of protective glass, straining to see every detail.

The more Anderson studies the photographs, the more he is convinced they are pictures of *him*. The more he studies the settings, the more he sees himself inside them. When he looks at the picture that shows him arm in arm with the senator, he can almost smell the senator's expensive after-shave. When he examines the picture that shows him sitting on a park bench, he knows how the weathered wood of the bench would feel through his trousers and against his back. Taken together, the framed pictures show a person both attractive and admired, a person whose identity he would be almost eager to accept as his own.

Yet the person in the pictures remains unreachable. The barrier between Anderson and the images of himself on the wall is not the glass in the picture frames. It is not even the fact that these are mere images, whereas he is real. No, Anderson realizes, the real barrier is simply his memory. He has no memory to match the pictures, only memories that contradict them.

Anderson returns to the kitchen and pours himself more champagne. Then he opens the door to the laundry room and walks through it to the dressing room beyond. There, in one of the bookcases below the racks of clothes, are the photo albums he had discovered on his first visit. He takes out the one that seems most recent and carries it back into the kitchen.

Sitting down on the chaise longue in the breakfast area, Anderson begins paging through the album, studying every face, trying to find even one he remembers meeting. He stares obsessively at the pictures of 'himself,' especially the ones with other naked people. He turns repeatedly to the picture of the television anchorwoman, admitting to himself he feels a guilty satisfaction in seeing her needs so crudely satisfied.

When the food is ready, Anderson eats it, hardly noticing how it tastes. As he eats and drinks, he continues to turn the album pages. The images haunt him, even when he looks away. They threaten to follow him even into his dreams.

Drifting on the edge of sleep, Anderson feels disturbed at how easily these pictures have taken hold of his imagination. The physical circumstances they portray are much further from his experience than the physical circumstances of the pictures mounted on the exercise room wall. Yet Anderson is sure he knows the feel of every texture, the sound of every action.

Are these pictures less alien than they had first appeared? Is this nightmare, into which he has been plunged, more his own than he has been willing to admit?

C H A P T E R   1 1

Anderson awakes with the album still beside him. His back is sore and his burned arm aching. He realizes he has spent the night on the lounge in the breakfast area. He must have fallen asleep while still looking at the photos. His joints all feel stiff, and his clothes, grubby. Beside him, on the low table, he sees the empty trays from the 'gourmet' dinner of the night before. He swings his legs off the chaise longue and rests them on the floor. In front of his feet, he sees the empty champagne bottle.

Remembering that he drank the whole bottle, Anderson is surprised he doesn't feel worse. His head seems remarkably clear. But there is no comfort in this clarity. In the morning light, he is painfully aware that he doesn't belong here.

He struggles to his feet and staggers into the laundry room. There, he removes his clothes, taking care to place the contents of his pockets—the wallet, key, ibuprofen, and note from Shannon—on the counter. Naked, except for his bandage, he passes through the dressing room and heads for the master bathroom.

When he emerges a half hour later, he has showered, taken some more painkiller, changed his bandage, and shaved. This time, he has no hesitation about choosing clothes from Peterson's wardrobe. He dresses quickly, in much the same sort of apparel as the last time. Checking his appearance in the mirror, Anderson is once again surprised at how good he looks. He picks out a sports coat that goes with his trousers and shirt, but after trying it on, leaves it hanging over the back of a chair.

He walks back through the laundry room, stopping to put the wallet and other items back in his pockets. Then he looks around the kitchen, trying to find something to eat for breakfast. After his large meal the night before, he is satisfied with Amaretti, but needs something to help him wake up. He finds a coffeemaker and fiddles with it until it begins to operate.

While the coffee brews, he walks back to the living room and peers cautiously out the window. There is no sign of the person who was watching from the parked car the night before. Anderson is well aware there could be other watchers, less easy to spot. But he is somewhat relieved the obvious one is gone.

He opens the draperies, letting daylight flood the living room. Once more Anderson is struck by the richness of the furnishings. But this time the subtly erotic art works seem to have taken on additional meanings.

For anyone aware of being portrayed in Peterson's photo albums, the art works would be reminders of how Peterson has seen them and of how Peterson has preserved them on film. If Peterson invited his 'friends' from the albums to a party in this room, those 'friends' would feel threatened, almost subliminally, with public exposure. Perhaps, they would even feel that their most private moments were on display.

But why would Peterson want to create this effect? Was he simply carrying out a kind of symbolic or psychological revenge? Staging an artistic exposé of the 'cultured society' that had stripped him of his academic degrees?

Or was there a more immediate reason? Was Peterson reminding these people of their vulnerability in order to keep them in line? In order to make them cooperate with some project of his?

Anderson looks around the room, realizing how little he understands of what is going on. He still has no clear idea of why Peterson was so desperate to change places with him. He has no idea of why he was attacked in his friends' home, no idea of why Jack and June are now dead.

If Anderson is going to have any chance of straightening things out with the police or finding his friends' killer, he must find out what Peterson was up to.

He goes out into the entry hall and examines the mail that had arrived the day before. He discovers it includes another envelope full of money—about two thousand dollars' worth. As before, the bills are new, but the serial numbers are not consecutive. The paper slip reads *III—T.S.*

In search of further clues, Anderson sets about examining the contents of Peterson's apartment more thoroughly. He wanders from room to room, looking for cabinets and drawers that might contain something revealing. He peers behind the pictures and bookshelves, trying to find a safe or secret compartment. But there doesn't seem to be anything significant that he hadn't spotted on his first search.

The most suspicious items Anderson can find are still the parcels of money. Although he had dismissed the idea earlier, Anderson wonders if Peterson might have been involved with drugs after all. If Peterson had become sufficiently embittered after his experience with the university, building up a drug network involving some of the more affluent neighborhoods in the Twin Cities might have seemed justifiable to him.

It's true that the way the money is delivered in the mail doesn't seem consistent with a drug business. But maybe Peterson had invented a way of doing large scale drug deals by mail order. Certainly, if Peterson had gotten involved in a drug war, that would explain why he might want to be thought dead.

The problem is that, except for the cash and a few books on pharmacology, Anderson can't find anything in the apartment to suggest the drug trade.

The most striking thing about the furnishings continues to be the way the extremely sensual or sybaritic is mixed with the extremely technical or intellectual. It's as though Peterson had been trying to dwell exclusively among things beyond the reach of ordinary people. This makes a certain sense, given Peterson's personal history.

But it raises again the other question: having taken the trouble to create such an environment for himself, why would Peterson be so eager to leave it? Why, in particular, would he go so far as to arrange his own 'death'?

The phone rings in Peterson's office. Anderson wonders if he should answer it. He doesn't want to do anything that might raise an alarm. On the other hand, if there is any chance the call will reveal what sort of business Peterson was in, it might be worth the risk. The problem is that impersonating Peterson over the phone might be harder than doing it in person. Would people mistake his voice for Peterson's if they didn't see him *looking* like Peterson?

He ponders the question for a couple more rings, then picks up the receiver. "Hello," he says gruffly, making his voice hoarse.

There is a moment's hesitation at the other end. "Who is this?" a man asks.

"Who do you think?" Anderson says in the same hoarse voice, forcing a cough.

"This is Dick Haugen. You got a cold or something?"

"Just an allergy."

"Oh, sorry to hear that. Hope it gets better. Listen, we've got a problem down here."

Anderson holds his breath. Evidently the call is business rather than pleasure. Just what Anderson had hoped. "What sort of problem?" he asks carefully.

"It's this new operation. We've got the chemistry essentially right. But the product consistency is way off."

Anderson's pulse rate increases. It sounds as though the fellow is talking about some kind of laboratory. Could the 'product' in question be drugs?

"Can't you take care of it?" Anderson asks.

There is a long groan at the other end of the line. "I don't know where to start," the caller says. "Come on, help me. *You're* the genius."

Anderson tries to guess what is expected of him, but hasn't enough clues to go on. He needs an excuse for delaying any action, while still extracting as much information from the caller as possible. "I wouldn't be able to get down there right away," he says. "Maybe you could describe the situation over the phone."

"Who said anything about coming down here?" the caller replies, sounding puzzled. "I just need your best guess as to what's going wrong. If I can't sort it out after you've pointed me in a likely direction, I can always get back to you. I mean, if you're not too busy."

"Okay, what's the deal?" Anderson knows that by asking this question he might be setting himself up to be exposed as an impostor. But he doesn't see any other way to get the information he wants.

The man on the phone line takes a deep breath. "Here's

where we're at. We're synthesizing a polymer. Step-growth type. Solution process. Medium viscosity at the stage we're talking about, but increasing fairly rapidly." The voice pauses, apparently waiting for an acknowledgment.

Anderson doesn't remember what a polymer is, but it doesn't sound like a drug. Maybe this phone call is innocent after all. He tries to think how he should handle it. If he remains noncommittal, he might still be able to learn something without arousing suspicion. "Okay," he says, keeping his voice neutral.

"We're using a new type of tubular reacter," the voice continues. "It's designed something like an extruder, but with a much greater diameter. A central, rotating shaft. Close-clearance, helical impellers. Steady rate of flow. Surprisingly low shear factors. Good heat control." Again, there's a pause.

Anderson feels he should say something more. "So what's the problem?" he asks.

"The problem is that the residence time distribution is much too wide."

Anderson has no idea what this means, but he figures it never hurts to ask for a problem to be reformulated. "What are you asking?" he says.

"Well, we need to reduce the backmixing. But we can't figure out where we're getting the unexpected turbulence."

There is another pause. Anderson is sweating now. All he can think of is to get the fellow to define the problem in greater detail. Didn't the caller say something about heat? "What did you say about temperature?" Anderson asks aloud.

"It's pretty optimal," the voice replies. There is another . pause. Then a sharp intake of breath. "Oh, I see what you mean. You think we're getting hot spots we're not detecting."

"It's something to consider," Anderson says cautiously.

"Peterson, you really are a genius! I'll check it out right away."

Anderson can't help smiling. He feels brilliant. "Glad to be of help."

"Just one other thing," the man says.

"Yes?"

"I'm having a little trouble getting this quarter's payment together." The man's voice suddenly sounds tight and dry. He clears his throat. "Would it be all right if the payment arrived slightly late this time?"

All at once, the call doesn't seem quite as innocent. This Haugen must be one of the people sending Peterson money. How would Peterson deal with the issue of late payments? "How late?" Anderson asks.

"Not more than four weeks."

Anderson doesn't want to seem either too tough or too easy. He lets the silence grow, until it begins to seem awkward. "Okay," he says finally, trying to make his voice hard. "If it's really necessary."

"Thanks. I'll make sure it's in the usual form. And thanks again for the help with the polymer synthesis. I knew you wouldn't let me down."

Anderson hears the phone at the other end being hung up. He replaces the receiver and stands there thinking. The tone of the call had been very odd. The man seemed to treat Peterson with a mixture of whining and fawning. Yet despite the man's apprehensions about asking to pay late, Anderson could not detect any serious fear or underlying resentment.

Looking around the office, Anderson tries to remember where in the apartment he has seen books on chemical engineering. He can't immediately visualize them, but he decides the logical place would be next door in the 'high tech' study.

After a few minutes' search, he finds them. They fill a shelf and a half just below the books on applied physics and mechanical engineering. In their midst is a Ph.D. dissertation that sticks up higher than the rest. The name in gold lettering on the spine is "R. Haugen."

Anderson pulls this volume off the shelf. Its title is *Analytic Distinctions between Turbulence and Chaos in Chemical Mixing Theory.* Thumbing through the pages, Anderson sees that it consists largely of equations. The table of contents includes sections on "Generation Sequences for Turbulence" and "Generation Sequences for Chaos." Both are broken down into a number of subsections.

Anderson is very puzzled. He turns back to the title page and checks the author's name a second time. It is indeed "Richard Haugen."

So why, if this guy is an expert on turbulence, is he asking Peterson about it? And how could the fellow have overlooked a source of turbulence so obvious, even Anderson could stumble on it?

Even the fact that Peterson has a copy of the man's Ph.D. thesis seems odd. Thinking it over, Anderson realizes he has never before seen a Ph.D. dissertation outside of a university library, except perhaps for a spare copy in the possession of the student who wrote it. Presumably, this bound thesis on chemical engineering was a gift to Peterson from Haugen himself. That would mean they were extremely close friends. Perhaps they were college roommates or something and had exchanged dissertations in memory of their student days.

But as Anderson looks around the room, he spots several other Ph.D. dissertations. They are scattered widely among the other books, but easy to pick out because of their large size and similar bindings. Surely Peterson couldn't have been such close friends with each of these people!

Perhaps Peterson simply admired certain dissertations and wanted to have copies of them around. Anderson has some vague recollection that copies of dissertations can be ordered from somewhere in Michigan. But he also remembers that those copies arrive in the form of microfilms or Xeroxed editions. Peterson's copies, in contrast, are bound just like the originals. Where does one order those?

The doorbell rings, interrupting Anderson's thought.

Anderson has no intention of opening the door. He does not want to be caught again in Peterson's apartment, and the second attempt on his life has made him doubly cautious. But he is terribly eager to collect any information he can on Peterson's visitors, so he moves quietly into the front entry hall to listen.

The doorbell rings a second time. Then he hears a woman's voice. Shannon! The memory of her seductive face and body is more than he can resist. His face warms with pleasure.

When he undoes the latch, however, Anderson finds someone completely different. The woman is very tall and slender. She wears a tailored suit with a square shouldered jacket and a pleated skirt, ending a little below her knees. Her blouse is a brilliant white, and her velvet tie is formed into a bow like a ribbon. It is hard to tell what sort of build she has beneath the tailoring, but she does not seem at all bony or flat chested. Hanging from her arm is a large, flat portfolio, with a handle that allows it to be carried like a suitcase. Everything about her signals 'businesswoman.'

Seeing him in the doorway, she starts back slightly, her eyes wide with surprise. Then she smiles and shakes her head. "You know, for a moment, I didn't recognize you," she explains with a laugh. "Without the beard, I mean."

"How have you been?" Anderson asks, hoping to divert her from his appearance.

"Fine," she says, still staring at him.

Anderson is suddenly very aware that all Peterson's former acquaintances have been accounting for the apparent alterations in his appearance by the fact he no longer has a beard. Feeling foolish not to have seen it sooner, he realizes this was the reason Peterson had arranged for them both to be shaved. Such a big change would inevitably distract people from any smaller ones.

This time, however, Anderson wonders if the absence of a beard will be enough. The woman seems to be studying his features with unusual attention. His body tenses. If she recognizes he isn't Peterson, she might scream or turn and run. He, too, would then have to flee.

But the woman continues to smile. "It's amazing how much it changes the appearance of your eyes," she says finally.

"Well, yours are as bright as ever," he says.

She gives him another look of surprise. "Why, thank you," she says, catching his eyes with hers.

Anderson realizes he almost made a serious slip. Peterson was obviously not in the habit of handing out compliments. Anderson seems to have gotten away with it this time only because the woman is so obviously delighted.

She steps toward him and stretches her neck to kiss him on the cheek.

Then, before he has quite realized what she is doing, she sweeps past him into the apartment. "I've got some real goodies for you today," she says, flourishing her portfolio. "Just the kind of thing you like!"

She heads directly for the living room, apparently familiar with the layout. Anderson can think of nothing else but to follow.

Once inside, she kicks off her shoes. "God, I love your carpeting! It's a real erotic experience."

Anderson walks behind her into the room and watches her prop the portfolio against one of the footstools. "This collection has just come up for sale. I'm pretty excited about it, but I need your opinion."

As she speaks, she steps behind one of the high backed chairs and, using it as a screen, wriggles out of her panty hose. "I hope you don't mind the informality," she says. "It's just too warm for these today."

"Make yourself at home," Anderson says with an expansive wave, aware that this is what she has done already.

The woman steps out from behind the chair and tucks the hosiery into her jacket pocket. Then she pauses to straighten her skirt. "Ooh, that feels better," she says, caressing the carpet with her feet.

Anderson notices that her legs are so well tanned and so closely shaven, it would be difficult to tell whether she was wearing stockings without looking at her toes.

She bends over and unzips the portfolio. "You know, if I acquire this collection, you may even want to buy a couple of these pieces yourself." Throwing the portfolio open, she removes a stack of large pictures. "Anyway, I think you'll find them intriguing."

She sits down on one of the footstools that stand in front of a pair of easy chairs, gesturing for Anderson to take the other stool. He does as she indicates.

She ruffles quickly through the pictures, checking that everything is in order. As she does this, Anderson gets a brief glimpse of them. They seem to be art works of a fairly traditional sort. Not paintings, but prints and drawings, mostly without color. The actual pieces the woman is holding are not the originals, but huge photographs mounted on stiff paper.

"I don't know if I should put in a bid for the whole collection," she says, "or try to talk the owner's agent into splitting it up. Tell me what you think. If I do ask for the collection to be split up, I need to know which pieces I should buy."

She lays the first three pictures across the carpet in front of him. Then, pausing to check his reaction, she hands the rest of the stack to Anderson. The edges of the photos are already fanned out, to make it easy for him to continue laying them down. Anderson obliges the woman by spreading further photos along the floor, letting them fall one by one, casually overlapping each other. Judging by the number on the floor in front of him and the thickness of the pile in his hand, there must be about three dozen pictures in the collection.

Anderson is relieved to discover he at least knows what country and era the pictures come from. They are French and from the period known as "Rococo." The pictures present an idealized picture of French society in the time before the Revolution. Every scene possesses an atmosphere of elegance and gaiety, but there is always something contrived about it.

For a moment, Anderson is surprised he can identify the style so easily. But then he realizes it is familiar from old Hollywood movies and picture books he had as a child. The fashions had made an impression on him, because they were so elaborate and elegant. The decorative style had appealed to him, because it was so remote from the Protestant austerity of his grandfather's house.

While Anderson is handling the pictures, the woman shifts her position from the footstool to one of the easy chairs. Then she reaches forward with her bare foot and drags the footstool out of the way. This gives Anderson more room to lay out the photographs, but still allows her to see what he is looking at.

At first, Anderson is so concerned with sounding as though he knows something about art, he can hardly focus on the pictures. "Interesting technique," he mutters inanely, unable to think of anything better.

This is followed by a long silence, while the art dealer waits for him to say something more definite. Anderson begins to sweat. He continues to lay the photos slowly across the floor, trying desperately to think of comments that will allow him to keep up his impersonation of Peterson. But nothing comes to mind.

With the art dealer there beside him, Anderson feels under much more pressure than when he was speaking on the phone earlier. Still, he is not ready to give up. Visual art is hardly as foreign to him as chemical engineering. And having the pictures in front of him at least gives him something to go on.

He forces himself to concentrate on the pictures themselves, to study the images in order to see what they might be saying.

Each time Anderson hesitates over a picture, the woman murmurs a name, which he assumes belongs to the artist. "Gravelot . . . Jean-Michel Moreau . . . Eisen . . . Marillier . . . Augustin de Saint-Aubin . . ." But apart from enunciating these names, she says nothing to help him.

Most of the pictures show people in remarkably elaborate clothing or undressed amid piles of linen. The fabrics seem to receive as much attention as the human figures. The settings are sometimes hard to identify, but they usually seem to be gardens, bedrooms, or fantasy landscapes of clouds and seas.

The action in most of the pictures is essentially social. The images do not show warriors in battle, rulers wearing the emblems of office, or workers going about their jobs. They mostly show couples or small groups approaching each other by gestures or engaging in conversation. A few depict musical instruments being played, while the listeners whisper to each other or pass notes. A few others show people dressing or grooming themselves, while engaged in gossip or lively chat.

Because there is no way to tell what has happened earlier or what is being said, the reactions of the characters in the pictures are often mysterious. A woman, for example, might be announcing something with a placid expression, while some of her listeners recoil in horror and others dissolve in laughter.

After Anderson has noticed several pictures that are mysterious in this way, it suddenly dawns on him that many of these engravings are illustrations to stories, either cut from books or intended to go with narratives already familiar to the viewer.

He decides to take a chance by expressing this thought. "It' s a shame to divorce some of these from the narratives," he comments.

"Oh, do you think so?" the woman replies. "I like them better when they're a little ambiguous."

Anderson decides his last remark has passed muster. But he

needs to figure out more about what is happening in the pictures, if he is going to be able to keep up the deception.

The relationships in the pictures that are easiest to guess seem to involve differences in social status. In some pictures, the central figures are observed or assisted by other figures who seem to be of lesser importance. Sometimes these lesser figures are chambermaids or young women who seem to be enjoying the intrigue. Other times the lesser figures are cherubs.

It occurs to Anderson that the central figures surrounded by cherubs are probably supposed to be the gods of classical mythology. He remembers hearing that artists in earlier centuries often portrayed their contemporary subjects as gods in order to flatter them and to have an excuse for painting them naked.

As Anderson becomes more aware of the nudity in certain pictures, he realizes that many of the others seem to have erotic motifs as well. At first, this is just a general impression. The foliage in the pictures looks like frilly underwear. The skirts and petticoats look like disordered bed linen. The bed linen looks like clouds or like a storm tossed sea. The more Anderson examines the overall effect of the pictures, the more everything in each scene appears to merge into a tumbling, seething anarchy of erotic opportunities.

In this anarchic mass, voluptuous bodies are thrown surprisedly to the surface or coyly uncovered in the deeper recesses of the pictures. The paleness of long protected flesh is suddenly exposed amid the darkness of fabrics, waves, or leaves.

Anderson wonders, for a moment, if these erotic motifs were put there intentionally by the artists, or if an evening looking at Peterson's photo albums has simply made him overly sensitive to such things.

Then he comes to some pictures where the erotic theme is too obvious to be an accident or an unconscious effect.

In one of the engravings, the man is sliding home a bolt on a bedroom door, trapping a woman inside the bedroom with him. This ensures the couple's privacy and indicates metaphorically what he has in mind. The woman is struggling to stop him, but her expression indicates a certain complicity.

"That one deserves its fame, doesn't it?" the art dealer remarks.

"Yes, it does," Anderson replies, trying to sound as though he is looking afresh at a picture with which he has long been familiar.

"Of course, Blot's engraving is a mirror image of the painting," the art dealer adds. "That alters the emphasis somewhat. But it's still exquisite, isn't it?"

A particularly delicate drawing shows a young woman in a garden surprising a man by creeping up on him from behind and squeezing his bottom. This time, it's the young man who seems to forfeit his composure.

"The fellow selling this collection claims that's part of the lost erotic series by Watteau. But I think it was done a generation later. What do you think?"

Anderson decides to be a little bit mysterious. "It's awfully good for a student," he says.

"Whose student?" she asks, suddenly intent. "Boucher's?"

"That's a good guess," he says. He turns slightly to catch her reaction. The woman beams, like an eager pupil complimented on getting the right answer.

In another of the erotic engravings, a young man has just succeeded in digging through the numerous layers of skirts and petticoats enveloping a young woman's thighs. This leaves her most intimate parts exposed, but practically everything else covered.

"That's allegedly engraved by De Ghendt after a painting by Baudouin, but there's no record of Baudouin's original."

"There probably *was* one, though," Anderson says, figuring it's a safe bluff.

"Yes, I suppose there was," she says, accepting his judgment.

Anderson shuffles through the pictures, laying them out and picking them up again. He tries to put the ones together that share a common quality or style. He dissolves his own categories and groups in order to make new ones. He doesn't know what he is doing.

A number of pictures show women in their private chambers, doing things they wouldn't want men to see.

One of the few colored engravings shows two women comparing their bosoms with the aid of a table mirror. One of the women wears an elaborate feathered hat, and both wear full, floor length skirts in cream and pale yellow.

"That's supposed to be by Janinet after Lavreince," the woman informs him. "I imagine you've seen other versions of it."

Anderson makes an affirmative noise.

Another striking engraving shows a woman lying on her back amid crumpled bedding and voluminous draperies. Her breasts are exposed, and she is bare from the waist down. Her legs are in the air, and on her feet she balances a little dog.

"That's my favorite," the woman comments. "I know some critics have claimed it's a variation by the engraver. But it's so delicious, I can't believe it's not based on another lost original by Fragonard himself."

When Anderson has arranged a number of the pictures into the groups that seem to go together, he notices that something remarkable is happening: certain pictures are beginning to seem much better to him than others.

The drawing in some seems very fresh and assured, as though the artists know exactly what they are trying to achieve. Every detail in these pictures seems to contribute to the overall effect. The drawing in other pictures seems mechanical or tentative, as though the artists are simply copying someone else's work. The components of these pictures seem to have been added piece by piece, without ever being made into a consistent whole.

Before this perception can fade, Anderson goes through the pictures again, moving without pause from one to the next, but not too fast. This time he simply sorts the pictures into two piles, the good and the less good.

"Oh, you're a darling," the art dealer murmurs behind him. "That's exactly what I had hoped you'd be willing to do for me."

Trying not to lose his concentration, Anderson continues until he has sorted through the entire collection. Then he picks up each of the two piles and goes through them again, checking for a certain degree of consistency. Two of the pictures in the first pile now seem less of a piece than the others, so Anderson transfers them to the other stack. One of the pictures in the second pile seems to have a kind of vitality that others placed with it completely lack, so Anderson moves it back to the first pile.

Surveying his selections, Anderson has a sudden wave of confidence. The choices he has made don't seem to be an expression of his own tastes or interests. The choices he has made simply seem *right*.

"Nearly two thirds of them seem to be good ones," he comments, weighing the two stacks of photographs in his hands. "So you might want to bid for the whole collection."

The woman's reply to this last comment sounds more like a moan than a murmur of assent.

Anderson looks up to find her sitting in the chair with her head tilted back and her eyes nearly closed. She has one leg draped over the arm of the chair. Her skirt is still covering her thighs, preserving a degree of modesty. But she has her hand between her legs and is stroking herself.

Anderson is too surprised, at first, to say anything. But he is too fascinated to look away.

After a moment, she notices him staring at her, completely dumbfounded. She makes a soft, chuckling sound. "I'm just trying to save time," she explains.

Utterly taken aback, Anderson tries to guess how Peterson would have responded. "You're very considerate," he says finally.

"Anyway," she adds, running her eyes over his face and torso, "it's a real turn-on to find you looking so different. It's like getting ready to do it with a stranger."

Anderson suddenly realizes the outcome of this situation is something she is taking for granted. It seems any visit by a woman to Peterson's apartment has a certain predictable outcome.

"Aren't you going to help?" she asks.

"I'm not sure what sort of help would be appropriate this afternoon."

"Those engravings over there should give you a couple ideas."

She straightens the leg draped over the chair arm, extending it into the air and pointing her toes. Her pleated skirt falls back, exposing her thigh and panties. Her upper thigh is wider than he would have expected and, despite its tan, looks very naked. But the length of her leg makes it perfectly proportioned.

Anderson notices she is expecting a reaction. He tries to look at her with Peterson's eyes, responding more forcefully, as he imagines Peterson would have done. "You look better than any etching," he says, momentarily forgetting his resolution to avoid compliments.

"Well, aren't you nice," she says, genuinely pleased. Her hand goes once more to her crotch.

Anderson experiences a curious feeling of freedom. He suddenly knows he could do anything he wanted with this woman. Furthermore, he has a feeling he could do it without incurring any responsibility. Because it would not be he, Anderson, who was doing it. It would be Peterson.

The woman senses his excitement. She smiles and pulls at the end of her velvet bow with her unoccupied hand. The tie falls loose. Then she begins undoing the buttons of her blouse. When she reaches the waistband of her shirt, she pushes the top of the blouse to the sides, so he can see her tanned breasts swelling over the edge of her white bra. The remaining buttons and clasps are outside her reach. "I can't do much more without your help," she says.

Despite his excitement, Anderson realizes he is not really ready for what is being offered. "It's hard to resist," he says. "But I've got some other things I have to do."

"Can't you do me first?" she asks.

He shakes his head. "Sorry. Not right now."

She sighs and stops stroking herself, but continues to lie there, looking invitingly open. "Do you want me to schedule an extra session, or should I just come back next month as usual?"

"I'll see you next month."

She shifts to a sitting position and begins rebuttoning her blouse. "You'll probably see me a lot sooner. I have an invitation to the Lundgrens' cocktail party."

Anderson is relieved she still sounds cheerful. "You *do* look very appealing," he assures her.

She stands up and straightens her clothes. Her face is slightly flushed. "If I pull some stranger into a broom closet later today, it's going to be *your* fault," she says.

When the woman has left, Anderson discovers she has left behind a large check made out to Peterson.

People seem in the habit of giving Peterson money. And offering him their bodies. And asking his advice on incredibly technical questions.

Peterson, for his part, seems to have been able to answer all their questions and to meet all their sexual expectations.

Once more, Anderson feels a twinge of envy. Whatever he was up to, it strikes Anderson that Peterson was a person *worth* murdering, unlike some nonentity like Anderson himself.

But what about these people offering payments to Peterson? Were they the sort worth murdering or capable of murder? Was one of them the nightmare figure who broke into his dreams and tried to smother him? The faceless creature who caused the death of his best friends?

Suddenly, Anderson has an idea. Taking the check with the woman's name printed on it, he goes to the shelves holding Peterson's art books. Sure enough, there is a copy of her Ph.D. thesis: *The Iconography of 'Abstract' Detail in the Later Interior Designs of Robert Adam.* The university where it was submitted was Wisconsin, rather than Minnesota. But apart from some minor differences in format, it is bound just like the chemical engineering thesis Anderson had been examining earlier.

Anderson walks back to the entry hall and takes another look at Peterson's mail. He collects a number of the signed checks and arranges them in alphabetical order. Then he walks around Peterson's bookshelves looking for dissertations by people whose names are on the checks. After a few minutes, Anderson has found several that match. Since the majority of the payments are in cash and only accompanied by initials, this seems like a significant number of matchups between checks and dissertations.

The initialed slips accompanying the cash are less decisive, but when Anderson compares several of those to the dissertations, he finds that they, too, seem to correspond.

Anderson smiles at the idea of it. Evidently, if you sent Peterson enough money, he would honor you by keeping a copy of your Ph.D. thesis on his bookshelves. The humor of the gesture probably appealed to him.

But there obviously had to be more to it than that. In order to get a clearer picture of what Peterson was up to, Anderson decides he will need to find out more about Peterson's associates.

He returns once again to the piles of mail in the entry hall.

This time, he turns to the 'social' part of Peterson's mail. After a few moments' search, he finds the invitation from the Lundgrens. This must be the party the art dealer had mentioned. The address is on the West River Parkway, overlooking the Mississippi, a couple of miles to the south. The inscription on the card says 'cocktails and a light buffet.'

The invitation is for 5:30 that very evening.

CHAPTER 1

The door to the Lundgrens' house is dark and imposing. Anderson studies the area on each side of it, but is unable to find a doorbell. He decides the heavy brass knocker must be more than ornamental. Lifting it a couple of inches and letting it drop produces a satisfying 'thunk.'

Almost at once, the door is opened by a boy of high school age. He wears a dark suit that is slightly too small. Anderson can't tell if this is the Lundgrens' son or just someone hired to help with the party. "Hi, how are you?" Anderson says.

The boy doesn't reply, but simply stands to the side, gesturing for Anderson to enter. "Help yourself to a drink," the boy says.

Anderson passes through the vestibule, into the large front hall. It is paneled in dark wood and deeper than it is wide. Although it is not crowded, there is a good deal of noisy activity.

According to the time listed on the invitation, the party has been in progress for nearly a half hour. Most of the guests are probably already there, but a few recent arrivals are still checking their appearances in the mirrors just inside the door. Judging by the sounds coming through the large archway to the right, there must be forty or fifty guests. Maybe more.

For a moment, Anderson has doubts about whether he should have come. With so many people present, the chances he will be exposed as an impostor are surely increased. If someone questions his presence or denies he is Peterson, he has no idea how he will handle it.

But he tells himself the possible gains are worth the risk. Even if he is exposed, it seems doubtful anyone would make a public scene by preventing him from leaving or calling the police. In the meantime, every conversation he gets through undetected should provide valuable information about Peterson and his friends.

Anderson hesitates a few seconds longer, studying the gently milling crowd, then takes a deep breath and plunges in.

Straight ahead, at the back of the hall, is a table covered with a white linen tablecloth and rows of champagne glasses, already filled. A woman standing by the table sees to it that each guest has a drink as soon as he or she arrives. Another young man is helping her. He pours soft drinks or whiskey for people who don't want champagne.

Anderson makes his way to the table and picks up a glass of champagne. He drinks most of it and hands it back for a refill before moving on, glass in hand. His hands are shaking, but he figures the champagne will help.

Turning toward the big archway, Anderson sees a well tanned, white haired man looking at him and grinning. Anderson walks over and shakes his hand. Up close, it is apparent the man is only a little older than Anderson. But the man has the sedately mild manner of someone who has been rich and powerful for many years.

"We're awfully glad you could come," the man says. "No one seems to have seen you since spring."

"I've been up north a lot," Anderson says. "It's very re-newing. But I'm glad to be back."

"Well, you look good." The man stands there inspecting him and nodding.

It's not the sort of scrutiny Anderson wants to encourage. "Who are all these people?" he says, gesturing toward the crowd.

The man looks where Anderson is gesturing, then turns back, eyebrows raised. "You ought to know. After all, most of us first met each other at your parties."

"I don't recognize *all* the faces," Anderson says, hoping this is plausible.

"There are a few new people," the man admits. He glances through the archway, then suddenly smiles to himself. "Oh, I know who you've spotted. Come on, I'll introduce you."

They stroll through the archway into the large living room. After a few steps it becomes apparent they are headed for a young woman in a low cut, red dress. Anderson can see why someone like Peterson would want to meet her. Her charms are barely concealed by the red fabric. She sees the two men approaching and steps away from her companions.

"Sherry. I'd like you to meet our guest of honor."

Anderson looks sideways with a quizzical expression.

"Well," the man explains, "you're certainly our 'guest of honor' now that you've graced us with your presence."

Anderson can't tell if this is meant sarcastically or simply as an elaborate compliment. Before he can think of a suitable reply, the man is diverted by a tug on his sleeve. A woman in dark green whispers something in the man's ear.

"Excuse me, I have to talk to the caterers," he says.

"Good to see you," the woman says, kissing Anderson on the cheek. "I'm sorry to run off with my own husband, but we have a little crisis in the kitchen."

The two of them hurry away, leaving Anderson standing with the woman in red. "I'm—"

"I know who you are," she says.

"Are you new to the Twin Cities?" Anderson asks.

"I just moved here from Bemidji."

"Bemidji's a nice town."

"It's nice if you're a moose." The young woman smiles sweetly, but her eyes are hard.

A muscular young man with curly hair hands her a glass of champagne. "I got you a chair and some food," he tells her. "But it's getting cold."

"I'll catch you later," she says to Anderson, letting the young man lead her away.

Anderson steps back and leans against a wall, happy for an opportunity to survey the gathering. After his years of reclusive living, he feels disoriented by the profusion of voices and gestures. Yet he knows the scene in front of him is normal enough on the surface.

People are talking in small clusters in every part of the living room and on the terrace beyond. They are lively, but well behaved. All of them are drinking, and many hold plates of food as well. The women wear party dresses, and the men are in jackets and ties, but the atmosphere is informal. Everyone looks extremely prosperous.

Shannon is one of the few people Anderson can definitely recognize. She is once again wearing a black dress that leaves her shoulders bare. But this time, instead of straps crossing in front, there is curved panel of black tulle. This netted material covers the area below her neck and spans the gap made by her wide, plunging neckline. It is echoed below by a tulle ruffle along the hemline. In between, the dress clings tightly to Shannon's body. Anderson's breath catches at the sight of her.

She is engaged in animated conversation with an old man who holds on tightly to her arm. Catching sight of Anderson, she waves a greeting, but indicates she is unable to get away.

A number of other guests are vaguely familiar from the local television and newspapers. They are the sort who sit on the boards of corporations, serve on public commissions, and support the arts. If there is a mandarin class in the Twin Cities, this is a significant segment of it.

Much of the talk Anderson can overhear seems to be about sports. Not so much spectator sports, but the kind that the people talking participate in: sailing, tennis, golf, and horseback riding.

Out on the terrace, an older man is showing a young woman how to drive a golf ball with an imaginary club. He stands behind her with his arms pressed against hers and leads her in slow motion through the movement of a swing. She seems to be giggling, but Anderson is too far away to hear her over the noise of the party.

"I can't figure out why you look so different," a voice says near his ear.

Anderson is startled by the proximity of the sound. He turns to see a man with protruding eyes studying him from only a foot and a half away.

"It's not just the beard being gone, is it?" The tone is accusatory, but still uncertain.

Anderson decides to try brazening it out. "I've been getting a lot of exercise lately," he says. "How about you?"

"Oh, I've joined a health club myself. But I haven't undergone the amazing transformation that *you* have."

"You have to really work at it," Anderson says.

"Lots of us *work* at it. But it doesn't make us look like different people."

Anderson doesn't know how to deal with this conversation any longer. "Excuse me, I need some more champagne," he says. He holds up his empty glass, twirling it between his fingers. Then he steps around the fellow and heads back toward the front hall.

Joining the line at the drinks table, Anderson glances back through the archway. The man with protruding eyes is still staring after him.

Anderson feels a strong impulse to flee. But he is also aware he hasn't found out what he came for yet. It is obvious that the fellow suspects something. But maybe he will forget about it, if Anderson can manage to avoid him long enough. After considering his options, Anderson decides to stay a while longer.

A short, elderly gentleman, who is standing beside Anderson in line, gives him a conspiratorial look and beckons Anderson to lean closer.

For a moment, Anderson wonders if this man, too, has begun to suspect something. He bends down to hear what the man has to say.

"My wife doesn't know how to drink," the man confides with a thick tongue. "That's why she's always sober."

"I think you've figured it out," Anderson says.

He collects another glass of champagne and returns to the living room. This time, he makes his way farther into the room. He avoids the man with protruding eyes, hovering stubbornly near the archway. Several people make signs of greeting as Anderson passes by. But he nods hello without stopping.

Near the far end of the room, a pianist seated at a baby grand is turning rock and roll hits from the sixties and seventies into cocktail hour music. A few feet from the piano, along the wall, is one of the buffet tables. Above it hangs a large painting of deer in a forest.

Anderson goes over to the buffet and loads a plate with little squares of thickly laden toast. They are covered with shrimp, herring, and smoked duck, garnished further with tomatoes and ripe olives. Using the plate to protect himself for the moment from social encounters, Anderson settles against another wall to inspect the guests.

Now that he has seen more of them, Anderson is struck by how young they are. A few, like the man in the drinks line, are considerably older. But most of the people at the party are somewhere between their late twenties and early forties. They seem to have become successful at an unusually early age and with remarkable ease. There are no signs of wear in their apparel, no marks of anxiety in their faces.

For a moment, Anderson has trouble identifying what it is about these guests that makes them look so different from other groups he has observed. Then, in a flash, it comes to him: they seem to be people for whom happiness is normal.

Anderson hears a rustle at his side. He turns to see Shannon leaning against the wall, scanning the crowd as he has been doing. Her eyes are intent on the figures in front of her.

"Everyone loves them," she comments, "because they're rich."

Halfway across the room, a small burst of commotion draws their attention. It is an overweight man telling a story with flamboyant gestures. He puts his hands around his throat, puffs out his cheeks, and crosses his eyes. The half dozen people around him laugh heartily.

Anderson finds the demonstration disturbing, because it reminds him of being strangled or smothered. But he tries to conceal his reaction.

As the laughter subsides, the overweight man notices Anderson watching him. He snares fresh pineapple from a nearby platter and makes his way over to Anderson, eating the fruit on the way.

"Well, what do you think?" the man asks without further introduction. "Is our new heart valve going to be a winner?"

"Do *you* think it will be a winner?" Anderson asks, trying the most obvious method of dodging the question.

The man laughs as though Anderson has just said something witty. "Hey, what do *I* know? I'm just the head of the design team."

Despite the joking manner, Anderson can see the man is still waiting for a serious reply. But how could even Peterson discuss heart valves on an equal basis with someone who designs them?

Not knowing what else to say, Anderson goes for the obvious. "I'm sure you'd know the relevant factors better than I would."

The man looks bewildered. "Didn't you get the test data I sent you?"

Anderson doesn't want to deny receiving it, but he can't pretend to have read it either. "I haven't had time to study it yet."

"So how long would it take you? Five minutes?"

"I've scarcely had time to glance at it."

"Just give me your initial impression," the man persists.

"My initial impression is that there's a vast difference between having a good product and getting it adopted." Anderson doesn't know where this came from, but it seems an appropriate thing to say.

"Damn. I was *afraid* you'd say that." The overweight man strikes his own hip with the bottom of his fist. "Okay, thanks. We'll do something to cover ourselves in case the approval process takes longer than projected."

Wondering how Shannon is taking all this, Anderson turns back in her direction. But Shannon is no longer there.

Instead, Anderson is greeted by the woman from the drinks table. She refills his champagne glass and then moves on.

"Hey, there's Julianne!" the overweight man exclaims. He rushes forward to greet a tall, blond woman with an amazingly wide mouth.

Anderson takes the opportunity to slip away. He walks over to the piano and stands near it, in a position that suggests he is interested in the music. "Can you play some Rodgers and Hart?" he asks.

The pianist nods cheerfully and switches to "My Funny Valentine." In his version, it sounds remarkably like the song by Richards and Jagger he had been playing a moment earlier.

From his vantage point near the piano, Anderson can once again study the crowd. He still needs to get a clearer idea of who these people are and what their relationship was to Peterson.

His attention is caught by a wave of activity only a few yards away. The woman in dark green, who is apparently Mrs. Lundgren, is introducing a late arrival to the other guests. He seems to be a foreigner and is determined to get everyone's name.

This is the sort of opportunity Anderson has been waiting

for. He pretends he is looking for someone in the crowd and strolls forward until he can hear the introductions. The names are Scandinavian and German, with a couple of English and Irish ones mixed in. Two of the five names Anderson catches sound like ones he has been expecting.

Without changing his expression, Anderson slips his hand inside his jacket and extracts a sheet of paper folded lengthwise. This is a list he made before leaving Peterson's apartment. It consists of the authors and titles of the dissertations among Peterson's books. There were a total of twenty-six Ph.D. dissertations and five master's theses. These had been submitted for degrees over a period of eight years.

Out of the thirty-one people on the list, Anderson has already talked to three: the chemical engineer who telephoned Peterson's apartment, the art dealer who came by for a visit, and Lundgren, who must have been the man greeting people in the front hall.

Holding the folded paper close to his chest, Anderson glances down at it. Both of the names he thought he recognized are indeed there, and a third as well. This suggests that the guests at the party include a considerable number of the people whose dissertations stand on Peterson's shelves and who were regularly sending him money. All these people must know at least one of the secrets Anderson is after. But what could he say that would lead them to reveal it?

As Anderson is tucking the list back inside his jacket, a hand grabs him by the elbow. This is just at the edge of Anderson's burn, and he jumps slightly at the pain.

"Sorry, I didn't mean to startle you," a man says. "I just wanted to tell you that you got it right, as usual. The impellers weren't drawing the heat off as efficiently as we had thought."

Anderson realizes this must be Haugen, the chemical engineer who had called Peterson about the turbulence problem. He seems to be Anderson's age, but already going bald. Knobby features and a short, thick beard give his face an elfin look.

"I'm glad you got it sorted out," Anderson says.

"Well, we haven't gotten the process working yet. But at least we're getting there."

A woman standing at the chemical engineer's side rolls her

eyes. "I keep telling my husband he shouldn't be discussing business at a gathering like this, but he says everybody else does."

"Don't worry," Anderson says, giving her a reassuring smile.
"I don't mind."

For a moment, their eyes lock. Anderson realizes he has seen
her before. Then, with a flush of embarrassment, he remembers
where. She is one of the women featured prominently in Peterson's photo album.

Without taking her eyes off Anderson's, the woman picks up
a long slice of pear and slowly inserts the whole thing into her
mouth. The gesture reminds Anderson unavoidably of a specific
photo in which she was demonstrating her erotic skills. Her male
companion's head and shoulders were outside the frame, but
Anderson remembers thinking the rest of the body could easily
be his own.

The chemical engineer is still speaking, but, for a moment,
Anderson has lost track of what the man is saying. The woman's
eyes sparkle as she swallows the pear in one gulp. Apart from
that, she wears an expression of exaggerated innocence.

"I really appreciate your advice," Haugen says warmly.

"Always happy to help," Anderson replies.

"See you soon, then," the wife offers suggestively, as the couple strolls on.

Anderson stares after them. Does the chemical engineer
know of his wife's relationship to Peterson? Nothing Anderson
can spot in the man's behavior indicates he suspects, but it's
impossible to tell for sure. If Haugen does know what his wife
has been doing, it occurs to Anderson that this would give him a
powerful motive for murder.

Anderson looks around the room. He is suddenly very aware
that the person trying to kill Peterson was probably someone in
Peterson's circle of acquaintances. If so, that person is likely to
be here at this party. Anderson's pulse quickens. If he knew what
to look for, he might be able to pick out that person this very
moment.

He scans the assembled company, trying to imagine each
guest in a motorcycle helmet, attempting to smother him. But the
helmeted image seems too remote from the well dressed figures,
the violence too much of a departure from their polite behavior.

Turning slowly where he stands, Anderson sees the art dealer who had visited Peterson's apartment with the portfolio of Rococo prints and drawings. She is about fifteen feet away, surrounded by a trio of male admirers. The dress she is wearing for the party leaves her shoulders bare.

Anderson notices how muscular she is. He realizes he is not even sure that the person in the motorcycle helmet was a man. A woman as strong as the art dealer could be a fierce combatant in motorcycle leathers.

The art dealer sees Anderson staring at her and raises her champagne glass in greeting.

Anderson raises his own glass in response.

A passing waiter thinks Anderson is signaling for a refill and hurries over to pour him more champagne. Anderson nods his thanks, but resolves to drink more slowly. His head is less clear than it ought to be.

Someone jostles him from behind, causing him to spill some of his champagne. "Oh, I'm terribly sorry," the man says.

"That's all right," Anderson replies.

"I was hoping to bump into you," the man continues, "but not quite so literally." He pats Anderson's dripping hand with a cocktail napkin. Then he leans forward intently. His boyish face is shiny with drink. "I need to get your take on the currency markets in relation to precious metals," he says.

Anderson is by now used to these approaches, but he doesn't feel up to bluffing his way through a discussion of economics. "I'll talk to you about it later," he says.

"There are just a few variables I don't know how to estimate," the man persists.

"Later," Anderson says firmly. He turns and makes his way back to a nearby wall. At least in this position, people won't be able to come at him from all sides.

Leaning against the wall, Anderson tries to see the gathering through Peterson's eyes. He remembers the arrogance of Peterson's comments in the *Minnesota Daily* all those years ago. He imagines the condescension with which Peterson would regard the people seeking his advice. These are the people who possess the degrees and public recognition Peterson had been denied. Yet they seem in constant need of his help.

How would Peterson have felt while he helped them? What would he have found to enjoy in a party like this? Would he have experienced a kind of satisfaction in his superiority to the other guests and their implicit acknowledgment of this superiority? Or would he have been looking for other satisfactions?

As Anderson watches, he notices the party subtly shifting into another gear. The guests have now been drinking long enough to show the effects of alcohol. Their voices are growing louder, their gestures broader.

His attention is drawn to the young woman in the low cut, red dress. The one from Bemidji. She leans over to chat with some people who are sitting down, resting her elbows on the back of a low backed easy chair. This makes her bosom hang forward, so that it is almost falling out of her top. She seems to be striking this pose intentionally. Anderson finds it hard to look at her without thinking of ripe fruit, but he still finds her very attractive.

Was this what Peterson would be looking for at a party? Was it what he, as Anderson, would be looking for?

There is a rustle at Anderson's elbow. He becomes aware that Shannon is standing beside him, following his gaze. She looks up at him with an appraising smile, then swings her eyes back toward the woman in red. The woman's breasts bulge more than ever. "Quite a show," Shannon murmurs, lifting her glass. "Have you had her yet?' "

"What do you mean?" Anderson stammers.

Shannon's eyes are full of mischief. "Have you screwed her yet?" she asks in a low voice.

Anderson doesn't know how to reply. He was taught, growing up, that a gentleman doesn't answer such questions, even in the negative. "I've barely met her," he says.

Shannon smiles, looking at him skeptically.

Anderson tries to imagine how Peterson would have reacted, but he doesn't know how to begin. "I was just admiring her dress," he adds.

Shannon takes another sip from her drink. "You'd like to screw her, though, wouldn't you?" She waits for his reply, obviously enjoying herself. Her eyebrows are raised, and the tip of her tongue is touching her upper teeth.

Anderson is completely at a loss. He has never even used the word 'screw' the way she is using it. "Can I get you another drink?" he asks.

But Shannon is not to be diverted. "Look at her twitching her fanny. She really wants it, doesn't she?"

"Come on, Shannon." He tries to sound bored, but he can't conceal his discomfort.

Shannon laughs at his embarrassment. She studies him with narrowed eyes. "I bet you were imagining it just now. Getting her bent over like that. Cupping those fat breasts from behind. Fingering those big nipples. Hearing her gasp . . ."

Anderson notices that Shannon's own nipples are getting erect as she teases him. He swallows more champagne than he intended. He wonders desperately what Peterson would have said at this point. "I wasn't thinking of that," he says.

"No, of *course* you weren't," Shannon comments with a smile.

She turns around to survey the room, stepping slightly in front of him. As she does this, she reaches behind her back and runs her hand over the front of his trousers. "Oh, my goodness," she coos ironically. "What a surprise!"

Anderson blushes furiously. He looks along the wall to see whether her gesture was observed, but realizes her body had blocked it from view.

Turning back toward him, she beams with satisfaction at having made her point. "You *should*, you know."

"I should what?" he asks.

"You should screw her," Shannon says softly. "After all, that's what she'd like to do to you."

Shannon turns and walks away, ostensibly to refill her glass, but mostly to show Anderson the saucy wiggle of her hips.

Anderson follows her with his eyes until she disappears into the crowd. Then he looks back at the people nearer by.

A dozen feet from where Anderson is standing, the man with protruding eyes is sitting down, watching him. Their eyes meet for a brief moment. Anderson wonders if the man heard Shannon's lewd remarks or saw her grope him. The thought embarrasses him. But he decides the incident wouldn't do his credibility any harm.

The man with protruding eyes apparently takes the moment of eye contact as an invitation to resume their earlier conversation. He gets up and begins making his way toward Anderson, staring fixedly at him as he approaches.

Anderson tries to make an evasive movement, backing off toward the door to the terrace. But a cluster of guests gets in his way.

The man catches up to him. "Are you going to the opening of the opera next week?" he asks.

"I don't know," Anderson says. "I'd have to check my calendar."

The expression in the man's eyes tells Anderson he has made a mistake. "I thought you had total recall for things like that," the man says.

Anderson thinks fast. "I had someone else making some arrangements for me while I was up north. I don't know yet exactly what's been planned." As he says it, Anderson realizes he is inadvertently telling the truth.

Apparently, the man finds this explanation sufficient, because he nods understandingly. "Well, if you *are* going, let me know if you'd like to have dinner with us afterward."

"Thanks," Anderson says. "I'll do that." He nods at the man, giving him a grateful smile, and resumes his progress toward the terrace.

Near the sliding doors, he sees that the foreigner is being introduced to some more of the guests. This time, it is a large man with wire rimmed glasses who is performing the introductions. Anderson moves forward to where he can hear the names. He takes the sheet of paper from his jacket pocket as unobtrusively as he can and scans it to see if any of the new names are on it. There are three more matches.

At this point, Anderson has identified nine guests whose graduate dissertations are on the shelves of Peterson's apartment. He is willing to bet that the other people who have asked him for advice are also represented there. The party seems to be littered with guests whose academic work Peterson had known intimately.

Anderson steps out on the terrace, looking for a secluded corner. He spots some empty lawn chairs and walks over to them.

Sitting down where he hopes he will be inconspicuous, he takes out the list of dissertations and examines it further.

Drawing conclusions from the list is difficult, because the subjects are so technical and the fields of study so remote from anything Anderson has studied. Lundgren's dissertation, for example, seems to deal with the aerodynamic stability of small planes at very high speeds. But the approach is so abstract, it had taken Anderson several minutes to figure out even that much.

The one dissertation Anderson thinks he might be able to decipher is in his own former major, sociology. Its title is *The Circulation of Elites as a Result of Observable Changes in the Distribution of Residues.* Anderson is not sure what this means, but he recognizes the technical terms. They come from the sociological theories of somebody named Pareto.

During his sophomore year, Anderson had attended a class in the history of social theory, which covered the fellow. As far as Anderson can recall, Pareto described society as consisting of mindless masses exploited by equally mindless elites. Both groups, Pareto claimed, are dominated by irrational prejudices or 'residues,' which they are unwilling to acknowledge. Hence, they conceal these 'residues' with elaborate rationalizations or 'derivations.' The result, according to Pareto, is that everyone lives in a condition of total hypocrisy.

Anderson remembers the theory better than most, because he had found it rather shocking. In fact, at the time, it was the most cynical account of human affairs he had ever encountered.

Gazing at the page, Anderson notices that the author of the dissertation is one of the guests he had heard being introduced a few minutes earlier. It occurs to Anderson that if he talked with this person, he would not need to do quite as much bluffing as in most of his recent conversations. Maybe that would make it easier to explore the man's relationship to Peterson.

Anderson gets up from the lawn chair and goes back into the house. He spots the author of the sociology dissertation engaged in conversation with a woman whose wavy, reddish hair falls most of the way down her back. Her hair makes her unmistakable. She is another of the women who had posed for Peterson's photo album.

As Anderson walks toward the couple, he finds himself vividly recalling one picture in particular. It shows her standing with her head tilted, so that her hair falls to the side of her body. She smiles seductively at the camera, while she gathers her pale lime skirt in one hand and slides it up her hip—high enough to reveal she's wearing nothing underneath. The wispy patch between her legs is the same reddish color as the hair flowing down from her head.

Anderson tries to put the image out of his mind. He concentrates instead on the man he wants to talk to. The fellow has the kind of beefy build that will turn to flab as he ages, but right now seems bursting with health. Anderson wonders if the woman with reddish hair is the man's wife. After a moment's reflection, he decides it is unlikely, because the man is flirting with her so energetically.

The couple notice Anderson's approach and turn to greet him. Anderson bends forward, so that the woman can kiss him on the cheek. She is wearing a rather clingy, dark blue dress.

"You know, that's almost as good a color for you as pale green," Anderson comments.

The woman laughs, obviously catching the reference. "How nice of you to remember," she says.

Her smile makes Anderson feel pleased with himself. He realizes his remark was exactly the sort Peterson would have made. Patting her affectionately on her upper arm, Anderson turns to her companion. "You're looking very fit," Anderson says.

"You too," the man replies.

"I was thinking of you just the other day," Anderson continues. "After I came upon something by Pareto."

The man looks blank. "Who?" he asks.

"Pareto, the Italian sociologist."

"Oh, yeah, I remember." The man smiles and nods, as though the recollection is a happy one. "There were lots of references to him in my Ph.D. thesis."

"I was recalling the way you analyzed social mobility in terms of Pareto's concepts."

This time the man looks distinctly puzzled. "Wasn't he the guy who wrote about residues and deviations?"

"Derivations," Anderson says.

"What?"

"He wrote about residues and *derivations.*"

"Too bad," the woman comments. "Deviations would have been a lot more fun."

"What I wanted to ask you," Anderson persists, "is whether you think Pareto's work really remains relevant, now that we've got so many more concepts for analyzing the way culture shapes behavior."

This time the man looks distinctly irritated. "Why are you asking me? *You're* the one who knows all that stuff."

There is a long silence. "Yes, I guess you're right," Anderson says finally. He smiles cheerfully, to let the man know he's off the hook. "Have you noticed where they're serving those little Swedish meatballs?" Anderson asks.

"There's another buffet in the dining room," the woman says. "Here, I'll show you."

"That's okay," Anderson says, putting up a hand to stop her. "I'll find my way."

He walks back through the living room to the front hall. There, opposite the archway to the living room, he finds the doorway to the dining room. Inside, a large table covered with white damask holds silver chafing dishes. In addition to tiny Swedish meatballs, they contain baked salmon and sliced Canadian bacon. There are also vegetables and rice. A number of people are waiting to serve themselves, but they are too intent on the food to do much talking.

As Anderson stands holding a plate, he goes over his last conversation in his mind. His first impulse is to dismiss the man with the sociology doctorate as an idiot. But he knows this would not be accurate. True, the fellow is remarkably ignorant of his own academic specialty. And he seems unable, on short notice, to rise to even a modest intellectual challenge. But this does not mean the man is incompetent at routine professional tasks. It merely means he lacks the intellect to deal with problems that are more unusual or require an extra degree of depth.

Judging by the conversations Anderson has had with them or overheard between them, the rest of the people with dissertations on Peterson's shelves are not very different. What is striking about these people is not that they are distinctive in any way. It is their utter *lack* of distinction. They do not seem to be especially intelligent. They show no signs of being creative or original. It is very difficult, for example, to imagine any of them writing the kind of heavy-duty dissertations found in Peterson's apartment. The more Anderson thinks about them, the more they all seem like pretentious frauds.

Suddenly, Anderson's vague suspicions condense into a definite hypothesis. He is now convinced that he knows what Peterson's racket was. Peterson must have used his extraordinary abilities to write dissertations for other people, just as he had once used those abilities to take exams for them. He probably sold the dissertations to graduate students who lacked the ability or the discipline to produce work of a high enough standard by themselves. Faced with the prospect of their graduate studies going to waste, many students would have jumped at the chance to buy a top quality dissertation, containing original contributions. If they needed it, Peterson probably coached them through their orals as well.

Later, as the Ph.D. holders went on to successful careers, Peterson probably used the same dissertations as a basis for blackmail, with further career help thrown in as a sweetener. Most of his 'clients' were in fields where the licensing requirements and professional liability laws would prevent them from operating without a valid degree, even if they were known to do first rate work. Others were academics or high ranking civil servants who were expected to be exemplary in their professional conduct. Since Peterson's name was already blackened by scandal, he would have nothing to lose by revealing his own role in these people's careers. His hold over them would have been complete.

Anderson has no trouble imagining how it might work. The payments Peterson demanded were probably based on what the individual clients could afford. The actual blackmail rate was probably a percentage of their quarterly income. It would also have made sense if Peterson's clients were offered a choice between paying in cash at a lower rate or paying by check at a higher one. Those who paid by check probably claimed the payments as a business expense for their income taxes, listing Peterson as a 'consultant' or 'manager.'

If anyone had ever challenged him to a showdown, Peterson probably wouldn't have needed any special documentation to prove himself the author of the dissertations. He had put his personal stamp on all of them simply by making them so abstruse. The people who had submitted them for degrees probably couldn't even follow the abstract reasoning they were pretending was their own.

Anderson wonders if the pornographic photos were also used for blackmail. He decides that they might have been, but that it probably wasn't necessary. After all, a minor sex scandal would be painful, but something most of these people could survive. Losing their professional credentials and careers would be a much bigger disaster.

Gradually, as he thinks it through, Anderson appreciates what a nice set up Peterson had. On the basis of Peterson's mail for the last three months, Anderson estimates that the income from his thirty-one clients must have been nearly a million dollars a year. As the clients became older and more successful, this figure would have kept going up. The fringe benefits from controlling so many influential people would also have been considerable. The sexual favors the women in the group were providing for Peterson were probably only one of many services he was in the habit of demanding.

To Peterson himself, the set up must have seemed not only justified, but ironically appropriate. Society had deprived Peterson of credentials that he had earned, so Peterson had retaliated by providing other people with credentials that they hadn't earned. And, of course, he made them pay heavily for it.

"Are you all right?" a voice asks.

Anderson looks up and sees Shannon. "I'm fine," he says. He realizes he is sitting on a chair along a wall of the dining room. A plate of meatballs is balanced on his knee, untouched. He tries one and finds it cold. "I was just thinking about something."

Shannon sits down beside him with a sympathetic smile. "This party isn't very stimulating for you, is it?" She looks around at the other people in their vicinity. "Maybe I could do something to make it more interesting."

"I've been finding it interesting enough, actually." Despite his other concerns, it is hard for Anderson to avoid staring through the sheer material spanning Shannon's plunging neckline.

"How about that woman with the lace sleeves? She just moved here this summer." Shannon turns back to Anderson to gauge his reaction. "She has the kind of body you like. Lush breasts over a flat stomach, the mound between her legs neatly trimmed—"

"I don't know which woman you mean."

"That one over there. In the yellow dress with lace sleeves and the ultra high heels." Shannon nods toward the door leading back to the front hall. "She's started going to the same fitness club that I do." A slow smile spreads across Shannon's face. "I think she could be quite diverting."

"Why do you say that?" Anderson studies the woman in question. She is standing in the front hall with her legs well apart, tilting her head forward to hear a story. From what Anderson can see of her face, the woman is very pretty, with large eyes and full lips.

"She likes parading around the ladies' locker room with no clothes on. I think she finds it exciting." Shannon's own eyes look large and moist. "In fact, she'd probably like to make it in a threesome. Or at least do it with you while I watched."

Anderson feels his face grow warm. He hopes he isn't blushing. Peterson's sexual activities are still something he doesn't entirely understand. "Why would she be so interested in me?"

Shannon raises her eyebrows and purses her lips. "Well, you're awfully attractive. You've got a sexy reputation. And"— she hesitates—"you're known to have a lot of influence with her new boss."

"I suppose that would help motivate her."

Shannon smiles. "She'd be motivated on *several* levels. Shall I try to set something up?"

Anderson shakes his head. He sets his plate of cold meatballs on the radiator cover behind him. "Not just now, thanks."

"If she doesn't appeal, I can suggest a couple of other candidates." Shannon's breasts strain bewitchingly at each side of her neckline as she turns to look further.

Anderson tries to think of a way to change the subject. Then he realizes there is another opportunity here, beyond the sexual one. "Wait a minute," he says, "who is this woman's new boss?"

"Our host. Mr. Lundgren."

"Have you seen him in the last few minutes?"

"Sure. He's back by the other buffet."

It occurs to Anderson that if Peterson has set things up the way he suspects, his 'clients' should be more motivated to please him than anyone. By applying some pressure to someone like Lundgren, Anderson should be able to test his deductions.

"Excuse me. There's something I need to find out from him."

Kissing Shannon lightly on the cheek, Anderson gets up and heads back to the living room.

Lundgren is standing near where Shannon had last seen him. He grins again as he sees Anderson approaching. "Did you find something to eat?" he asks.

"The food is great," Anderson assures him.

"Anything else I can do for you?"

Anderson looks him over. "Actually, I just thought of something. There's a woman in the front hall wearing a yellow dress with lace sleeves. I believe she works for you."

"Yes, that's Linda Fagerstrom. What about her?"

"I think you should give her a raise. Say, a thousand more a month."

Lundgren's face goes blank, but his eyes grow more alert. "I didn't realize you had a personal interest in her."

"I don't. But I think anyone who can balance that gracefully on heels that high deserves an extra thousand."

"Oh. You're joking."

"No," Anderson says in a matter-of-fact tone, "I'm not."

"I think there's something here you don't understand." Lundgren puts his hand on his own chest, his fingers splayed. "*I'm* not the one who decides the salary level for her job."

"You could. You will."

"The departmental budgets are already allocated for the next six months."

"Then you can do a little *re*-allocating."

"I can't just increase her salary on your whim."

"Why not?"

"I'm a corporate officer. I have responsibilities."

"Ah, a good point," Anderson says. "You're in a very responsible position."

"I'm glad you can see that."

"I suppose a company like yours must carry a lot of professional liability insurance."

"Yes, I guess we do."

"And there's probably a clause in the policy about your obligation to take 'all due precautions' in your engineering and designs."

"I suppose there is."

"Well, if you were examining a claim, would you consider that having someone like you in charge is taking 'all due precautions'? I mean, considering the way you earned your engineering degree."

Lundgren goes rigid for a moment, then looks away. "Okay, okay."

"Or should I say, 'failed to earn'—"

"You've made your point."

"You know, under the circumstances, you should be grateful this woman is willing to work for you."

"But how do I justify a pay increase to my business associates?"

"Give the woman some special duties, say, in public relations. Then explain that the salary increase would be appropriate, given her new duties."

"It would be difficult to make them accept that."

"But you'll do it. Won't you?"

"Yes."

Anderson turns and walks away. He feels intoxicated. He is not sure if it's a result of the champagne or of his new sense of power. As he moves through the crowd, he spots two more women and one man whom he thinks he recognizes from Peterson's photo album. The idea of these guests stripped naked for his amusement is beginning to seem almost natural to him. The whole party seems to revolve around his interests and his powers. The women all seem to be his for the taking. The guests all seem to know he controls their income and their status. Everything they have achieved depends to some extent on him.

A short, sturdy woman approaches him with another request for advice. Anderson smiles at her, barely listening. He is vaguely aware that she's asking him a complicated question about epidemiology. But he pays more attention to how she looks than to her explanations. He decides she is rather pretty, despite her squat build.

"What I need to know," she concludes, "is whether that sort of sampling procedure would give us sufficient data for estimating the tertiary vectors."

After his previous successes, impersonating Peterson, Anderson is confident he could handle her questions. But he realizes now that he doesn't have to. As long as he is taking the place of Peterson, these people are at his mercy far more than he is at theirs.

"I'm sorry. I'm tired of answering questions tonight. Can't you figure it out for yourself?"

The woman is taken aback. "I suppose I could," she says. "But it would take me weeks. I might even have to do a trial survey. Couldn't you just tell me the answer now? I'm sure it's obvious to you already."

Anderson smiles and shakes his head. He walks on, leaving her standing there, frustrated. Thinking for a moment about her question, he is surprised to discover he actually understood most of what she was saying. He even has a strong feeling that the sampling procedures she described would be inadequate. She needs to go back and rethink what she is doing.

Recalling the other conversations he has had that day, his sense of exhilaration grows stronger. He feels almost as though he *belongs* in this role. He feels charged with energy from the force with which he has been asserting Peterson's position, the resourcefulness with which he has been acting Peterson's part. It's as though he had been going through life with all these latent powers which are only now being activated.

If only he could figure out which one of these people is trying to kill him! He keeps suspecting each party guest of hating him, but he can find no evidence for it. As he passes slowly through the room, the people he hasn't spoken to yet make welcoming gestures. They seem genuinely glad to see him, eager to be close to him. The ones he was willing to greet earlier, or who were confident enough to approach him, smile warmly as though hoping he might join them again.

A passing waiter holds out a tray of glasses. Anderson hesitates, then accepts one. As he takes a sip, he feels as though he is toasting himself. Champagne has never tasted so good to him.

Up ahead, Anderson sees that a woman has stepped out to waylay him. It is the wife of the chemical engineer. Looking at her from a few feet away, Anderson can see that she is a little too small in the bosom and a little too wide in the hips, but she carries her body with a confidence that makes it attractive.

"You've been neglecting me," she says coyly as he draws near.

"Not intentionally," Anderson replies. "I've just been busy."

"It's been months," she pouts. "You haven't phoned me in months."

"How's your husband doing?"

"Oh, you know him. I think he's happier when someone else is satisfying my little cravings. That way *he* doesn't have to."

They both turn as they sense the approach of someone else. It's the man with protruding eyes. He looks fixedly at Anderson. "I've figured out your secret," he announces.

"What do you mean?" Anderson's heart rate soars.

"What you've been up to. Why you've virtually been in hiding lately. Why you look so different."

Anderson holds his breath. His eyes automatically seek the nearest exit.

"What are you trying to say?" the woman asks.

The man with protruding eyes looks smug, his gaze never shifting from Anderson's face. "You've had cosmetic surgery!"

"Oh, Mel—" the woman groans, apparently embarrassed by this social lapse.

But the man will not be subdued. "I'm right, aren't I? You've had your face done."

Anderson relaxes enough to breathe, but can't yet manage a reply.

"Why on earth would he have his face done?" the woman asks, springing to his defense. "He looked wonderful already."

"To look younger. To conceal the effects of his decadent lifestyle." The man grins widely. "It catches up to everyone eventually."

"Well, I don't see anything wrong with it," she says. "Women have plastic surgery all the time. I think people should look as good as they can."

"The surgeon did a great job. I'll give you that."

The woman leans forward for a closer look. "I certainly can't spot the scars."

Anderson is extremely uncomfortable at being examined this closely. He had better extricate himself from this situation before he really *is* revealed as a fraud. Lifting his eyes to the people around them, he tries to think of an excuse to end this conversation.

Then the obvious way out occurs to him. He will simply make his farewells and leave the party altogether. He has gotten most of what he came for, and staying longer might be pressing his luck too far.

"It's been nice talking to you," he says. "But I have to be going now."

With a smile and a little nod, Anderson pivots and walks away. Carrying his champagne glass in front of him, he moves back into the front hall. He sets his glass on a tray of empty ones. It still has champagne in it, but Anderson knows he has now had more than enough.

Turning back toward the front door, he sees the Lundgrens standing there, bidding people good-bye.

"Thank you for the lovely party," Anderson says.

"A pleasure to have you," Lundgren replies.

"You really should come more often," his wife adds. "We hardly ever see you anymore."

Anderson studies their faces for signs of resentment or other concealed emotions, but the couple seems completely sincere. He can't decide if Lundgren is exercising remarkable control or if the man has already taken Anderson's demands in his stride.

Lundgren's wife leans forward and kisses Anderson on the

cheek. Then the couple turn their attention to the next set of departing guests.

From somewhere to the side of him, a man tugs at Anderson's jacket. "Hey, are you leaving already?"

"I'm afraid so."

"But I haven't even talked to you yet."

"Another time."

"I just wanted to tell you I'm ready to kill you."

Anderson freezes. He can't believe the man is actually speaking these words. "What did you say?"

"I said I'm ready to kill you."

"Why?"

"Why not? I've come close enough before."

"Why are you telling me this?"

"To psych you out." The man is visibly gloating. "Don't look so surprised. You've known this was coming."

"But why you? Why now?"

"I'm ready, that's all."

"I don't understand."

"I did the two week camp this year. My serve is so much better, you won't even recognize it. When I got back I beat Ingersol in three straight sets! Ingersol!"

"You're talking about tennis."

"I'm not talkin' tiddlywinks."

Anderson has a sense of relief, but he feels his muscles beginning to tremble. "Well," he says as evenly as he can, "I'll look forward to meeting you on the court."

The man holds up his index finger. "Your reign as top player in our group is over, Peterson." The man disappears into the dining room.

Anderson tries to conceal the fact that he is shaking. His nerves have finally had it. He has to get out of there.

A number of people stand between Anderson and the front door, trying to say all the things they didn't get around to saying earlier.

Anderson eases through, making an effort not to get drawn into conversation. In front of him, several people are putting on light coats or jackets before stepping outside. Anderson tries to slip between them, but a woman steps backward, bumping into him.

"Oh, I'm sorry," she says, as Anderson helps her regain her balance. "I didn't know you were there."

Anderson looks down at her upturned face. It is startlingly familiar. Then he realizes why. She is the television anchorwoman who had reported on his grandfather's death all those years before. She is the woman featured so memorably on Peterson's wall and in Peterson's photo album.

"Long time, no see," she says, stepping backward again, so that her body is pressed against his.

"Long time," he agrees.

"Say, did you notice the news item about that fellow Anderson?"

"Who?"

"You know, that guy who looked like you."

"No. What about him?"

"He was drowned about three days ago."

Anderson looks at her, afraid for a moment she suspects something. But there is no sign of special knowledge in her face. She is obviously just mentioning the news item as something of passing interest.

"That's too bad," Anderson says.

"Why do you say that?"

From her sudden question, Anderson realizes it is not the sort of thing Peterson would have said, but he doesn't see any way out of it. "It's always too bad when people die that young," he comments lamely.

"Depends on who they are." She looks up at him again, but focuses now more on his jawline than his eyes. "I like you without the beard."

"Thanks."

"Call me sometime." She gives him a little pat, then turns back toward the front hall, apparently looking for the person she came with.

Anderson steps past her and out the front door. He notices the freshness of the night air. There was hardly anyone smoking at the party, but it occurs to him that a crowd that size still uses up lots of oxygen.

Anderson is relieved to be out of the Lundgrens' house. But he also has a sense of accomplishment. He feels that he is finally getting control of things, that he is handling these people from Peterson's circle brilliantly.

He is so pleased with himself that he barely notices the motorcycle starting up down the block.

C H A P T E R 1 3

With a bounce in his step, Anderson walks down the slate walkway leading from the Lundgrens' front door to the street. It is not completely dark yet. The sky is still a pale blue and reflects enough light to make all the features of the landscape clear. Most of the street lamps are on, but at this point in the evening their light is not yet necessary.

The Lundgren place overlooks the Mississippi River with only the roadway and a narrow strip of parklands in between. But the late summer foliage is still so thick, the river itself is not visible from Anderson's vantage point.

Across the road is a narrow stretch of green lawn with a concrete sidewalk and an asphalt bicycle path running through it. Beyond this lawn are the trees and sumac that mark the beginning of the steep drop to the river.

Anderson crosses the road and turns left along the river, heading upstream in the general direction of Peterson's apartment. For most of the day, he has been immersed in the role of Peterson. But as he walks along in the cool evening air, Peterson's world suddenly seems to fade away.

When Anderson was a child, his mother had once taken him for a walk along this riverside parkway. He remembers her warning him to stay out of the woods, because the steep muddy banks occasionally give way to sheer rocky cliffs. She warned him, too, about the vagrants who live down on the river flats. They sometimes do bad things to children, she said. Anderson had no idea what these bad things could be, but he imagined the vagrants throwing children in the water and hurling stones at them while they drowned.

It feels good to Anderson to be moving outdoors. He

stretches his legs and walks with long strides. Periodic gaps in the vegetation allow glimpses of the opposite bank and the water far below.

Stretching across the river a few blocks ahead is the Franklin Avenue Bridge, perhaps the most spectacular of the many spans across the upper Mississippi. Three gigantic arches of concrete support the roadway that runs from high on one bank directly across the valley to the same level of the other bank. The middle arch is so big, it vaults the entire waterway. A navigation light, marking its apex, is suspended beneath the bridge by a metal rigging. The glass bulb already glows red, despite its not yet being dark.

Anderson walks up the long, gentle ramp to Franklin Avenue, crosses the street, and then heads across the bridge on the upstream side. There are four lanes of traffic on the roadway across the bridge, with a wide sidewalk on either side. A concrete barrier runs along the outside edge of the sidewalk, reaching almost to knee height. On its top is a double railing, consisting of two fat, bluish gray pipes. Anderson runs his hand over the railing as he strolls along, enjoying its pleasant, grainy texture.

The large spaces between the railings offer spectacular views of the river and its tree lined banks. Upstream a considerable distance from the Franklin Avenue Bridge is a lower bridge for the interstate highway. Farther upstream, visible under this bridge, is the paddle wheel steamer the University of Minnesota uses as a showboat. Some of the university buildings can be seen high on the bank above it. Beyond the showboat's moorage, the river disappears in a short S-curve.

By leaning his head out past the railing, Anderson can look almost straight down. Far below, he sees a pair of barges, pushed by a tugboat. Nearer the bank is a rowing team from the university, out for an evening practice. The vertical drop makes Anderson shiver. He is suddenly aware there is nothing beneath the massive concrete roadway but open space.

In the fading light, the street lamps on either side of the bridge look beautiful to him. They are mounted on slender octagonal posts that arch high over the roadway. These graceful posts, in turn, rest on concrete pedestals that jut out beyond the railings of the sidewalks every sixty feet or so. Against the twilight sky, they appear more decorative than functional.

Anderson is just past the midpoint of the bridge, enjoying the views, when he hears the sound of a motorcycle coming up behind him. It shifts gears, revs its engine, and accelerates. Something about the sound is odd, but Anderson can't think what it is. Then he realizes that, judging from the direction of the noise, the motorcycle is driving in the wrong place. Anderson is walking on the left side of the bridge. The traffic coming toward him from behind should be on the other side, well off to his right. But this motorcycle sound is coming from the near side, directly in back of him.

Anderson turns. The motorcyclist is wearing black leathers and a helmet with a tinted visor. The visor is down. Anderson recognizes the figure as the same one he fought in the burning house, the same one who caused the death of his friends. This time, the faceless figure is riding straight at him, swinging a pipe.

Anderson dives forward. He can't fall fast enough. He senses the heavy pipe swishing down at him, grazing his back. Then he is catching himself with his hands, hugging the gritty pavement. He hears the motorcycle, now in front of him. He realizes it is past, that the pipe has missed him.

He scrambles to his feet, lifting his head in time to see the motorcycle slowing down at the far end of the bridge. The helmeted figure is turning his machine around for another pass. He throws his body back, yanking on the handlebars, bucking the front wheel up onto the curb. Then he leans forward, hips in the air, as the back wheel follows.

Anderson hears the engine gunning. The bike comes back toward him, this time on the sidewalk. Anderson looks frantically around. There is no place here to escape the swinging pipe. He feels horribly exposed.

He runs back twenty feet or so to one of the places where a concrete lamppost support protrudes beyond the railing. Scrambling over the railing, he grabs the octagonal post. Then, pivoting around it, he crouches down and leans back, away from the bridge. This leaves his hands around the post and his feet wedged against its base. His body extends out into space, high over the distant water.

Looking back toward the motorcycle, he sees the pipe swinging outward and downward in the biker's hand. He slips his own hands downward at the last moment and hears the pipe clang against the steel post, barely missing his fingers.

Pulling himself back upright, Anderson watches the motorcycle thirty-five yards or so down the bridge, slowing for another turn. He looks desperately for somewhere to run, realizing how totally vulnerable he still is. There seems to be no cover, nothing to hide behind. Then Anderson spots a metal apparatus of some kind outside the railing, back in the very middle of the bridge. It's the lighting rig he had noticed earlier!

He swings back around the lamppost, plants his hand on the railing, and vaults over it. This lands him back on the sidewalk. There is an ominous roar in the distance. He turns and sees the motorcycle coming toward him again. He sprints down the sidewalk, heading toward the motorcycle—but also toward the lighting rig.

For a moment Anderson thinks he will not be fast enough, that the motorcycle will beat him to the midpoint of the bridge. Then he spots the heavy seam in the pavement and realizes he is there.

He climbs over the railing and crouches down, holding on with one hand, while groping for the lighting rig with the other. A flat metal bracket about ten inches wide extends downward more than a dozen feet. Jutting out from it are short struts that support a metal rod, running downward in front of the bracket. Anderson leans out into space for a better look. A dozen feet below him, the metal rod connects to an additional pipe, supporting the navigation light.

Anderson gets his feet on either side of the metal rod. Then, as fast as he can, he lowers himself down over the side of the bridge, until he can grab the top of the rod with his hands. Once he has a firm hold, he lets his feet swing back against the flat metal bracket. He pushes himself away from the bracket with his feet, while pulling himself toward it by his grip on the rod. This gives him enough traction to control his descent.

Up on the bridge, he hears the motorcycle skid to a halt, its engine suddenly silent. Anderson tries to climb downward faster, but his dress shoes are too slippery. For a moment, he clings precariously to the vertical rod, while his feet slide uncontrollably over the bracket's surface. Then, just as he is about to be dangling by his hands, his feet hit another set of struts. Wedging his shoes against these, he is once more able to lower the top part of his body.

As his torso approaches the level of his feet, he is forced to move his feet below the struts. But this time, he pushes his body farther out from the bridge, to get better traction. He is now leaning far back into space, with nothing underneath him, except the river, a terrifying distance below.

Overhead, he hears the scrape of metal against concrete. He lifts his eyes to see the helmeted figure leaning over the railing. Anderson is now below the level of the roadway. But he knows this is not far enough. Struggling to maintain his grip on the lighting rig, he eases himself down farther.

Leather creaks above him. Glancing up, Anderson sees only a silhouetted shoulder. Then the pipe on a long, leathered arm swinging through the air. It misses his head and body, but clangs against a metal strut. This sends a shock wave reverberating through the whole framework, jolting Anderson's arms and shoulders, as though he had struck the blow himself.

A second blow comes whistling over his head, glancing lightly against the rigging. It doesn't produce the shock wave the first blow did. But it is lower and frighteningly close.

Seeing that Anderson is out of reach, the biker draws back and disappears from sight. But Anderson knows this is only to get into a better position. The attack is far from over.

Anderson struggles to climb lower. He is now several feet below the underside of the roadway. This portion of the lighting rig is not bolted directly to the concrete, but hangs in space, several yards out from the giant concrete arch that supports the roadway from underneath.

Anderson looks frantically about for something further to climb on. He spots a set of long metal braces running horizontally from the flat metal bracket to the side of the concrete arch. One pair is at the level of his head, the other near his feet. They angle off in each direction, so as to form a huge triangle that would keep the lighting rig stable in heavy winds.

If he could get his arms around one of the upper braces, he

would be able to rest his feet on the brace that runs parallel to it a few feet below. This would enable him to move along the metal braces and to retreat under the bridge.

Beneath the bridge, where the braces are fastened to the giant arch, Anderson sees a possible refuge. Instead of resting directly on the arch, the roadway is supported by massive concrete crossbeams. This leaves a considerable space between the arch itself and the roadway above. If Anderson could climb from the metal braces onto the arch, he would be in a position to wait out his attacker indefinitely.

Anderson begins to ease himself over toward one of the braces. But before he can get to it, the faceless figure reappears above him. The attacker is now bent over, almost prone, reaching between the concrete barrier and the lowest railing. The pipe whistles back and forth just above Anderson's head, getting closer with each swing. Anderson realizes he won't make it to the parallel braces if the pipe comes any nearer.

The menacing pipe is slightly to his right, so Anderson moves left. He reaches out toward the parallel braces with his left arm and leg. As he does this, he props his right foot against a bolt end and grips the vertical rod tightly in his right hand. He pivots in the direction he is reaching, swinging his forearm around to brace it against the metal bracket. The move is instinctive.

But disastrous. Anderson has neglected to consider the burn on his right forearm. As the blistered flesh connects with the metal surface, the unexpected pain sends his muscles into a short, reflexive spasm. This loosens his grip at the very moment when he needs it most. The metal rod slides from his hand. His body falls back. His foot slips sideways off the bolt end.

Suddenly, the lighting rig is beyond his reach. There is only a vast open space around him. Anderson is falling.

He has a curious sensation of being out in the air. He realizes once again how high he is above the water. He has plenty of time to feel himself dropping, to watch the water below gradually growing closer.

He pumps at the air with his arms, trying to remain upright as he falls. He struggles to keep his legs underneath him and to bring his feet together. He has some vague idea that if his feet break the water first, he will have a better chance of surviving.

Then, all at once, he seems to be falling faster. The water below is rushing up to meet him. He has run out of time. Run out of everything.

The impact with the water's surface crumples his legs and slams him in the groin. It pounds him in the diaphragm, pushing the air from his chest. It yanks his arms upward. It punches his head from beneath his chin and behind his neck. It compresses him and stretches him at the same time.

Plunging downward through the water, Anderson feels as though huge rollers are wringing him from the sides. But wringing the water into him, not out of him. It shoots up his nose and is forced into his mouth. It blasts through his clothes and assaults his eyes and ears.

His eyes feel blinded with watery light. His ears deafened with watery noise. He is in a swirl of bubbles, but they are hard, rather than soft. His arms feel pulled from their sockets. He is buffeted and squeezed. He feels the precious air escaping from his mouth.

His momentum carries him to the bottom, where his feet plunge into the mud. The prolonged crash he has been hearing is replaced by a numbing silence. It is as though he has already lost consciousness or gone deaf. But he can still tell he is sinking in the murk, and he can still register the water's coldness.

He feels the current sending him into a slow cartwheel. The top of his body is tilted sideways, until it is completely horizontal. His feet are pried out of the mud. His legs are picked up and slowly thrown over his head.

He tumbles like a piece of wet debris. A cloud of silt surrounds him. He no longer has any notion of which way is up toward the air, and which way down toward the riverbed. Everywhere around him, there seems to be nothing but mud. He can smell it, taste it, feel it in his teeth. The mud is his comforter. There is no other refuge.

It is only a kind of half-conscious reflex that brings him back to the surface before his lungs have drawn in the turbid water. He doesn't even realize he is there until he hears his own coughing and gasping. It is as though he is listening to himself and watching himself from a great distance. Perhaps, from the bottom of the river.

Then, gradually, his consciousness seems to rejoin his body. He sees his surroundings from the vantage point of his own eyes. He realizes he is bobbing at the surface of the water and that he is being swept off downstream.

For a few minutes, he drifts along in a daze, stunned and numb. He has all he can do to keep his head above water. It is difficult to move any part of his body. He feels as though his arms are tied behind him. His face is periodically turned beneath the surface.

There is a moment when he can't get the air he needs, when he feels as though he is drowning all over again. Somehow he finds the strength to kick. His head emerges, but he still feels smothered.

He discovers that his arms really are tied behind him. The jacket he was wearing has slid off his shoulders and partway down his arms. It is turned almost inside out. But it is still caught around his elbows and forearms.

He gets the cuff of his left jacket sleeve in his right hand. With tremendous exertion, pulling and twisting, he manages to wrench his arm free. Then he brings the jacket around in front of him. Heavy with water, it threatens to drag him under. His burn hurts him, even in the water, as he struggles to free his right forearm. But finally, as he turns and sinks, the jacket comes loose and falls away.

Anderson notices that his feet feel different from each other. He reaches down and discovers he is still wearing one shoe. The other shoe must have stuck in the river bottom. Without bothering to untie it, he pries the shoe off with his hand.

Now that he is free of the shoe and jacket, swimming becomes somewhat easier. Without really thinking about it, Anderson begins to stroke toward shore. But he makes little progress. The swirling waters make it hard to keep swimming in the same direction. The current of the river sweeps him back toward midstream.

It is hard for Anderson to keep his eyes open. His arms and legs are growing increasingly numb. The sky is growing increasingly dark.

As he begins to abandon all efforts, he hears a voice. It is calling out to someone. Gradually, Anderson realizes it is aimed in his direction. It is calling out to 'Peterson.' Calling out to him.

He swims toward the voice. It seems important to reach it, but he is afraid he will be swept on by. He begins to exert himself harder, struggling against the water, battling the cold currents pulling him along.

The voice comes nearer, grows louder. It shouts encouragement. The encouragement of a cheerleader from a swim meet long ago. The encouragement of a coach. The encouragement of a friend. It tells him he can do it, that he has the strength, that he is almost there.

He strokes harder, longer, deeper. His hand hits sand, then his arm and elbow, then his chest and face. He is on a sandbar, run aground, beached.

He lies there, clinging to the shore. His eyes are closed. He wants to put his head down and go to sleep. But the voice still urges him on. He begins to crawl forward. Then hands are helping him. Gentle hands, but firm.

Anderson moves along on his hands and knees. He feels himself being part guided, part lifted, out of the water. The sandbar turns into a narrow beach. At first, there are clay and weeds, mixed with the coarse sand. Then the surface becomes rougher. It is covered with smooth stones, driftwood, and occasional bits of debris. Anderson smells the stink of dead fish.

His arm is being pulled over a friendly shoulder. He is on his feet now, still scrambling with his hands, but almost walking. He makes his way through tree sized pieces of driftwood, scattered along the high water mark. Beyond them is the remains of a long dead campfire. The association of the charred logs with heat makes him aware of how cold he is.

His companion helps him over a low dune that separates the beach from some woods beyond. Anderson is shivering too violently to walk steadily. Twice, he falls and has to be helped up again. The ground changes abruptly as they leave the open sand and begin moving between the trees and bushes. His wet, stockinged feet are poked and stabbed by the twigs and dead branches that snap explosively underfoot.

Then, a short way into the woods, the ground becomes softer. It is a dirt road, with patches of mud in the low spots. To Anderson's feet, it feels like a caress. His rescuer leads him along it, past places where the road has almost grown over. In the shadow of the trees, it is now almost completely dark.

All at once, his rescuer stops. Anderson leans sideways against a warm metal surface. He hears a car door open and realizes he is propped against the hood. Then he feels himself being helped inside. He slumps in the seat, shaking. His rescuer tilts the seat back as far as it will go, then throws a raincoat over him. Car doors slam, and the engine starts. A current of warm air from the car heater begins blowing across him.

In the closed space of the car, Anderson recognizes a scent he has smelled before. The warm air begins to revive him. He opens his eyes, looks over, and recognizes his rescuer as Shannon.

She turns sideways to see how he is doing. Noticing his confused expression, she reaches over and touches his cheek reassuringly.

He smiles weakly in response, then curls sideways, closes his eyes, and lets go of everything. At first, his body shakes more than ever, but Anderson no longer struggles against it. A few moments later, he begins to relax.

As he lies there, almost unconscious, he feels the car bouncing along the dirt road. After a short distance, the vehicle reaches a paved surface. Then it climbs sharply and swings around a hairpin turn, before reaching a level street with sounds of traffic.

Riding beside her, Anderson feels a rush of gratitude toward this woman who has come to his aid. But he is puzzled that she should appear so opportunely.

When he opens his eyes again, they are on a well-lit city street. At first, Anderson just lies there, observing Shannon drive. He studies the expert way she uses the manual shift, caressing it in her hand between gear changes. Her dress has been badly ripped during her efforts to rescue him, and it has slid most of the way up her thighs. He watches in fascination as the muscles of her legs tighten and relax, pumping the clutch and brakes.

She swings her gaze sideways and catches him staring at her legs. "You seem to be reviving," she comments wryly.

It takes him a few seconds to find the energy to speak.

"Thank you for rescuing me," he says finally. "I might have drowned without you."

"I don't know about that, but you're welcome."

He is comforted by the sound of her voice, but has to ask her about what's troubling him. "There's something I don't understand."

"Yes?"

"What were you doing there?"

She smiles at him before replying. "I was feeling amorous. I saw you leaving the party alone. So I followed you."

"Where were you? I didn't see you."

"I was half a block behind you in my car. I was going to offer you a ride. But before I could get into a position to do it, you were attacked."

"Did you see who did it?"

"I couldn't see the face."

"Did you see any other signs of who it might have been?"

She shakes her head. "It looked like a member of a motorcycle gang." She falls silent for a moment, apparently thinking it over. "The whole attack seemed senseless, the way he went about it. It must have been a drug addict. Or some kind of maniac, out for kicks."

"I suppose it must have been," Anderson agrees. It seems useless to attempt an explanation.

"I was afraid the fall from the bridge would kill you. It's so high. Then I saw you downstream, bobbing on the surface. I think I started crying. I was so relieved you were still alive."

"I almost wasn't," Anderson says. He braces himself as Shannon brakes for a stoplight. "What happened to the character on the motorcycle?"

"He just roared away. By that time, I had pulled over and gotten out. I tried to call down to you. But you were too far away to hear me."

"It wouldn't have mattered. I'm not sure I was even conscious at that point."

"You seemed to be swimming, but the current was sweeping you downstream. I knew I'd have to hurry to pull you out. I think I set a speed record for that stretch of the West River Parkway."

"How did you know where to intercept me?"

"Oh, that beach with the sandbar is just a few blocks from where I grew up. The river makes a slight bend at that point. I used to play there as a child."

The car goes over a pothole. Anderson can't help groaning.

"Hang on," Shannon says. "We're almost there."

Anderson looks out the window. He sees a huge complex of brick buildings and a sign that says something about 'Outpatients.' "Where are you taking me?"

"To the hospital, of course."

Anderson can't conceal his horror. "I can't go there."

"But you're hurt."

"If you take me to the hospital, I'll have to spend half the night being questioned by the police. I'll recover faster if I can just get some rest at home."

"What if you have internal injuries?"

"If I develop any symptoms of internal injuries, then you can take me back to the hospital. Or they can send an ambulance."

"Okay. If you're sure that's what you want."

Shannon drives past the Metropolitan Medical Center, swings around the Metrodome, and cuts over to Washington Avenue, a couple blocks from the Whitney Hotel. The nearby buildings are dark and traffic sparse. From there, it's just a short drive up to Hennepin Avenue and across the bridge over Nicollet Island to Peterson's apartment building.

Shannon stops in front of the building's entrance and climbs out. She walks around and opens the door on Anderson's side.

He swings his legs around, but is still stiff and weak. It is only with difficulty that he can even lean forward.

She drapes the raincoat around his shoulders, then takes hold of his arm to help him up. It is the one with the burn.

Anderson recoils in pain. "Higher up," he gasps. "Hold it higher up."

She changes her grip on his arm and hoists it over her neck, so she can support him in a standing position. Reaching back with her foot, she kicks the car door closed.

By this time, the doorman has seen them and hurried out to help. "Mr. Peterson!" he exclaims. "Are you all right?"

"I'm fine," Anderson assures him.

The doorman looks touchingly upset. "Here, let me give you

a hand." He takes Anderson's left arm and puts it over his shoulder. "You're soaking wet."

"I had a little accident, that's all. I was fooling around by the river after a few drinks, and I fell in."

"Do you want me to call a doctor?"

"No, I'll be fine. I'm just cold and stiff."

With Anderson's arms hooked over their necks and shoulders, Shannon and the doorman walk him into the building. The doorman holds the front door for them with his free arm and leg. Then, inside, he assumes more of the burden. He is solidly muscular and about the same size as Anderson, so it is not difficult for him.

When they get to the door of Peterson's apartment, Anderson takes his right arm off Shannon's neck and digs in his pocket. The trouser pocket is twisted sideways inside his trousers, but the keys and wallet are still there. The wallet is a soggy lump. Grimacing at the effort, Anderson extracts the key and opens the door.

Shannon gropes for the light switch and gets the entry hall lamps to go on. Then she turns to the doorman. "Thank you. I can take him from here."

"Okay," the doorman says, letting Anderson lean against her. "But give me a call, if you need any more help."

She pulls Anderson clear, so the doorman can close the door, then helps him farther into the entry hall. "Remind me the way to the master bathroom," she says. "You know, the one with the amazing shower."

"It's through the living room, then down the hallway."

She leads him across to the living room door, helping him balance with a hand around his hip. "Where's the light switch?" she asks.

Anderson reaches for it himself. Numerous lamps go on in the space beyond, as though the switch has called the room into being.

With Shannon still supporting Anderson by the shoulder, the two of them continue across the end of the living room and down the central hallway. Shannon finds the switch that illuminates the hallway without having to ask. But near the end of it, she hesitates again. "Which way now?"

"It's to the left, through the exercise room and the Jacuzzi room."

Anderson feels able, by this point, to walk by himself, but he is enjoying the physical contact with Shannon too much to mention the fact.

When they reach the bathroom, they pause for a moment while she kicks off her high heels and helps him shed the raincoat. Anderson takes the wallet and keys from his pocket and places them on the counter beside the sinks. Then Shannon takes him around the tiled partition into Peterson's large shower.

Inside the shower, she lowers him onto the soft plastic webbing of the chaise longue. Stepping back toward the wall, she pulls on the control that turns on the water. A moment later, Anderson is deluged with the warm spray. He realizes, as he feels it soaking through his clothes, why Shannon has brought him directly here. The hot pulsing water is exactly what he needs.

"How do you adjust this thing?" she asks.

Suddenly, Anderson knows he has to concentrate. To remain convincing as Peterson, he must get these things right. "You tilt the lever on the wall to move the center of the spray."

Almost as soon as he has said it, he feels the jets of water aiming more directly at the spot where he is sitting. Then the streams fall back slightly, creating a space around his upper body that is no longer under bombardment.

"You seem to have mastered it," he says.

"It's wonderful," she replies. She steps through the streams into the relatively clear area around him. "You've got to get rid of these clothes, though." She reaches down, undoes his tie, and pulls it off. Then she bends over, unbuckles his belt, and helps him out of his trousers.

Straightening up again, she steps back to dodge some of the arcs of water that splash against the chaise longue. Anderson looks appreciatively across at her. The light in the shower room is subdued, but much brighter than in Shannon's car. Anderson can see now that her elegant dress has practically been destroyed. It is smeared with mud and torn most of the way up her leg. The netted ruffle at the hemline has been pulled loose too.

Shannon reaches behind and pulls at a short zipper. This loosens the dress in the middle. Then she bends forward, crossing her arms, and takes the hem in her hands. She pulls the dress up and over her head, turning it inside out in the process. Slipping the last of the dress off her wrists, she tosses it aside.

Underneath, she is wearing no slip or underpants. But there are flesh colored pads wedged under each breast. They are shaped something like oversized orange slices and seem to float there defying gravity.

She notices him staring at them and laughs. "I need something to hold my breasts in place, if I'm going to wear an outfit like that. It's a great style for showing off. But I think it was designed for women with smaller bosoms. Or implants."

She lifts a breast with one hand and pulls the pad off with the other. It makes a gentle tearing noise, indicating it was being held in place with an adhesive. Then she repeats the process with the other one. With the pads off, her breasts do not look significantly smaller or lower. But they do jiggle and sway more.

Anderson decides they are much sexier in their uncontrolled condition. Gazing at Shannon through the splashing water and rising steam, he notices that the image is like some of the Rococo engravings he was looking at that afternoon. "You look like Venus Amid the Sea Mists," he comments.

She throws him a kiss. "Hold that thought," she says, and slips out of the room.

While she is gone, Anderson finds it hard to think of anything other than the contours of her body and the sparkle of her eyes.

After a couple of minutes, she returns with a bottle of cognac and a soft dish-towel. She is shivering and stands for a moment under the spray to get warm. But she is careful to keep the towel dry. "That's the most astonishing wine cellar I've ever seen."

"I'm very proud of it," Anderson says.

She uncorks the cognac and hands the bottle to Anderson. He expects the liquid to be a shock to his mouth and throat, but it goes down easily. After several swallows, he hands the bottle back to Shannon.

Crouching beside him, she wets part of the towel with the cognac, then uses it to wipe the scrapes on Anderson's face.

When she is finished with those, she unbuttons his cuffs and the front of his shirt. "Show me where it hurts," she says, sliding it off his shoulders.

Anderson sits up and helps her remove the shirt from his arms and back. He hears her gasp aloud when she sees his bruises and burn.

"How did you get those?" she asks in a horrified tone.

Anderson doesn't see any way to avoid acknowledging it. "That maniac has tried before," he says. Anderson can tell from her eyes that Shannon is deeply troubled by this revelation. But she refrains, for the moment, from asking the obvious questions.

"Here, let me look at that," she says, reaching for his injured arm. She rests the burned part across her leg. The gauze bandage has come loose and slipped up around Anderson's elbow. It is soaking wet and connected only by one remaining strip of tape. Where the bandage used to be, the pieces of skin on top have turned a dark brown color and are coming loose. Underneath, the flesh is a raw pink. Exposed once again to the air, it seems to sizzle with heat.

Shannon removes the soggy gauze. Then she begins cleaning the burned area, blotting away the streaks of dirt and picking off the loose bits of skin. She pauses occasionally to moisten the dish towel with more cognac. Her movements are deft and professional.

"Where did you learn how to do that?"

"I don't know. From my mamma, I guess."

She positions his arm in space, keeping it clear of the spray. "Hold it like that for a moment." She stands up, turning away. "I hope you have a well stocked medicine cabinet." She vanishes again in the mist.

A few seconds later, she is back with the burn ointment. She crouches down again and takes his arm in her lap. Biting her lips in concentration, she spreads the ointment rapidly across the burn.

As she works, Anderson admires the way her eyebrows arch over her stunning brown eyes, the way her breasts hang forward in graceful curves, the way her stomach is slightly furrowed in a vertical line. "Your mamma must have been a beautiful woman," he comments.

Shannon's lips relax at the memory. "I suppose she did look pretty good. She always had lots of boyfriends."

"What happened to her?"

"Oh, she lives in Stillwater now. She takes good care of herself. She probably still has lots of boyfriends."

Shannon covers the ointment with gauze. Then she begins covering the gauze loosely with strips of adhesive bandage, using the dispenser edge to tear them off.

"What about your father?" Anderson asks.

"I never knew him. He was the second of my mamma's three husbands. After three divorces, she stopped marrying them."

Anderson tries to imagine Shannon as a little girl. "Was that hard on you?"

"No. Boyfriends are much better to have around than fathers."

"Why?"

"They're nicer. They were always bringing us presents and taking us out to dinner. Especially, when they were happy." Shannon smiles to herself. "Mamma was good at making them happy."

"Why were there so many of them?"

"Mamma got restless, I suppose. And she had terrible taste in men. She was always attracted to guys without any money or power."

"And you?"

"I don't have any problems that way."

Shannon puts aside the bandage dispenser and smoothes down the last end. No part of the gauze is now left exposed.

Anderson inspects her work. "That looks almost waterproof."

"Not really. But we're trying to protect it from the air, so there's no point in leaving openings for it to breathe." Shannon stands up. "Now let me see your bruises," she says.

Anderson sits up and puts his legs over the other side of the chaise longue, so that his back is turned toward her.

Shannon sits down beside him, facing the opposite direction. She finds a clean area on the dish towel and moistens it with cognac. Then she begins cleaning the bruises and scrapes on Anderson's back.

When she gets to the place where his skin was split by the fire poker, Anderson winces at the sting of the alcohol.

"Here, let me kiss it better," she says. She bends over and puts her mouth on the bruise, first licking, then gently sucking at it. Slowly, she moves the length of it, causing him a mixture of pain and arousal. When she is done with that bruise, she moves on to the others on his back, doing the same thing. He shivers noticeably as she works her way along the bruises on his tailbone. It is not a shiver that comes from being cold.

"Does that help?" she asks.

"I don't know," he says, "but I like it."

She reaches around and puts a hand on his chest. With a gentle pressure, she pushes him back into a reclining position. Then she leans over him and applies her mouth to the bruises on his chest and side.

As she does this, Anderson reaches down and strokes her breast, first encompassing as much of it as he can in the wide circle of his fingertips, then drawing his fingertips slowly together, so that they meet at her nipple.

Shannon moans softly in response. She moves her mouth across his chest until she is sucking his nipple, while he continues to stroke hers.

After doing this for many long seconds, she gets up and fetches a tube of 'body shampoo' from a rack on the wall. She squeezes some of the thick gel onto Anderson's chest. It feels cold as it splatters across his skin.

She drops the tube on the floor, then sits down again beside him and begins working the gel into a lather. "What was *your* childhood like?" she asks.

"Pretty normal, I guess. Except that I spent a lot of time reading. I needed books, books full of information and concepts, as much as other people need food."

Hearing himself say it, Anderson is sure it is true. He notices, with some surprise, that there are many things about Peterson he does not need to be told.

Shannon looks thoughtful. "That fits with something I've heard people say about you."

"What is that?"

"They say you love the money, the power, and all the other benefits you've acquired by being able to answer difficult questions; but most of all—more than any of these things—they say you love the questions."

Anderson smiles. He is sure that is true too.

He also realizes there is an opportunity here. Even if Shannon didn't know Peterson very well, she might have heard other things about Peterson that would help complete his picture of Peterson's personality. "Have you heard any other comments about me, ones that sounded especially interesting or insightful?"

Shannon spreads the lather lower across Anderson's stomach and onto his thighs. "I've heard that you regard yourself as superior to conventional morality, that you have no moral inhibitions."

"What do you think about that?"

"I think it's very sexy." She begins working her hand between his legs, using the foam as a lubricant.

"What else do they say about me?"

"They say that you really are some kind of superman. But obviously, you can't be."

"Why not?"

"If you really were a superman, you wouldn't be insecure enough to be asking these questions." She gives him a dimpled smile, delighted at having scored a point, then cups him in her hand and gives him a gentle squeeze. "Don't worry, that touch of vulnerability makes you even sexier."

"I think you need a good scrubbing yourself," Anderson says. He picks the tube of body shampoo off the floor beside him and squeezes a large dollop onto his hand. Then he reaches out and begins spreading it over her breasts.

"Ooh, that *is* cold," she says. But she leans toward him, so that he can reach her better. After a few moments, she begins to tremble in response to his touch.

"I dreamed about you a couple of nights ago," Anderson says.

Shannon giggles. "Was it a wet dream?"

"Not as wet as this."

"Was I good?"

"You were trying to save me from drowning. I was being

smothered in pine needles, and I felt your hands reaching out to me. Only, I didn't recognize you at the time."

Shannon's eyelids are now lowered. She seems to be concentrating on the sensation of his fingers as they gently fondle her smooth, slippery skin. She breathes through her mouth.

"I dreamed about you, too," she says, without opening her eyes.

"What were we doing?"

"We were vacationing together at a tropical resort. It was beautiful. There were palm trees and flowering bushes. Everybody was rich, and everyone loved them."

"Like the people at the party tonight?"

"Oh yes, they were all there."

"Did I love them too?"

"You mostly loved the bimbos down on the beach." Her eyes open with a look of amusement. She gets up to rinse off.

Anderson follows. The effort of standing is hard for him. But he doesn't want to lose contact with her body.

She turns away from him, so that her breasts are pointing toward the spray, letting the water cascade over them.

He steps toward her and embraces her from behind.

She presses backward against him, resting her round bottom against his thighs and tilting it from side to side.

He runs his hands across her neck, over her breasts, and down her stomach.

"That's what you kept doing in my dream. To the bimbos in their bikinis. To all the Minnesota bimbos. Who wanted to get screwed."

She turns and bends over, resting her arms on the back of the chaise longue.

"Come on, do it now. Screw me. Screw me the way you'd screw the bimbos."

Anderson hesitates.

Shannon's hips lift slightly as she flexes the muscles in her legs. "Screw me the way you'd screw that bimbo from Bemidji."

Anderson feels a wave of uncontrollable desire. He leans forward and eases himself into her. He cups her breasts from behind. He looks down over her shoulder at the front of her exquisitely shaped legs.

"Yes. Do it. Screw me."

They begin to move rhythmically in the spray. The water splashes across them. Every sensation seems to reinforce the sensual effect. Anderson feels as though he is inside one of the erotic, Rococo engravings. Not just inside it as a character, but inside the very textures and folds of the surfaces it portrays.

After a few minutes, Shannon begins forcing the pace. Her movements get shorter, harder, faster. She pounds her most delicate parts against him with a kind of frantic energy. She moans and cries out in so loud a voice, the sound of the spray seems to diminish almost into silence.

Anderson feels a wave of pleasure rolling out from inside of him. His body begins jerking spasmodically. The rush of the water, of his own body, and of Shannon's frenzied movements all become inseparable. Shannon's moans reach a crescendo.

Then, slowly, the movement, the sounds, the energy, all subside. Anderson steps back, separating their exhausted bodies. He staggers, grabbing the back of the chaise longue for balance, and grins sheepishly.

Shannon puts her arms around him and kisses his chest. They stand holding each other in the hot mist. Then she helps him out of the shower and throws a robe around him. She reaches back in and turns off the water.

Anderson sits on the counter between the sinks. Shannon examines herself in the mirror. They both smile at the wild tangle of her hair.

As Shannon shifts her attention to Anderson's face, her expression grows wistful. "I'm afraid I've got a special work assignment to prepare for tomorrow morning," she says.

"You can't go home now," Anderson tells her.

"Why not?"

"Your dress is too torn and dirty to put on."

"So?"

"What would you wear on the way back?"

Shannon laughs. "My raincoat and high heels."

She goes and picks them up from the floor. She puts her arms through the sleeves of the coat and steps into the shoes. Then she holds the sides of the coat out from her body and does a little bump and grind. With the dark coat behind her light skin, she looks far more naked than she did with nothing on.

As she does up the buttons, Anderson starts to protest, but she silences him by placing her fingertip against his mouth. "It won't be for long," she says. She reaches up and kisses him, firmly and thoroughly, pulling lightly on his lips as she draws away. "I'll make sure the door is locked. Don't take any risks, okay? I mean, don't go anyplace where a maniac could get at you."

"I'll be careful," Anderson assures her.

She gives him a broad smile, but her eyes are troubled. Then she leans forward and kisses him one more time before stepping out of the room.

Her presence is so strong, it's a few moments before Anderson realizes she is gone. He turns and stares at himself in the mirror. It looks strange to see himself there, wrapped in so luxurious a robe. Yet he feels relaxed and almost at home.

He hears a low beeping noise and sees a flashing light in the mirror. He turns and spots a telephone in the opposite wall. It's the same color as the tile on which it's mounted.

Anderson steps over and picks up the receiver, remembering to make his voice hoarse. "Hello," he says.

"It's you, isn't it?" The voice on the other end speaks in a muffled whisper.

Anderson's hand tightens around the receiver. The sound of the voice alone is enough to bring the tension back to his body. Is this a call Peterson would have been expecting? "What do you want?" he asks.

"I just wanted to compliment you on your swimming ability," the voice says. "And your diving—that was even more impressive."

"Who *is* this?" Anderson asks. From the whispering tone, he cannot even tell if the voice belongs to a man or a woman.

"There's nothing you can do, you know. You can't go to the police. You can't complain to anyone. You're fair game."

"What's this about?" Anderson asks, trying to sound reasonable. "If you're upset about something, I think we should meet and talk about it."

"We're past that now. Long past."

Anderson is desperate to find out something more, to hear anything at all that would help him deal with this. "If you would just explain—"

But he gets no further. There is a click, then silence on the other end.

Anderson hangs up the phone, his hands shaking. He tries to connect the whispering voice to one of the people he has met as Peterson, one of the people, presumably, at the Lundgrens' party. But there doesn't seem to be anything to go on.

He is now certain he understands why Peterson wanted to fake his own death. One of Peterson's 'clients' was apparently trying to kill him. The pressure of blackmail had presumably become too much. Perhaps the client was in a financial bind that could be alleviated by eliminating Peterson's 'fee.' Perhaps the client had developed too much resentment toward Peterson over the passing years. Perhaps Peterson had demanded sexual or other favors that someone had found intolerable.

Whatever the exact motive, Peterson obviously felt in danger from some source he could neither avoid nor neutralize. Hence, Peterson wanted to disappear in a way that would guarantee he was not pursued further. By appearing to die, Peterson would have prevented anyone from trying to track him down. By taking Anderson's place, he would have also been moving into a ready-made identity. In many ways, Peterson's scheme for faking his death must have seemed a perfect solution.

But Peterson didn't arrange his death entirely by himself. There had been other people helping him, other people who must have had some idea of what was going on. Would these accomplices have known additional details of his scheme? Details, for instance, that might reveal which client was trying to kill him? Details that would point to the person responsible for the deaths of Jack and June?

Anderson thinks once more of 'Brian,' the huge man who had actually abducted him. He thinks of Trudy, the co-ed with the innocent face, who had let herself be used as bait. He thinks especially of Gretchen, the girl with the heart melting smile, the one he had run into again at the university.

He checks the clock on the bathroom wall. After all that has happened to him, he is surprised to discover it is only 10:15. If Trudy and Gretchen had gone to their neighborhood bar that evening, they might still be there.

Battered and exhausted though he is, Anderson resolves to try tracking them down that very night.

Walking into the bar, Anderson grows tense. He realizes this is partly because the place once again looks the way it did the night he was kidnapped. There is no harsh daylight now to spoil the warm, congenial atmosphere. The rougher edges and dingier corners are all concealed by soft shadows. But Anderson's memories make this picturesque effect seem more sinister than the daytime one.

The table where Gretchen and Trudy had been sitting when Anderson met them is now occupied by three fraternity boys. They wear pale blue sweatshirts with the emblem of Phi Delta Theta. A dozen empty beer bottles litter the tabletop between them. The boys are flirting with two women in their thirties, sitting at another table a few feet away. The women look like underpaid secretaries, but they seem to be in control of the situation.

One of the women shifts her attention to Anderson as he strolls by, but he avoids meeting her eyes. A conversation with a friendly drinker is not what he needs right now. She opens her mouth as though she recognizes him and is about to speak, but then thinks better of it. After a puzzled moment, she turns back to the college kids.

Anderson thinks he may have seen her in this bar when he was here before. She probably notices that he looks familiar, but is thrown by the elegant clothes and the absence of a beard.

It occurs to Anderson that if *he* might have occasionally been mistaken for Peterson before this current nightmare began, Peterson might also have been mistaken for him. Their dress and habits would have been very different, but Peterson must have occasionally crossed through Anderson's world. Does this mean that people tried to start fights with Peterson in the months after the television publicity? Was Peterson accused of murdering his grandfather by sentimental drunks? Despite all that has happened since, Anderson finds the idea funny and smiles to himself.

A stylish young man thinks the smile is meant for him and beams back. But Anderson disappoints him by continuing his tour of the drinking areas.

Satisfied that Gretchen and Trudy are nowhere to be seen, Anderson makes his way back to the bar. The bartender he spoke to the day before is not on duty. But Anderson approaches another one. "Excuse me, have you seen Gretchen and Trudy tonight? I was supposed to meet them, but I'm terribly late."

"They're not here."

"I can see that. I just wanted to know if you'd noticed them earlier this evening."

"They were here a while ago, but they left."

"Any idea where they might have gone?"

The bartender folds his hands across his chest and looks blankly at Anderson. "Someplace other than here."

Anderson decides he is unlikely to get anywhere by becoming angry. He takes out a ten dollar bill and places it on the counter. The money is still soggy, but Anderson doesn't think the bartender will mind. "I really need to find them," Anderson says. "So I can apologize for being so late."

The corners of the bartender's mouth twitch slightly, but he gives no other sign of having seen the money. "I might have heard them mention a pizza."

Anderson turns his head toward the front door, trying to remember where the nearest pizza parlor would be. When he looks back, he notices the ten dollar bill is gone. "Which is the most likely place?"

"Take your pick. There are three joints within two blocks."

"Okay. Thanks."

Anderson leaves the bar and walks along the street to the pizza restaurants. He stops in front of each and studies the customers through the windows. The eating areas are not large, so there is little chance of his missing anyone as he peers inside. He sees no sign of Gretchen or Trudy.

Anderson feels discouraged. If the girls went to a pizza place farther away, there would be too many possibilities for him to check. He decides he will have to come back another night. Either that, or try to trace Gretchen through the archaeology department.

He wonders if that is really what she is studying. The archaeology department is housed in the university building he saw her go into. But passing it on the way to another class might have suggested the idea of archaeology to Gretchen, without its being her real specialty. Of course, if she was intentionally serving as bait, even her appearance on campus as a student could be a hoax.

Turning over the possibilities in his head, Anderson wanders on down the street. Despite the hour, there are quite a few students about.

It is Trudy he sees first. She is using chopsticks to lower a long, stringy piece of meat into her mouth. Her head is tilted back, and her chin makes little quivering movements as she catches the meat with her tongue. It's an irresistibly sexy action.

She is sitting in the window of a Vietnamese restaurant. Across the table from her is Gretchen. The girls are both wearing tight fitting jeans for the cooler evening. Trudy is in a blue chambray shirt with dramatically full sleeves. Gretchen wears a ribbed cotton turtleneck that highlights the contours of her chest.

The floor of the restaurant is three or four steps above street level, so the two girls look as though they are sitting in a framed picture. Anderson wonders what Peterson's lustful art dealer would call this style if it were a painting. 'Photo-Realism,' perhaps.

Near the top of the window, a sign reads "Late Night Take Out." The girls are positioned under this and a little to the side. Next to them is a huge ceramic planter filled with silk flowers. Below the planter is another sign with smaller lettering. It reads "Vietnamese Smorgasbord Every Sunday."

Anderson decides the girls are prettier than any models a Photo-Realist would choose. He climbs the steps to the door and enters the restaurant. Waving aside the waitress who comes to greet him, he goes over to the girls' table. Without waiting for an invitation or even a greeting, he sits down between them.

Trudy looks startled and starts to rise from her chair, looking for help. It is obvious she doesn't recognize him.

But Gretchen knows him at once. "Hey, it's the champion swimmer," she says, grinning. "The one who sometimes has strange men chasing him."

Trudy takes another look at Anderson and relaxes, dropping back into her seat. "The one who organized all those amazing practical jokes."

Gretchen nods. "The one who invented that remarkable cocktail."

Anderson looks intensely at each of them. "The one you almost got killed," he says.

Gretchen and Trudy stare at him a moment, then dissolve in laughter. "It's not *our* fault you drank that concoction so fast," Gretchen says.

Trudy tilts her head toward him, raising her eyebrows. "It was your own recipe, after all."

"What went into that cocktail, anyway?" Gretchen asks. "Aquavit?"

Anderson looks first at one, then at the other. "I don't know what went into your drinks, but mine had some kind of drug in it."

Trudy laughs again. "I know the feeling. It happens to me every New Year's Eve. It's usually the fifth drink of the evening."

"No," Anderson says firmly. "Mine really was drugged. Chloral hydrate or something."

Gretchen and Trudy look blank.

Anderson puts his hands on the table and leans forward. "Am I supposed to believe you don't know what I'm talking about?"

Gretchen turns to her companion. "What do you think, Trudy?"

"I don't know what he's talking about." Trudy digs in her bowl with her chopsticks and extracts a bundle of dripping noodles.

Gretchen turns back to Anderson. "Neither do I."

"How about your pal Brian? Have you seen him lately?" There's a hard edge to Anderson's voice.

"I haven't seen him," Trudy replies. "Have you, Gretchen?" She lowers her chin and tucks the noodles into her mouth.

Gretchen shakes her head, still facing Anderson. "Why should we see him? He was your friend, not ours."

She begins stirring through her food with her chopsticks, looking to see what might be buried underneath, then glancing over at Trudy's bowl. "We ordered completely different things," Gretchen explains, "but these two dishes look exactly the same."

"I'd never met him before that evening," Anderson says.

Gretchen looks up at him with a sudden frown. "What were you doing, then? Playing a part? Was that what you were doing on campus too?"

"I suppose I *was* playing a part that evening. But I wasn't the only one."

"Don't look at *us*," Trudy says. "We didn't pretend he was an old friend."

"But you knew him, didn't you? You knew him and pretended you didn't."

"We never met him until that evening," Gretchen says.

Anderson struggles to keep his voice casual. "You're sure? There wasn't some kind of prior relationship?"

Trudy's nose wrinkles in distaste. "He's not exactly our type."

"We just had a couple drinks with the man," Gretchen says. "We never saw him before. We never expected to see him again."

"So why were you acting so friendly?" Anderson studies Gretchen's face, then Trudy's. He senses some kind of tension in their eyes, but can't identify it.

"Maybe we were *feeling* friendly," Trudy says defiantly.

"Come on! Nobody acts that way toward someone they don't find attractive unless they've got a special reason."

"How do you know we didn't find him attractive?" Trudy asks.

"You just admitted as much!"

There's an awkward silence. Trudy and Gretchen exchange looks. Trudy pokes at her food with her chopsticks.

Gretchen stirs uneasily in her chair. "He paid us," she says.

Anderson stares at her. "He *paid* you?"

"Don't look so shocked!" Trudy says. "It wasn't as though we were being prostitutes or anything."

"He offered us fifty dollars apiece just to sit at his table and talk to him." Gretchen says it in a matter-of-fact voice, but avoids Anderson's eyes.

Trudy is less bothered. "He described it as a modeling job. He said no sex was involved. Not even any improper conversation."

"We could leave at any time, if we felt uncomfortable," Gretchen adds.

Trudy gestures up the street with her chopsticks. "The people in the bar know us, so we thought it would be okay."

"He just wanted us to look decorative and act sexy," Gretchen says.

"Did he say why?" Anderson asks.

"He said it was a kind of joke," Trudy answers. "To impress an old buddy of his."

Gretchen smiles. "You were the old buddy."

"We didn't accept his offer until he pointed you out," Trudy adds, obviously eager to please.

Anderson doesn't know whether to believe them. "Was there any special reason he mentioned for wanting to impress me?"

Gretchen looks at Anderson, her gaze once more unwavering. "He said you used to kid him about his lack of success with women."

"Even though," Trudy interjects, "he said *you* were the shy one."

"He told us," Gretchen continues, "that he wanted you to think, in the years since he'd last seen you, he'd acquired this amazing power over the opposite sex."

Trudy takes a chopstick in each hand and holds them apart. "He just wanted to show off a little."

"We went along with it as a kind of dare," Gretchen says.

Trudy smiles, putting her chopsticks together again. "He was very funny and charming."

"I'll bet he was," Anderson comments.

"He was!" Trudy insists.

Gretchen takes a sip of her tea. "It was actually a lot of fun, until you started feeling ill. Then he left to take you home. We didn't see him again after that."

Anderson decides to say it again, although he knows they

won't believe him. "He *didn't* take me home. He took me off to be killed."

This time the girls both stare at him. If they aren't ready to accept what he is saying, they at least realize he expects to be taken seriously.

"Why would Brian want to kill you?" Trudy asks. "I thought you said you didn't know him."

"I don't know why he did it. I'm trying to find out."

Gretchen puts her cup aside and leans back in her chair. "What do the police say?"

Anderson takes a deep breath. "I have reasons for not involving the police."

"What sort of reasons?" Trudy asks.

Anderson considers telling them, but he can't think where to begin. "It's too complicated to explain."

The waitress comes by with a fresh teapot. She refills the girls' cups and sets the pot on the table. Then she puts an empty cup in front of Anderson. "You like to order food now?" she asks.

"No, thank you," Anderson says.

Gretchen is inspecting him with narrowed eyes. "This is one of your practical jokes, isn't it?"

"I don't play practical jokes." As he says it, Anderson realizes how little reason they have to believe anything he says.

A wry smile begins to spread across Gretchen's face. "Brian got us to do something slightly outrageous by paying us. Now *you've* probably bet him that you can get us to do something even more outrageous by spinning us a story."

"Where is he now?" Trudy asks. "Waiting outside?"

"It's nothing like that."

"I don't think this joke is as funny as your other ones," Trudy says.

"This isn't a joke. I was kidnapped and nearly murdered."

Trudy frowns. "Then you should go to the police."

Gretchen puts her hand on the table to emphasize the point. "If this isn't serious enough to warrant involving the police, you shouldn't be making a fuss about it."

There is a moment's silence.

Then Trudy relaxes into a smile. "You probably just misunderstood Brian's efforts to help you."

Taking her cue from Trudy, Gretchen relaxes too. "You were pretty intoxicated, you know."

Anderson feels a wave of anger at the excuses they are making on his behalf. "What *is* this?" he demands. "Do you really think I've been imagining things?"

But his frustration only makes Gretchen act more sweetly 'reasonable.'

"If you're not playing a practical joke," she says, "then I think you've gotten a little too caught up in whatever game you *are* playing."

Trudy reaches forward and touches Anderson's hand with her fingertips. "You're not having some kind of drug reaction, are you?"

"You just need to relax a little," Gretchen continues in a soothing voice. "You know, get some perspective on things. You seem to be losing track of what's real."

Anderson looks from one to the other. He can't think of any arguments to convince them. Then he gets an idea. "Here, let me show you something."

He withdraws his hand from Trudy's, stands up, and takes off the sports coat he is wearing. He drapes it over the back of his chair.

The two girls push themselves back from the table, apparently afraid he might do something violent. "Better take it easy," Gretchen warns him.

Anderson moves carefully, so he won't frighten them into retreating further. He turns slowly around until he is facing away from them. Then he pulls his shirt out of his trousers. He lifts it halfway up his back, so the girls can see the split skin and the bruise left by the blow from the fire poker.

"Is that real enough for you?" Anderson asks in a soft voice. "That's part of what they did to me, when they were trying to kill me."

He lowers his shirt and turns back toward the girls. Then he tucks his shirt tail back in his trousers and sits down again. He unbuttons the cuff on his right sleeve and rolls it back. He puts his arm on the table, so the bandaged side is up. Using his fingernails at first, he gets the fingertips of his other hand under the lower end of the bandage and gives it a firm yank. It peels back, exposing the burned flesh underneath.

Once again he makes an effort to keep his voice gentle. "Do you think I'm imagining that? Or that I'd mutilate myself for a practical joke?"

Gretchen and Trudy stare at him, horrified. There is a long silence. "Okay, I was wrong," Gretchen says. "You're not making it up. You really *have* been hurt. Maybe you even had men chasing you. But *we* didn't have anything to do with it."

Anderson presses the bandage back into place. "You set me up for it," he says. "That man 'Brian' couldn't have gotten me out of there the way he did without your help."

Trudy draws her fists to her chest, one above the other. "We had no idea what he was up to!"

"Maybe not," Anderson says. "But you're still partly responsible."

"What do you want from us?" Gretchen asks.

"You could answer my questions, for one thing. I need to find out what this guy 'Brian' was up to, and why he picked you to help him."

Trudy's face goes slack, but her eyes are intense. "He picked us because we were in a party mood."

"He picked us because of the way Trudy was dressed."

"Gretchen—!"

"All right, it was because of the way *both* of us were dressed."

Trudy makes a face at Gretchen, then looks directly at Anderson. "He picked us because we were there."

"Are you really students? Theater and archaeology majors?"

"Yes," Trudy says.

"Of course," Gretchen affirms.

"We didn't say anything that wasn't true," Trudy continues, somewhat indignantly.

"You're sure you didn't have any previous contact with this fellow 'Brian'?

This time, it's Gretchen who looks steadily at Anderson. "We're sure."

Anderson sits back, intentionally reducing the pressure. "Did you two grow up around here?"

"My parents have a farm near New Ulm. Trudy is from Golden Valley."

"Why did you decide to become an archaeologist?"

Gretchen smiles. "My parents keep asking me that. They have what you might call 'traditional values.' They think if a girl goes to college, she should become a nurse or a grade school teacher. I'd go crazy."

"But why archaeology?"

"I'm not sure. My parents are convinced it's due to the corrupting influence of public television."

"Come on, Gretchen!" Trudy protests. "Your parents respect what you do, even if they don't understand it."

Gretchen looks at Trudy, eyebrows raised, then turns back to Anderson. "Trudy idealizes my parents," Gretchen explains. "She's a wealthy suburbanite, who grew up watching *Little House on the Prairie*. She thinks of my parents as 'noble tillers of the soil.'"

"Well, they are!" Trudy exclaims. "My parents just care about money."

"Do you suppose mine don't?" Gretchen asks.

Anderson turns toward Trudy. "What do your parents think about your studying theater?"

"Oh, they're all for it. They think it will help me marry an entertainment lawyer."

"The two of you seem to be good friends."

Gretchen looks affectionately at Trudy. "We're very different, but we like doing things together."

"We share a taste for amusing conversations," Trudy adds.

Anderson feels as though he is beginning to understand them. "Like the one you were having with me the night we met."

Gretchen nods. "Exactly."

"Do you share an apartment too?"

"No," Trudy answers, "but we live only two blocks apart."

"Can I have your addresses and phone numbers? In case I think of something else I need to ask."

There is a long silence. Trudy looks questioningly at Gretchen. Gretchen gazes off across the restaurant.

"Come on. You owe me that much."

"Okay," Gretchen says, turning back to Anderson. "You may

be right. I guess you could track us down if you wanted to anyway." She reaches for her purse, hanging from the back of her
chair, and takes out a notebook and pen. Resting the notebook
on the table, she writes down their addresses, tears off the page,
and hands it to him.

Anderson folds it and puts it in his pocket. As he is doing
this, he hears a rapping on the plate glass window. He looks up to
see someone outside waving at him. A young man with a
ponytail.

"A friend of yours?" Anderson asks.

"That's Benny Olson," Trudy says, waving. "He's a painter."

The young man points to himself and then to the empty chair
at their table, raising his eyebrows.

Trudy nods affirmatively.

Anderson watches as the young man goes around to the entrance, up the steps, and into the restaurant. Every movement
the fellow makes seems to express a bounding vitality. But when
he arrives at their table, he suddenly becomes tentative. "Mr.
Peterson?" he says, half in question, half in greeting.

"How *are* you?" Anderson asks, with forced enthusiasm.

"Just fine," the painter says. "And how are *you*, Mr. Peterson?"

"Call him 'Andy,' " Trudy says.

The young man looks puzzled, but eager to comply. "How
are you—Andy?" he asks awkwardly.

"Surviving."

"You two look great as usual," the painter says, turning
toward the girls. "Every time I see you I regret giving up figura-
tive work." He steps around Trudy to sit in the empty chair on
the window side. This puts him directly across from Anderson. "I
didn't know you knew Gretchen and Trudy," the painter comments.

"We just met recently," Gretchen explains.

Anderson looks at the fellow, trying to size him up. The man
is a few years older than the girls, but younger than Anderson.
He is large and blond. Apart from the ponytail, there's nothing
'artistic' about his appearance.

"You know," Anderson says, addressing the painter, "I was

just trying to figure out when you and I first met. Do you remember?"

"How could I forget? It was in the Lamberton Gallery. I had five paintings in their spring show that year. You said you liked them and asked to meet the artist. It made me feel real important. Do you still have the one you bought?"

Anderson smiles and nods. "It's hanging on the wall of my apartment right now."

Trudy looks at Anderson, then at the painter. "It sounds as though you're old friends."

The painter grins. "We've run into each other at a lot of gallery openings." He turns to Anderson. "But I haven't seen you in over a year."

"I don't get out to the galleries as much as I used to," Anderson says.

The painter turns back to Trudy. "Have you got any shows coming up?"

"I just did an audition for one of Anouilh's early plays." She breaks into a big smile. "It had this long stretch where I had to act without any lines. Here, look at this. See if you can tell what's going on." Trudy begins going through a series of physical reactions and changing facial expressions, without saying a word.

Gretchen laughs at some of Trudy's more extravagant facial contortions.

Anderson decides there is nothing more to be discovered from these students. Apparently, they really are just what they claimed to be. They don't seem to have any idea of what Peterson was up to. Tracking them down seems to have been a dead end.

"Excuse me," Anderson says, "but I've got to be going." He gets up to leave.

"I'm sorry if we caused you any trouble," Gretchen says. "You can call us, if you like."

Trudy reaches forward and gives Anderson's hand a reassuring squeeze. "You take care now."

"It was nice talking to you again," the painter says. "Say 'hello' to Shannon for me."

Anderson goes rigid. Slowly, he lowers himself back into his seat. "How do you know Shannon?"

"You introduced her to me that first night I made your acquaintance. Of course, I've talked to her a number of times since."

"When?"

"Oh, just on the same occasions when I've seen you."

Anderson tries to behave casually. "We were together?"

"Sure. I think the two of you have been together every time we've met. Until tonight, of course."

Speaking with great care, Anderson asks the crucial question. "How long ago *was* it that you and I first met each other?"

"Let's see. It must have been nearly three and a half years ago."

"And you're sure Shannon was with me then?"

The painter nods. "She's not the sort of woman one forgets. I was doing my 'Mysteries of Women' series at the time. I remember thinking what a great model Shannon would make. If she hadn't been with you, I would have asked her to pose for me."

"Do you remember Shannon's last name?"

"Sure. It's Crosno, isn't it? Something like that."

"How about her address?"

The painter looks confused. "I don't understand. Oh, you mean when she's not at your place?"

"That's right. Do you know it?"

"I don't know her exact address. I've never exactly been on her guest list or anything."

Anderson leans forward. "But you have some idea where she lives?"

"Sure. A friend of mine once went to a party she gave at her place instead of yours. I suppose you were on one of your trips or something."

Anderson stares intently at the painter. "Where was it? Where did your friend say Shannon lives?"

"He said she's got one of those expensive apartments near Orchestra Hall. On Marquette. 'Marquette Place,' I think it's called. But why are you asking me this?"

Anderson takes a deep breath. "There's been a serious misunderstanding. I need to find out where it started."

With no further preliminaries, Anderson gets to his feet. He is too distracted by what he has heard to say anything more. He stumbles out of the Vietnamese restaurant and walks up the street in a daze. He does not know what to make of the painter's remarks, but he realizes they have some startling consequences. If Shannon had known Peterson intimately for some time, she could not have mistaken their identities. She must *know* he isn't Peterson.

But if that's the case, then everything Shannon has said and done in his presence has been part of an elaborate charade. Could she be that good an actress? And if she is, what is Shannon up to?

Anderson knows he is on the track of something crucial, but it is not what he wanted to discover.

He finds himself once again in front of the bar where he was kidnapped. He turns and walks in. Just inside the entrance, he spots a pay phone. Underneath it is a shelf holding phone books. Anderson studies the battered spines and pulls out the one he wants. Searching the white pages, he finds an entry for 'Crosno, S. 1314 Marquette Ave.' The location sounds right. He considers dialing the number, but phones for a taxi instead.

He goes back outside to wait. The sound of a motorcycle starting up a block away puts him into a sweat. But it's just a gangly college boy out on a date with his equally gangly girlfriend. Anderson's muscles gradually relax after it sputters past. But his mind remains feverish.

A yellow cab with a checkered stripe shows up a few minutes later. Despite the hour, Anderson gives the taxi driver Shannon's address near Orchestra Hall.

"Looking for some excitement tonight?" the driver asks.

"No," Anderson replies. "I don't think I could handle any more."

"Well, if you're ever looking for some, give me a call." The driver reaches back, extending a business card between his second and third fingers.

Anderson takes the card and puts it absentmindedly in his pocket. "Thank you," he says.

The traffic is light, and they are soon approaching the high rise building where Shannon has an apartment. Just before they reach it, the taxi is slowed by two cars turning down the side street, toward the adjoining parking ramp. From where the taxi pauses, Anderson can see that the apartment building has an elaborate lobby manned by night staff. "Just pull up here on the street," he says, handing the driver a folded ten dollar bill.

The driver does as Anderson asks. "Have a good night, sir," he says, as Anderson climbs out.

"You too," Anderson replies.

Standing on the sidewalk, Anderson surveys the physical layout. He is suddenly very apprehensive about going inside. He knows he is moving toward a critical confrontation, but he has no idea what form it will take. His senses seem abnormally acute. He is eager for any clue that might give him some notion of what he is walking into. He wants to know what kind of people live in this building. He wants to know the ways in and out.

His attention is caught by a sculpture located directly in front of the entrance. For a moment, Anderson is too fascinated to look anywhere else. It is a bronze statue of a nude woman. She is standing on one leg, holding a large bird of prey on sticks over her head. Surrounding her is a circular fountain. The bird looks as though it is focused on something out in front of it and is unaware of how much it is being controlled by the woman. The woman's skin looks bare and vulnerable. It provides a jarring contrast to the violent shapes of the bird's talons and beak. Yet her nude flesh seems to be the thing that links her to the bird. It is what makes her the bird's master.

With a slight shudder, Anderson shifts his gaze from the sculpture to the entrance itself. This end of the building is supported by massive pillars, so that the front doors are actually tucked well underneath it. To the right of these doors is a curved, brick facade with the words "Marquette Place—Luxury Apartments" spelled out in large, milk white letters. To the left is a windowed waiting area, deserted at this hour.

The doors in the middle are the only obvious way in from the street. At another time of day, Anderson would have been able to tag along behind a tenant with a key. But at this hour, he sees no alternative except to approach the front desk. He detours around the sculpture and goes through the doors. This puts him in a glass vestibule, with a window to his right, where the desk clerk can look out at him.

Anderson walks over to it, expecting he will be asked to explain his business. But the clerk is evidently satisfied by the expensive clothes Anderson is wearing. He buzzes Anderson through.

Entering the lobby itself, Anderson finds himself facing a mirrored wall lined with decorative furniture. The night clerk is around to his right, behind a long brick counter, set on a diagonal. He stands up as Anderson approaches.

Behind the clerk is a bank of fifteen small video monitors. They show black and white images from security cameras around the building, including a view of an indoor swimming pool. The top three screens flick automatically from one location to another. No people are visible in the pictures.

"It's the latest style in programming," the night clerk says. "Video minimalism."

"Looks very restful," Anderson comments.

The clerk laughs. "You got that right."

"I'm here to see Shannon Crosno. My name is Peterson."

The night clerk consults a long sheet of cardboard encased in plastic, then reaches for a phone. "I have to phone up to clear it," he explains. He dials a number and waits.

Through the nearby windows, Anderson sees a car pulling out of the adjoining parking ramp. The desk clerk must know who it is, because he glances back, but pays no further attention.

"Hello," he says into the telephone. "I have a Mr. Peterson for you." There is a pause. "No, he's right here in the lobby." This statement is followed by a longer pause. "All right, I'll send him up."

The clerk puts down the phone and tells Anderson the apartment number. "The elevators are down there," he says, gesturing. "I don't think the lady was expecting you."

Anderson walks in the direction the clerk had pointed. This takes him past the mirrored wall, down a corridor extending away from the front desk. A short distance along it, he comes to three elevators. The middle one is standing empty, doors open. Stepping inside, Anderson finds himself surrounded entirely by mirrors. Even the ceiling is covered by one. Anderson tries not to look. The multiple images are too unsettling. He presses the button for Shannon's floor. Her apartment is more than two thirds of the way up the thirty-five story building.

Anderson emerges on her floor. In front of him are windows, offering dazzling views of the lights outside. But the lighting inside the building is so subdued, the green carpeted hallways seem almost dark. Cautiously exploring, Anderson comes to the apartment with Shannon's number. It is one of the corner ones directly above the building's entrance. Anderson is about to knock when her door swings open.

Shannon stands there in a clingy chemise, silhouetted by the light coming from inside. "This is certainly a surprise," she says.

"I'll bet it is," Anderson replies.

She steps forward and kisses him, but Anderson doesn't respond. "Well, come in," she says, standing aside. "Can I get you a nightcap?"

Anderson shakes his head and walks past her. There is a tiny kitchen just inside the door to the right. Beyond it, through a serving bay, Anderson can see the living room.

Shannon closes the door behind him. "Let me know if you change your mind," she says. "I'm opening a bottle of Chardonnay." She goes to the refrigerator and takes one out.

Anderson walks past the kitchen, into the living room. The space is small, but the views are spectacular. In one direction, sliding glass doors open onto a balcony with the entire skyline of downtown Minneapolis beyond it. In the other wall, a large window offers a vista that stretches all the way to downtown St. Paul, several miles away. Far below, connected by a skyway over the street, is the sprawling mass of the Minneapolis Convention Center.

Although the living room is well illuminated by track lighting, Anderson notices when one of the lights behind him goes off. He turns to see what Shannon is doing.

She emerges from the kitchen carrying a glass of wine in her right hand. With the light now in front of her, Anderson can see much better what she is wearing. It is a silky black garment, much like a slip. It hangs from the thinnest of spaghetti straps. Her bosom is encased in a decorative web of lace with so many open spaces, her nipples are clearly on display. The filmy skirt that follows the contours of her body begins just below her breasts and ends in mid-thigh.

Anderson wonders whether she put this outfit on after the

desk clerk phoned up to her. He decides she probably did. It doesn't look like the sort of thing a woman would wear unless she were expecting a certain kind of visitor.

Shannon stops halfway across the floor. She seems to see the tension in Anderson's body. She backs slowly away from him, toward the dining room, until her legs bump against one of the low backed dining room chairs. She rests her bottom on the chair's back. Sipping her wine with elaborate casualness, she draws one knee forward until it is in front of the other.

Anderson is very aware that everything she does is an elaborate performance. Even now, she is striking a pose she knows will be flattering. He takes a step toward her, fists clenched. "You've been lying to me all along, haven't you?"

"What do you mean?"

"You weren't a stranger to Peterson's apartment when you went there three nights ago. You'd been there hundreds of times before."

"So?"

"So you weren't getting to know Peterson for the first time. You had a long standing relationship. You were Peterson's mistress! You'd been his mistress for years."

"It would be four years in November."

For a moment, Anderson is too horrified to speak. This is what he feared, but didn't want to face. It means all her apparent affection for him was a total sham.

When he finds his voice again, it is bitter. "You were faking all of it, weren't you? Pretending you'd never been in the apartment before, acting as though you were seeing the entry hall for the first time, asking where things were located, where the light switches were, where the bathroom was. It was all just a lousy performance."

"I thought it was a very good performance," Shannon murmurs. She takes a large sip of her wine.

Anderson feels an impulse to knock it from her hand. But he is still reeling from the things she has so casually admitted. "You knew I wasn't Peterson. You've known it all along."

"I knew something had gone wrong. The plan obviously hadn't worked the way it was supposed to."

"Then you knew what Peterson was up to? You were in on that too?"

Shannon sets her wine glass on the table behind her. "Of course." She speaks gently, but wears an expression of growing pride.

Anderson stares at her, trying to connect her beautiful features to the ugly acts he suspects she was involved in. "Don't you feel any shame?"

"Why should I?"

Anderson's throat goes dry. He must swallow before he can speak further. "What Peterson was doing was criminal. Doesn't that bother you?" He hears his own voice sounding hoarse and shaky. "It was murder!" he almost shouts. "Do you think I haven't figured it out? Peterson was planning a murder, wasn't he?"

Shannon folds her arms, tucking them under her breasts. "Yes, that was part of the plan."

"He was going to fake his own death and take on someone else's identity—my identity!"

A trace of a smile plays across Shannon's mouth. "You've got most of it figured out."

"But you weren't just a bystander, were you? You were his accomplice."

Shannon puts her leg out sideways to brace herself better. "There was no way to set it all up without me."

Anderson suddenly recalls the sounds that had filtered through to him while he was drugged. He remembers the rendezvous he had overheard, the snatches of conversation that had become entangled with his own memories.

"My God, you were *there*!" he exclaims. His eyes go to her throat and mouth as he thinks of the tones her voice can make. "I'm right, aren't I? You were the woman I heard in the pine forest. It was *your* voice calling out, talking with Peterson, arguing about how to do things. *You* were the one laughing. Laughing, while I was lying there helpless!"

Shannon looks proud, defiant. "Someone had to meet the detective we hired to do the snatch down in Minneapolis. So I did that part. None of it would have been possible without me. I was the one who shaved off that beard. I was the one who drove the station wagon north."

"To the nighttime rendezvous."

"That's right. When we got the body out of the car, it took both of us to drag it down to the lake. And it took both of us to cover up the tracks we made dragging it. I helped change the wallets and arrange everything else. By the time I headed back to the Twin Cities, almost everything was done. Except for the drowning itself."

"It must have been quite a shock to see me back at Peterson's apartment."

"I was a nervous wreck. You must have noticed that I was shaking." She runs her fingertips over her upper arms, as though feeling for goose bumps.

"But why did you behave the way you did, when you saw me there? You knew Peterson intimately. You must have noticed something was different the moment you got up close."

"I noticed something was different when I was still halfway up the hallway. You were staring at me so strangely. As though you'd never seen me before."

"So why did you do what you did? Why did you behave as though I were Peterson?"

"I behaved as though you were Peterson, because you *are* Peterson!"

Anderson hears a rushing sound in his head and ears, as though a waterfall were roaring through them. But every sound Shannon utters, as she continues to speak, remains distinctly audible.

"You're *not* Anderson," Shannon says. "Anderson's been dead since you killed him! You're *Peterson!*"

Anderson tries to steel himself against Shannon's statements, to keep the very sounds from entering his body. Yet as soon as Shannon has said the words, he feels as though they are already inside him, as though he has expected to hear them all along.

"I knew something was wrong," Shannon continues, "when you didn't meet me at the airport the way we'd planned. So I went back to the dinner party as though nothing had happened. You can imagine how hard it was to keep my mind on the conversation."

As she speaks, the rushing sound in Anderson's head seems to grow louder. But Shannon's voice grows louder with it. His senses seem to be amplifying everything. But he is also aware that, outwardly, things remain as before.

Shannon is clearly conscious of the effect her words are having, but the only visible sign is the stillness of her body as she speaks. "After the party, I couldn't stand it any longer. I had to know what happened. I drove by Anderson's house, but it was all dark. Then I drove by your apartment and saw the lights on."

Memories from Anderson's first exploration of Peterson's apartment come flooding into his mind. Then comes the image of Shannon, walking down the hall, moving steadily toward him as he tries to leave the apartment, trapping him inside.

Shannon stares at him as though she can tell what he is thinking. "When you looked at me so oddly, I thought at first you were starting that love game we used to play. You know, the one where we would act as though we were meeting each other for the first time. As though we were each beginning a love affair with a stranger. It seemed a charming way of dealing with our anxieties, a romantic way of remembering how we used to seduce each other."

Her eyes are wide, her expression intent. "But this time it wasn't a game for you. You seemed to be taking everything at face value. At first, I couldn't figure it out. You seemed so fragile, I didn't dare say anything that would change the mood."

She pauses, studying his eyes, then goes on. "Gradually, it became apparent you were suffering some kind of temporary amnesia. The trauma of having to kill someone was obviously too much for you."

Anderson hears the waterfall noise grow louder again. He feels transparent to it, so that he catches little of its force. But the roaring flow is still strong enough to drive him backward. He puts a foot behind him to brace himself, to keep from falling.

Shannon extends a hand as though to steady him. But she still leans on the back of the chair, remaining a greater distance away than their arms can reach. "I didn't want to do anything that might push you into a total breakdown. So I just played along, thinking it would be better not to challenge you prematurely."

Shannon pauses again. With her other hand, she eases herself gently forward, off the chair. "I thought you'd just snap out of it after a few hours. But you didn't."

She stands there, prepared to come to him. But she makes no further move. "It took me a while to figure out what had happened. I mean psychologically. But gradually I began to understand. Your idea of yourself as Anderson was a delusion created in response to the trauma and guilt you felt committing the murder."

Anderson feels himself physically stagger. The rush of water through his mind is pushing him off balance.

Shannon steps toward him, yet still stops short of actually touching him. Her voice is gentle and understanding. "The physical resemblance, which gave you the idea in the first place, encouraged you to identify with your victim. When you realized you had actually killed Anderson, you must have felt as though you had killed yourself. That made you panic and try to run away, rather than carrying out the rest of your plan."

Anderson tries to shake his head in denial, to shake the water from his brain, to shake off the words that are gradually saturating him.

But Shannon continues in the same steady voice. "Since that morning, when you ran away, you have been denying your role in Anderson's death. You've been denying it by trying to take Anderson's place—at least in your own mind. This has led you to construct an elaborate delusion. Applying your genius to the construction of an 'Anderson personality.' But that is *all* it is. A temporary delusion."

"No," Anderson says, finally managing to speak. "That's not possible. I have Anderson's memories. I know what his childhood and adolescence were like, what *my* childhood and adolescence were like."

Shannon shakes her head, her eyes moist. "You're a genius. You're inventing those memories as fast as you need to remember them."

"But they're too vivid," Anderson says.

"Are they? Can you really remember Anderson's childhood or teenaged years that clearly? Are you sure the vivid details aren't ones you've been adding from other experiences? Experiences you've had at other times, other places?"

As she says this, Anderson tries to refute her in his mind. He tries to find one memory so distinctive, it could only be Anderson's, one memory so vivid, it could not be imagined, one memory so perfectly intact, it could not be constructed out of other experiences. But all his memories as Anderson seem to dissolve as fast as he can call them up.

Shannon seems to sense his uncertainty. She puts out a hand, finally, to steady him. But she continues her inquiry. "And what about the answers you've been coming up with, when people ask you questions? Answers in so many fields. Where have those answers been coming from?"

She leans toward him, her face now close to his, her eyes almost filling his eyes. "How else could you have played the part of Peterson so successfully? How else?" She pauses, then speaks the words he can't refute. "It is because you *are* Peterson."

Anderson is shaken to the core of his being. His mind tries to take on the implications of what she is saying. Could he actually be this person everyone takes him for? Could he be Peterson? As the idea sinks in, Anderson realizes he is no longer sure of anything. He feels himself crumbling from within, swept off, one piece after another, by the treacherous current that seems to be streaming through everything.

Shannon guides him to the couch, easing him down into the cushions. Then she sits beside him, carefully leaving a space between them.

"Here, look at these." She reaches down and unzips the outside pocket of a travel bag sitting on the floor. Slipping her hand inside, she extracts some documents and hands them to Anderson. "I was supposed to give you these at the airport."

He takes them. The top one is an airline ticket. He opens it with trembling hands and sees that it is in the name of 'Anderson.' The other document is a passport. He stares at it, his hands now shaking almost uncontrollably, afraid to look inside.

"You were going to use those to travel with, once you had been pronounced legally dead." Shannon takes the passport from him, opens it, and hands it back.

The name is his own. 'Anderson.' The picture, too, is his. But it shows him once more with a beard.

"Look closely," Shannon says, pointing to the picture. "That's not actually you. That's Anderson."

He turns the page more toward the light. The bearded picture in the passport does look slightly different from him.

"See what I mean?" Shannon says. "This is Anderson's passport, not yours. But you look so much alike, no immigration official would ever notice the difference."

Anderson stares at the picture in horror. This must be the face of the man he drowned.

"You see, I did everything you asked. If you would only come to your senses and accept yourself as Peterson, you'd see how loyal I've been."

She moves closer on the couch. "You shouldn't feel so bad about killing Anderson," she says. "After all, Anderson himself was guilty. He was guilty of murdering an innocent old man! Everything you've done was justified! You arranged an 'accidental drowning' for Anderson, just as Anderson did for his grandfather. Anderson deserved to die!"

Her words are like torture to him. "No," he says in a hoarse whisper. "Anderson didn't deserve to die!"

He gets up, still clutching the strange documents. For a moment, he sways, uncertain of his balance. Then he turns and staggers out the door.

C H A P T E R   1 5

Anderson awakes in Peterson's bedroom. His head is throbbing. It is early morning. Through the Moorish windows at the end of the room, he can see that the sky outside is barely light.

He gets up and staggers through the dressing room into the bathroom. This headache is worse than any he can remember. The bathroom lights seem so painfully bright, he can hardly open his eyes. He navigates by squinting at the floor and groping along the walls with his hands.

He finds it difficult even to locate the washbowls. Only his memory of the room allows him to keep his sense of direction. Clinging to the counter for support, he opens the medicine cabinet and finds the amber vial of pills prescribed for Peterson's migraines. He puts two of them in his mouth and swallows them by slurping water from the tap.

Unable to think of anything else to reduce the pain, he makes his way back to the bedroom. The padded floor seems almost liquid in its softness. He crosses it with difficulty and lowers himself onto the bed.

His sleep is disturbed by nightmares. At first, they seem like ones he has had before. Dark dreams of drowning and northern lakes. But then they turn more abstract.

Anderson dreams he is physically dissolving. He dreams his own boundaries are softening, blurring, becoming indistinct. He dreams the individual parts of his body are disintegrating, melting, becoming liquid. As his body parts dissolve, they go through a stage of being grainy. They disintegrate, not into blood or shredded tissue, but into crystalline particles, like dissolving sugar.

At first, he tries to surrender to the process, to lose himself in the liquid flow. He has no energy left to fight the currents in which he is caught. He only wants them to reach their end, to stop.

Yet even as he feels himself disintegrating, he achieves no peace. The liquid into which he is dissolving pulses with tension. Waves of pressure surge across it. Tides of pain torment it. The pressure seems to become almost mathematical, the pain a matter of correlated variables. He feels caught in a web of equations, tortured by numbers.

These are someone else's dreams, someone else's nightmares. They are the nightmares of an engineer or mathematician, the nightmares of Peterson.

For a time, as he realizes this, the pain subsides. Then the pressures build again. The connections between his elements are strained beyond endurance. Abstract forces blast him with their blind precision. The residues of his existence become ever more dispersed. Only in his agony, does he retain any identity.

Anderson tries to control these dreams. He tries to choose resistance as the easier course. But he is no better at controlling the processes than he is at surrendering to them. The currents in which he is caught are too ethereal to resist. Matrices engulf him. Abstract formulas redistribute him. He is reduced to data that is being lost as fast as it is created. He feels himself spooling off into space, spooling off into realms forever inaccessible. The pain he feels and the peace he seeks eventually become indistinguishable.

When Anderson wakes again, the headache is gone. But he is almost too groggy to move. He rolls onto his elbows and knees, then, faint from the movement, ducks his head to let the blood flow back into it. His right arm throbs where it presses against the mattress, so he shifts the weight to his hands. This makes him aware that his whole body aches.

For a moment, he is almost surprised to *have* a body. It seems remarkable to him that he can span the space under his chest. He feels his hands and knees resting on the bed and marvels that he can support himself that way.

Then, gradually, he becomes more aware of his environment. He realizes he is still in Peterson's bedroom. He gets to his feet and, supporting himself with the aid of walls and door frames, stumbles to the bathroom.

Stepping into the giant shower, he turns the water on full and directs it toward where he is standing. The powerful streams bombarding him bring back a rush of fragmented memories. Memories of falling, of river bottoms, of dark, smothering water. Memories of spray, of erotic splashing, of wet, soothing hands.

Anderson blasts the memories away by shifting the temperature to cold. Then he cuts off the water entirely and emerges, dripping and slightly shivering. A brisk rub with one of Peterson's towels brings the circulation back to his skin.

Feeling better, but still disoriented, Anderson studies himself in the mirror. He looks older and more tired than his memory of himself. He seems to have suffered a migraine.

But this can't be right. Anderson is not a migraine sufferer. Peterson is the migraine sufferer.

He tries to see himself as Peterson.

Despite the difficulties Peterson seems to be in, the prospect is not altogether unappealing. In addition to the wealth and sexual opportunities available to Peterson, Anderson has been enjoying a profound sense of freedom in the Peterson role. As Peterson, he is constantly being threatened with things he doesn't understand. Yet he feels more in control of his life as Peterson than he ever did as Anderson.

The bathroom phone begins ringing with its low, beeping tone. Anderson hesitates before answering it. He looks at the clock and sees he must have slept through most of the day. It is now nearly 3:30 P.M.

Anderson takes a deep breath. Then he picks up the receiver and says, "Hello."

"Hi. This is Shannon." Her voice sounds concerned, but otherwise normal. "How are you feeling?"

"Sore. Stiff. Confused." The words come out with difficulty.

"Listen. The police have just been here. Detectives Berglund and Holmquist. They asked me a lot of questions."

Anderson is now fully awake. "About what?"

"You, mostly. Your personal habits. Your business dealings."

"What did you tell them?"

"Not much. I pretended you only use me for sex. They were so impressed with my figure, I think they believed me."

Anderson tries to guess why the police would be interviewing Shannon. "Did they concentrate on anything specific?"

"No. But they wanted to know about any friends you might have on the police force or in the mayor's office."

"Why would they ask about that?"

"I'm not sure. But it sounds as though someone higher up doesn't want you investigated. I overheard them grumbling to each other, while I was making them coffee. Apparently, the word in the police department is to leave you alone. These detectives don't know who's responsible, but they're angry about it."

"It doesn't sound as though they're taking the warning very seriously," Anderson says.

"Well," Shannon replies, "they were interviewing *me* instead of you. That's something." She pauses for a moment, then continues. "I guess, by warning them off you, someone has inadvertently made you the center of their investigation. They probably won't be able to get any cooperation from the rest of the department. So you're probably safe from other surveillance. But the two of them are obviously going after you as hard as they can."

"Great. Just what I need."

"It's funny. They seem to suspect you of killing Anderson."

"What's funny about that?"

"To have them get to that point so quickly! After all your careful planning! After you and I went to so much trouble to send them in a different direction!"

Anderson decides to put a stop to this.

"Shannon. I *know* I'm not Peterson. I might be a little disoriented at the moment, but there is solid evidence I couldn't be Peterson. In fact, there are details that could only be explained if I'm Anderson."

"What are you talking about?"

"Last night, before I went to your apartment, I tracked down the girls who were involved in the kidnapping. Their names are Gretchen and Trudy. I recognized them from my memory of them in the bar. We talked about the night I met them. My recollection of our conversation is completely consistent with theirs. Don't you see? That was a conversation Anderson had *before* he was kidnapped. I must have been the one who was there. I must be Anderson."

"No," Shannon says firmly. "You've got it wrong. I'll tell you what happened. Before the kidnapping, you received surveillance photos of several girls Brian proposed to use as decoys. After the kidnapping, he phoned you and gave you a complete report. He told you which of the girls were actually used. *That's* why you could recognize them. He also told you everything that was said. *That's* how you could reconstruct the conversation."

"But there's physical evidence too."

"What physical evidence?" Her tone is scornful. "If you mean that your clothes are too large, forget it. You've lost so much weight while you've been going through this ordeal, it's amazing they fit you as well as they do."

How did she know this was what he had in mind? For a moment, Anderson is stumped. Then he remembers the shoes. Peterson's shoes are much too big for him. Surely he couldn't have lost enough weight to make that big a difference in his feet. Anderson decides to mention this.

But Shannon is still a jump ahead of him. "Your shoes," she says. "Have you noticed those? You always insist on buying them too wide and a half size too big. After your recent weight loss, I bet they hardly fit you at all."

How could she tell his shoes were too big? Anderson realizes Shannon has managed to turn his evidence around. It now seems to indicate the opposite of what he had first thought.

"Look, you've got to snap out of this," Shannon says. "With the police investigating you, it's too dangerous to be operating with delusions."

"I'm not operating with delusions."

"Everybody who knows you recognizes you as Peterson. *You're* the only one who's having trouble accepting it."

"That's because I'm *not* Peterson."

"You couldn't be anybody else. You're simply too good at being Peterson. Even though you're a genius, I bet you're not half as convincing when you act the part of Anderson."

As she says it, Anderson remembers having this very idea, while he was talking to Freilinger. And it was Freilinger, he recalls, who had first denied to his face that he was Anderson. The recollection makes him tremble.

"The way you speak," Shannon continues. "Your voice, your vocabulary, your inflections—it's all Peterson, not Anderson."

This reminds Anderson of something even more disturbing. Of June telling him over the phone that his imitation of Anderson's voice wasn't that good. June, too, had refused to recognize him at first as Anderson. He feels his confidence crumbling.

"You know I'm right, don't you?" Shannon asks.

"No. What you're saying is impossible." Desperate to find something to refute her, Anderson searches his mind for recent occasions when he has been accepted as Anderson.

With a flood of mixed emotions, he recalls his evening with Jack and June the night of the fire. June had accepted him readily enough when she saw him. Jack had comforted him in his distress. Surely, *they* would have known if he weren't Anderson. Yes, that's it! That's something which proves he's Anderson!

"I visited some good friends after the drowning," he tells Shannon. "How could I have fooled them into thinking I was Anderson, if I were Peterson? Wouldn't I have said or done things that would make them suspicious?"

"When had they last seen Anderson?" Shannon asks.

Anderson remembers Jack and June saying they hadn't heard from him in nearly a year. "It had been a while," he admits, "but I'd known them for years. If I weren't Anderson, they would have suspected something."

Shannon hesitates, but only for an instant. "How can you be so sure they *didn't*?" she asks.

Memories of the evening come pouring back. Anderson recalls Jack's moment of uncertainty, when Jack had first opened the door. 'It *is* you, isn't it?' Jack had asked. The recollection is unsettling, but Anderson tells himself Jack's reaction was only natural, considering Anderson had lost his beard and been reported dead.

Then a more chilling memory comes to him. Anderson recalls June looking at him strangely later in the evening. 'You seem different,' she had said. 'It's your voice, I guess.' To Anderson, this memory of June's stare is the most devastating thing of all.

Shannon seems to know from his silence that her point has gone home. When she speaks again, her voice is once more soothing. "You were probably still pretty upset when you visited Anderson's friends. You wouldn't have been very good at interpreting their reactions. And they would have been making allowances for your unusual state of mind. Do you see what I'm saying? You shouldn't let yourself be misled by the fact you got through that evening without being exposed. It doesn't mean anything."

There is only one thing left for Anderson to fall back on. "I don't *feel* like Peterson," he says. His voice sounds plaintive, almost whimpering.

"Darling," Shannon murmurs, "you don't have to be afraid. You don't have to handle this alone. I can take care of you. The police won't be a problem. I know how to get us of out of this. Just let me guide you until your memory comes back."

The tone of her voice offers comfort. The things she is saying offer a direction, a course through the confusion.

Anderson feels an almost overwhelming urge to surrender himself to her care. Yet he can't do it as 'himself.' He can only do it as some hypothetical 'Peterson.'

"I can't accept what you're saying. I can't do what you ask."

"Just consider it, okay? Promise me you'll consider it." This time her voice is almost a whisper.

There is a long silence. "Okay, I'll consider it," he says.

He imagines he hears a sigh of relief on the other end of the line, but he cannot be sure there really was one.

"Be easy on yourself," Shannon says. "You've been through a lot. You need to let yourself recuperate. Use the Jacuzzi. I'll call you again in a couple of hours."

Shannon makes a kissing sound into the phone, then hangs up.

When he puts down the receiver, Anderson feels more shaken than ever. He stares vacantly into the mirror, his mind elsewhere. It is the small details that preoccupy him.

He wonders, in particular, about the shoes. Was there some point at which Shannon could have felt the toes of Peterson's shoes, while he was wearing them? Some moment at the party, perhaps, when she could have rested her foot on his? Obviously there might have been, even if he can't remember it. If there were such a moment, that would have tipped her off to the fact that his shoes were too big. A woman as clever as Shannon could then have seen the opportunity to turn this to her advantage.

As he goes over them in his mind, none of Shannon's arguments seems conclusive. But then, none of Anderson's do either.

He continues to stare at the mirror. The reflection of his face reminds him of the passport photo Shannon had shown him the night before. He had taken the passport with him when he left her apartment. What had he done with it after that?

Returning to the dressing room, Anderson finds the clothes he had pulled off before climbing into Peterson's bed. They lie heaped on a chair and strewn across the floor. Tucked among them are the passport and the airline ticket.

Anderson extracts these documents and sets them on another chair. Then he dresses himself once more in clothes from Peterson's wardrobe. This time, he chooses a cream shirt, tan trousers, and the pair of brown shoes that seems smallest. He also picks out a brown sports coat, but he sets it aside for the moment.

He goes through the pockets of the clothes he was wearing the previous evening and removes the wallet, the apartment key, and the miscellaneous scraps of paper. These, he puts in the pockets of his fresh apparel.

Checking his appearance in one of the floor length mirrors, Anderson notices he needs a shave. He takes the passport with him into the bathroom. While he shaves, he sits and studies it. He compares the photograph on the third page of the passport to his image in the mirror, paying special attention to things like the contours of his ears and the shape of his nostrils. There are some slight differences!

Anderson gets excited. For a moment, he believes he has discovered something truly revealing. Then he thinks about it longer and begins to wonder if it proves anything at all. Peterson could have stolen Anderson's passport, figuring the subtle differences in their appearances would never be noticed. In that case, the difference between the passport photo and his own face would show that he is Peterson. On the other hand, Peterson could have applied for a passport in Anderson's name, supplying his own picture to the government agency. Then the difference between the passport photo and his own face would show that he is Anderson. There is no way to tell from the passport photo which of these things is true.

But Anderson decides it still might teach him something. Finished shaving, he carries the passport into the workout room. He holds the passport picture beside the photographs mounted on the wall and tries to decide if they match. The lighting and the glass over the framed photos makes it difficult to compare the details. So Anderson takes several of the photographs off the wall and removes them from their frames. He carries these into the office and puts them on the desk.

Then he goes back to the dressing room and takes out one of the photo albums. From behind the protective plastic, he removes some of the photographs that seem to provide the best views of his face. He also removes a few in which he is featured less prominently, choosing them almost at random. He brings all the photos he has removed from the album back to the office. Sitting down at Peterson's desk, he compares them with the passport picture and with each other.

Most of the larger images of his face seem slightly different from the image in the passport. This suggests that these photos from Peterson's apartment are of one person, presumably Peterson, while the photo in the passport is of another person, presumably Anderson. Since his own face is more like the photos in the apartment than the photo in the passport, it suggests that he is indeed Peterson.

But studying the photos longer, he notices something else. Some of the images from the album and from the workout room wall seem to be the *same* as the image in the passport. In fact, as Anderson examines the photos more closely, he is gradually able to divide them into two piles: those that match the passport photo, and those that match his own face, as he sees it in the mirror. This suggests that some of the pictures in the apartment have somehow been tampered with or faked.

If this is the case, then some of the pictures in the album and on the wall are of Anderson, and some are of Peterson. But which are which? His head is spinning. He feels as though he is caught in a whirlpool with nothing to grab hold of.

Even the idea that the photos were faked suggests more questions than answers. How, for instance, was it done? Where did the forger get the pictures of Anderson to use as raw materials?

Anderson stares at the two stacks of photos, feeling more perplexed than ever. His original idea had been to use the photos to verify his identity as Anderson. But the more he looks at them, the more he doubts this identity.

Trying desperately to find evidence that would prove he is who he thought he was, Anderson opens the lower drawer of Peterson's desk and goes through Peterson's bills one more time. In the middle of the pile, he comes across the old dental bill. Anderson is about to ruffle past it, when something stirs in the back of his mind. He remembers reading that dental records can be used to identify bodies too burned or decomposed to be checked by other means. If the technique works with dead bodies, it should certainly work with a live one!

Anderson reaches for the phone and dials the number printed on the bill. He hears his heart pounding as the sound on the line indicates the number is ringing.

"North Hennepin Dental Clinic," the receptionist says cheerfully.

"I'd like to see one of the dentists," Anderson says.

"Have you been a patient here before?" the receptionist asks.

"Yes, I have," Anderson says, giving Peterson's name.

There is the sound of pages being noisily turned at the other end. "We have an opening in five weeks," the receptionist says. "On Monday morning at eight-thirty."

"I was hoping to get in right away," Anderson explains. "I'm in considerable pain."

"Oh, dear," the receptionist says sympathetically. "We're just closing for the day. I'll see what I can do." There is a thump as the phone is set down on a blotter, then a long silence.

While he waits, Anderson pushes the photographs in front of him into a single pile. He takes a large brown envelope out of a drawer holding stationery and puts the stack of photographs inside it, along with the passport. After a minute or so, he hears the phone being picked up again.

"Are you phoning from home?" the receptionist asks.

"Yes, I am," Anderson says, puzzled.

"You're less than five minutes away," the receptionist explains. "If you can get here within fifteen minutes, Doctor Gustafson will wait."

"Thank you," Anderson says. "I'll be there in five."

He hangs up the phone, picks up the envelope, and hurries back to the dressing room. There, he pulls on the brown sports coat and grabs the airline ticket. He tucks the ticket in the envelope on his way to the front door. As he is about to leave, he hesitates, wondering whether he should take the envelope with him. He decides it would probably be safer on the table with Peterson's mail. He puts it there and then goes out, pausing to double lock the latch.

As he passes through the lobby, the doorman offers to call him a taxi. But Anderson waves the offer aside, saying he won't be needing one.

Outside the building, Anderson turns left and walks rapidly along North East Main. He keeps to the middle of the sidewalk, listening for motorcycles and watching for other avenues of attack. The skyline across the river and the buildings closer at hand all have a different look to him than they did the last time he walked this route. This time, he is unnerved, not by their strangeness, but by their familiarity.

He passes the bus stop across the street, crosses First Avenue, continues another block to Hennepin Avenue, and turns left again. From there, it is only another three or four blocks to the address printed on the dental bill.

The clinic is up a flight, but the entrance is clearly marked and the stairway brightly lit. Anderson hurries up the stairs and goes through the door into the waiting room. Inside, he sees the usual plastic chairs and low tables with old magazines.

The receptionist observes him through a window in one wall, a look of cheerful concern fixed permanently on her pert blond features. "Mr. Peterson?" she asks.

Anderson nods.

"We're all ready for you." She opens the door beside her window and leads him down the hallway to the second operatory.

"Make yourself comfortable," she says, gesturing toward an ancient looking dental chair.

Anderson sits down and leans his head against the paper covered headrest.

The receptionist puts a large green napkin under his chin and fastens it in place with plastic clips on a light metal chain. She raises the chair with a foot pump. "Doctor Gustafson will be with you in a moment," she assures him, leaving him suspended in space.

A few minutes later, the dentist appears. "What seems to be the trouble?" he asks, putting on a pair of latex gloves.

"I'm afraid it's not as urgent as I thought," Anderson says. "I was getting a lot of pain. But after I phoned you, it went away."

"That's often what happens," the dentist says cheerfully.

"I think the pain is brought on by changes in temperature. If I avoid things that are very hot or very cold, I don't feel it."

"Let's take a look," the dentist says, picking up a tiny mirror and a hooked metal probe.

Anderson opens his mouth.

The dentist adjusts the light and looks inside.

"Any sensitivity there?" the dentist asks, prodding a molar.

"A little," Anderson replies.

"How about here?" He taps his instrument in another place.

"Nothing," Anderson assures him.

The dentist turns aside to consult a yellow paper dental chart. He takes out a pencil and makes some notations on it. Then he looks in Anderson's mouth again.

Anderson expects some kind of reaction. Surely, the dentist has discovered by now that his teeth do not match Peterson's records. Anderson has even prepared a story, explaining that he is the 'other Peterson.'

But the dentist continues to examine Anderson as though everything is normal. Whatever chart he is consulting apparently shows Anderson to be Peterson.

"Where, exactly, was the pain?" the dentist asks.

"I'm not sure," Anderson replies.

"You've been doing a pretty good job of flossing," the dentist tells him, reaching for another instrument. This one has a curved shape with a flat metal blade on the end. The dentist rubs some spots near the gum line, then squirts them with water. "Rinse and spit," he says.

Anderson does.

The dentist continues looking at Anderson's teeth and makes some more marks on the chart. There continues to be no sign that anything is out of order.

Anderson finds himself accepting the apparent medical evidence. The clinical surroundings seem more real to him than he does to himself. The possibility that he really is Peterson seems to be turning into a medical fact.

After a few more pokes and prods, the dentist puts down his instruments and snaps off his gloves. "You probably don't have a serious problem, but there are a couple of things we still need to check."

He takes out a prescription pad and scribbles on it. "It's a little too late to do anything more tonight. Most of the clinic is already shut down."

Anderson clears his throat. He wants to ask the dentist to take a second look, to make extra sure the records match his mouth. But he knows this is silly. If he weren't Peterson, the difference between his mouth and the records should have been obvious.

The dentist looks up from his writing and gives Anderson a weary smile. "The hygienist and the lab assistant have already gone home. You only caught me because I had to go over some insurance records."

He tears off the prescription and hands it to Anderson. "These are for the pain. But if you avoid temperature extremes, you probably won't need them." The dentist moves out of sight, then reappears holding a sample tube of special toothpaste. He hands it to Anderson. "Use this when you brush, in place of your regular brand."

"Just brush as usual?"

"That's right." The dentist unclips the napkin and touches something with his foot that makes the chair sink to the floor. "I want you back for full mouth X-rays tomorrow morning. Or as soon as possible, if you can't make it then. You can set a time with the receptionist on the way out."

Anderson can hardly believe the appointment is over. "Thank you for seeing me on such short notice," Anderson says.

"No problem." The dentist steps into the hallway and stands there at an angle that subtly directs Anderson back to the reception desk.

Anderson walks slowly in the direction the dentist had indicated. In this clinical setting, he finds himself confronting the purely practical problems of being Peterson. He realizes he is now afraid of being trapped in the Peterson identity. Peterson is under investigation for murder. People have been killed, and Anderson is partly responsible. But he does not feel guilty in the way the police will claim. Whether he is Peterson or not, he does not want to be sent to jail for Peterson's crimes.

He sees that everything tying him to the Peterson identity could easily become a danger to him. The dental records, for example. They could trap him permanently in the role of Peterson. He must try to get his hands on those records! If he could somehow destroy them, he would be eliminating one of the chief pieces of evidence identifying him as Peterson.

But how could he do it?

Anderson becomes aware he is lingering in the hallway. The receptionist is staring at him from her post at the reception desk.

"I'm sorry," Anderson says. "I was thinking about something." He walks the rest of the way down the hallway. Most of the clinic is already dark. He enters the waiting room and steps over to the opening where the receptionist looks out.

She smiles at him, but her eyes are tired. "If I can make an appointment for you, we can all go home." She opens a large, leather bound appointment book and picks up a pen.

"I'll be moving to a new city soon," Anderson says.

The receptionist looks up at him with a serious expression. "If you put off treatment, your condition could get much worse."

"I understand that. I'll get my teeth fixed here before I leave." Anderson hopes this sounds sufficiently reassuring. "I just wanted to ask you about getting my records transferred to my new dentist."

The receptionist's face returns to a smile. "We'd be happy to mail them on for you."

"It would be a lot more convenient," he says, "if I could take them with me."

The woman gives Anderson the indulgent look that professionals use for laymen. "We normally send them directly to the new dentist."

"The thing is," Anderson explains, "I don't know who that's going to be yet. But it sounds as though I'll need dental treatment as soon as I arrive. If I were carrying the records with me, I could get that treatment without any further delay."

"So you want us to release your records directly to you?"

"That's right."

"Just a minute. I'll have to check with Doctor Gustafson."

The receptionist is gone for several minutes. When she returns, there is a subtle change in her manner.

"Doctor Gustafson says you can take your records with you. But I'm afraid the only ones we'll have for you are the X-rays we're about to take and the chart he began today."

"I don't understand."

"Some of our records were destroyed during a recent burglary. Yours, unfortunately, seem to have been among them."

Anderson becomes very still. "This clinic was burglarized?"

"It's awful, isn't it? The way they break into places these days. Apparently, they were after drugs. When they couldn't find the kind they wanted, they vandalized the office."

"Does this mean the doctor didn't have any records on me when I came in today?"

The receptionist resumes her indulgent, professional manner. "Your dentist has to update your records every time the condition of your teeth changes."

"But he didn't have any old records to start with this time?"

She looks at him more intently, aware she is being pinned down. "No—I told you—the records were lost. But don't worry. It's not going to cost you any extra to have him make a new chart. And the new X-rays would have to be done anyway."

The implications of this sink in. There was no medical evidence here identifying him as Peterson. As far as the dental records are concerned, he could just as well be Anderson.

Then he realizes something else. The fact that the clinic was burglarized could itself be a clue. Peterson might have arranged the break-in to eliminate any records that would show Anderson's body was not Peterson's. If this were the case, then Anderson's dentist would probably also have been burglarized.

"How common are burglaries of dental clinics?"

"This was our first one. But I understand some of the other clinics in the city have been robbed three or four times already. It's a problem that just got serious recently, when the rate of drug addiction soared. Now everybody's installing security systems."

The difficulty facing Anderson is that even if Peterson were responsible for the records being destroyed, he could still be Peterson. The fact that Peterson might have gone to extraordinary lengths to carry out his scheme doesn't refute anything Shannon said.

The receptionist's pen taps a spot in the appointment book. "We could fit you in at nine-fifteen tomorrow morning," she says. "Can you manage that?"

"I'm afraid I'll have to check my calendar and get back to you," Anderson says.

The receptionist gives him an impatient look. "Doctor Gustafson says he needs the X-rays done as soon as possible."

"I'll phone you," Anderson says. He gives the receptionist an apologetic smile and leaves the waiting room.

CHAPTER 16

Reaching the street outside the dental clinic, Anderson finds himself uncertain what to do next. He feels as though he is moving through a landscape that has been subtly rigged with practical jokes and funhouse illusions. But the jokes and illusions are a matter of life and death.

Across the street, a block and a half away, is a neon sign reading "Cocktail Lounge." Anderson looks cautiously up and down the street, then heads over toward it.

Inside, the furnishings are very different from a student bar. Everything is upholstered in simulated red leather. An aging woman with an overripe figure sits at a piano that doubles as a bar top. She croons songs of lost love popular forty years earlier. A big polka dot bow in her yellow hair matches the pattern on her low-cut dress. Around her sits a circle of maudlin drinkers. Some of them hum the tunes along with her.

Anderson chooses a table as far from the music as possible. A waitress appears and sets a cocktail napkin in front of him, along with a little dish of peanuts. Anderson orders a double bourbon and soda.

While he waits for his drink, he tries to figure out how his experience in the clinic changes things. When Anderson had first heard that Peterson's dental records were missing, he had felt relieved. But when he thinks about it longer, he finds the idea increasingly unsettling. He does not want to be trapped in the Peterson identity. But he wants any doubts about his identity to be eliminated, at least from his own mind.

The fact that Peterson may have been systematically destroying or altering all the relevant medical records makes Anderson wonder what proof of his identity might remain. If Peterson was being as thorough as it sounds, would there be any records beyond his reach that could still be trusted?

Peterson had 'clients' in government jobs, who would do almost anything he asked. Hence, he might have even arranged for 'corrections' to be made in things like police records. The prospect makes Anderson feel almost dizzy. Even if he *is* Anderson, his police records, including his fingerprints, might show him to be Peterson.

What other documents do people leave behind as they go through life? Anderson takes out Peterson's wallet and examines the credit cards. One of them, he notices, was issued by a local bank.

Spotting a telephone back by the men's room, Anderson waves at the waitress. "Could you give me change?" he asks, holding out a dollar bill.

She smiles, takes the bill, and puts four quarters on the table. "Here you are, honey," she says with a smile. "I hope you catch her in an understanding mood."

Anderson is confused. "What do you mean?" he asks.

"Sorry, just a joke. I figured you'd be calling your girlfriend or your wife. I was wishing you luck."

"I don't have a girlfriend or a wife."

She looks at him with new interest. "Maybe I could do something about that."

Anderson manages a smile. He realizes the woman is quite pretty, if a little on the plump side. "Thanks, but not tonight."

The waitress stands there a moment studying him. "Let me know if you change your mind," she says. She gives him a large, deliberate wink and goes happily on her way.

Anderson gazes wistfully after her, but can't forget his immediate predicament. He notices that his drink is sitting in front of him untouched. He dumps a healthy dose of it down his throat, catching the ice cubes against his upper lip. Then, taking his drink with him, he walks back to the pay phone. No one is sitting at the nearby tables, so the area is relatively private.

After checking the telephone directory, Anderson dials the number for the bank that issued Peterson the credit card. It is well past banking hours, but a recorded voice offers him a list of services he can access by selecting different numbers on the phone dial. Anderson picks one that seems to offer the possibility of a live voice. When a woman answers, he gives Peterson's name and asks to speak to someone in personal accounts.

"I'm sorry," she says. "The bank is closed for the day. If you telephone tomorrow morning, I'm sure someone will be able to help you."

"This is very urgent," Anderson tells her. "Could you check, please, if anyone is still there who could help me right now?"

The skeptical sigh at the other end of the line is clearly audible. "What is the nature of your problem?"

Anderson takes a deep breath. He knows he had better come up with something convincing. "The bank was supposed to send me some documents this afternoon by express courier, but they never arrived. I have to have them right away. If one of the people who handles my accounts is still there, it might be possible to avoid some serious legal repercussions. Otherwise things could get complicated."

The woman doesn't reply at first, but Anderson can hear her breathing. He is sure it is the implicit threat of legal action that is making her hesitate.

"I'll see if I can locate anyone," she says finally.

The woman's voice is replaced by modern classical music, full of cheerful fanfares for the brass and low warbling melodies for the woodwinds. Through the telephone earpiece, it is all weirdly distorted. The music ends as abruptly as it began.

"Mr. Peterson?"

"Yes."

"This is Carol Dorfer. How can I help you?"

Anderson decides to continue with the same story. He figures if he can keep these people at the bank on the defensive, they might reveal some of what he needs to know.

He makes his voice polite, but firm. "I was supposed to receive copies of my account records by four o'clock this afternoon. They haven't arrived."

"That's strange. We sent copies of all your records by special messenger this morning."

Anderson is too stunned at first to speak. "What did you say?" he asks.

"You should have received the documents you requested before noon," the woman says.

This makes no sense to him. How could she have fulfilled a request he never made? She might be lying to cover up a possible mistake by the bank. But why would she assume the bank had made a mistake? Anderson wonders again if he is going crazy.

He tries to get a grip on himself. "You sent those records to me this morning, you say?"

"That's right," she replies. "To your address on North East Main. We got them off less than an hour after you left."

Anderson feels increasingly bewildered. "After I left where?" he asks.

"After you left the bank."

Anderson finds it hard to breathe. He didn't go to any bank this morning. He was in bed with a paralyzing migraine. The other man who looked like him is dead. Who could she be talking about?

"You saw me at the bank this morning?"

"Yes. I was the one you talked to." The woman on the phone is beginning to sound puzzled and slightly impatient.

Anderson realizes he needs to say something reassuring. "I'm sorry. I guess I forgot your name. It's been so hectic lately, I hardly know whether I'm coming or going."

"I understand," she says, her voice softening.

He doesn't want to make her suspicious, but he has to get some idea of who might have been posing as Peterson. "Did I look a wreck when I stopped by the bank?"

"You looked fine to me, Mr. Peterson." She is obviously amused by the question. "A little windblown, perhaps."

Anderson has got to get more out of her than this. "I know this sounds odd—but could you tell me how I was dressed?"

"You were wearing a black leather motorcycle suit."

As soon as she says it, he has an image of his faceless assailant. But he tries to keep himself from jumping to conclusions. "How do you know it was a motorcycle suit?"

"You were carrying a motorcycle helmet."

"I see. Thanks."

What Anderson needs now is a description of the man's face. But he can't think of any plausible reason for having her give him one. At least, he has found out that the motorcyclist is a man. Until this moment, he wasn't even sure of that.

The sound of the woman's voice brings him back to the subject of the call. "I can't imagine what happened to the records we sent you," she says. "Would you like me to make another set of copies and send them off now?"

Anderson wonders if this would give him the lead he seeks. "Which copies, exactly, did you send me?"

"Everything you asked for. All the records that would correspond to those you lost in your fire."

"The lists of transactions involving my accounts?"

"Yes, and the billing records for the safe deposit boxes you gave up in June. Just as you instructed."

Anderson can't understand why someone who has been trying to kill him would want those out-of-date financial details. "I guess you'd better send me additional copies of everything right away."

"I'll get to it tonight, Mr. Peterson."

Anderson suddenly feels guilty for putting her to so much trouble. "Tomorrow morning will be soon enough. Now that I know you're taking care of it."

"I'm awfully sorry about the delay. If the documents were somehow delivered to the wrong address, the courier service will retrieve them."

"I'm sure you'll get it straightened out."

"Is there anything else I can do for you?"

"No, thank you, Ms. Dorfer. You've been extremely helpful." Anderson hangs up the phone.

For a moment, he just stands there, staring into space. Then he goes back to his table and orders another double bourbon. While he sips it, he gazes at the door where he came in. Somewhere out there is *another* person impersonating Peterson. A person who has been trying to kill him, just as he killed the person he took for Peterson. Does that other person look like Peterson too? Is that other person as beset by uncertainties as he is?

Anderson sits there in the dark, trying to grasp what this additional impersonator might mean. He has a fantasy in which he imagines dozens of Peterson impersonators moving through the city, all looking alike, all being mistaken for each other. They multiply indefinitely, like images in funhouse mirrors placed face to face. Anderson can't tell one from another. In his fantasy, they are so much alike, he can't even tell which one is the original. But then, as he watches them, they do something mirror images never do, even in the wildest of funhouses. The impersonators break ranks and go running off in different directions.

Anderson shakes his head, trying to clear the imaginary figures from his mind. But it is hard to make them go away completely. He realizes he might be blamed for any further crimes committed in Peterson's name—as well as any past crimes. He feels as though his personality has divided and gone out of control.

As he struggles with these ideas, his mind feels obsessively active, while his body remains almost immobile. Thoughts go racing through his brain at a tremendous pace. But they don't seem to get anywhere. They merely go round and round. Anderson drinks to slow them down.

Afternoon turns to night. The waitress who was bringing him drinks goes off duty and is replaced by another. The drinkers sitting around the piano seem to trade places with each other. They request the same songs all over again. The clownlike singer croons on. The bar gets noisier and more crowded.

Anderson looks around the room to steady himself. Suddenly, his heart seems to jump. Sitting alone on the far side of the room is Holmquist. The detective is facing toward him, a drink in his hands. As Anderson watches, Holmquist takes a sip, letting his gaze slide past the tilted glass, toward Anderson's table. There is no eye contact, but Anderson knows the detective would only be there for one reason. To keep him under surveillance.

Moving unsteadily, Anderson gets to his feet. He drops some money on the table and heads for the front door. There is no sign that Holmquist is following. Reaching the pavement, Anderson sets out on foot across the few short blocks to Peterson's apartment building. He scans the sidewalk and street, ready to take evasive action at any moment. He avoids anyone who could be a plainclothes policeman. He avoids even the most innocuous looking pedestrians.

He has been drinking very slowly, so he is not very drunk. But he is not up to any further interviews or other encounters. He certainly does not want to meet anyone right now who might know Peterson. He doesn't think he could bring off another impersonation in his present condition.

He slips almost furtively into the building. He is relieved to see that the doorman is not at the front desk. At Peterson's door, he fumbles with the key for a few moments, because of his unsteady hands. But he still gets inside without meeting anyone.

Back in the apartment, Anderson goes directly to the kitchen. He starts the coffeemaker. Then he opens the freezer to find some frozen food. The package he chooses is labeled "Polenta Casserole with Onions and Bacon." Anderson isn't sure exactly what this is. The picture on the front of the package makes the dish look like scalloped potatoes, but potatoes aren't mentioned in the ingredients list.

He removes the baking dish from the cardboard package. The directions say to make slits in the foil top before putting the casserole in the oven. Anderson rummages in the kitchen drawers, looking for a knife. The first one he finds is a large butcher's blade. He uses it to cut the foil, then lays it on the counter beside the baking dish. Consulting the package again, he sets the oven temperature.

While the oven is preheating, Anderson goes around to the master bathroom. He splashes his face with water. He looks at himself in the mirror. The water streams down his cheeks and drips from his chin.

He notices one of the bathroom drawers is slightly open. He doesn't remember leaving it that way. A linen hand towel has been pushed up, preventing the drawer from closing. Anderson straightens it and slides the drawer shut.

He leaves the bathroom and begins walking back toward the entrance. As he passes each room, he reaches inside and turns on the lights. At first, he thinks he is imagining things. But the evidence quickly mounts. In nearly every room, there are unmistakable signs that the place has been searched. Furniture is slightly out of alignment. Pictures are no longer perfectly level.

Anderson is now feeling deadly sober. He enters the office with the antique medical equipment and begins opening the drawers in Peterson's desk. Just as he expected, Anderson finds the contents of the desk noticeably out of order.

He wonders if the police are responsible. Perhaps this search is just part of their investigation. If Shannon is right about the detectives being told to lay off, they might have trouble getting a search warrant. But perhaps Holmquist and Berglund have been doing some illegal snooping on their own.

Then, as Anderson looks in the drawers, he realizes some things are actually missing. The credit cards and identifications he remembers seeing in the top drawer—they are no longer there! Surely the police wouldn't confiscate those without notifying him.

Looking further, he notices some of Peterson's old utility bills are also gone. Who would be interested in those?

For a moment, he is puzzled. Then it occurs to Anderson that the culprit might be the *other* person who was impersonating Peterson, the person who was going after Peterson's financial records.

If this is also the man who was trying to kill him, does this mean the killer has changed tactics? Is he now less intent on murder? Or will he still kill Anderson as soon as he gets whatever else he is after?

Returning to the kitchen, Anderson notices that something else looks odd. At first, he can't think what it is. Then he realizes that one of the objects he had left on the kitchen counter a few minutes earlier has disappeared. The butcher's knife.

For a moment, Anderson thinks he has truly lost his mind.

Then he realizes there is another explanation: the intruder is still in the apartment. Worse, the intruder is now armed with a knife.

Anderson looks around for something he himself could use as a weapon. The only thing he can see is a copper frying pan hanging from the rack over the butcher block table in the center of the room. Moving as silently as he can, Anderson takes the pan off its hook. It has an unusually long handle. Anderson gets a firm grip on it and weighs it in his hand. With its thick copper bottom, the frying pan is suitably heavy. Anderson figures that if he has to use it to defend himself against a knife, he will at least have some chance.

Holding the frying pan above his head, Anderson moves toward the door to the central corridor. He leans forward and peers down it. There is no one in sight. But the empty corridor looks dangerous. Every door along it could provide an opportunity for ambush, a place where someone wielding a knife could get close without being seen.

Still moving as quietly as he can manage, Anderson crosses the corridor into the exercise room. This gives him more space, room to pivot and strike before a knife could reach him. But he remains enormously vulnerable.

What Anderson needs is a weapon that would give him more reach, one that would allow him to strike a blow without getting within knife range. The only thing like that he can think of are the golf clubs in the closet off the entry hall. The problem is to get there without being caught off guard.

Avoiding the corridor, Anderson slips through the door to the high tech study. There is no sound apart from his own breathing. He creeps sideways through the room, turning his head from side to side, so that he can watch each door.

Suddenly, there is a flash of activity just outside his field of vision. He whirls and prepares to strike. But just before his frying pan connects with a glass sphere, he sees that the movement is only a cluster of electron beams responding to his proximity. For a few seconds, his heart is beating so loudly, he feels he must have betrayed his position. But replaying the incident in his mind, he realizes it took place in total silence.

He moves up against the wall that adjoins the doorway to the office. This allows him to see diagonally into the room before stepping into it. Circling around to the other wall adjoining the doorway, he repeats the procedure, looking through the crack left by the door hinges. There is no sign of anyone lying in ambush, so he eases himself through the doorway.

Inside the private office, Anderson maneuvers around the desk, so he can keep his back to the outside wall. To protect himself, he finds he has to keep track of the door he came from, the door to the little hallway leading to the main corridor, the door to the small bathroom, and the door to the snooker room. Struggling to do this, Anderson realizes that one of the oddities of Peterson's apartment is the unusual number of doors. He is accustomed to rooms with one door or very large rooms with two. But the majority of Peterson's rooms have three doors, and this one has four. He realizes this is probably psychologically significant, but has no time to ponder it. At the moment, he can only regard each door as a physical avenue of attack or escape.

While shifting his eyes between doorways, he tries to spot a better weapon among the antique medical instruments. But despite their ominous appearance, none of them looks as though it would be very effective against a large butcher's blade.

The position of the furniture makes it difficult to see ahead into the snooker room, so Anderson darts through the door as fast as he can, pivoting only when he gets to the snooker table. Once again, he finds himself alone.

By now, he is getting shaky from the strain. He has no idea if the person with the butcher's knife is waiting for him somewhere ahead or moving from room to room as Anderson is doing. Each time he peers through a doorway, he has the curious feeling he is about to encounter his own reflection. He imagines seeing himself as he would look in a mirror, but with no mirror present. The only way he expects his double to be different is that the double will be carrying a knife.

When his eye falls on the long, wooden snooker cues, he realizes one of these might be effective in holding off a butcher's blade. They are not heavy, but they would certainly give him plenty of reach. He moves cautiously to the rack at the far end of the table. Holding the frying pan to the side with one hand, he reaches for a cue with the other.

In the silence of the apartment, the sound of cracking wood is like a gunshot. Anderson is not even sure what he did to cause it. But the wood panelling on which the cue rack is mounted acts like a giant sounding board. Anderson freezes, waiting to see if the noise he has made will have any consequence.

It is not long in coming. From somewhere near the door between the living room and dining room, he hears something bang against one of the built-in cabinets.

This tells him the intruder's location, while confirming that the intruder knows his. No reason now to move slowly! The only imperative is to change his own location as quickly as possible.

Leaving the snooker cue balanced halfway out of the rack,

Anderson runs quietly through the adjoining lounge and into the front entry hall. He finds the bag of golf clubs just inside the closet. With trembling hands, he extracts the driver that looks heaviest. This time, he has better luck than he did with the snooker cue. The club comes out of the bag silently.

He hears movement now in the snooker room. Armed with the golf club and standing in the wider space of the entry hall, Anderson decides to wait for the intruder. If he is facing a man with a knife, his odds should be fairly good. He is determined to get a look at this would-be double, this person who has apparently been trying to kill him, this person who is responsible for the death of his friends. He has vague thoughts of putting the man out of commission once and for all, perhaps even of killing him.

Then Anderson hears a gun being cocked.

This is more than he can handle. Whoever the intruder may be, if he is cornered, he is likely to start shooting. That would make Anderson's golf club useless.

Anderson tiptoes to the entry hall table. He picks up a packet of money and the large brown envelope containing the photographs and travel documents. Then, as quietly as he can, he leaves the apartment.

Once in the outside corridor, he pulls the door tight and runs as fast as his shaky legs will carry him. He gets out of the building without seeing anyone.

Out on the street, he realizes he is still carrying the golf club. He throws it down the bank toward the river.

Then he goes off in search of sanctuary.

C H A P T E R   1 7

Waiting in front of Gretchen's door, Anderson feels himself being inspected. He tucks the large brown envelope under his left arm, where he hopes it will be less conspicuous. The peephole level with his chest lights up, grows dark, then lights up again. Anderson fidgets uncomfortably. After a moment, he hears the sound of a metal chain being unfastened. Then the knob turns and the door swings open.

Gretchen stands in front of him, wearing a quilted, pale blue bathrobe. It goes well with her golden tan and honey blond hair. Her hair is pinned up in back, giving her a slightly formal look, despite the casual way in which it was done.

"Well, if it isn't the swimmer!" she exclaims, looking wary, but amused. "I suppose your car broke down just as you were passing my door."

"I came here to see you," Anderson replies.

The quiet intensity of his voice makes her pause. "Why so serious? Did someone try to kill you again?"

Anderson looks at her with worried eyes and a sheepish smile. "I'm afraid so. Something like that, anyway."

"You know, you do look awful." She leans forward slightly and lifts her head.

Anderson realizes she is sniffing him. He hopes he doesn't smell too bad.

"You smell of whiskey," she says. "But you don't seem drunk."

"I'm definitely not drunk. I just need to talk to you."

"About what?" she asks.

"I'm not sure. Maybe nothing in particular. Maybe everything."

She studies his face, as though trying to read his mind. "Why me?" she asks.

"There is no one else I've seen recently whom I trust."

"I seem to have caused you nothing but trouble. Why would you trust me?"

"I guess I just decided to." It's as close to the truth as anything he can think of saying. He is relieved that she doesn't reject it immediately.

"Hey, Gretch," a male voice calls from somewhere behind her, "is everything okay?"

"No one's attacking me yet," she calls back.

"Damn," the voice says, in a tone of exaggerated disappointment. "Well, let me know as soon as they do."

Somewhere down the apartment's hallway, Anderson can hear female giggles. These are followed by a male voice making a shushing sound.

"That's my roommate's boyfriend," Gretchen explains. "He's a martial arts freak, but he's frustrated because he's never had a chance to use his skills in a real life situation."

Anderson tries to look as unthreatening as possible. "If you're that well protected, maybe you could let me in."

Gretchen hesitates a moment longer, then stands aside and gestures for him to enter. "You do realize how late it is, don't you?"

"I'm sorry, I guess I didn't." Anderson steps into the apartment's hallway, then stands aside so Gretchen can pass by him after closing the door.

Despite the modesty of Gretchen's bathrobe, it is hard for him to ignore the way her body is proportioned. She leads him partway down the hallway, then turns left into the living room. Walking behind her, Anderson observes the way her calves taper gracefully into slender ankles. She is wearing fleece lined slippers, made of soft leather, dyed pale blue.

The decor of the apartment reminds Anderson of his own student days. Posters from old movies decorate the walls. Macramé cradles fastened to the ceiling support ceramic bowls holding spider plants. The bare wood floors are stained by spilled beer. Nothing seems destructible, because everything is already a wreck. Yet everything is vaguely tasteful, even artistic.

It is the kind of environment Anderson associates with happy memories, memories of the time before the drowning of his grandfather sent him into semiseclusion, memories of parties and of laughter.

But are these really happy *memories*? Or are they only happy imaginings?

He tries to recall some student occasion so concrete, it could not be a mere imagining. But as soon as he makes the effort, he catches himself choosing plausible details to round out the mental picture. There is no circumstance in his mental imagery he might not be concocting, no texture or contour he can trace with confidence to a particular time and place.

As he tries to control his growing panic, he becomes aware that Gretchen is staring at him.

She has stopped halfway across the living room and turned around to face him. Her expression makes it clear she is aware of his distress, but is unsure how seriously to take it. "Can I get you something to drink? Herbal tea? Coffee? A beer?"

Anderson struggles to get a grip on himself. "A cup of coffee would be great."

He expects her to go and get the coffee, but instead she continues to examine him.

"You look as though you're losing weight," she says. "Have you had any proper food lately?"

"I can't remember," Anderson admits.

Gretchen gives him a disapproving frown. "I'd better get you something to eat." She walks back to the door of the living room. "Come on," she says, gesturing over her shoulder.

Anderson follows her down the hallway to the kitchen at the back of the apartment. There is a bread baking machine sitting on one of the counters, but otherwise the fittings are fairly old fashioned. High cupboards line the walls, and an old kitchen table stands in the middle of the floor. A colorful plastic table-cloth is spread across it. The room's woodwork is covered with so many layers of white paint, it is difficult to guess what the original trim was like.

"Have you been living here long?" Anderson asks.

"Since the end of my junior year."

Gretchen bends down and opens one of the cupboards below

the counter top. She takes out a large wok. It is Teflon on the inside, with an orange finish on the outside. She puts it on the electric stove and turns the burner to high. Then she takes a bottle of peanut oil out of the cupboard and pours a little onto the Teflon surface.

She goes to a large freezer across the room and removes a Ziploc bag of beef, already cut into thin strips. She puts this on the counter by the stove. Then she opens the refrigerator and begins taking out assorted vegetables. She sets these in the sink, turns on the faucet, and begins washing them.

"Can I help?" Anderson asks, putting his envelope on a nearby shelf.

"I'm counting on it," Gretchen replies. She takes a cutting board off a hook on the wall and removes a knife from a wooden rack. She hands these to Anderson.

He puts them on the kitchen table. The table is too low for him to reach comfortably from a standing position, so he pulls out a chair, and sits down.

Gretchen puts some celery stalks she has just washed on top of the cutting board. "You can discard the ends. Then cut the rest into narrow slices."

She sets a large platter on the counter beside the wok and lays a wooden spatula across it.

Anderson begins slicing the celery. "Are these the right size?" he asks.

"Perfect," Gretchen says. She scoops up the chunks of celery he has already cut and dumps them on the large platter.

"I really appreciate what you're doing," Anderson says. "Seeing me and feeding me this late at night. It's more than anyone would have a right to ask."

"I don't know about that," Gretchen says seriously. "I seem to have set you up for some trouble. I might not have understood what was going on at the time, but I think I still owe you something."

By this time, the wok is hot, and Gretchen adds the frozen beef. It pops and sizzles, but Gretchen is expecting this and dodges the spatters. She takes out a pepper mill and grinds it over the wok. Then she adjusts the heat and gives the mixture a quick stir, pushing the pepper into the meat with the wooden spatula.

As the meat fries she returns to washing vegetables, but she reaches over every few seconds to turn the beef or push it around.

"Your friend Shannon is out of town, I suppose." She says it with elaborate casualness, while facing the stove.

Anderson is not sure how to answer. "No," he says carefully, "I think she's still here."

"Benny Olson says she's very beautiful."

Anderson tries to be noncommittal. "There are other beautiful women."

"It must be nice to have the sort of relationship you have with Shannon. Going to galleries together and such."

Her persistent tone of 'cheerful unconcern' makes Anderson feel increasingly uncomfortable.

"Look," he says finally, "I can't satisfy your curiosity about the sort of relationship I have with Shannon, because I don't *know* what sort of relationship I have with her. I only know I don't trust her."

"Is that why you haven't gone to see her tonight?"

Anderson gives her a patient smile. "I didn't come here as a substitute for seeing her. I came here because I wanted to see you."

"You're welcome to tell me about your romantic problems if you want. But I might not be a great listener at the moment. I've got some pretty serious problems of my own."

Anderson looks up to see her tearing some dark green leaves off some fat, white stalks. She seems to be expressing some of her own frustrations by the energy with which she does this.

"Are yours romantic problems?" Anderson asks.

"No, mine are career problems."

Gretchen sets the leaves on the platter by the wok. Then she puts the stalks on his cutting board. "Quarter inch slices, cut at a diagonal," she says. "You can discard the lower ends."

"What is this vegetable?" Anderson asks.

"Bok choy. A kind of Chinese cabbage. Just what you need to get your digestive system back in shape." Gretchen takes a small paring knife from one of the kitchen drawers and uses it to trim some mushrooms. As she does this, she dips them frequently in the cold running water.

"So what are these career problems of yours?" Anderson asks. He puts the question to her out of politeness. But, as soon as he hears himself speak, he realizes he is more than a little interested. In fact, he is desperate to hear about some problems other than his own.

"My problems would probably seem boring to anyone else. They all have to do with my supervisor, Professor Kolstad, and some trouble I've been having with him."

Anderson feels a sudden chill. He recognizes the name from Peterson's world. One of the academics for whom Peterson had supplied a dissertation is named Kolstad. "Is this the Kolstad who did the work on Pre-Columbian pottery?"

Gretchen stops what she is doing and looks around at him. "I'm surprised you've heard of him. His work isn't that well known outside the field."

"I don't know anything about his work. I've just come across his name. What kind of problem are you having with this Kolstad?"

"I'm supposed to be working on my doctoral dissertation, but Kolstad keeps blocking my research. He refuses to give final approval to my dissertation topic. He refuses to endorse my grant applications. He even refuses to write the letters of introduction that would allow me access to the excavations."

"But if he's your supervisor, why would he want to stop your work?"

"I don't know. It's all rather mysterious." Gretchen looks at him for a moment with raised eyebrows, apparently uncertain how to explain. Then she collects the sliced bok choy stalks from the cutting board. She dumps them in the wok, along with the celery Anderson had cut before. Then she adds a spoonful of tan paste from a jar in the refrigerator.

"What's that?" Anderson asks.

"Gingerroot," Gretchen replies. She takes two small garlic cloves from a box in the cupboard, rinses them under the running water, and then puts them on the cutting board.

"Chop these?" Anderson asks.

"Yes, as fine as you can."

When he has done this, she picks up the cutting board and scrapes the garlic bits into the wok. Then she sets the board in front of Anderson again.

Anderson catches her eye as she does this. "Tell me about this mysterious behavior on the part of your supervisor."

"I hardly know where to start."

"Try to start at the beginning."

Gretchen looks thoughtful. "I suppose it all begins with Kolstad's own doctoral dissertation. It was on Maya pictorial ceramics. He treated the pictures and diagrams on Maya vases as texts, connecting them to the *Popol Vuh,* the Maya's sacred book. He analyzed the 'pictorial discourse' in what he called a 'structural linguistic' manner. The component images were treated like words, the larger pictures like sentences. Kolstad's analysis focused on 'the syntax.' It was brilliant."

Anderson can't help smiling. It sounds as though Kolstad had been landed with a typical Peterson thesis: ingenious, provocative, and extremely abstruse. "It must have been an unusually abstract piece of work," Anderson comments.

"I suppose it was," Gretchen says. "Kolstad worked everything out with a kind of symbolic logic. Most people in the field found it hard to understand. But Kolstad's results were very exciting. They included some remarkable conclusions about the mental world of the Maya."

Anderson tries to decide if he would have been capable of writing such a dissertation. The fact that the thesis sounds so difficult to him suggests that he isn't Peterson. But he hesitates to say he couldn't have written it. He has certainly done other things in the last few days he wouldn't have thought possible.

"What's happened in this field *since* Kolstad's dissertation?"

"Quite a bit," Gretchen replies. "The most important thing is the enormous progress that's been made in the decipherment of Mayan writing. It hasn't made the earlier work in the field obsolete, but it has made us see it all in a new light."

"So where do you come in? What does your work try to accomplish?"

"I guess you could say it picks up where Kolstad's thesis left off. The decipherment of the Maya script makes it possible to go much further in the analysis of the ceramics. So by using the techniques Kolstad introduced, I've been able to come up with many more conclusions about Maya mental categories."

Gretchen picks up some mushrooms she has trimmed and puts them down on the cutting board. Beside them, she sets a handful of water chestnuts.

"Do you want these halved or quartered?" Anderson asks.

"Either would be fine."

Anderson cuts the mushrooms and water chestnuts into quarters.

Gretchen picks up the cutting board and pushes the pieces into the wok.

As Anderson thinks over what Gretchen has told him, he begins to see the nature of her problem with Kolstad. She keeps expecting him to behave like the man who wrote the ground breaking dissertation. But the real Kolstad is actually a very different sort of person. "I guess you assumed Kolstad would support what you've been doing."

"I thought he'd love it!" Gretchen exclaims. "All my work is really just an extension of the theories he himself propounded. I wouldn't have known where to begin without him. Yet Kolstad doesn't seem to have any sympathy for what I'm trying to do. I can't figure it out. Sometimes, when I try to ask him about the project, he doesn't even seem to understand it!"

Anderson has to stop himself from laughing out loud. How exquisitely Peterson had contrived his revenge! By making his dissertations so intellectually difficult, Peterson had made it impossible for an academic 'client' like Kolstad to come up with comparable work on his own. The more attention a client's dissertation received, the more he would be reminded of own limitations.

Of course, the drawback to Peterson's scheme is that it could make things hard on people like Gretchen, who thought their professors would be interested in real scholarship. "What a disappointment for you," Anderson says sincerely.

"It gets worse! Kolstad is now making all sorts of lame excuses for opposing my research proposals. His excuses are so feeble, I should be able to just laugh them off, but people seem to be taking them seriously. There's a very real danger that he's going to wreck my reputation in the field before I even have one."

Gretchen removes the wok from the burner. She opens the refrigerator and takes out a bottle of sauce with a Chinese label. She pours a hefty helping of this into the wok. It hisses and boils. Then she takes a half-finished bottle of German wine from the refrigerator and adds some of this to the wok as well. When the mixture has stopped making bubbling noises, she puts it back on the burner.

"What kind of excuse is Kolstad using to oppose your work?"

Gretchen rolls her eyes. "Kolstad now claims the pictorial ceramics are the product of an elite class and do not reflect the culture of the society as a whole. That's complete nonsense, of course. No elite has ever been able to maintain that separate a culture. But even if it *weren't* nonsense, it would hardly be reason for vetoing the study of these ceramics. You can't dismiss the culture of the people running things on the grounds that they are the people running things!"

"It's hard to believe Kolstad would get anywhere with that argument."

"Oh, he's got other arguments too. He says the 'structural linguistic' analysis of these ceramics is too speculative and theoretical to be part of scientific archaeology. That's also ridiculous, because I start and end with observable data. Every theorist has to! No one would consider a theory otherwise."

"Surely, you can point that out."

"I keep trying to! But then Kolstad introduces the argument he considers the real clincher. He says the key ceramics of this type were obtained by looting and that to study them is to condone art theft. He says his professional ethics prevents him from supporting work like mine. Can you imagine?! That policy would make half the antiquities in the world's museums out of bounds for scholars!"

The mixture in the wok is by now boiling again. Gretchen adds a sizable quantity of pea pods, which she had been washing and trimming earlier. She gives these a good stir, then covers the wok.

"It sounds as though all Kolstad's attacks on your work could be used equally well to attack his own early work."

"Oh, he admits that. But he says his own work was only partly tainted, because he was merely introducing these ideas as a possibility, whereas *my* work, because it goes so much further in actually applying them, is *all* tainted."

"If this Professor Kolstad is so opposed to what you are doing, why don't you just tailor your thesis proposal to suit his wishes? Why are you so devoted to this one particular subject?"

Gretchen looks shocked. "I've been working on it for nearly three years! It's the best work I've ever done. Do you expect me to throw it all away?"

Anderson raises his hands as though they could protect him from the fury of her response. "I'm just trying to understand the reasons you're caught in this bind."

Gretchen relaxes slightly. "Actually, it's not just a matter of the work I've put in. There's more to it than that. Apart from the *Popol Vuh,* these pictorial ceramics I've been studying are the best available source of information on the central myth of the Maya."

Gretchen lifts the cover off the wok, taking care not to be scalded by the steam. She adds the leaves she had torn off the bok choy stalks. Then she gives the mixture another stir and covers it again.

"What's so important about this myth? Why is it central?"

"It's the Maya's own account of their past."

"What sort of things do they say about their past?"

"Well, part of the myth is like Genesis. But there are some big differences. One difference is that the Maya believed there were a number of gods interacting with each other before the creation of man. Another difference is that the Maya didn't believe that man was created in one try. They believed there were successive attempts to create man and successive floods that washed them away."

Anderson becomes alert. After his own near drownings, the mention of successive floods catches his attention. "Tell me more about these floods and creations," he says.

Gretchen turns toward him, her cheeks dimpled with pleasure, and her eyes glowing with enthusiasm.

Anderson can see he has said exactly the right thing.

"In the beginning," she says, "there was only water. Then the gods began their creative efforts. First came the man of mud, who had no strength. This type of man was wiped out by a flood. Then came the man of wood, who had no proper feeling. This type of man suffered a rebellion in which his utensils rose up against him. Then he, too, was wiped out by a flood. Finally came the man of dough, who could be repeatedly remolded. This type survived, but with his vision impaired."

Gretchen lifts the cover from the wok. She takes a can of mixed nuts and sprinkles them liberally over the steaming food. Then she turns off the burner and takes out a large dinner plate. She piles the contents of the wok onto the plate and sets the heaping plate in front of Anderson. It makes an appealing pattern of greens, yellows, and browns.

"Would you like a fork or chopsticks?"

"I think I'd be better off tonight with a fork."

Gretchen hands him one from a nearby drawer and sets a glass beside his plate.

Anderson holds a forkful of the food in the air to let it cool, then puts it in his mouth. The taste and texture is full of contrasts. It is spicy, but mild. Moist, but crispy. "This is wonderful!" he exclaims between chews.

"I'm glad you like it," Gretchen says, genuinely pleased at his response. She takes a can of beer from the refrigerator and opens it. Then she picks up his glass and pours the beer down its side, so it doesn't foam. When the glass is full, she sets the can beside it.

Anderson is by now enjoying the food, but he is also fascinated by her enthusiasm and by what she has been telling him. He has no conscious knowledge of the Maya or of their mythology. But each thing Gretchen tells him seems to possess a dreamlike familiarity. He wonders if the 'Peterson' who wrote Kolstad's dissertation is so remote from him after all.

Gretchen rinses the wok with water. Then she squirts a little detergent into it, scrubs it around with a brush, and rinses it again. "What's really important, for my purposes, is the mental framework hidden in the myth. While the gods of the Maya were carrying out their various tasks, they were also laying out the moral and physical world of the Maya. The myth that's recounted in the *Popol Vuh* is the best key we have to Maya culture."

She opens a beer for herself, sits down in the chair opposite Anderson, and begins sipping from the can.

Anderson tries to look at her problem as objectively as possible, focusing on the practical aspects. "If you know this myth so well from the *Popol Vuh,* why do you need to study these ceramics of yours?"

Gretchen smiles. "It turns out that the pictorial ceramics have some big advantages over the *Popol Vuh* itself. For one thing, they diagram certain relationships better. So they provide a key for interpreting some vital parts of the myth. For another thing, they include many incidents not mentioned in the surviving portions of the *Popol Vuh.* So they're an irreplaceable source in themselves."

There is a positive energy in Gretchen as she talks about archaeology that Anderson finds irresistibly appealing. He loves the way she forgets herself as she expounds her ideas. He loves, in particular, the way she extends her leg beyond the side of the table, the way she makes circles with her toe as she talks.

"What would you want to do next?" he asks. "I mean, if your supervisor were supporting you, instead of getting in your way."

"I want to find out if my deductions actually hold up." She gestures with her hands to convey her excitement. "I've figured out a way to test some of my conclusions by checking them against the physical evidence at the excavations."

"How, exactly, would you do that?"

Her eyes sparkle with a special eagerness. Once again, Anderson knows he has asked exactly the right thing.

"By taking advantage of something very peculiar in Maya culture," she explains. "The Maya believed that if certain art objects were used for a time by royalty, these objects accumulated a special potency. They even portrayed this potency in their paintings by means of a particular symbol called a 'personification head.' When the potency was unwanted or became so intense as to be dangerous, the Maya would try to release it or remove it by vandalizing their own art works. They would deface their carvings, drill holes in their painted pots, smash the faces of their statues. The way they did this and the sequence in which they went about it could be very revealing. It should confirm or refute some of my deductions about their cosmology."

"It sounds like a brilliant idea to me."

"Unfortunately, it's an idea that's more difficult to pursue than it sounds. You see, most archaeologists have ignored the vandalism. They have repaired the artifacts, and they have photographed or drawn them in ways that conceal or minimize the damage. Often, when there was natural or accidental damage, they haven't distinguished this properly from the intentional damage. The result is that instead of providing me with the data I need, the field archaeologists have actively concealed it."

"So what do you want to do?"

"I want to go back over the excavations and study, not the monuments and artifacts themselves, but the *damage*. The holes, the breaks, the cracks. In other words, I want to test my conclusions by examining the patterns of intentional destruction."

"You don't need to make any new excavations?"

"No, I just need to examine the existing excavations in a new way."

"What do you need in order to do that?"

"I need my supervisor's approval of my dissertation topic. I need his support on my grant applications, so I can get the money I need to do the work. And I need his help in getting permission to do the on-site tests and measurements. But it all seems hopeless. This crazy position he has adopted means he's blocking everything."

The unfairness of her predicament pulls her up short. For a moment, she seems on the verge of tears.

Thinking back over what Gretchen has told him, Anderson realizes that Kolstad is being threatened with more than embarrassment. If Gretchen focuses enough attention on Peterson's abstruse concepts, it will become increasingly evident that Kolstad doesn't understand those concepts. From there, it is just a short step to recognizing that Kolstad couldn't have written his own dissertation.

No wonder Kolstad is blocking her research! He feels threatened with total exposure, with complete professional disgrace!

Fortunately, the same fears that have turned Kolstad against her work could also be used to make him support it. All Anderson has to do is contact Kolstad as 'Peterson.' Faced with the certainty of what Peterson could do to him, the risk from Gretchen's work will seem like a mere inconvenience.

"Listen," Anderson says. "There's something going on here I know a bit about. I can't explain it right now. But I can assure you this grief you've been getting is only temporary. In the very near future, you're going to be able to go ahead with your research, exactly the way you want."

"There's no way you can guarantee something like that."

Anderson leans forward and touches her arm. "There is. It will happen. I promise."

Gretchen stares at him wide-eyed, eager to believe what he is saying. But then she seems to decide he is being irrationally optimistic. What could he possibly know of Kolstad? Her look of hope fades. "I hope you're right," she says wistfully.

Anderson finishes the last of the stir fry. He is surprised at how fast it has disappeared. "This food was really wonderful," he says.

Gretchen gets to her feet and picks up his fork and plate. She splashes them with water, adds a couple of drops of detergent, and scrubs them with a brush. Then she rinses them off and puts them in the dish rack.

"I'm afraid it's past my bedtime. I've got to go to work tomorrow."

Anderson gets to his feet as well, but stands there awkwardly. "There's a problem with my apartment. I can't go back there tonight."

Gretchen studies his face again for several seconds, then looks directly in his eyes. "You're welcome to sleep in my room as long as you stay outside my bedcovers and don't try to make any sexual advances."

"Thank you. I'll obey the rules."

"Remember, I've got friends down the hall. If I let out a scream, the one who's a martial arts expert will come in and break all your bones." She smiles as she says it, but isn't entirely joking.

"I'll keep that in mind," Anderson says, sliding his chair back under the table.

Gretchen leads him down the hall to her bedroom. "Make

yourself at home," she says, opening the door for him. Then she disappears into the bathroom a few yards up the hall.

Anderson steps inside and looks around. Her walls are decorated with posters. He is surprised to see that several are of rock stars. Two of them are unfamiliar to Anderson, but the others were actually more popular in his student days than in hers. The remaining posters are more what Anderson was expecting. They show Central American pyramids, calendars, and figurines. Several were advertisements for airlines and travel agencies. The remaining couple were announcements of museum exhibits. When Anderson surveys the total effect, the juxtaposition of modern performers and ancient artifacts seems to suggest a network of esoteric connections, stretching across the distances of culture and time.

Gretchen's books create much the same impression. There is a sizable collection of popular novels, including a number of bodice rippers and some science fiction. But there is an even larger collection of books on Mesoamerican archaeology. These books are supplemented with numerous loose leaf binders filled with handwritten notes and huge stacks of Xerox copies taken from excavation reports and journal articles. The scholarly effect is softened by a makeup table covered with lotions, brushes, and other feminine supplies. But scanning the room, it would be difficult to say whether Gretchen was more immersed in her own time or in an alien past.

When Gretchen comes back a few minutes later, Anderson takes his turn in the bathroom, washing himself and cleaning his teeth as well as he can without a brush. He checks the dressing on his arm, but it seems to be okay.

Returning to her room, Anderson finds Gretchen already in bed. The only light still on is a lamp on her bedside table that was made from a Chianti bottle. The bed seems roomy enough for two, so Anderson climbs carefully onto it, taking care not to bump against her. He stays outside the covers as she requested, but pulls the extra blanket over himself.

When it seems clear that she is comfortable having him there, Anderson slides up toward her pillow and, as she shifts position, places his arm gently around her shoulders.

Gretchen stares off into space, her mind obviously still dwelling on her career predicament. "Sometimes I think of abandoning archaeology altogether. But I'm reluctant to let all my past efforts be for nothing."

Anderson studies her profile. The first smile lines are beginning to form at the corner of her eye. He realizes they will make her face look even more attractive as she gets older. He wonders what he could say that would reassure her about her work. "It's important to be able to build on the past, to use the past to illuminate the present."

"But maybe I'm *too* concerned with using the past. Maybe that's why I got involved with archaeology in the first place. Maybe I've taken the wrong direction."

"There's nothing wrong with the direction you've taken. It's the people around you who have gotten out of kilter."

Gretchen rolls toward Anderson and kisses him full on the mouth. It is a moist, yielding, passionate kiss, with nothing held back. He feels the solid pressure of her tongue and lips against his tongue and lips. He feels her extraordinary breasts pressing against his chest. He feels her hips nestled against his own.

Anderson feels a powerful impulse to yank down the covers, to tear off her nightdress, to touch her body everywhere. But he remembers his promise, and, trembling almost from head to foot, he restrains himself from moving anything but his mouth. The kiss goes on for several minutes, growing ever more intense.

Then, as suddenly as she had turned toward him, Gretchen breaks it off and turns away. "Thank you," she says softly, when she has caught her breath.

Anderson is not sure if she is thanking him for his restraint or for the kiss. Perhaps it's his reassuring words before the kiss that made her feel grateful. He doesn't dare ask.

For a few minutes, Gretchen is silent. Anderson shifts his head slightly to look at her and sees that she has fallen asleep in his arms. A wave of tenderness sweeps through him. The sexual attraction he has felt each time he has seen her is still there. But it has now become only one of several ways in which he feels drawn to her.

Moving as gently as possible, he reaches across her and turns off the light. She doesn't stir. He finds himself hoping intensely that all goes well for her. He is glad he will be able to help by getting Kolstad to cooperate.

Anderson stays awake as long as he can, clinging to this feeling of simple good wishes and companionship. While the moment lasts, he has a sense of peace. But he is exhausted and soon succumbs to his dreams.

They are turbulent and filled with Shannon. Anderson dreams he is having sex with her in some woods. They are naked, but sweating profusely, and the leaves and twigs are sticking to their backs. Suddenly, the two of them are interrupted by a face-less figure in motorcycle leathers. The motorcyclist scolds Anderson with a voice like that of Anderson's grandfather. He threatens Anderson with punishments too terrible to be named. Then, when he has finished his angry tirade, the figure removes his helmet to reveal his face. The face is Anderson's.

As he dreams this, Anderson is racked with guilt, but he is unable to let go of the images. He feels as though portions of the dream are not his own, that they belong to someone else. But he is not sure which portions. He sweats as though in a fever.

Gretchen becomes aware of Anderson's troubled sleep and moves to comfort him. Her arms go around his neck, and her lips kiss the side of his face. In her embrace, Anderson is able to relax once more. For a time, his sleep is blessedly dreamless.

When he awakes the next day, Gretchen is no longer beside him. Anderson gets up to look for her. He puts on his shoes and opens the door to the hall. There is no one in sight, but he hears faint sounds coming from the back of the apartment.

Anderson walks down the hall and looks into the kitchen.

A young man is bent over, peering into the refrigerator. Hearing Anderson behind him, he whirls and goes into a martial arts stance. The refrigerator door stays open behind him. The fellow is Anderson's size, but hardly more than a kid.

Anderson is not frightened, but he is careful to make no sudden movements. "You must be the boyfriend of Gretchen's roommate. I heard you call out to Gretchen, when she let me in last night."

The boy slowly relaxes and assumes a normal posture. "I'm sorry. You startled me. Gretchen isn't in the habit of having overnight visitors."

"Where is she, by the way?"

The boy takes a carton of yogurt out of the refrigerator and closes the refrigerator door. "She left for work about an hour ago."

"Where is she working these days?"

"The same place. Harry the Health Nut's."

"Harry the Health Nut's?"

The boy smiles. "You know, the natural food co-op over in St. Paul."

"Oh."

"My name's Eric," the boy says, offering his hand. "What's yours?"

Anderson hesitates. "Andy," he says finally, giving the boy's hand a firm shake. "Pleased to meet you."

The boy gestures at the cupboards. "I'm afraid most of the food in this kitchen is intimidatingly good for you. But you're welcome to anything you can find that appeals."

"Thanks. I'll have some low fat granola or something."

The boy tears the top off the yogurt carton and takes a spoon from the silverware drawer. "Can I help you with anything else?"

"Not really." Anderson hesitates. "Unless you'd like to sell me one of your shirts."

The boy looks at him quizzically. "You want the shirt off my back?"

"No, any shirt would do. I just need a clean one."

The boy laughs. "And here I was thinking you liked my taste in clothes!"

"I love your taste," Anderson assures him. "But my real problem is I've got some important business to do this morning, and I don't have time to shop or go back to my apartment."

"I'd be happy to lend you anything you need." The boy begins cheerfully spooning the yogurt into his mouth. Evidently, being associated with Gretchen is all the character reference Anderson needs.

"I'm not sure when I'd be able to get the clothes back to you."

"Don't worry about it."

"You know," Anderson says, "I don't want to take these

clothes I've been wearing with me. Do you think you'd have any use for them? They're dirty now, but they've barely been worn."

"Are you proposing a trade?"

"If you like."

The boy looks more closely at what Anderson is wearing. "That shirt of yours is pretty classy."

"You're welcome to the pants as well, if you'd like. I'm afraid they're rather wrinkled, but they should look good when they've been laundered."

"I don't have anything of comparable quality to offer you."

"It doesn't matter. Anything clean will do."

"All right, it's a deal." The boy puts his spoon in the yogurt carton and sets the carton on the table. "Come on," he says. "Let's see what we can find."

Anderson follows him down the hall to the room he apparently shares with his girlfriend. Inside it, the furnishings are almost spartan in their simplicity. Except for one thing. On every surface, there are furry stuffed animals. Not just teddy bears, but zebras, camels, pigs, raccoons, seals, kangaroos, ducks, alligators, and others.

"Quite a zoo, isn't it? Two years ago, my girlfriend told me: 'If you want to sleep with me, you have to sleep with them.' I said I thought I could get used to it." The boy turns back and gives Anderson a cockeyed grin. "But I haven't."

He pulls open a drawer and takes out a pair of green denim trousers. "How about these?"

"They look great," Anderson says.

"And these?" the boy asks, adding a purple pastel shirt, brown socks, and orange boxer shorts.

"They're all perfect," Anderson affirms.

"Hey, maybe you *do* like my taste. My girlfriend says I'm color blind. You can put the clothes you're leaving behind in the bathroom hamper."

"I really appreciate this," Anderson says, heading for the bathroom.

"No problem. It's a good trade."

Anderson comes out of the bathroom fifteen minutes later, newly showered and crisply attired.

The apartment is now completely silent. Either everyone has left for the day or else they are sleeping soundly.

Anderson shaves with an electric razor he finds in Gretchen's room. It is apparently designed for women's legs, but it works fine on Anderson's face.

When he is finished shaving, he puts on the brown sports coat he was wearing when he arrived and retrieves the large brown envelope he had brought with him. He feels surprisingly refreshed.

He thinks about the kind of health food breakfast he'd be likely to find in this apartment. Glazed doughnuts sound better.

Making sure the apartment door is locked behind him, Anderson sets out to find some.

C H A P T E R   1 8

Anderson is still eating a doughnut when he pushes on the glass
and steel door of a local camera shop. The shop is located halfway between Gretchen's apartment and the university campus. A
chime sounds as the door swings inward, but there is no other
acknowledgment of Anderson's arrival.

The walls of the shop are lined with glass cabinets, displaying
cameras, tripods, lenses, light meters, slide projectors, carrying
cases, boxes of film, and other photographic supplies. The backs
of the cabinets are all mirrored to make the space seem bigger
and to show the reverse sides of the merchandise.

Anderson is very aware of his own reflections as he moves
deeper into the shop. There seem to be an infinite number of
them. They remind him of his own drunken fantasy in which
Peterson impersonators were multiplying indefinitely.

Free standing glass counters run along one side of the shop
and across the rear. Behind one of them sits a man reading an
article on ice fishing in *Field and Stream.*

Anderson extracts some of the larger photographs from the
envelope he is carrying. The top one is the photo that shows a
United States senator hugging Anderson's arm affectionately,
while looking desperate for Anderson's approval.

Anderson lays the photographs down on the counter top beside the spot where the man is sitting. "I was wondering what you
could tell me about these," he says.

The man looks up reluctantly from his magazine. His face is
heavily lined. Despite his thick brown hair, it is obvious he is in
his late sixties. "That doesn't look like the sort of order we normally handle. You got a receipt?"

"These aren't from your shop," Anderson explains. "At least,

I don't think they are. If you can spare me a minute, I was hoping to get your technical opinion of the work."

The man sets down his magazine. He picks up the photographs, glances quickly at them, and drops them back on the counter. "It's good work. Very professional. Do you have a studio?"

"I didn't take these. Actually, I was hoping you might be able to give me some clues about the photographer who did."

The man turns over the top photo and examines the back. "There's no way to tell who took them."

Anderson takes the photos and lays them down in a long row. "Do you notice anything odd about these pictures?"

The man leans forward to examine them. "Nope. Good focus and exposure. Nice tones and saturation in the prints. Skillful retouching. It's competent work, but nothing unusual."

"What, exactly, was retouched?"

"Can't tell. That's why it's good work."

"If you can't tell, how do you know these pictures *were* retouched?"

"They just look that way."

Anderson tries to control his impatience. "Is there anybody in the Twin Cities who might be able to tell me more about these? Some technical specialist or something?"

"You might talk to Procolor."

"What is Procolor?"

"They're the processing lab most professionals in town use when they're not too worried about costs. They're downtown on Hennepin. Right across from the Orpheum Theater."

"Thanks. I might try them."

"Ask for Sonia Larson. Waste as much of her time as you can. Don't tell her who sent you."

Anderson gives the man a wry look, gathers up his photographs, and leaves the shop.

Twenty-five minutes later, he arrives by bus on Hennepin Avenue. He gets off near the corner of Ninth Street. Straight ahead is the Orpheum Theater, its marquee announcing a touring production of *Guys and Dolls*. Across the street is a windowless bookstore selling pornographic magazines and videos.

For a moment, Anderson wonders if the man in the camera

shop has misdirected him, perhaps as a joke. Then he sees the rainbow colored sign for Procolor on the building beyond.

Entering through the parking lot door, Anderson finds the interior of Procolor a disorienting exercise in graphic design. Red, yellow, and blue stripes stretch horizontally overhead, punctuated by neon signs. Gray counters with black-and-white trim parallel these stripes below. There seem to be plenty of clerks, all dressed in sweatshirts, jeans, and running shoes. But everyone looks busy.

Anderson hesitates, wondering which counter to choose. "Processing" is written in blue neon tubing over the left hand counter, where two clerks are filling out forms for customers handing in rolls of film. "Order Pickup" is written in red tubing over the center counter, where one clerk is handing out huge white envelopes labeled "Procolor" and another is restocking a refrigerated film case. "Prints" is written in blue tubing over an archway that opens to the right. There, four clerks are manning color copiers, paper trimmers, and other devices laid out behind a longer counter.

Anderson walks through the archway into the "Prints" department.

One of the clerks detaches herself from a copying machine and hurries over. "Can I help you?" she asks.

"I'd like to see Sonia Larson, if she's available right now."

"She's up in the processing lab. I'll tell her you're here, but she's very busy this morning." The clerk picks up a telephone and pushes one of the buttons on top of it. "Perhaps I could help you," she says, as she waits for the phone to be answered.

Anderson takes out the same photos he had shown the man in the camera shop. The one of him with the senator is still on top. Anderson sets the photos on the counter.

There is a rattle in the clerk's telephone receiver. She turns away slightly as she speaks into it. "There's a man here asking for Sonia. No, I haven't found out yet. All right, I'll tell him." She hangs up the phone. "Sonia will be down shortly. But she'll only be able to give you a minute or two of her time." The clerk looks at Anderson expectantly.

Anderson pushes the photographs toward her. "Can you tell me anything about these?"

The clerk picks the top print and looks at it closely. "These are well done," she comments. She feels the paper, then turns the print over to inspect the back. "I think this is our processing and printing, but I can't be certain."

"If Procolor did do these, is there any way you could find out *who* you did them *for?*"

"Not really. We don't label our prints, so there are no records to show who sent them in, or when, or anything else like that."

"But you think this is Procolor's work?"

The clerk shrugs her shoulders. "Looks like it."

A slightly older woman appears behind the clerk. She is tall and regal looking. "I'm Sonia Larson. Can I help you?"

"I'm trying to find out anything I can about these photographs. Where they came from. Who took them, if possible."

The woman picks up the first couple of photos and looks at them briefly before dropping them back on the counter. "Nobody 'took' them. Somebody 'made' them."

"You're saying these are fakes."

"Not exactly. They just don't show real situations."

"What do you mean?"

The woman pushes the edges of the pictures with her fingertips, spreading them out. "These are actual photographs, rather than, say, airbrush art. But they're mostly composites."

Anderson looks at her intently, but says nothing.

The woman points to the photo on top. "This one, for instance. It was made from at least two separate exposures on two separate negatives."

"How can you tell?"

"A couple of things. Look at these faces, for example. They're not shown in the same perspective. This face was taken with a high quality telephoto lens from maybe forty feet away. This other face was taken with a fairly ordinary lens from only eight or ten feet." She lifts the photo closer to her eyes. "Say, that's you, isn't it? With a beard."

"You said 'a couple of things.' "

"Sure, look. The lighting is also different. The key light for this man's face would be right about here. Whereas the key light for your face would be slightly lower and more to the side. Over this way someplace. Where have I seen that man before? Oh, I know. He's a senator, isn't he?"

"How about the background?"

"I can't tell about the background. It's too flat. But the flag and the rostrum are probably from the same negative as the senator. The lighting is consistent, anyway." The woman pauses and laughs.

"What are you laughing at?"

"Well, it appears that someone has concocted this photograph in order to put you in a very compromising position." She laughs again. "They want it to seem as though you're friends with a senator."

"How about these other photos?"

She looks at her watch. "I'm afraid I've got to go check color gradients up in the lab. If you've got more questions, why don't you try asking the studio that sent these in for processing?"

"I was told there were no records that would show who sent them in."

"There aren't any records. But I'm pretty sure these photos came from Personality Event Photography. I don't remember them doing composites much, but otherwise this looks like their work."

"Who are they?"

"They're a local outfit. They specialize in candid location jobs, but they've also got a regular studio over in the warehouse district." The woman leans over and types something into one of the computers.

"What are 'candid location jobs'?"

"At the lower end of the market, they're weddings and bar mitzvahs. At the upper end, where PEP operates, they're mostly public relations events organized by big corporations." She pauses and smiles, as though remembering something she doesn't want to describe. "PEP is a very 'fast track' outfit."

"Why 'fast track'? What makes them different from their competitors?"

"They're just very good at what they do. A corporation can tell them exactly the kind of photographs they want, and PEP will get them—without interfering with the 'spontaneity' of the occasion."

"In other words, they photograph staged events so they don't *look* staged."

"Precisely."

The woman picks up a business card for Procolor, turns it over, and writes the address for Personality Event Photography on the back. After checking the computer screen, she adds two phone numbers underneath.

"The number on top is their regular business phone," she says. "The one on the bottom is for urgent messages after business hours."

Anderson glances at the card. The bottom number looks like one he has seen recently. But he doesn't remember actually dialing it. He tries to recall the possible circumstances. The memory makes his jaw muscles tighten. "Would Shannon Crosno be connected with this outfit, by any chance?"

"Sure. It's her operation. I think she owns it."

Anderson takes a deep breath. He looks again at the address the woman wrote on the card. 420 North Fifth Street. "This place is within walking distance, isn't it?"

"I suppose. It's at the corner of Fifth Street and Fifth Avenue. That's about eight blocks from here."

"In the warehouse district, right?"

"That's right. You go up Hennepin to Fifth Street, then left four or five blocks. It used to be a good area to have lunch, but the restaurants over there are getting too expensive now."

"Thank you," Anderson says. "I really appreciate your help." He turns and leaves.

As he walks up Hennepin Avenue, it occurs to Anderson that the busy Ms. Larson seemed to have a lot of time for him after all. He realizes belatedly that she was probably angling for a luncheon invitation. He feels he has been socially clumsy, but knows he can't worry about it now. He has to decide what to do with his new information.

The fact that the studio he has been seeking belongs to Shannon puts some of the physical clues he has been following in a new light. Evidently, it was Shannon who contrived the misleading photos of Anderson in Peterson's apartment. She took photographs of the face he has identified as his own and inserted them in photographs where he wasn't present.

Were these composites simply one of Peterson's devices to make sure Anderson's body was identified as Peterson's? If so, doesn't this demonstrate that he really is Anderson? Doesn't it show that his face could only be inserted into Peterson's world through fakery?

Or is there another explanation? Perhaps these photographs are simply 'trophies,' like the military medals that also decorate Peterson's walls. Perhaps Peterson had Shannon make them as a sort of private joke, as a gesture of contempt toward the kind of photos ordinary people use to demonstrate their importance. If that is the case, then perhaps he really is Peterson after all.

The one person who he knows has the answer is Shannon. His pace quickens as he thinks about confronting her. He intends to make her reveal everything this time, every detail of Peterson's life and schemes. He will shake the truth out of her if he has to.

He turns down Fifth Street, dodging impatiently around the people on the sidewalk who get in his way. One is a vagrant with a long, gray beard, who wanders drunkenly in front of him. To Anderson, he looks like the wreck of a river god.

Closer to First Avenue, the pedestrians grow more stylish. Most are on their way to business luncheons. Anderson is now in the area that used to consist of old warehouses, but later became fashionable for businesses with connections to the arts. In addition to offices and restaurants, it is home to dozens of art galleries, like the ones Peterson used to visit with Shannon. Anderson wonders if the Lamberton Gallery, which Gretchen's friend mentioned, is among them. It seems likely.

After Second Avenue, the pedestrian traffic on Fifth Street diminishes. The roadway becomes a bridge that stretches nearly three blocks over parking lots and railroad tracks. Just past the end of the bridge, Anderson sees the address he is looking for.

It's an eleven story building of red brick, covered with large, many-paned windows. These were obviously designed to let as much light as possible into the studios and workshops within. The main entrance is around the corner on Fifth Avenue, near an elevated roadway, passing over the street. As Anderson heads that way, a truck roars across, silhouetted briefly against the sky. Otherwise, the streets in that direction seem deserted.

Before he goes in, Anderson walks a few steps farther, so he can get a glimpse of the building's far side. Loading docks for trucks extend the length of it, but none of them is in use at the moment. Back at the entrance itself, there is a green canvas awning over the doors and a new ramp providing access for the handicapped. Everything seems strangely peaceful.

The silence is broken by two girls who burst from the building, chattering loudly about their favorite binge foods. Their strikingly chiseled features, peculiar makeup, and amazing youth mark them as models on a break from a photo session.

Anderson goes in where they have just come out. A security guard is sitting in a windowed room overlooking the entry, but he pays no attention as Anderson walks by. Straight ahead, opposite the doors, is a black mirrored wall. Anderson sees his own reflection looking ghostly in the darkness.

The managers of the building have obviously made an effort to give it an attractive lobby. There are lush plants, thick carpets, comfortable chairs, and good woodwork. But the effect is spoiled by the roar of ventilation fans and the utilitarian look of the corridors beyond.

Anderson finds a passenger elevator just inside the entrance, to the left of a glass wall. He takes it to the floor indicated by the office number he was given at Procolor. Stepping out, he finds himself at the end of a long corridor. It is painted white, with a tan stripe running along the walls at the top of the widely spaced doors. Overhead are bare pipes and fluorescent light fixtures. The doors themselves are double-width and made of light colored wood. Beside each one is a black plastic sign with white lettering, bearing the name of the tenant.

Anderson walks quietly along the corridor. There is a pleasant odor of industrial solvents and photographic chemicals. He passes a large freight elevator and rounds a corner. The corridor widens. A short distance beyond, he sees the sign for "Personality Event Photography."

Taking a deep breath, he knocks on the door. There is no answer. He turns the knob and finds it unlocked. Cautiously, he pushes it open.

He finds himself looking in on an office with desks and personal computers, a copier and a coffee machine. There is no one in sight. Large glass windows are set in the far wall. It is hard to tell what is beyond them, because there are venetian blinds on the other side of the windowpanes, and the blinds are closed.

Anderson steps inside for a closer look. He calls, "Hello," in a low voice, but there is no response. Then he sees a door in the same wall as the windows. It must lead to a studio space beyond. He goes over to it and puts a hand on the knob. It is locked, but the door has not quite closed, and the latch has not clicked into place. When Anderson pulls, the door opens. He balances the envelope he is carrying on the corner of a nearby desk, so both hands are free. Then, grabbing the door by its edge, he draws it slowly toward him.

The first thing he notices, as the door swings wide, are the strange sounds coming from inside the studio. Moans and grunts of exertion, recognizable as human, but completely inarticulate. Padded surfaces absorbing low velocity impacts. At first, Anderson thinks he is hearing an athletic workout. But something about the sounds is distinctly odd.

Wondering what he is hearing, Anderson slips inside. He finds himself in a sort of vestibule, formed by draperies and screens hung from beams overhead. The immediate space is relatively dark, but the materials surrounding it are light in color. Anderson eases the door shut behind him, then turns toward the source of the sounds. What he sees makes him freeze in midstep.

On the broad, white surface in front of him is a kind of pornographic shadow play. Two life-sized human shapes are visible in profile, one clearly male, the other vividly female. The male figure looks huge, monolithic. The female figure facing him is composed of undulating curves. Her back is arched, accentuating the shape of her bottom and pushing her bosom farther out and higher.

The two figures are upright, but merge at the hips. They lean backward and farther apart, then forward and closer together. Their movements are uninhibited. The male figure's hips thrust forward and back. The female figure's breasts bounce up and down.

As Anderson watches in silence, he realizes this shadow play is being projected by accident from the other side of the photographer's backdrop. The figures causing the shadows are in the position that would normally be occupied by the models. The lights are those the photographer might use to illuminate his subjects. The couple have simply chosen this somewhat theatrical setting for a sexual interlude. They probably have no idea they could be observed.

Anderson walks softly to the right hand edge of the backdrop and parts the curtains where they join at the corner. Despite the shadows he has just been watching, he can hardly believe what he sees. The man and woman are naked in the blaze of spotlights.

The woman is Shannon. She is being held out in front of the man, as though on display. Her legs are wrapped around his hips. Her eyes are closed, and her hair hangs loose. Sweat glistens on her bobbing breasts. Her nipples are dark and their tips extended. The muscles across her stomach tighten and relax as her torso is raised and lowered.

The man is turned away, so Anderson cannot see his face. But his identity is unmistakable. No one else Anderson has ever seen could look so enormous. No one else Anderson has ever known could suspend Shannon in front of him with so little effort.

The man stands with his legs slightly apart. He has a hand on either side of Shannon's waist. With regular, rhythmic movements, he pumps her body up and down. It's as though he were using the lightest setting for biceps on an exercise machine. He moves mechanically, as though in a trance.

Anderson is transfixed. He can't seem to move or speak. He can only stare at the strange conjunction of bodies. The gross, white flesh of the man called Brian makes Shannon's long and healthy figure look small and downright frail.

As Anderson stands there watching them, Shannon's eyes open slightly. She sees him. Her gaze locks with his. She seems to look deep into his eyes. Her eyes remain glazed, her eyelids partly lowered. But there is no doubt about what she is seeing.

With each pumping motion, Shannon's head tilts slightly back and forth. Her mouth is open. A series of low sounds, half moans, half cries, seem to come from her chest. Yet her eyes never leave Anderson's.

The movements of the big man's arms seem to quicken. The

sounds Shannon is making seem to be urging him to greater efforts. For the first time, his breathing becomes labored.

Then, still staring into Anderson's eyes, Shannon begins to come. Her body bucks, as she gasps for air. Her movements grow more violent. Finally, as her head is thrown more wildly about, her eyelids begin to close again. But Anderson knows the only thing she is seeing as she reaches her climax is his face watching hers.

For Anderson, the sight would be traumatic, except that it seems to be happening on some film set, not there in front of him. His deeper emotions seem to have gone numb. He is fascinated by what he is seeing, but it is an academic fascination. He is aware of being sexually aroused, but it is a kind of impersonal arousal.

As Shannon recovers from her climax, her eyes again open. Her lips remain parted as she strains to catch her breath. But gradually her face becomes more composed. She looks at Anderson with an expression suitable for a social occasion, as though nothing out of the ordinary were taking place.

Brian remains oblivious to what is happening. He continues to pump her up and down. Now that Shannon is no longer contributing to the motion, the movement becomes much more subdued. But the rhythm itself doesn't falter.

Shannon puts her hand on Brian's arm, as though to restrain him.

Brian realizes something is wrong. He slowly ceases the pumping motion, then turns to see where Shannon is looking. His face registers no surprise at the sight of Anderson, but he eases Shannon off and sets her on her feet.

"I see you remembered the way to my studio," Shannon says, conversationally. She bends over and picks her panties off the floor. Her breasts hang forward once as she does this, then forward a second time as she leans down to put on the panties. As usual, she seems to linger a moment longer than necessary in each of the positions that displays her body to best advantage.

Brian does not turn around, but simply squats to retrieve his clothes and begins pulling them on. His underpants are still inside his enormous blue trousers, and he steps into them both at the same time. He wrestles his partially buttoned, white dress shirt down over his head.

Anderson can't understand their behavior. Why don't the two of them act more embarrassed, considering what they were doing when he walked in? Why isn't Brian more embarrassed simply to see him again? "You're the thug who kidnapped me," he says to the man called Brian.

The big man straightens up, stretching to his full height. He looks at Shannon with raised, but angry eyebrows. The muscles in his arms tense up.

Shannon picks up a lacy bra that hooks in front. She fastens it around her rib cage, then pulls it up over her breasts, wiggling from side to side, to settle them into it. "I warned you he's been having trouble accepting things," she says.

Anderson realizes she is talking to Brian. He looks at the kidnapper, then back at her. "You can't deny what you did," Anderson says.

"We did exactly what you asked us to do," Shannon replies, reaching down to pick up her blouse. "Brian has collaborated with PEP on a number of assignments in the past. His work has always been outstanding." She puts her arms through the blouse's sleeves and begins buttoning it. "When you needed someone to snatch Anderson for you, he was the obvious choice. He did the job with his usual efficiency."

The big man is still staring angrily at Anderson, but as Shannon speaks, he relaxes slightly. "I am not a thug," he says finally, through clenched teeth. "I am a licensed private investigator. I have a master's degree in criminology." He pauses and looks Anderson directly in the eye. "And I wrote every word of my thesis myself."

Shannon laughs as though Brian has just said something very funny. Anderson wonders if she is on the verge of hysteria. Then her mirth subsides, and she looks at Anderson with sympathetic eyes.

"Whatever else we may have done," she says earnestly, "we have always been your loyal employees." She makes a gesture with her long, bare leg, pointing her toe and turning the inside of her thigh toward him. Then she picks up her skirt and steps into it.

"Why should I believe anything you say?" Anderson asks.

"Come on! You know we're not the *real* enemy." She twists her torso sideways to reach the zipper on her skirt. "Brian's far too big to fit inside that motorcycle suit. And *I'm* the one who rescued you when that maniac tried to kill you."

"What about the photographs in Peterson's apartment? I know you faked those so it would look like they included me."

"I only produced the photographs you asked for, to include what you wanted them to include. I made photographs for *your* apartment, to *your* specifications."

"If I were Peterson, why would I need those photographs to be faked?"

"You like things faked!"

"Show me the original exposures, then! Show me the photographs you used to make those fakes! Have you still got them? I want to see where the images came from!" He looks around the studio and spots a row of filing cabinets beneath a counter running along the far wall. "Are they in those cabinets over there?"

Anderson walks over to one of the filing cabinets and pulls open a drawer. It is filled with hanging files bulging with material. The tabs at the top edge of each file are labeled only with code letters and dates. Anderson takes out a file and dumps it on the counter. Sheets of contact prints come spilling out, alternating with envelopes holding the corresponding negatives.

Even at a glance, it is apparent that the tiny pictures in this pile show buildings and cars, not the kind of images Anderson is seeking. He pulls open another drawer at random. He grabs a file from that drawer, too, and dumps it on the counter. This time, the contact sheets go cascading down to the floor.

"You won't find anything you're looking for in there," Shannon says.

Anderson yanks open another drawer. His latent anger comes bubbling to the surface. "I have a right to know what's going on!" His own words sound inadequate as he hears them. His frustration adds to his anger.

He begins pulling open one drawer after another, grasping the files several at a time, dumping them on the counter and on the floor.

"That's enough of that," Brian says. He grabs Anderson by

the shoulder from behind, squeezing Anderson's muscles and bones with his immense hand as he pulls him slowly back from the filing cabinets.

The physical contact brings memories from the night of the kidnapping flooding into Anderson's mind. Memories of how Brian conned him, drugged him, manhandled him, delivered him to be drowned.

Anderson swings his elbow down and back, propelling it deep into Brian's belly. This causes the kidnapper's grip to loosen enough so that Anderson can break away.

But Anderson's freedom is only momentary. The kidnapper is on him again almost at once, grabbing Anderson's arm and twisting it backward. With a slow, but irresistible movement, he drags Anderson back from the filing cabinets and turns him around.

Anderson tries to pull his arm away. But it feels as though it is caught in a giant wrench. He realizes there is no point in wrestling with someone as big as Brian. He needs a weapon.

But what could he use? On the opposite side of the studio is an enormous mass of chicken wire netting, used to make contoured backdrops. Beside it are rolls of fabric and a table littered with spools of straight wire.

Closer at hand, but still beyond reach, are three spotlights supported by their own stands. All three are switched on. They give off so much light, it is difficult to look at them without being blinded.

Twisting sideways, Anderson sees a wooden stool and a camera tripod, only about eight feet away. The tripod looks heavy. If Anderson could get hold of it, he could at least improve his odds.

Realizing he wouldn't be able to move Brian more than three or four feet, Anderson lunges in the opposite direction, toward the filing cabinets.

Brian pulls him up short and drags him even farther back.

This puts Anderson within five feet of the tripod. His arm feels as though it's about to come out of its socket. His burned forearm aches where it presses against his own back. But Anderson knows this is his best chance. He tilts the upper part of his body back toward Brian and reaches out for the tripod with his leg.

He misjudges the distance. The tripod slides farther away. But he catches a leg of the wooden stool with his toe, drawing it closer, before Brian wrenches him upright again.

The kidnapper switches to a tighter grip, putting his other arm around Anderson's chest. Anderson spins sideways, but can't get free.

Held this close to Brian's body, Anderson smells the big man's sweat. He can't help visualizing what the man was doing to get so overheated. He experiences a delayed response to the idea of Brian and Shannon having sex. A wave of rage rolls through him. He feels as though he is the one who has been violated.

His eyes seek out Shannon. She stands strangely immobile, watching the men's struggle with an expression of profound concentration. Anderson can't tell if she is more concerned for Brian or for him.

Filled with renewed anger, Anderson throws his body first one way, then the other. This forces Brian to take short steps, in order to maintain his balance. After three or four tries, Anderson is able to get his hand on the wooden stool. He lifts it in the air and, with a slight toss, slides his hand down the leg. This moves his grip farther away from the stool's seat.

Tightening his fist around the leg, Anderson swings the stool violently upward and back, so that it just clears his own head.

There is a satisfying impact as the wooden seat connects with Brian's skull.

Anderson can't see Brian, but he visualizes the way the man looked pumping Shannon up and down. He repeats the blow twice more. Brian's grip finally loosens enough to let Anderson break away. With his arm almost useless from pain, Anderson dives for the nearest spotlight.

Brian scoops up the wooden stool that Anderson has just dropped and hurls it at Anderson's back. The stool strikes his shoulders with surprising force.

But Anderson, in the meantime, gets hold of the rod supporting the spotlight. He whirls it around as though he is going to strike Brian with it, slowing its movement only at the last moment.

Brian puts up his arms to defend against the blow, then catches the lamp's reflector in his hands. The hot metal sears his fingers and palms. He lets out an involuntary cry and releases the metal, his face contorting more with anger than with pain.

Anderson remembers how Brian had kicked him in the side when he was lying helpless in the parking lot beside the bar. He presses the lamp forward again, until its metal surface connects with Brian's face.

Brian bellows in pain and staggers backward, his face blotched with crimson where the metal has touched it.

Anderson is startled to see the effect of his actions. He realizes he is capable of a ruthlessness he had never before suspected. When Brian comes at him again, he deliberately plants the hot metal where it will cause the most damage.

Brian cries out, louder than ever.

But this time, Brian manages to grab the cooler supporting rod. With his greater strength, he drives the lampstand back toward Anderson, slamming the base against Anderson's chest.

Anderson falls backward, landing hard on his tailbone, his earlier bruises adding to the pain.

Brian raises the lampstand, preparing to smash it into Anderson's head.

But Anderson rolls sideways as the blow falls and scrambles to his feet behind the mass of chicken wire.

Brian advances at him bare handed, ready to crush him with his fingers.

Anderson grabs the wire netting and flings it across Brian's body. Then, as Brian continues to advance, Anderson tears some of the coiled straight wire off its cardboard spool. As Brian reaches toward him, Anderson tosses the loose wire at Brian's head, getting some of it over Brian's shoulders and around his neck. Pivoting around the big man and throwing out more coils, Anderson gets him thoroughly tangled in the fencing wire and chicken netting.

For a moment, Anderson has a satisfying sense of superiority. By using his wits and seizing the initiative, he has overcome Brian's mindless strength. He glances to where Shannon stands watching, pleased that she is witnessing his triumph. The prospect of Brian advancing on him is now almost amusing.

But when Anderson tries to back off, he finds that he himself is now entangled in the mass of metal strands. He can't take more than two or three steps before the wires pull him up short. They bind him to his antagonist, stretching and contracting with a jangling sound every time either man moves.

Anderson finds if he pulls the wires as far as they will go, he can keep beyond the reach of Brian's long arms. He can even swing the wires around, forcing Brian to keep turning. But Anderson can't get away from him. It seems only a matter of time before Brian closes the gap.

As Brian moves toward him, Anderson uses the slack in the wires to dodge around the metal table. He tries to keep the table between him and Brian, hoping it will help protect him from Brian's crushing grip. But the wires catch on the table and begin sliding it sideways, forcing Anderson into a frantic scramble. The maneuver is awkward, but, for a moment, it seems to be working.

Then Brian plows directly into the table, pushing it with him, reaching across it. There is a loud scraping noise as the table and the mass of wire are propelled along the floor.

Anderson keeps backing away, but finds himself against the wall. The table smashes into him at waist level, pinning him against the brick window casing.

Brian works his arm through the tangle of wire. He gets a grip on Anderson's belt and begins twisting it to apply pressure. It feels to Anderson as though he is being cut in half.

But Anderson is simultaneously able to tighten the wires around Brian's neck. The big man flexes his neck muscles to withstand the tension on the wires. But the individual filaments begin cutting into his flesh.

"Hey, Shannon," Brian calls in a choking voice. "Help me a little here."

"What did you have in mind?" Shannon asks.

"There's a gun," Brian croaks. "In the holster by my suit jacket. Go and get it. Put it in this lunatic's ear."

Shannon disappears from Anderson's sight. There is the noise of another stool being knocked over, followed by the sound of a snap being undone. Then Shannon reappears, holding a pistol. The gun looks very shiny, but rather small. Shannon holds it high and well out from her body. She reaches forward, taking care not to get caught in the tangle of wire.

Anderson senses the gun moving closer to his head. He anticipates the feeling of cold metal against his ear. There is no point in carrying this fight any further. His muscles prepare to surrender.

But Shannon doesn't put the gun in Anderson's ear. She puts it in Brian's.

A look of confusion enters the kidnapper's eyes. He appears as though he is about to speak, but doesn't know what to say.

Anderson leans away, trying instinctively to get as far away from the gun as he can. He is now in less of a crouch than Brian, so he is looking down slightly at Brian's ear.

Shannon says nothing. She merely pushes on Brian's ear with the barrel of the gun.

Brian does not resist the pressure. His head tilts sideways until the gun is pointing almost straight down.

Shannon's finger tightens on the trigger. The gun fires.

The abrupt sound is not especially loud. But it is followed by an absolute silence.

There is no further movement. The tangle of wires holds Brian in the same position he was in before the shot was fired.

For several seconds, the only sound Anderson hears is the thumping of his own heart. Then there is the sound of air rushing into his lungs, as Anderson begins to breathe again.

Shannon remains remarkably still. She looks deeply thoughtful. After a few moments, she removes the gun from Brian's ear. This causes Brian's head to shift slightly.

There is a smell of gunpowder. But nothing else. Only an unnatural stillness.

With the gun now out of the way, Anderson can see the small bullet hole. It is right next to the normal ear hole. Blood oozes from the new hole, filling the cup of Brian's ear and trickling down Brian's massive neck. But there is surprisingly little bleeding.

Anderson finds his mind shutting off all emotion, reasoning as coldly as a computer, running through the mechanics of the situation.

When Shannon had pulled the trigger, Brian's head was the highest part of his body, and his ear was the highest part of his head. The bullet went directly into his brain. His heart must have stopped almost instantly. The position of the body and the stopped heart would account for the lack of bleeding.

The lack of bleeding means Brian is dead.

Shannon wipes the end of the gun barrel against Brian's shirt. Then she takes the gun and tucks it away in her purse.

Anderson remains where he was, tangled in the wire, propped against the table. The same thoughts go round and round in his head. He is too stunned to move.

Shannon is silent for a while longer. Then she reaches out and touches Anderson's arm. She tilts her head toward him and looks into his eyes, her own eyes intense and moist.

"It's Brian's fault," she explains in a low, steady voice. "He was using his knowledge of the murder to blackmail me. He forced me to have sex with him just now. He boasted about the power he had over us. He was going to blackmail you as well. He said he could prove you drowned Anderson. I had no alternative. I had to shoot him. It was for your sake."

Without taking her eyes from his face, she opens a drawer in the table and fumbles inside. Finding what she is looking for, she removes it from the drawer. It is a pair of shears. She uses them to cut the tangle of wires away from Brian's body.

With the wires no longer supporting it, the body begins to slump toward the floor. Shannon grabs the shirt collar, struggling to keep the head higher than the rest, so that it doesn't bleed on anything. "Help me with this," she says. "He's too heavy for me."

Anderson untangles himself from the wires. The table presses toward him as Brian's body leans against it. Anderson slowly squirms his way out from between the table and the wall.

"I can't hold him alone," Shannon warns.

Anderson staggers around and puts his shoulder to the body. It flops over toward him as it slides down the table leg. Anderson finds he has to sit against the body on the floor in order to keep it upright. But he is hardly aware of what he is doing.

"I love you," Shannon says. "Don't worry. I'll make sure you don't get prosecuted for this or anything else. After all, we're in this together." She stops and gives him the sweetest of smiles. "You killed Anderson and concealed the murder with my assistance. Now I've killed Brian, and I'll conceal the murder with your assistance."

Anderson stares at her in a state of shock.

She gets up and begins digging in one of her storage bins. "If we put the body in a giant plastic bag and stash it in my store-room, it won't be found for months. My bank pays the rent on the studio automatically. You and I will be long gone."

Shannon returns with a large bag of dark gray plastic. She puts it over Brian's head, pulls its lower edges outward in each direction, so that they go over Brian's shoulders, and begins working the bag down over his torso.

"Help me do this," she says. "Lean him that way, like this. Now the other way."

Anderson is still too stunned to say anything. In a kind of daze, he carries out the few simple actions Shannon asks of him. He tilts the body first one direction, then the other, so that she can slide the bag farther over it.

Shannon gets the bag down as far as the body's hips. "Okay," she says. "You can let go now."

As Anderson relaxes his grip, she gives the body a hard shove. It slides past the table leg and falls flat, so that it is lying on its back.

"Now I need you to lift the hips," Shannon says.

Anderson stands up and straddles the corpse. He gets both hands around Brian's belt and, using his legs as much as he can, he lifts upward. The weight of the dead body is enormous. Anderson's muscles are shaky. He is unable to get Brian's hips off the floor. But he manages to raise them enough so that Shannon can slide the edge of the bag farther underneath.

"We need another bag," she says, getting to her feet.

Anderson looks up and sees that the plastic bag is already pulled tight over Brian's head.

Shannon returns with another bag and begins sliding it over Brian's feet. With Anderson lifting, as before, she gradually works the plastic up past Brian's hips. When the plastic pulls tight, she fetches a roll of packing tape and begins taping the edge of the outer bag to the inner bag. "Help me turn him over," she says, as the tape reaches the side nearest them.

Anderson kneels on the floor beside her, and the two of them lift and push. For a long moment, it seems as though Brian's body is going to roll back on top of them. But they finally succeed in turning it over. Shannon continues her efforts with the tape, sealing the two bags tightly together. She uses the same shears that she used on the wire to cut the tape. When she has finished she stands up and surveys her work. The entire operation has been remarkably tidy.

She goes over to one of the full length cupboards and takes out a large, canvas drop cloth. Struggling to control its bulk and weight, she wrestles it over to where Brian's body is lying encased in plastic. "Does this look familiar?"

Anderson is still too shaken to figure out what she is talking about. "What do you mean?" he asks.

"It's the same cloth we used for transporting Anderson," Shannon explains, unrolling it beside the body.

Looking at it more closely, Anderson can see that the canvas is streaked with dirt and spotted with pine sap. "Why did you keep it?" he asks.

"You told me to hide it," Shannon says. She pauses and turns toward him as though she has just realized something she wasn't aware of before. "I guess you anticipated a further need for it."

Anderson is aware she is giving him an accusing look, but he has no idea whether he deserves it.

"Help me get him onto the canvas," she says. "But be careful not to puncture the plastic."

The two of them push at the body, until it rolls onto the big drop cloth. Then they take hold of the cloth's edge and lift as hard as they can. This makes the body tumble farther, so that it ends up in the middle of the canvas.

Shannon notices a spot where the plastic has stretched thin. She peels off several strips of packing tape, cutting them with the shears, and using them to reinforce the damaged area.

Satisfied that the body is now well wrapped, she takes a quick turn around the studio. She sees Brian's suit coat lying over a chair and his shoes on the floor beside it. She stows these items in a smaller plastic bag and tosses it on the canvas with the larger ones. Then she checks to see if she has missed anything else.

Apart from the file drawers and the objects disturbed in the fight, everything seems to be in order.

She straightens up the area where Anderson and the kidnap-per had fought, putting the lamps back where they belong, dragging the wire out of the way, and pushing the table back into place.

Her face takes on a blank look of total attentiveness. She walks back and forth giving everything a final inspection. There seem to be no drops of blood on the floor, no real signs of the murder that has just taken place. She looks at the piles of spilled files, but evidently decides to leave them as they are.

"Okay, I think we're ready to go," she says. She folds the sides of the drop cloth inward, so that they cover the body. "My storeroom is at the loading dock level."

"What if someone sees us?" Anderson asks.

"They'll never guess what's in the canvas." She puts her purse strap over her head and shoulder, so that her purse is secure, but out of the way. Then she grasps the edge of the drop cloth nearest the door.

Anderson takes his position beside her, and, together, they begin dragging the body toward the exit. They back directly into one of the hanging cloths, and it slides over them as they pull their load farther.

Passing through the door into the outer office, Shannon spies the large envelope Anderson had been carrying when he arrived. "Is that yours?" she asks.

"It's the photos," Anderson replies. He has a moment of fright, as he realizes how easily he could have left it behind.

Shannon picks up the envelope and sets it on the rolled canvas, so that they are dragging it with them as they continue on their way.

Getting their load around the desks and out the door takes some maneuvering. But they manage it fairly quickly. Anderson stands sweating in the hallway, while Shannon turns off the lights and locks the studio door. Voices and laughter come from another doorway only fifteen feet away. But no one looks out.

They begin dragging the body down the hallway to the freight elevator. The doorways they actually have to pass are blessedly closed. The canvas makes considerable noise, but it slides well on the worn-out floor tiles.

As Anderson watches it being pulled along, he has sudden flashes of being transported in a similar way himself. But was *he* actually the one on the canvas? Or was he merely watching the process and imagining what it would be like?

When they reach the freight elevator, Shannon uses her key to summon it. There is an agonizing wait, while the car comes lumbering up. Finally, it arrives. The outside doors open vertically from a chest-high seam, the top one rising, the bottom lowering. Inside is a safety door made of wire mesh. Shannon raises it manually with the aid of a cloth strap.

The floor of the elevator car is finished with battered, wooden boards, running diagonally across the surface. With Shannon pulling beside him, Anderson tugs the canvas onto it. Feeling shaky, he leans against the side wall and finds it is covered with reddish gray carpeting. It disorients him further.

"Is that you, Shannon?" a voice calls.

Shannon hurries toward the sound. "Hello, Lorraine," she answers, out of sight down the corridor.

"What you doin', girl?" the voice continues.

Anderson looks for a way to start the elevator, but he sees that the heavy brass controls inside need a special key, just like the control outside.

"Just hauling out some used props," Shannon's voice says.

"You throwing stuff away?" the strange voice asks hopefully.

"No, just putting some things in storage," Shannon replies.

"Need any help?" the voice asks, growing closer.

"No, thanks. I can handle it."

"Well, you take care of yourself, honey," the voice says.

"You too," Shannon replies. She backs into the elevator, reaches for the cloth strap dangling from overhead, and yanks the safety mesh shut. Then she shoves her key into the lock and pulls back on the control lever. The elevator car jolts slowly downward.

When they've reached the lowest level, Shannon aligns the elevator floor with the one outside and hoists open the doors. Anderson looks out. They are in a large, dimly lit area lined with numerous storage rooms. Some have wire mesh fronts, while others have ordinary looking walls, with wide, wooden doors. Only a few have solid metal walls with heavy steel doors.

Between the storage rooms, wide passageways, designed for

forklift trucks, extend in all directions. Wooden loading pallets are stacked in the larger area closer at hand.

"My storeroom's down that way," Shannon says, pointing.

They drag the body off the elevator. The floor at this level is rough and dirty. It makes pulling the canvas much harder. In a few moments, they are breathing heavily.

Anderson moves as though in a dream. None of this seems real to him. The dingy setting seems to be something streaming past him, rather than something he is walking through.

As they pass over a particularly rough patch, the envelope balanced on top of the canvas falls to the floor. They stop while Shannon retrieves it.

Anderson notices they are near the loading docks he saw from outside the building. Close by are a cluster of garbage bins and a row of recycling containers, divided into sections for cans, brown glass, clear glass, and green glass. The whole area reeks of rotting oranges and sour milk.

When they have dragged the drop cloth a little bit farther, Shannon stops to unlock her storage room. Anderson is relieved to see it is one of those with a solid metal wall. With a last burst of effort, they get their load through the storeroom door.

Looking around the interior, Anderson sees it is lined with metal shelves holding photographic supplies. Leaning against the shelves are lampstands, tripods, and long cardboard tubes. A bare bulb, dangling from the ceiling, provides light.

The loosely folded canvas lies in the middle of the room, directly below the light. Anderson stares at the cloth surface, finding it hard to believe that Brian's body lies inside. It is almost as easy to imagine the canvas contains his own.

"Come on," Shannon says, taking Anderson by the arm. She reaches up to turn off the light bulb, then leads him back through the door into the public passageway. He hears the door clang shut behind them.

Shannon closes the heavy steel hasp, slips a padlock through the staple, and clicks the lock shut. With a vigorous tug, she verifies that it won't be opened easily without the key.

Then she takes Anderson's arm, guides him physically to a door that opens onto the parking lot, and loads him into her car.

CHAPTER 19

t is several blocks before Anderson is even aware that he is riding in a car. Then he gradually recognizes where he is. They are making their way slowly through the traffic and stop signs of downtown Minneapolis. The buildings outside are familiar to him, but Anderson feels strangely insulated. As though the atmosphere outside were denser than air.

He turns his head toward the driver's seat, where Shannon is sitting. Once more, his attention is caught by her long, slender legs, by the flex of her calves as she works the clutch and brake.

Shannon reaches down, as he watches, and grasps the hem of her skirt. With the most casual of motions, she yanks the skirt higher, making it easier for her legs to move and exposing more of her thighs.

"What are we doing?" Anderson asks.

"Right now? We're driving back to your apartment."

Anderson remembers the circumstances under which he left it, the way he had to flee from the intruder. "It's not safe there," he says.

"We have some business there to take care of."

"I don't think it's a good idea," Anderson insists. "The apartment has been searched recently. Someone else has a key."

"The police?"

"No. I think someone was inside the apartment while I was there yesterday evening."

Shannon reaches over and pats Anderson's leg. "I've still got Brian's gun," she says soothingly. "If someone is in the apartment when we arrive, I'm sure I'll be able to hold him off while we make our getaway. If the apartment is unoccupied, we'll simply put the dead bolts on from inside. Whatever happens, we'll be fine."

As he listens to Shannon's words, Anderson realizes he is now quite frightened of her. The very comments she makes to reassure him have something chilling about them.

It occurs to him that the lawyer's description of Anderson as a 'manipulative personality' actually fits her much better. In fact, he realizes, Shannon is the most extreme example of this he has ever known. No deed is unthinkable to her, if it gets her what she wants.

He studies her beautiful profile, trying to guess what she is planning next. "You've always got things figured, don't you?"

She looks back at him with her head cocked and her eyebrow arched. "I just try to remember the things you've taught me."

Through the car window, Anderson recognizes the suspension cables of the Hennepin Avenue Bridge. He realizes they are now only a few blocks from Peterson's apartment. The idea of going back there fills him with dread.

He considers asking Shannon to let him off. He could take a taxi directly to the airport. He still has thousands of dollars in the pocket of his sports coat. He could travel a long way. He has some vague idea of starting over somewhere else.

But Anderson knows trying to do that would be even crazier than what he is doing now. If he ran away at that moment, he would always have to worry about someone coming after him. He would never really be free of the nightmare he is in. He would always have doubts about who he is and what he has done.

By staying with Shannon, at least for the time being, he might find some of the answers he needs. She must know, for example, whether or not he really is Peterson. She must know more about Peterson's affairs than she has so far revealed. If Anderson is ever going to extricate himself from this situation, rather than just hide from it, he will need her help.

Then, of course, there is the other thing. The thing he is reluctant to admit even to himself. If he is frightened of where this woman is taking him, he is also frightened of leaving her. His body aches at the thought of being separated permanently from hers. Even though he has just seen her kill a man, he still finds her sexually fascinating. It is a fascination he cannot shake off.

A sudden silence and lack of motion interrupts his thoughts. Anderson realizes they have parked outside the apartment building. When Shannon climbs out of the car, Anderson follows her example. He walks beside her to the building's entrance and helps her push through the door.

Entering the lobby, Anderson hears the doorman playing his guitar. The beat of the song is fast, but the chords seem plaintive.

The doorman looks up when they enter and greets them with a nod. "Hello, Mr. Peterson. Good afternoon, Ms. Crosno." He pulls the guitar strap off his neck and leans the instrument against the wall. "Say, Ms. Crosno, how did that zoom telephoto work out? You know, that big monster you needed a special case to transport."

"It worked out just fine," Shannon says. "It took the place of three other lenses, so it wasn't really more to carry."

"I bet you had to take on extra work to pay off the price of that beauty."

Shannon shakes her head in amusement. "Not as much as you might think."

Anderson looks from the doorman to Shannon, then back to the doorman. "I'm surprised you're so concerned about Shannon's business."

The doorman breaks into a big grin. "Ms. Crosno is one of my favorite people. She has even made valuable contributions to my development as an artist. Not as obvious as *your* contributions, of course. But very important." The doorman folds his hands across his chest in a gesture of pride. "When they write my biography, they're going to say: Mr. Peterson was his mentor; Ms. Crosno was his muse."

Shannon beams at him, as though genuinely flattered. "How nice of you to say that."

The doorman reaches beneath the counter and takes out a stack of mail. "This is the mail that's arrived since you last collected it."

"That's something I wanted to ask you about," Anderson says. "Where is the mail stored after it's delivered?"

"I lock it in this cabinet under the counter."

"Who else would have a key to that cabinet?"

"Nobody. Nobody at all."

"Is there any other way someone might be able to get to the mail between the time it is delivered and the time a resident picks it up?"

"I suppose it might be possible, if the mailman was early, and if I was away from the desk for a few minutes when he arrived. But it would be very difficult."

"How about documents sent by courier?" Anderson asks.

"Anyone delivering special or registered mail would be sent directly up to the apartment, unless I had been given special instructions."

"Have there been any deliveries like that recently?"

The doorman looks puzzled. "Sure. Don't you remember? You must have had three or four just since you've been back. Why, I sent someone on up to your apartment only yesterday."

"What time was that?"

"About lunch time. Twelve-thirty, maybe one o'clock. Not much later."

Anderson nods, realizing the delivery must have been intercepted while he was still asleep. The person responsible was either very daring or completely unfraid of running into him. "Okay, I just needed to check. Say, how is your music coming?"

"Great. I'm still struggling with the last couple melodies. But I think I already have most of what I need for my first album."

"That's great news," Shannon exclaims. "Hey, maybe I could do the album cover."

"Would you?" The doorman's eyes glow with excitement. "With your photographic skills, I bet you could make me look really famous. You know, wind blown and well groomed at the same time. Like the guys in *Rolling Stone*."

Anderson nods enthusiastically. "This is something we'll *definitely* have to talk about." He takes Shannon's arm and leads her away, before the doorman can come up with any further ideas.

They walk rapidly up the marble stairway and down the blue carpet. As they approach the door to Peterson's apartment, Anderson is relieved to notice he still has the envelope of photographs under his arm. Shifting it to the other side, he takes the apartment key from his pocket and undoes the lock.

Shannon takes Brian's gun out of her purse. She holds it in front of her, ready to threaten or fire.

"Don't worry," she says in a low voice. "I know how to use these things. One of Mamma's boyfriends was a gun freak. He got a real kick out of teaching Mamma's little girl how to shoot."

Anderson opens the door to the apartment, swinging it wide, but keeping as quiet as he can.

Shannon steps in ahead of him. She takes a few steps in each direction with her gun pointed at the doorways. Then she gestures for Anderson to follow.

He pulls the door shut and tags along behind her. The lights in the apartment are still on, so despite some shadowy areas, it is not hard to see. They move quickly through the entry hall into the lounge with the hunting pictures. Anderson feels a special sympathy for the scenes they portray, but he is not sure whether he feels more like the hunters or the hunted.

With Shannon leading the way, they continue cautiously from room to room. Shannon sheds her shoes, so she can move more silently. Anderson leaves his envelope on the snooker table, so that his hands are free for sudden movements.

Gradually, they develop a rhythm of darting quickly into each successive room, then slowing down once they are inside it. The deeper they go into the apartment, the more silently they move.

As far as Anderson can tell on a quick inspection, everything is exactly as he had left it. There is no sign of an intruder.

They circle through the bedroom and return to the kitchen via the laundry room. The oven is still on, and the uncooked casserole is still sitting beside it. A few inches away is the butcher's knife, exactly where Anderson last saw it. For a moment, he wonders if the whole episode with the intruder was simply a paranoid delusion.

"I need to check something," Anderson says.

Leaving Shannon in the kitchen, he walks back to the office and looks in the desk where the extra credit cards and identifications had been, before they were taken. He finds them still missing. Anderson feels almost relieved. If his memory of the desk drawer is accurate, this at least confirms the apartment was robbed.

He wonders if the intruder will have explored Peterson's other papers. He returns to the front entry hall and examines the piles of mail. The majority of the envelopes and checks from clients seem undisturbed. But the envelopes that held the cash have all disappeared.

Anderson can hardly believe it. He ruffles through the mail again, looking for the envelopes with the telltale bulges and the ends cut open. But there can be no doubt. Over a hundred thousand dollars is missing. It's as though it had never been there.

Anderson walks back into the living room just as Shannon is entering from the dining room. In one hand, she holds an open bottle and two champagne glasses. In the other hand, she carries a champagne bucket, containing a second bottle surrounded by ice.

"Are you okay?" she asks, setting the bucket on a long, narrow table. "You're not still worried about an intruder, are you?"

"I'm fine," Anderson answers. "There are just a lot of things I need to figure out."

Shannon pours champagne into both glasses and brings one over to him. Her movements are as seductive as ever. "Could I help?"

"I'm sure you could. But I'm not sure how." He looks around the bookshelves, noticing the telltale dissertations. The actual contents of these dissertations are no more meaningful to him now than they were before.

"If I *am* Peterson, then I'm still suffering from some kind of amnesia. At least as far as Peterson's affairs are concerned."

"I'm sure the amnesia will only be temporary."

"You offered to guide me. Maybe you could help me remember things. Maybe you could fill in some gaps until my memory returns."

Shannon sits down, crossing her legs. "I'll help you any way I can. Where would you like me to start?"

"I need to know more about my business operations."

"I'll be happy to tell you everything I know. But there are some aspects of your business you never explained to me."

"As I understand it, I've been blackmailing all these people whose dissertations I wrote."

"That's right."

"I demand quarterly payments. These payments are a percentage of my 'clients'' income. Some of them write me checks and declare it as a business expense. Others pay cash and keep our relationship a secret."

"You've got that all exactly right. You see what that shows?! You're getting your memory back."

"It doesn't show anything of the kind. I found the checks and cash in Peterson's mail. I noticed the original dissertations scattered through his bookshelves. It wasn't very difficult to make the connection and deduce what's going on."

"But did you really deduce it? Or did you *remember* it?"

"I told you, I have no memories of being Peterson. I deduced everything."

"I don't think any of your deductions were as obvious as you suppose. Did you really have enough evidence to go on? Or were you jumping to conclusions with the aid of your unconscious knowledge?"

"I explained to you how I figured it out."

"It would have taken a genius to figure it all out that quickly with so little to go on!" Shannon pauses. A slow smile spread across her face. "But then you *are* a genius, aren't you?"

"That's specious reasoning."

"Is it?" Her eyes sparkle. "Would Anderson have used a word like 'specious'?"

"Anderson wasn't uneducated."

"That's not what I asked." She pours herself more champagne, then holds out the bottle.

Anderson extends his glass, letting her fill it. "All right," he says, "let's go back to assuming that I *am* Peterson. How do these different people I'm blackmailing regard me? Which one might have given me reason to fake my own death?"

"I'm afraid I have no idea."

"Didn't I voice my suspicions before we went ahead with the plan? Come on, you were my accomplice! I must have given you some pretty definite reasons for taking such drastic measures."

"I know that something specific happened back in the spring. But you wouldn't talk about it. You told me it would be better if I didn't know."

"What did you *think* happened? You must have had some idea."

"At the time, I was mystified. But now I think it must have

been the first attempt on your life. I think the person in the motorcycle gear tried to kill you. But I don't know who that is. And I don't know why you decided to fake your death instead of neutralizing that person in some other way."

"How did I regard these various people I blackmailed? Didn't I talk about them?"

"Oh, you talked about them, all right. But rarely in personal terms. To you, they were like laboratory specimens. Living examples that you used to support your observations about society."

"And what were my 'observations about society'?"

"You liked to point out that your own experiences were extreme, but also typical."

Anderson looks at her skeptically. "How could I possibly claim my experiences were 'typical'?"

"You said a handful of people in every society generate all the concepts, insights, or ideas that everyone else uses as they go about their daily activities. In other words, from a cultural standpoint, society owes everything to a few creative intellects."

"Not a very unusual observation."

Shannon purses her lips. "Perhaps not. But you went on to draw a rather unsettling conclusion."

"What was this conclusion?"

"That the rest of the population are cultural parasites."

"That wouldn't be a very popular idea."

"No, people don't like to think of themselves as cultural parasites." Shannon smiles. "So they pretend that they are creative too. They 'express themselves' and imagine that this is equivalent to generating new thoughts. They restate other people's ideas in their own words and pretend they have invented them. They become poseurs."

"That seems harmless enough."

"You said it was better than harmless. You said it was extremely useful."

Anderson frowns. "Why?"

"Because it creates the illusion that there are numerous creative intellects around, instead of just a few."

"What makes that so useful?"

"It prevents the genuine creative intellects from provoking

too much resentment. And it allows them to survive by extortion."

"Why extortion?"

"Genuine creative intellects seldom get paid directly for their contributions. They only get paid indirectly, through foundation grants, research posts, and other such devices. You said the way they arrange these payoffs is by threatening the poseurs."

Anderson shakes his head. "I don't understand. What do the creative intellects threaten?"

"They threaten to tell the truth. To expose the cultural poseurs for what they are. To point out where the ideas people pretend are their own really come from. To show how little such people understand the ideas they pretend to have generated."

"So I claimed that what I am doing is standard operating procedure for creative thinkers?!"

"No. You said other creative thinkers are rarely as forthright as you are. But you said the bargaining power of creative thinkers in the real world is always founded on blackmail and intimidation. You said the salaries and royalties paid to creative thinkers are always hush money."

Anderson looks bewildered. "I don't remember any of this!"

"Yes, you do. You're remembering it piece by piece as I tell you."

"Let me see if I've got this straight. I claimed that all these financial payments I extort from people are just the royalties they owe me?"

"That's right. Except that the most valuable things they send you are not the financial payments. The most valuable things are their companies' business projections."

"You mean all those business reports that arrive here in the mail?"

"That's right."

"I'm afraid I put those reports aside without even looking at them. Why are they so valuable?"

"Because they're all confidential, in-house documents. They provide you with the advance information you use to plan your investments."

"You mean I've been making money in the stock market with inside tips?"

"I suppose some people might call it that. You said it was payment in kind. Information handed back for information handed out."

"It must have given me quite an edge in choosing when to buy and when to sell."

Shannon nods, reaching for the bottle. "That's why you're so much richer than any of your clients."

Anderson accepts a refill, then walks over to one of the huge, classical heads. He reaches up and runs his hand from its brow, across its unblinking eye, to the edge of its jaw. He looks at the other art nearby—the abstractly erotic figurines on the tables, the coyly lecherous paintings on the walls. He doesn't understand the details, but the overall decor is making more and more sense.

"These clients of mine must all want me dead."

Shannon shakes her head. "That's the *last* thing most of them want. They need you. They need the help you give them with their work."

"Then they must hate me even more. And the people whose pictures are in those photo albums must hate me most of all."

"You couldn't be more wrong. They love you."

"How could they, when I humiliate them?"

"You don't humiliate them. You liberate them."

"What do you mean?"

"Think what it's like for those poseurs when they go about their daily routines. They are constantly pretending to have knowledge and understanding they don't actually possess. So they have to be constantly on their guard, bluffing, dodging, sidestepping crucial subjects. If they ever slip up, they risk a degree of embarrassment you can hardly imagine. Think of the strain they're under!

"Now think of what it's like for them when they're in your presence. They don't have to pretend to be better than they are, because you already know the worst about them. They don't have to worry about doing anything that could later be used to embarrass them, because you already have worse ways of embarrassing them. They don't have to worry about maintaining your respect, because they know you have long since lost all respect for them.

"You see, despite your low opinion of them, these people know that you *accept* them. In your presence, they can relax, be themselves, let themselves go. For people who've been straining to maintain a pose, this is the greatest of luxuries. It's a luxury they can hardly ever allow themselves. But you make it possible for them!

"When they're with you they don't even have to worry about the further consequences of whatever they might do, because you're the one in control, the one who is always determining what will happen, the one who has final power over all of them! You provide them with what they most need. And they love you for it!"

Shannon pours them more champagne, finishing off the bottle. She sets it on the floor, looking distinctly smug.

Anderson knows he should be repelled by what she is saying, but he can't bring himself to feel that way. There is no real injustice in the society she is describing, because everybody is getting roughly what they deserve. If he is doing better than the others, it is because he is, in some respects, the most deserving. His genuine contributions justify his fortune, even if he does collect it in a roundabout way!

"Wait a minute," Anderson says. "If I have accumulated a sizable fortune, it wouldn't fit into a couple of briefcases full of cash."

"No, hardly."

"So what happened to the rest of the fortune? I certainly didn't intend to leave it behind. Where did I stash it? And in what form?"

"Those are questions I'd like answered too. In fact, that's why I insisted we come back to this apartment. It seemed the best starting point."

"What are you proposing we do?"

"I'm going to help you remember what you did with all that money. With both of us working together, I'm sure we can find it. Then I'm going to help you spend it."

"Why do you assume I'll go along with this?"

"Because we are going to have even more fun in the future than we had in the past."

"What sort of fun are you referring to?"

"All the fun we had with the poseurs. Especially when we made them abandon their poses. I was thinking of how entertainingly they could behave when they were completely free to be themselves. And the times I served as your photographer, documenting the more interesting moments."

"Tell me about those interesting moments."

Shannon takes a large swallow of champagne. "I guess my favorite ones involved your friend the TV anchorwoman. God, did she ever like to do it for the camera! You used to have me there photographing the action just so she'd carry on more. Surely you remember something of that! We used to let her have some of the Polaroids afterward, so she could take them home and admire her own performance."

Shannon smiles. "Remember that dance she did with a bottle? After she told us she wasn't wearing any panties that evening? Remember how she balanced the bottle on a footstool and began dancing over it? Gyrating her hips, lower and lower, until it began to disappear under her skirt?"

As she speaks, Shannon reaches out and picks up the empty champagne bottle. Lying back in her chair, she extends her legs, moving them wide apart. Then she reaches down and tucks the bottle under her skirt. Slowly, under the cover of the fabric, she begins to work the bottle upward.

"Of course, I haven't developed exactly the same skills." Shannon licks her lips. "Every girl has her own specialties."

From the way it presses against her skirt, Anderson can see that Shannon is working the tip of the bottle under the edge of her panties. Then she slides it over toward the middle.

"Remember how the bottle disappeared completely under her skirt? As she lowered herself over it? Twisting first one way, then the other? Going lower and lower? God, I'll never forget that look in her eyes as she *did it*!"

Shannon's own eyes widen, and she lets out a short gasp, as she penetrates herself with the bottle. "Remember the way she straightened up, and danced slowly away? With the bottle remaining out of sight?"

Anderson swallows. He can see that Shannon is easing the bottle farther into herself, advancing it with short, abrupt thrusts. He feels curiously detached, yet undeniably involved.

"It was quite a dance, wasn't it, darling?" Her eyes are glazed and her voice slightly hoarse. "And quite a vanishing act."

Anderson can feel himself perspiring as he watches.

Shannon takes her hand off the bottle and begins to straighten up. "Do you think if I practiced I could develop that kind of muscular control?" She hoists herself on the arms of the chair until she is upright. For a few moments, as she poses there, the bottle remains out of sight beneath her skirt. Then it falls to the carpet.

"I guess I need to keep working at it," she says with a grin. She walks over to the champagne bucket and begins undoing the wire on the second bottle.

As she does this, Anderson is aware that every move is calculated, every position sexually provocative. "You're doing it again, aren't you?" His voice sounds thick.

"Doing what?" she asks.

"Using sex to control me."

"Of course. And you love it." She pauses to undo a button on her blouse, looking over at him to gauge his reaction. "Don't you?"

She turns her attention back to the new champagne bottle, lifting the wire retainer off the end of it, then hoisting the bottle itself out of the bucket. After letting it drip a moment, she wraps it in a towel. Then she begins twisting on the cork.

Anderson walks over to her, holding out his glass. There is a soft 'thup' as the cork pops into her hand. Shannon tilts the bottle to fill Anderson's glass.

"I want to propose a toast," she says, pouring some champagne into her own glass. "To fortune—and to hell with fame!" She tips her head back and splashes the champagne into her mouth.

Anderson drinks at the same time she does, then lowers his glass thoughtfully. "That other person who has been impersonating me—he must be after the fortune too. That must be why this apartment has been searched and why the mail has been intercepted. He doesn't just want me dead. He wants my money."

"Everyone you know wants your money. They also want your power, your brains, your vitality, your body. I want them most of all. I'm willing to do anything to get them. Anything at all. That's why you find me so sexy."

Anderson sets down his glass. He reaches out and puts his

hand behind Shannon's head. Her hair feels soft and thick. He leans forward and kisses her.

She pulls away, interrupting the kiss. "Careful or you'll make me spill." She sets her glass on the table beside his.

Anderson realizes he is breathing heavily. He takes both her hands in his. He lifts her arms, holding them out from her body. He pivots, swinging her around with him.

"Take it easy," she says through pursed lips. She steps backward, curling her shoulders forward to give him a glimpse of her bosom.

But after her earlier behavior, Anderson is not in a mood to be teased.

He slams her up against the wall of books, pinning her arms up and back with his hands. Her hips push in the books on one shelf. Her head pushes in the books on another. He kisses her hard, almost bloodying her lip. Still startled, she tries to turn her head away, but his lips pursue her. He takes her lower lip in his mouth, drawing it across his teeth.

After a few moments, she begins to return his kiss, running her tongue along his upper lip. He lets go of her arm with one hand and puts his palm over her breast. As he fondles her through her blouse, she begins to respond to this too. Her back arches, pushing her breasts toward him. Her hips make a circular movement, rubbing her crotch against his thigh.

Then she turns her head more abruptly to break off the kiss. He hears her gasping as she tries to catch her breath. She puts out her free hand to push him back, trying to slow him down.

"Not yet," Shannon says.

Anderson feels a rush of impatience that she should still be trying to control him. He hooks his fingers over the neckline of her blouse and pulls violently downward, popping the buttons, tearing the fabric. Her eyes grow wide. The blouse falls open.

Her breasts are held high by the lacy bra, thrusting well out from her rib cage. He touches her nipples through the lace. They are hard. He slips his hand inside one cup of the bra, then lifts the bra upward. It flops loosely, across her upper chest, while her breasts bob resiliently below it.

Her eyes show fear, but also eagerness. "I want you to hurt me," she murmurs.

He reaches up and grabs the front of the bra, where it hooks together. With a sharp downward tug, he breaks the fastening, so that the lace cups fall to the sides of her chest. A short cry or moan escapes her mouth. Her deep, excited breaths make her breasts bound higher than ever.

He catches one nipple with his fingertips and pulls the breast inward, so that he can catch the other nipple with his thumb. For a moment, he admires the way the plump hemispheres overflow his hand as he holds them together. His eyes trace the long line of cleavage her breasts make in his grip.

"Hurt me," she says. "You know you want to."

He grazes her nipple with his teeth, causing her to cry out briefly. Releasing the wrist he was pinning against the bookcase, he slides his hand slowly down the tender side of her arm, under her shoulder, and around to her back. He pauses to pull her body toward him. Then his hand continues its course, curving its way lower.

He gives her bottom a rough squeeze. He tries to reach his hand between her legs from behind. But her skirt gets in his way.

"No, wait—" she begins.

But he ignores her. He pulls her away from the bookcase and turns her around in his arms, so that she is now facing away from him. With a sharp, hard movement, he pushes her back toward the bookcase.

As she tilts forward, she puts out her arms to catch herself. Her hands hit the books, pushing two sections of them all the way to the back of the shelves.

He reaches over and grabs the waistband of her skirt. Placing his other hand against the small of her back, he gives the waistband a violent, outward yank. The buttons and zipper tear as completely as the buttons of her blouse had torn a few seconds earlier. The skirt falls in a heap at her feet.

His hands slide around her waist, then up her stomach to her breasts, as he pulls her upright again. He cups her breasts with both hands from behind. Then he slides one hand up her throat, cups her chin with his palm, and inserts three fingers deep into her mouth.

At first, she gags and tries to push the fingers out. But then she relaxes and accepts them, caressing them from underneath with her tongue, holding them against the roof of her mouth.

He pulls his wet fingers from her mouth and runs his hand down her body until his hand is on her panties. He grabs her crotch from outside, feeling her through the thin, lacy fabric.

"Do your other women let you play this way? Will they go as far as I will?"

He moves his hand upward again until it is flat against her lower belly. Then he slides his fingers downward until they are deep inside her panties.

Her legs part as she steps sideways with one foot, trying to maintain her balance. His finger slips into her.

With one hand over her breast and the other between her legs, he drags her backward and sideways until they are up against the table. Releasing his grip, he pushes her forward.

The table edge catches her just below her hips. She falls across the tabletop, breaking her fall with her forearms, then lowering herself, so that she is lying on her chest and belly.

Anderson pushes her forward, so that she slides farther onto the table's surface. Her shoulder hits the champagne bucket, sending it tumbling onto the floor.

Shannon is now face down on the table. She turns her head, trying to see what he is doing. Her legs, from mid-thigh downward, extend over the table's edge. Her knees are bent.

Anderson reaches down and grabs her leg, just inside the knee. He lifts it to the side, so that it has the effect of rolling her over.

Shannon winces as her shoulder and bottom slap against the wood surface, but her eyes blaze with excitement. "Does your co-ed let you do this to her?"

It's a moment before Anderson realizes what she has said. "What co-ed?"

"The one you've been seeing recently. The one from the student bar."

"What do you know about her?" he asks, taken aback.

"I know she's got a big bosom. But her legs are shorter than mine." Shannon's eyes are taunting.

"She's not your concern," he says in a hoarse whisper.

Shannon slowly opens her legs, holding Anderson's gaze, her

expression challenging him to answer. "Will she do everything that I'll do?"

Anderson lets his eyes slide down Shannon's pale body. Her torn blouse and bra lie bunched behind her shoulders. Her only other garment is the dark triangle of her panties. Tiny pearls decorate it near its top and side. His jaw muscles tighten.

"Go ahead," she says. "Hurt me. It's what you want."

Anderson reaches out and tears the panties from her hips. The fabric is surprisingly strong, and it takes all his strength to do it.

She draws her legs up higher, in response to his violence. "That's right," she murmurs. "Hurt me."

Anderson leans forward, hooking his hands over the tops of her thighs. He pulls her toward him, until her hips are over the edge of the table. For a moment, he hesitates, looking down at her.

"Do it," she gasps. "Now. You know you can't wait."

He reaches down and undoes his trousers, tearing at his buttons and zipper as violently as he had torn at hers.

Her legs are open wide, but he pulls them farther to each side, opening them wider.

"Yes," she gasps.

Bending his knees, he pushes into her. A small cry escapes her as he does it.

Almost at once, he begins moving rapidly. Her body is jolted with the force of each thrust. His movements are vigorous, brutal. It is not a way he remembers ever having been before.

Shannon responds with a kind of exuberant intensity, grabbing at his arms, clawing at his chest. "Screw me!" she cries.

He lifts her legs over his arms, holding them up and to the sides. He pulls her hips more toward him. He throws his own body harder against her, thrusting deeper into her, pounding mercilessly at her.

With each thrust, she cries out. There are no longer any syllables in the animal sounds she is making. Each cry is halfway between a scream and a grunt.

His movements become battering, driving, as though he were trying to split her apart from inside. He doesn't know himself any longer.

Her eyes grow wider, then slowly close. Her cries become louder, then turn to pure gasps.

He hears his own gasps, joining at last with hers. He has lost himself completely. He has let go of everything.

When it is over, Anderson collapses against her. His chest is across her chest, his chin by her ear. They lie that way for some time, catching their breath, waiting for their heartbeats to return to normal.

When he moves enough to see her face, Anderson sees that Shannon's eyes are still closed.

Slowly, he pushes himself off her. He stands, looking down at her, not yet steady on his feet.

Already, he can see bruises forming. They are appearing at the places where he handled her roughly and where her clothes bit into her flesh as he was tearing them off. Her face is streaked with tears, her body marked with blotches of red.

Shannon opens her eyes. Gradually, she moves her back, stretching her shoulders. She stares up at him, her eyes large, locking on his. She opens her mouth to speak, but has to swallow and moisten her lips with her tongue before she can find her voice. Her eyes narrow. Her expression becomes a smile.

"Welcome back, Peterson."

nderson wakes to a faint smell of coffee and bacon. Although the odor is alluring, he does not go directly to the breakfast area. Instead, he showers, shaves, and dresses. After checking his appearance in the mirror, he transfers the wallet and keys from yesterday's clothes to his new ones. Finally, he decides he is as ready as he will ever be. Heading for the kitchen, Anderson realizes it's the thought of seeing Shannon that is making him apprehensive.

She is pouring coffee when he enters. "Good morning," she says, cheerfully.

"Good morning," he replies, taking the cup she hands him. He sits down at the table, then lifts his eyes to look at her.

She is elegantly attired in a tight, red jumpsuit. Seeing his surprise, she ventures to explain. "That collection of women's clothing in the dressing room isn't *all* lingerie."

"It looks good on you," he says, cradling his cup in his hands.

"Good enough to tear off me?"

Anderson stirs uncomfortably. "Wait until I've had some coffee."

She smiles at his embarrassment, then turns serious. "There's bacon in the microwave, if you want some. I have to go back to my studio one last time."

"Why?"

"To cancel my business appointments and to arrange for other photographers to take over my contracts. To shut things down."

"What if you don't?"

"If I don't, someone will start checking to see what's happened to me. They'll go to my apartment. They'll come here.

They'll find Brian's body in the next few days, instead of months from now."

"I guess you'd better go do it, then."

"I'm afraid it will take me three or four hours."

"I'll be waiting here for you."

Shannon leans over and kisses him, her eyes promising anything he might want from her. Then she heads toward the front of the apartment.

Anderson doesn't hear the front door close, but the absence of further sounds tells him he is alone. At first, the apartment seems almost startlingly quiet. Then the silence seems to conjure up its own distinctive sounds. The drip of the coffeemaker. The gurgling of the cooling system for the wine cellar. The whir of the dehumidifier near the Jacuzzi.

These sounds are soon joined by others from the recent past that begin seeping from the apartment's walls. Cries of violence. Moans of passion. Shannon's words from the night before begin echoing in Anderson's ears: Hurt me, hurt me. Welcome back, Peterson. Hurt me, hurt me. Welcome back, Peterson.

Anderson tries to make these echoes go away by concentrating on the here and now, by focusing on the physical details around him. But this only makes the other details of the previous evening all the more vivid.

He begins seeing things as well as hearing them. The bruises he remembers inflicting on Shannon's body give way in his mind to the bruises on the body of the drowning victim. The thought makes him shiver violently. Even if he might have been Peterson in the past, he knows he will never accept being Peterson in the future.

He walks down the hallway to the room with the snooker table. He picks up the large brown envelope of photographs he had been toting around the day before. He carries it into the living room, down the steps of the conversation pit, and over to the fireplace. The metal chimney suspended from the ceiling has a chain metal fire curtain hanging from it. Anderson slides it aside. He opens the envelope and dumps the contents on the floor. He picks out the passport and the airline ticket. He sets them on one of the carpeted steps a few feet away. Then he picks up the photos and the empty envelope. He puts these on the fire grate.

He walks back to the dressing room and gets the photo albums. He brings these back to the living room and dumps them on the grate with the loose photos. He goes to the exercise room and takes the photographs off the wall. One by one, he removes them from their frames. He carries the photographs back to the living room and puts those in the fireplace as well.

A handle on the chimney controls the damper. Anderson turns it carefully to the most open position. Then he looks around for matches. There don't seem to be any. But there is a lever on the base of the fire platform labeled "Ignition."

Anderson pulls the lever. A gas jet bursts into flame beneath the grate. The photos and photo albums catch fire almost at once. Smoke billows sideways and then begins to rise. There is a ticking noise as the metal chimney starts heating up.

As he watches the blaze, Anderson is startled by the ringing of a telephone, tucked discreetly under one of the ascending platforms. Even before he picks it up, it seems to have an accusing sound.

"Hello," Anderson says cautiously.

When he hears the muffled, whispering voice on the other end of the line, he is not altogether surprised. "You won't be able to keep it up much longer," the voice tells him. "You're becoming worn out. I've got you where I want you. You won't be able to defend yourself. I'm closing in for the kill."

"Wait a minute—" Anderson says, trying to establish a dialogue.

But the voice continues almost mechanically, building in intensity, growing more and more like a chant. "I'm going to come at you with the biggest knife you ever saw. I'm going to stick it between your legs and start carving upward. Your blood is going to flow like a river. It's going to spread around you like a lake. Your blood and all the pus inside you. It's going to all come pouring out. You're going to be drowning in it, you bastard. I'm going to carve you in two. You're going—"

Anderson hangs up the phone, as the voice continues its litany of violence. He feels a wave of delayed anger at the verbal assault. But it only strengthens his resolve to continue with what he is doing.

Moving faster now, Anderson goes around the bookcases collecting the dissertations. He carries them back to the fireplace and stacks them on the floor beside it. Then he returns to the shelves, looking for any he might have missed.

When he is sure he has collected them all, he begins destroying the volumes, one by one, using his bare hands. He splits their bindings, tears off their covers, divides their pages. He uses his foot to hold the dissertations down, so he can pull at them with both arms. He uses his hands to bend the pieces he is making, so they will no longer lie flat.

Every few minutes, he interrupts his work to add some of the pieces to the fire. With the photo albums already burning and the gas jet still switched on underneath, the dissertation pieces catch fire quickly.

As he nears the bottom of the stack, he comes upon the dissertation by Kolstad. It reminds him of Gretchen. The warmth in her smile when he first saw her across the student bar. The bounce in her walk as she was crossing the University of Minnesota campus. The enthusiasm in her voice as she spoke of Maya mythology. The tears that came to her eyes when she told of her academic frustrations. For a moment, he gazes at the dancing flames. Then he shuts the chain metal fire curtain on the blaze.

Carrying Kolstad's dissertation with him, he walks back to the study and switches on the computer, using a start-up floppy in the absence of any hard disk. When the screen shows it is ready, he loads a standard word processing program.

After a bit of trial and error, he drafts a brief letter to Gretchen's supervisor:

```
Dear Professor Kolstad:
    You must be aware that the career of a
teacher depends on the careers of his
students. Hence, I'm sure you are as eager as
I am to see Gretchen's research go ahead
without any impediments or delays.
                        Sincerely yours,
```

He leaves a few blank lines, so there will be room for his signature, then adds:

P.S.—My lawyers have been provided with the means to enforce my wishes in this matter, should anything prevent me from doing so myself.

He prints this off and carries it into the adjoining office, along with Kolstad's dissertation.

Taking a pen from the top drawer of the desk, he signs the letter with Peterson's name. Then he puts it in an ordinary envelope, seals it, and adds a stamp. Checking the University of Minnesota's listings in the phone book, he addresses the envelope to Professor Kolstad, c/o the Archaeology Department, Ford Hall.

Thinking of Gretchen and her research problems gives Anderson an overwhelming longing for her. With trembling hands, he takes the St. Paul telephone directory out of the lower desk drawer and looks up Harry the Health Nut's. It is on Grand Avenue, in one of the wealthier parts of the city. He remembers the street well. The shops along it tend to be self-consciously fashionable and expensive, but Macalester College is nearby, so there are also makeshift cafés and bookstores. Anderson dials the number.

As he waits for the phone to be answered, he pages through the thesis on Maya ceramics.

"Hello. Harry the Health Nut's." The voice is pleasantly feminine, but with nothing distinctive about it.

"Gretchen?"

"No, this is Regina."

"Is Gretchen there?"

"Just a minute, I'll get her. Who shall I say is calling?"

"Tell her it's the swimmer."

A few seconds later Gretchen's voice is on the line. "Hi. I was hoping you'd call."

"I was going to phone you yesterday, but things got out of control."

"Are you all right?" she asks.

"I think so, but I'm going to have to do something drastic."

"I've been worried about you. I feel terrible about the other night. You were the one in real trouble, and all I did was talk about my own problems."

"That's one of the reasons I phoned you. I've been looking into some things connected with your dissertation supervisor. I'm sure he'll change his mind about your work very soon."

"That's what you said the other night. But I still don't see how you can know that."

"Believe me. You've nothing to worry about as far as your research proposals are concerned."

"What about you? Are you going to be okay?"

"I've figured out what I have to leave behind."

"That sounds like a good start."

"But I can't move on without settling certain things first."

"I couldn't begin to guess what you're referring to. But, at some level, I think I understand. If I can help in any way, just ask."

"I might take you up on that offer."

"I hope you will. It's a very serious offer."

"Good-bye. Take care."

"You too."

Anderson puts down the phone. He picks up Kolstad's dissertation and gets to his feet. His eyes are drawn to the office furnishings. He stands there for a moment, slowly turning his head. Here and there, in the surrounding bookshelves, he sees the gaps left by the missing dissertations. They remind him of broken faces on Maya statues, of holes drilled in Maya pots. The missing bits are not numerous or extensive. But when they are gone, they seem to remove much of Peterson's power.

Anderson carries Kolstad's thesis back to the living room. He tears it into pieces. He adds them to the fire, along with the other dissertation pieces he hadn't added earlier.

Anderson stares at the rising smoke. The ritual vandalism is complete. His problem now is to deal with the person who has been trying to kill him, the person who has been making the threatening phone calls, the person who caused the death of his friends. Anderson can't leave this as a loose end. He must find out who is responsible. He must do something in response to the terrible things that have been done. And he must do it quickly, before the person responsible succeeds in killing him.

Anderson has no notion of how to go about this, so he asks himself how Peterson would approach the problem. Judging from his own dissertation, Peterson would probably see the whole situation as a game. He would then proceed to analyze it as a problem in game theory. This would show Peterson how to take control of the game.

But what *kind* of game is he being presented with?

Anderson tries different variations of the question. What kind of game is he himself supposed to be playing? What kind of game is Shannon playing? What kind of game, in particular, is the person who has been trying to kill him playing?

Suddenly, a possible answer comes to him. 'Treasure hunt'! The person threatening him is after Peterson's loot. Of course, someone is playing other games as well. But one of the key games is definitely 'treasure hunt.'

Okay, assuming the game is 'treasure hunt,' how would Peterson take control of it?

With some amazement, Anderson finds he has this answer as well. Peterson would take control of the game by taking control of the clues that guide the players in their search for the treasure.

How would Peterson take control of these clues?

By making them up! By simply *inventing* the clues that lead the players from one destination to the next. By inventing the treasure map.

Vague memories from his adolescence come back to him. Memories of a 'paper chase,' memories of 'capture the flag.' Pursuing 'treasures' or 'flags' was hardly as exciting as pursuing the opposite sex. But he remembers a distant time when he engaged in both pursuits with equal enthusiasm.

For a few minutes, he hesitates, wondering whether the memories coming back to him are Anderson's or Peterson's. Then he decides to postpone the question. As far as his immediate task is concerned, it doesn't really matter. The point is to think of clues, ones so enticing, no one in pursuit of a treasure could resist following them.

He returns to the office. Taking a sheet of paper from Peterson's desk, he draws an outline of the low promontory that forms the downstream end of Nicollet Island. He labels a street and a nearby bridge to make the location clear. Then he places a mark near the tip of this pointed piece of land. Beside it, he writes a set of numbers that could be coordinates of some kind.

Anyone visiting the tip of the island to see what these markings might mean could be observed from a distance and cornered there. By watching the relevant area, Anderson should be able to find out which client of Peterson's has been trying to kill him. Once he knows this, he will be in a position to scare the client off or to do some kind of deal.

The first step is to hide this 'treasure map' in a place where the fellow impersonating Peterson will find it. This hiding place will itself need to be watched, so Anderson will know when the map is picked up. It should also be a considerable distance from Nicollet Island, so Anderson will have time to position himself on the island before the impersonator can get there.

Anderson can think of only one place to leave the map that meets these requirements.

He folds the map and places it in the most expensive looking envelope he can find. He seals the envelope and writes Peterson's name on the outside. Then he takes out a plain slip of paper and writes down the telephone number for Peterson's apartment. He puts the envelope and the slip of paper in his jacket pocket.

Patting his pocket to make sure he still has the wallet and keys, Anderson leaves the apartment. The doorman is playing his guitar in the lobby. But Anderson hurries by with a wave, before the fellow can start talking obsessively about his future career as a pop star.

Out on the street, Anderson checks the taxi stand that services this apartment building and the adjoining one. He is in luck. A taxi is waiting.

Anderson hurries over and climbs in the back seat. "I'd like to go to Grand Avenue in St. Paul. But could you take the scenic route along the river and then along Summit Avenue?"

"If you want to go slow, it's going to cost you extra."

"You can go as fast as you like. I just want to take that route."

"Okay, you're the boss." The taxi pulls out from the curb.

"Oh, one other thing. Could you stop at a postbox, so I can mail a letter?"

"Anything wrong with that one there?"

"No, that's fine."

The driver pulls up so the mail chute is opposite the taxi's rear window. Anderson cranks the window down and deposits the letter to Professor Kolstad. "Thanks," Anderson says.

The taxi roars off, while Anderson peers out the rear window, trying to make sure he is not being followed. He sees nothing to worry him further.

In just over twenty minutes, the taxi pulls up in front of the health food co-op, where Gretchen works. Tracings in the brickwork show that it used to be a tailor shop, but a bright yellow and green sign announces that it is now HARRY THE HEALTH NUT'S.

Anderson gets out, asking the taxi to wait. He walks over to the shop's entrance, carrying his envelope, and pushes through the front door.

Inside the entrance is an antique cash register. A broad shouldered woman with a cheerful smile sits on a stool behind it. This is presumably Regina. Beside her is a huge, stainless steel urn with a spigot. It seems to be used for dispensing honey.

Anderson nods a greeting to the woman, then turns his attention to the space beyond. The shop is so narrow, there is only room for two aisles. The first is lined with plastic bins, arranged in four tiers, reaching from knee to chest height. The bins have hinged covers of clear plastic. They hold various kinds of grains, lentils, dried fruits, and nuts. Handwritten cards identify the foodstuffs: "PEARLED BARLEY," "COUS COUS," "ORGANIC MILLET," "FALAFEL MIX." Attached to each bin is a large plastic scoop for doling out its contents.

Above the bins against the outside wall are clear plastic hoppers for dispensing additional nuts and lentils. Things like garbanzo beans and sunflower seeds. In the middle of the shop is a Formica counter holding small paper bags and metal scales calibrated in kilograms. As Anderson looks down the aisle, a ponytailed man is using one these scales to weigh something that looks like blackeyed peas.

The second aisle is lined with wooden shelves, holding foods that have been already processed or are more perishable. The containers are mostly large glass jars and small cloth bags. Anderson notices coconut chips and wild rice pancake mix. Again, the labels are handwritten.

Across the back of the store is a large refrigerated compartment, divided into sections. One section holds round cartons of live yogurt, another jugs of unpasteurized apple juice. Gretchen is standing on a stepladder, restocking it. She wears a green sleeveless dress with a white blouse. As she sees Anderson approaching, she flashes him her incredible smile.

Anderson looks up at her, holding his breath. The personal feelings between them seem to require no words. It is only the practical business at hand that makes him speak. He extends the envelope.

"I need you to do three things for me. First, keep this envelope somewhere near the cash register. Second, turn it over to anyone who identifies himself as 'Peterson,' regardless of who that might be. And third, telephone me at this number as soon whoever picks it up has left the store." He holds up the slip of paper with Peterson's number.

Gretchen nods confidently. "That shouldn't be any problem." She takes the envelope and the paper slip.

"Don't let the person who picks up the envelope know you're making the phone call."

"I won't."

"It should happen tomorrow afternoon, but I'm not sure when. If you're going to be off duty at some point, can you have whoever is manning the front counter follow the same instructions? It's very important."

"Don't worry. It'll be taken care of. We used to have some hippie types who were a little too casual about instructions. But everybody who works here these days is extremely reliable."

"I really appreciate the way you're helping me."

"I know you've got to do this, whatever it is. But be careful, okay?"

"I will."

"That beating you took before looked pretty bad. These people you're dealing with could end up killing you, whether that's what they intend or not."

"I won't let it happen again. Not if I can help it, anyway."

"Are you sure you can't involve the police?"

Anderson shakes his head. "If you think people like Kolstad can be unreasonable, you should hear the kind of stuff the police can come up with."

"I guess you're the one who has to decide."

"One other thing. Don't believe anything you hear or read about me in the news. Anything at all. Regardless of what it might be."

"Okay, I won't."

"Thank you for everything," Anderson says. He looks at her a long moment. She seems inexpressibly beautiful. "Good-bye," he says. He turns and starts to walk away.

"Wait," she says.

Anderson stops and turns around.

Gretchen climbs off the ladder and walks toward him. She pauses a foot away and looks into his eyes. Then she reaches up, puts her arms around his neck, and kisses him. It is a kiss reminiscent of the one she gave him the night he stayed with her. Passionate, yielding, and unrestrained.

Finally, and reluctantly, they separate. Anderson goes back to his waiting taxi. "You can take me back by way of the freeway," he tells the driver.

This time it is only about twelve minutes before they reach Peterson's apartment. The time is less than Anderson expected, but it should still give him a sufficient head start, when the envelope is picked up. He pays the driver, tipping him generously.

Back in the apartment's high tech study, Anderson sits down at the computer. It is still on and still loaded with the word processing program. He leans over the keyboard and types:

```
Dear Mr. Peterson,
    Your sealed instructions were opened this
morning and put into effect at one o'clock
this afternoon.

    In accordance with these instructions, we
have placed the envelope that was on deposit
with us in the hands of the managers at 'Harry
```

the Health Nut's Natural Food Co-Op' in St.
Paul. They will release the envelope to you
when you introduce yourself to them and
present identification.

We are proud to provide special services
of this kind to so distinguished a customer,
and we hope you will think of us in the future
when you need further help with complex
transactions.
Sincerely yours,
Carol Dorfer, Accounts Manager

While this is being printed off, Anderson goes back to the
mail in the entry hall. Sorting through the envelopes, he finds
one from Peterson's bank that was not seriously damaged when
he opened it before. He brings it back to the study and pastes
several large denomination stamps on it, so that they cover the
old cancellations. He folds the letter, so it will fit in the envelope.
Then he flattens it out again and adds a scribble that should pass
for a signature.

For a few minutes, Anderson sits there studying his handi-
work. There is no letterhead, and the signature will not match
the ones on any other letters Ms. Dorfer might have sent. But
these things shouldn't matter. Even if the letter is recognized as a
forgery, it will still be seen as a possible clue to what Peterson has
done with his fortune. If the impersonator sees the letter, the
fellow will have to investigate.

The only tricky part might be allowing the impersonator to
see the letter without making him suspicious. But if the impersonator is intercepting Peterson's special delivery mail, that
should solve the problem. All Anderson will need to do is mail
the letter to Peterson's address. If Anderson arranges to be away
from the apartment when the letter is delivered, that will make it
easier for the impersonator to intercept it. The impersonator will
open the letter and go off to investigate.

Once the fellow starts following the false trail, Gretchen will
warn Anderson. Even if the impersonator races directly from the
natural food co-op to Nicollet Island, Anderson should have time

to get to the tip of the island first. From there, he should be able to spring the ambush however he chooses.

"Found something promising?" The voice comes from almost above his head.

Anderson jerks forward in his chair, then realizes the voice is Shannon's. He turns and sees her standing directly behind him. "You startled me."

"I'm sorry." Her eyes are on the letter.

Anderson waves it in the air. "Just one of those business reports that keep arriving in the mail." He folds it casually and tucks it into his jacket pocket, along with the envelope. "I've been thinking. If we knew which companies I held stock in, that might allow us to identify my broker. He, in turn, might be able to give us some information that would help us trace the money."

"Sounds like a good idea."

Anderson gets to his feet. "I think I'll stroll over to one of those brokerage firms on this side of downtown. I'll pose as a prospective investor and find out what kind of data companies keep on their stockholders. That will give us some idea of how to proceed."

"I'll come along."

"No," Anderson says, smiling. "You'd attract too much attention. Even with me there, the male brokers would be lined up three deep around you. Don't worry, I'll be back shortly."

Anderson gives her a quick kiss and heads off. On his way through the entry hall, he stops and places the letter in the envelope. Then he reseals it, using the residue of glue left on the flap.

As he goes out the front door, it occurs to Anderson that Shannon must have her own key. How else could she have walked in on him without warning?

He covers the two blocks to Hennepin Avenue, then starts across the bridge on the far walkway. This bridge is at a higher level than the adjoining river banks. It passes over Nicollet Island without providing access to the island itself. From this vantage point, Anderson will be able to look down on the island landscape. But he won't be able to reach it.

He knows that taking this route on foot makes him vulnerable to attack. But he figures it is worth the risk. He needs to survey the whole area where he will stage the ambush. He needs in particular to see all the approaches to the end of the island and the places where they could be watched.

On the first stretch of the walkway, Anderson can see the lower level bridge that leads to the island itself. It was built with iron girders in the late nineteenth century. There are other ways onto the island, so this bridge wouldn't be suitable for an ambush.

Continuing along the walkway, Anderson reaches the stretch where the Hennepin Avenue bridge is directly over the island. He stops and leans on the railing, checking in each direction for motorcycles. The scattered traffic appears innocent.

With occasional glances at the roadway, he studies the area below. The end of the island is less open than he remembers. Trees and park buildings interrupt the landscape. One of the buildings is huge and has a high wooden tower. It is labeled "Nicollet Island Park" in white letters rimmed with black. Beyond it are boardwalks and picnic facilities.

At first, Anderson is disconcerted by the clutter. He tells himself he shouldn't have trusted his memory so much. But the news isn't all bad. The extra trees and buildings will probably allow him to get closer to the island's tip without being spotted.

Farther downstream is the Third Avenue Bridge and beyond it the complex of locks and dams he observed from the Whitney Hotel. Even at this distance, Anderson can see the heavy mist rising above the torrents of surging water.

He studies the layout a few minutes longer, then continues along Hennepin. But not all the way downtown. When he reaches First Street, he turns left and walks the single block to the Central Post Office. There he mails the letter to himself by overnight registered mail. The clerk tells him it should arrive about nine the following morning.

Walking back from the post office, Anderson feels on top of things. He figures he has the rest of the afternoon to prepare for his encounter with the man who has been trying to murder him. He plans to go out later to buy a shotgun and binoculars. But first he needs to eat and to reassure Shannon.

When he returns to the apartment, she is waiting for him in the living room. "You were burning things, while I was out this morning." Her voice is neutral, her usually mobile face almost expressionless.

"I was just putting my affairs in order. Like you were doing down at your studio."

"Has more of your memory come back, then?"

"Not yet."

"Then how do you know you were burning the right things?" Her tone is still patient, but it is obvious she is struggling to keep it under control.

"I didn't burn anything that would help us trace the money."

"How do you *know*?" This time the challenge in her voice is unmistakable.

Anderson stares back at her, trying to decide how to keep her from taking charge. A bold move occurs to him. "Maybe I was wrong just now. Maybe more of my memory *has* come back."

The tactic seems to work. Shannon is momentarily at a loss. She looks bewildered, then frowns. "If you *can* remember—" she begins.

But the phone rings, cutting her off.

Anderson hurries to answer it before Shannon does. "Hello," he says.

"It's Gretchen. Your envelope was just picked up."

"What?!"

"Someone came by for it. Less than two minutes ago."

"I don't understand. How did that happen?"

"It was just the way you said. A man came in, identifying himself as Peterson. He held out credit cards and other pieces of identification with his name on them. You didn't mention anything about those, so I didn't look too closely. Then he asked if we had something for him. I said 'yes' and gave him the envelope. He thanked me and left."

"What did he look like?"

"Fairly tall, light brown hair, athletic build."

"How old?"

"I don't know. A little younger than you, I guess. But more worn looking."

"How was he dressed?"

"In motorcycle gear. Black leather. A helmet under his arm."

"Okay. Thanks a lot. I really appreciate this."

"You're welcome. Bye."

Anderson puts down the phone. He can hardly believe it. The letter addressed to Peterson could not possibly have been delivered yet! No one could have known about the other envelope. No one but Shannon and Gretchen.

The thought is frightening.

If the envelope really has been picked up by the impersonator, then one of these two women has just betrayed him. Shannon could have read the letter over his shoulder when she crept up behind him, then phoned the impersonator while Anderson was at the post office. Gretchen could have opened the envelope as soon as Anderson left the natural foods shop, then contacted the impersonator any time after that.

Anderson's mind reels. He has no idea whom he can trust. He feels his back breaking into sweat, his heart pounding.

But he pretends he suspects nothing. By a supreme act of will, he relaxes his muscles. "I have one more business appointment," he says, almost too nonchalantly. "Someone might become suspicious if I miss it. But it shouldn't take me long."

Shannon studies his features. "I'll be waiting for you," she says.

"By the way, have you still got that gun?"

"No, I decided I'd better get rid of it. I wiped it off and put it in the storeroom with the body."

Anderson nods, as though he approves. He leaves the room, before Shannon can ask him any questions about his appointment.

When he reaches the entry hall, he takes off his sports jacket, so he will have more freedom of movement. What he really needs is a gun, but there's no time now to get one. Seeing nothing better, he grabs another of Peterson's golf clubs, then hurries out the door.

Striding down the corridor, he weighs the club in his hand. It was the heaviest of the drivers in Peterson's bag. Although hardly a weapon Anderson would have chosen with a little more time, it feels long and solid enough to do the job. This time he is the hunter, not the hunted.

Knowing he must look odd, Anderson is ready with a joke about slicing his ball a long way off the fairway. But he makes it down the hallways and through the lobby without running into anybody.

Reaching the street, Anderson turns left and hurries along the river front on North East Main. A few cars pass him, but there's no one else on foot. After Hennepin, the street goes rapidly downhill, until it is only a few feet above the normal high water mark. Pushing down the incline, Anderson breaks into a run, holding the golf club in front of him like a drum major's baton.

He slows down again where the street levels off in front of the partially deserted buildings of the Riverplace development. Then he turns right across the old bridge. Despite the bridge's iron girder construction, the walkway beneath him is made of wooden planks. The resonant thud of his feet makes Anderson feel conspicuous.

Emerging from the old bridge, Anderson hurries forward to the cross street, then turns left toward his destination at the downstream end of the island. He jogs along the edge of a parking lot, past the building with the tower he had spotted from the bridge walk. Up close, he realizes it's an old warehouse, converted into a park pavilion. Through its many doorways, Anderson can see a large, open floor interrupted only by a few picnic tables.

He is nearing the end of this long pavilion, when he hears the motorcycle. It starts as a low growl somewhere far behind him, but grows rapidly louder. Without even turning to look, Anderson can tell by the sound that it's veering into the parking lot.

Almost by reflex, Anderson darts sideways through the nearest doorway. He scans the interior of the pavilion, trying to decide what possibilities it might offer. But it is clear at a glance there are hardly any. There is no place to hide, if the motorcyclist should look inside. There is no inconspicuous way to look out, to see what the motorcyclist is doing.

Anderson sprints across the concrete floor, heading for the doorways on the opposite side. Just as he reaches the far wall, he hears the motorcycle engine die. His last strides on the concrete echo loudly in the sudden silence.

Then he passes through the doorway and is suddenly aware of the river's roar. Here, in the open air, he feels even more exposed. But at least he has a chance of seeing the motorcyclist before the motorcyclist sees him. The building is now, presumably, between them. But if the biker heads directly for the tip of the island, the fellow will be coming around the end of the building any second.

Anderson looks frantically for cover. Straight ahead of him is the widest channel of the river. Along the shoreline are wooden decks with benches and picnic tables. These are separated from the water by heavy wooden railings with wire grids underneath to prevent people from falling into the rushing current.

Anderson can see no place to hide on these wooden decks. And there aren't enough people about to allow him to merge with a crowd.

To his left, near the tip of the island, the wooden railings give way to thick foliage. Metal signs warn of the water beyond. There would be places to hide among these trees and bushes, but then he would be hiding almost on the spot he had marked on the map. Instead of pointing the way to a nonexistent treasure, the map would be pointing the way to *him*.

Anderson searches for another alternative, but he can't find one. Knowing that he might be spotted at any moment, he plunges into the undergrowth.

He tries to protect his face with his arms and with the golf club. But the branches scratch his cheek and hands. He rolls sideways and looks back, trying to see if his body is shielded from view.

The motorcyclist is walking directly toward him.

Anderson braces for the attack. He can't see the figure's expression, because the visor on the helmet is still lowered. But the way the figure is moving conveys a kind of obsessive anger.

Gripping the golf club in both hands, Anderson prepares to swing from a prone position. He aims at the biker's shoulder, planning to put every bit of strength he has into the blow, as soon as the distance is right.

Then suddenly the motorcyclist is past him.

For a moment, Anderson thinks the helmeted figure is going to attack him from the other side. Then Anderson realizes the biker hadn't seen him. He hears the leather suited figure crashing through the underbrush, oblivious to the branches and brambles, protected by his clothes from the bark and branch ends. Then the sounds are lost in the sounds of the water.

Anderson catches his breath. He hardly dares move. He realizes gratefully that the roar of the river is covering the noises he must be making—the rasp of air being pumped in and out of his lungs, the crackle of twigs under his body. But if the biker were looking his way, any physical movement might reveal his position.

Anderson rolls onto his stomach, trying not to shake the undergrowth around him. Cautiously, he lifts his head.

The motorcyclist is nowhere in sight.

Anderson tucks his elbows under his chest. Pushing the golf club in front of him, he begins to crawl forward. At first, he encounters little more than brush and weeds. He eases himself over a discarded beer can and detours around a tree. Then, abruptly, the foliage ends. Only the open sky and the more distant river scenery are visible ahead.

Anderson lowers his body until his chest and stomach are flat against the ground. Slowly, he squirms forward, until he is at the edge of the vegetation. There the ground drops about five feet. The weeds give way to sand and gravel.

The only thing now left between Anderson and the river is the tiny tip of the island.

The motorcyclist stands at the water's edge. He is facing away from Anderson, about twenty feet away. His helmet is now off his head, dangling by its strap from his arm. In the motorcyclist's hand is the map Anderson drew. The fellow seems to be scanning the opposite bank, looking for something that might correspond to the coordinates Anderson invented.

Anderson realizes he may have only a second or two before the motorcyclist turns around. Trusting the sound of the river to cover his movements, Anderson scrambles to his feet. He slides down the bank and advances toward the figure in leather. He holds the golf club in both hands, tilting it back over his shoulder. He is ready to strike at once, if the man tries to attack or escape.

Anderson stops about eight feet away, so that he won't lose the advantage of the extra reach the golf club gives him. His arms begin to tremble. This leather clad figure in front of him is the man who was trying to kill him, the man who caused his friends to die so horribly, the man who was impersonating Peterson only minutes earlier. As the figure begins to turn, Anderson has a crazy fear that the face will again be his own, that the confrontation will be with himself.

But the face that comes into view is not Anderson's own. It is not even one of the 'clients' Peterson had blackmailed. It is the doorman.

This is the last person Anderson expected. For a moment, he doesn't know what to say or do. "You're—"

"I'm what?" the doorman asks, seeing his surprise. "A 'nobody'? A 'nonentity'?"

"No—"

"Somebody you thought you could take for granted?" The man's face contorts with rage. Tucking the map inside his jacket, he starts toward Anderson.

Anderson raises the golf club.

The doorman draws back, hesitant. Then he smiles. "I'm the most important person in your life. I'm the person who's going to end it."

Despite the threat, Anderson sees this is no monster. It is someone he knows, someone he can to talk to. The man's violent acts must be a response to something terrible Peterson did to him. Whatever it was, it's something Anderson wants to repudiate, something he wants no part of.

"I'm not the man you want to kill," Anderson says. "I'm not Peterson! I've only been impersonating Peterson."

Anderson expects the doorman's fury to diminish. At the very least, he expects him to feel confused.

But the doorman's eyes blaze more than ever. "Do you think I'm an idiot?! Of course you're not Mr. Peterson!"

Now it's Anderson who feels confused. "I don't understand—"

"You only fooled me that first evening. When you came by my desk the next morning, I could tell you weren't Mr. Peterson."

Anderson feels as though the current is pulling the ground out from underneath him. Everything he has been doing is based on the assumption that Peterson was the target of the attacks.

But now the doorman seems to be telling him the real target was Anderson himself.

"If you knew I wasn't Peterson, why have you been trying to kill me?"

"Because you took Mr. Peterson's life. You didn't just kill him either. YOU TOOK HIS LIFE!"

Anderson feels his arms trembling. He begins to lower the golf club, holding it with one hand, reaching out the other for balance. "There's been some kind of misunderstanding."

"Are you denying you killed Mr. Peterson?"

"Not exactly, but—"

"But you don't think you're guilty."

"No, I admit I'm responsible. It's just—"

"That's good, because I know you did it. You killed Mr. Peterson by drowning him. You did it in order to get your hands on Mr. Peterson's money. You're a murderer. You deserve to die."

"I didn't drown him for his money."

"No, that wasn't enough for you, was it? You wanted it all. His clothes. His apartment. His friends. Even his women."

As he speaks, the man unzips a jacket pocket and takes out a snub nosed revolver. He moves slowly, but by the time Anderson sees what he is doing, it's too late to stop him. The man lets the weapon dangle, pointing at the ground, but something in his manner makes it clear he intends to use it.

Anderson realizes his own actions are responsible for much of what is happening, responsible in ways the doorman doesn't even know. But it all seems to have gone wildly awry. He tries to think of some way to explain, some way to reach this man who wants to kill him. But no excuse sounds adequate.

"I never intended the impersonation to go on so long."

"I'm surprised you tried it at all. Did you think you could trick me that easily? I started working for Mr. Peterson years ago. I have worked for him in a number of capacities. Do you hear? A number of capacities!"

"I never doubted it."

"I handled special jobs. Things he wouldn't entrust to anybody else."

"I expect you did."

"Mr. Peterson was helping me with my music. Mr. Peterson

was a genius, you know. He said I had real talent. He said my songs were well worth his attention. 'Well worth'! He helped me make them beautiful. I was going to become a famous singer-songwriter!"

"I'm sure you were."

"If anyone deserves Mr. Peterson's fortune, it's me! That's why I decided to let you live a little longer. So I could find the money Mr. Peterson left behind. That money would be compensation for my lost royalties. Compensation for the fortune I would have made as a singer-songwriter."

"You could still be compensated in other ways."

"No. Nothing could compensate me for losing Mr. Peterson! I loved Mr. Peterson! Loved him, you hear?!"

"I know he was a friend of yours."

"He was the only one who saw I was special. Even when I was being a criminal to buy drugs, he saw what I could become. He saved me from a life without beauty. He showed me how to be creative. I could never do enough for him. Never!"

"But another murder—"

"I owe it to Mr. Peterson to kill the man responsible for his death." A kind of fatal resolve comes into the man's voice. "It will be the last of my special jobs for him."

Anderson senses the new tone and once again raises his club. "Killing me won't get you what you want."

"It will get me justice!"

"It's not the answer."

"Ms. Crosno deserves to die too. She thought she could latch on to me, just like she latched on to Mr. Peterson and then you. That's why she told me to check out the envelope left for you. But, as far as I'm concerned, Ms. Crosno is just a groupie. Did you know that she promised to have sex with me, if I helped her find out where the money went? She's not even a loyal groupie."

Anderson is not entirely surprised, but he still feels stung. It brings back the image of Shannon and Brian making love. It seems more vivid to him now than when it was actually happening. He remembers the casual way Shannon dismounted, her lack of embarrassment, her lack of concern for his feelings.

The doorman seems to sense Anderson's temporary vulnerability. He chooses this moment to make his move. He jumps back to widen the distance between them, letting his helmet fall to the ground. Then he raises the gun, using his free arm to steady his hand, moving the gun sight toward Anderson's chest.

Anderson is quicker than the doorman expects. As the gun comes up, Anderson steps forward and swings the golf club. His aim is true. He strikes the gun solidly with the club head, sending it sailing into the river.

The doorman screams and staggers sideways, clutching one hand with the other.

Anderson sees that the blow which hit the gun has also crushed the fingers which were holding it. For a moment, he feels almost in control of the situation. He stands back, watching, trying to comprehend what he has heard.

Then the spectacle of the doorman's pain reminds him of greater agonies. Suddenly, the rushing water seems louder. Anderson screams above it, as he advances again toward the doorman. "What about Jack and June? What about their unborn baby? Was it your duty to kill them too?"

This time, it's the doorman's turn to look confused. "Those friends of yours? That was an accident. They were just caught in the wrong place. *You* were the only one I was trying to kill. *You're* the murderer!"

The doorman dives forward, reaching out suddenly with his unharmed hand. He hooks the shaft of the golf club with his curled fingers. He slides them up the shaft and gets hold of the club head. With a violent, twisting motion, he wrenches it out of Anderson's hands.

Anderson finds himself unprotected, with the doorman ready to strike at him. His response is to dive for the helmet. He snares it with his hand as his body hits the gravel. Then, before he has stopped sliding, Anderson rolls to the side, getting his feet under his body. He straightens up, holding the helmet in front of him as a shield.

The doorman lashes out with the club, aiming at Anderson's head.

Anderson ducks, lifting the helmet at the same time. There is a whistling sound as the club comes whipping through the air, then a dull gong as it glances off the side of the helmet.

The doorman's arms twist back, like a batter's on the follow-through. He seems surprised at first that his blow has had so little effect. Then he adjusts his aim, swinging this time at Anderson's waist.

Anderson gets the helmet in front of the club. This time, when the club glances off, it hits Anderson's shoulder. Anderson tries to hide the pain, even managing a grim smile.

But the doorman is not deceived. "It's going to hurt more than that," he says. "After what you did to Mr. Peterson, you could *never* suffer enough." He aims the club lower still, aware now that even if the blow is deflected, it is likely to do considerable damage.

Anderson blocks the next blow so accurately, the deflected club misses him entirely. But this makes the club's impact on the helmet so direct, it jolts through his arms. Anderson has all he can do not to let go.

The doorman's next try is from the other side, and again Anderson blocks it. But this time the club's head bounces against his forearm where he was burned. Anderson can't conceal how much it hurts.

"That's what you deserve," the doorman grunts. "That's for Mr. Peterson."

Anderson swings the helmet, trying to go on the offensive. But the doorman's reach with the club is too great. Anderson is forced to draw back.

The two of them are now standing with the water to their side and shoreline curling around them. The wall of trees and brush shields them from the rest of the park. No one else is in sight.

"I'm going to beat your life right out of you," the doorman says. He takes a deeper breath, then starts swinging in a regular rhythm. He drives Anderson steadily back toward the water, shrewdly aiming his blows, so they'll be deflected against Anderson's burned arm.

Anderson withstands the attack for several seconds. But he is losing ground. The river is now only inches behind him. His back foot is already wet. Anderson struggles to keep from falling. He flails the air. His guard is lowered.

The doorman raises his arms for the final blow.

Then someone screams, "Drop it!"

It's a voice like a television cop's, commanding, shrill. For an instant, the doorman hesitates, trying to spot its source. His gaze shifts sideways.

Anderson dives forward. It's a move so unrestrained, his feet leave the ground. With both hands on the helmet, Anderson extends his arms. His elbows lock straight as the helmet connects. It hits the doorman's mouth, slamming his face from nose to chin.

The doorman's eyes close as he falls back, stunned. The club flies loose. He topples backward into the water.

Anderson almost falls into the river after him. But then he regains his balance. He stands there bent over, trying to catch his breath. His eyes are on the doorman, who is drifting farther away.

Only gradually does Anderson realize he has knocked the doorman into the river. Anderson feels a certain satisfaction in this, since the doorman had earlier caused Anderson to fall into the river.

But Anderson doesn't feel anything has been settled. After all, how will he deal with the doorman when the man emerges from the water? Will their conflict resume where it left off? Will Anderson have to try to kill him?

As Anderson thinks these thoughts, he suddenly realizes that the deed is done. The doorman is moving faster and faster. He is being swept into the dam intake.

Anderson watches with morbid fascination. The doorman is sucked down the chute. It is only the first of the many water-works. Anderson knows what this means. The doorman will be smashed and pounded by the terrible forces of the falling water. The churning turbulence will dash him again and again against the concrete barriers. The pressure of the current will drive him against the steel grids that cover the inlets for the hydroelectric turbines. Nearly every bone in the man's body will be broken.

Standing there, listening to the roar of the dam intake, it dawns on Anderson that he has just killed a man. A moment of shaking, sweating terror jerks through his body. Then a wave of revulsion.

Anderson bends over and vomits. He does not lose every-thing in his stomach. But he is in the grip of a nausea he cannot control. He feels faint and shaky. His field of vision contracts. Then, slowly, the nausea passes. His vision clears, and he looks once more at the rushing water.

Anderson realizes that he has experienced this sort of terror and revulsion once before. It was when he drowned the man who was trying to drown him. The feeling is unmistakable. It is the feeling of having killed another human.

Immediately after this realization comes another. He has *only* experienced these feelings *once* before. He may have killed twice, but not three times. He certainly did not kill the old man in the Anderson family albums.

"Are you all right?"

Looking up, Anderson sees Shannon standing beside him. She has walked down the shoreline to this point from the other direction. It was her cry that had saved him.

Although she is obviously addressing Anderson, she is not looking at him. She is watching with a fascination equal to his own the spot in the river where the doorman disappeared.

"I wasn't responsible for my grandfather's death," Anderson says.

"Of course not."

"I thought for a long time I might have been. But now I'm sure I wasn't."

Shannon is now looking down at him with an expression of concern. "Are you sure you're all right?"

"I'm fine."

"You didn't get hit on the head or anything?"

"No, just beaten on the arms and legs." Anderson gets stiffly to his feet, wiping his mouth with his hand.

Shannon puts her hand on his arm to steady him. "I should have warned you about the doorman. He was a drug addict, you know. I'm afraid he had been getting increasingly paranoid."

Still holding him by the arm, she steps around, so that she is looking directly into his eyes. "When you started acting so different after killing Anderson, the doorman thought you must be a different person. I tried to calm him down and get him to see things more realistically, but he thought I was making advances."

Anderson steps back slightly. Then he turns and bends down. He rinses his hand in the river.

When he straightens up again, Shannon puts her hand once again on his arm. "I should have told you how he was behaving. But it never occurred to me that he would be capable of violence. I thought, as you did, that the real threat was from one of your clients."

She steps in front of him again, searching his eyes with hers. "That's why I followed you here. When you said you had a business appointment, I thought you were meeting with a client. I was afraid you might be in danger."

Anderson studies Shannon's face, trying to guess what she is thinking.

She seems genuinely relieved that he was not seriously hurt. Certainly, no one could seem more tender or caring.

Anderson does not let on that he knows she was playing both sides. At least, at the crucial moment, Shannon sided with him.

"My car is here in the parking lot," Shannon says. "We need to go back to your apartment to collect your travel documents and some clothes. Have you got some cash there too?"

"There should still be quite a bit in the pockets of my sports jacket," Anderson answers.

Shannon takes a few steps, then stops, waiting for Anderson to follow. "It'll just take us a minute to grab that stuff. Then I think we'd better head for my apartment. Unless you've got a better idea."

"Not at the moment," Anderson says, starting in the direction she has indicated.

They walk toward her car in silence, leaving a considerable space between their bodies. This time, they sense, there will be no love-making.

Anderson can't decide what his relationship is to Shannon. He has been with her now for many hours. He is eating breakfast in her living room, after spending the night beside her. But the more he sees of her, the less he feels he knows her.

He turns away from the windows and studies the color prints she has chosen for her walls. They are reproductions of lush paintings, showing palm trees and romantic villas. Pinks and reds shimmer against backgrounds of blue and green. Elegantly attired people sip cocktails on terraces overlooking the sea. It's the world she described from her dreams. Yet what does it truly mean to her?

"Come in here!" Shannon calls from the kitchen. "They've got you on television!"

Anderson sets down his coffee and hurries in to where Shannon is standing. She is watching a small television set mounted on a shelf between the stove and the sink. The screen is filled with a picture of Peterson in full beard.

Attending more to the sound, Anderson hears the anchorwoman noting that Peterson "is the sixth person to die this month in an accident on a Minnesota waterway." At first, this sounds like old news, but Anderson can't figure out why the woman is saying 'Peterson,' rather than 'Anderson.' Then Anderson realizes she is talking about something that has just happened, not the drowning of a week before.

The voice coming from the set has the perky, melodious quality typical of morning television, but it sounds slightly strained. "A man who left the limelight to others, Peterson was perhaps best known as a high level consultant to local businesses and as an avid patron of the arts."

While the voice continues, the accompanying picture switches to a videotape, shot from a helicopter. It shows the Mississippi River from the air, tracing its path slowly downstream through the more built up part of the city.

"Police believe that Peterson was strolling by the river near his North Minneapolis home yesterday afternoon, when he lost his footing and fell in. From there he was swept into the complex of dams at St. Anthony Falls. The State Department of Natural Resources issued a statement today reminding Minneapolis residents that the stretch of the Mississippi near Nicollet Island is particularly treacherous, due to the rapid current, dams, and locks. Police were alerted to the possibility that a body had become trapped against one of the dam's gratings, when a university rowing team out practicing yesterday evening found a human arm floating several hundred yards downstream. Peterson's body was recovered in the early hours of the morning by city workers, aided by experts from the Northern States Power Company."

From the videotape of the river, the picture switches to another still photo of Peterson, this time at a formal ceremony, surrounded by public figures.

"When informed of Peterson's death, Minneapolis Mayor Don Fraser said, 'I am sure the entire city will join me in regretting the passing of a man who has done so much to advance local culture.' Senator Dave Durenberger said, 'The state of Minnesota has lost a man of remarkable gifts; he will be greatly missed.' "

The camera draws back from the still photo to reveal the anchorwoman reading the story in the foreground. It is the same one who had reported on Anderson's family tragedy all those years ago, the same one whose sexual exhibitionism had featured in Peterson's album, the same one whose bottle dance Shannon had recreated so vividly two nights before. The woman's eyes are filled with tears.

"The arrangements for memorial services have not yet been announced, but they are expected to be held at Mt. Olivet Lutheran Church." For a moment the newswoman's eyes lose their focus, and she seems in danger of marring her performance with a genuine display of emotion.

Then she swallows and goes on. "In another water incident

384 ■ SCOTT BORG

yesterday evening, a Minnetonka resident lost control of a power boat carrying eight children—"

Shannon reaches over and turns off the television. "I don't understand. Why did they identify the body as yours?"

"The doorman was passing himself off as Peterson. It was part of his efforts to trace the money."

"But why were the police fooled after he was dead?"

"He was carrying some of Peterson's credit cards and other identifications. The zippered pockets in his leather suit would have kept them from being lost. The credit cards and identifications were all plastic or plastic sealed. I guess they survived the effects of the water."

"I suppose his face was battered to the point where it was no longer recognizable."

"I suppose."

"His coloring and size were roughly the same as yours."

Anderson nods soberly. "All the circumstantial evidence would have indicated the body was Peterson's."

Shannon picks up the coffeepot and carries it back into the living room.

Anderson follows.

Shannon pours hot coffee into Anderson's cup, then refills her own. "How soon will they discover their mistake?"

"I don't know. I imagine the Minneapolis Police are a lot more efficient than the sheriff's departments in rural Minnesota. If the doorman has a police record, they might match his fingerprints with those of the body in the next day or two."

"What if the doorman doesn't have a police record?"

"Then they might never discover the body is his."

"Someone will notice he's missing."

"True."

"They'll connect his disappearance with your death, because he works in your building."

"They won't know for sure there's a connection."

"But they'll probably notice that the apartment is in a rather disordered state, that things are missing." A smile spreads slowly across Shannon's face.

Anderson can't see why she is amused. "What are you suggesting?"

"That will give them the explanation they'll be looking for. They'll think the doorman looted your apartment after your death and then fled. If they suspect you were murdered, they'll blame him. You'll be in the clear. As long as you drop out of sight."

"What if the doorman *does* have a police record and the police *do* correct their identification of the body?"

"Then the police will want to ask you a lot of questions."

"I don't think I could handle that."

"Then you'd better not let them find you."

"You mean, regardless of what happens, I'd better drop out of sight."

"Do you see any alternative?" It is not a rhetorical question.

Anderson thinks about it a moment before replying. "Not really," he says.

Shannon shakes her head regretfully. "I knew we'd have to run for it. I was just hoping we'd be able to stay around long enough to figure out what you did with your fortune."

"Maybe we'll be able to trace the money from a distance. Hire a private investigator or something."

"God, I hope so. Anyway, the important thing now is to get out of here. To get out of the country."

Anderson walks over to the window between the living room and the dining area. It faces toward downtown St. Paul. Farther away in that direction is the Minneapolis–St. Paul International Airport.

"We better use the passports and air tickets we've already got," he says. "I don't see any way of getting another passport on short notice."

"You mean you'll travel as Anderson?"

"Why not? If they think Anderson is dead, they won't be looking for him."

"How about Anderson's passport? Do you think there's any danger it's been declared invalid? I mean, since Anderson is legally dead."

"I don't see how they could check every obituary in America against the list of currently valid passports." Anderson tries to remember something about passport controls, but nothing comes to mind. "I suppose there's a risk that Anderson's passport could be caught, but I don't think it would be a very big risk."

"I suppose the sooner we get out of here, the safer it will be."

"Do you know when the flights leave?"

Shannon smiles. "You had me check all the times, remember?" She looks at her watch. "There's one about an hour and a half from now."

"Let's be on it."

With Anderson following her almost reflexively, Shannon hurries down the short hallway to the room that serves as her den. Despite the fact it is almost as large as her bedroom, it seems to be used primarily as a dressing room. She takes out a suitcase and begins filling it with clothes, removing the hangers and laying things flat, but making no effort to smooth or fold. When the suitcase is half full, she takes out her camera and lens cases. She puts these inside and stuffs clothing around them.

Anderson goes back to the bedroom and puts his shaver and toothbrush back in the suitcase he had packed the previous evening at Peterson's apartment. Then he snaps it shut and carries it to the front door.

Shannon walks past him headed for her bathroom and returns in a matter of seconds with her arms full of bottles, a tote bag, and a makeup kit. She adds these to her suitcase, and, a couple of minutes later, is dragging it out into the hall.

Returning to the dining area, Anderson collects the sports jacket he'd left draped over the back of a chair. He puts it on, peering in the breast pocket to be sure it holds his passport and airline ticket, and patting his side pockets to verify they are still full of money.

Shannon, meanwhile, is making sure everything in the kitchen is switched off. "We can take my car to the airport."

"Have you got your ticket and passport?" Anderson asks.

"Of course," Shannon answers, checking in her purse.

Anderson picks up the suitcases as Shannon opens the apartment door. Her case is twice as heavy as his. He carries both cases down the dimly lit corridor to the elevators.

Shannon locks her door and joins him. They ride the elevator down to the ground floor without speaking further. Seeing their reflection in the mirrored walls of the elevator car, Anderson notices they make an attractive couple.

When the doors open, Shannon steps forward to stop them from closing, while Anderson picks up the suitcases. He glances left, toward the lobby, as he starts out of the elevator.

Near the front desk are Berglund and Holmquist. They are facing the other way, interviewing the clerk, but easily recognizable.

Before the suitcases have even cleared the elevator door, Anderson is stepping back in again.

Shannon looks puzzled and starts to lean forward, but Anderson grabs her before she has put her head out.

"The detectives!" he hisses.

"Damn!" Shannon stares wide eyed into space, then hits the button for the second floor. The doors begin to close almost at once.

Anderson feels a crazy impulse to laugh. "If they see me, I'm going to have a hard time explaining why I'm still alive."

"They won't see us," Shannon says. "We can get out of the building through the skyway."

The elevators open on the second floor, revealing an expanse of windows. Shannon picks up the smaller suitcase Anderson packed, while Anderson takes the larger one Shannon packed. Together, they get quickly off the elevator. There is no one in sight.

"Stop there!" Anderson says, as Shannon starts forward. "If we go across the skyway now, they might see us from one of the downstairs windows."

Shannon freezes, looking uncharacteristically rattled. "What are they *doing* here?" she asks.

"Investigating 'Peterson's drowning,' I suppose. They already associate you with me. They probably want to ask you if you've noticed anything suspicious lately."

"I think we should go. They're probably waiting for the elevators by now."

"Okay, but walk slowly and keep your face turned away from the building."

Anderson and Shannon cross the skyway and take the stairway down to street level. This puts them in front of the Minneapolis Convention Center, across the street from Shannon's building. They peer cautiously through the exit, but see no further sign of the detectives.

"What now?" Shannon asks.

Anderson's mind races as he tries to evaluate their options. "Taking your car would probably be less risky than trying to get a taxi. The problem is to reach it without attracting the attention of the desk clerk."

"If we cross the street a few yards to the right, I don't think he can see us."

"Okay, let's try it," Anderson says.

He holds the door for Shannon to go first. The two of them walk up the sidewalk, then across the street, doing their best to look nonchalant while toting suitcases. As they enter the parking ramp, they can see the desk clerk through one of the windows. He is facing the other direction, engrossed in a phone conversation. Shannon's car is only a few spaces from the street entrance. They hurry over to it. She sets the suitcase she is carrying beside it and unlocks the trunk. Anderson hoists the luggage inside, while she starts the engine. In a few seconds, they are driving away, headed for the freeway.

"I don't think he saw us," Shannon says.

"I hope not," Anderson sighs.

Although there is considerable traffic, Shannon's skillful driving gets them to the airport in roughly twenty minutes. She takes the exit for the Hubert H. Humphrey Terminal, where international charters and flights to Latin America generally depart. It's a modest building on the opposite side of the airport from the big domestic terminal.

"We've got nearly an hour," Shannon says, looking at her watch. "I'll go put the car in long term parking. You take the bags and wait for me inside."

"Are you sure that's a good idea? If someone identifies me as Peterson, there could be trouble."

"Relax. There aren't that many people who've seen you since you shaved off your beard. And that picture of you they broadcast is very misleading." She swings into the drive that runs next to the terminal and pulls up in front of an entrance.

Anderson gets out. When Shannon pops the trunk, he

removes the suitcases and closes the lid. Before he has even picked them up again, Shannon drives off.

Looking cautiously around, Anderson notices a huge veterans' cemetery across the roadway. He hopes it's not an omen. With unsteady legs, he carries the suitcases through the automatic doors.

Inside the terminal, his first impression is one of emptiness. There are few travelers to interrupt the wide expanses of linoleum and carpeting. The most striking activity is on the video monitors that hang in pairs from the ceiling, scrolling and blinking in a regular rhythm, announcing arrivals and departures.

Anderson realizes this lack of traffic means there is less chance of running into anyone who could recognize him. But it also means there is no crowd in which to hide.

Straight ahead of Anderson is a newsstand doubling as a gift shop. A sign above it advertises duty free items. He carries the bags over and pretends to inspect the selection of magazines and newspapers. It occurs to him that 'Peterson's drowning' might be reported in the later editions of the local papers. But Anderson doesn't dare check for the story, for fear of calling attention to it.

"There'll be magazines and newspapers on the plane."

Anderson turns and sees Shannon beside him. "We'd better hurry," he says. "Don't international flights require passengers to be there an hour in advance?"

"No one is going to turn us away for being a little bit late if we've got first class tickets."

"But won't we be safer once we're in the boarding area?" Anderson looks nervously each way. He knows he is acting furtive, but by now he has no idea how to act normal.

Shannon is more patient. "If we wait until the last minute to check in, there'll be less time to examine our documents. The more the airline personnel have to hurry, the less attentive they'll be."

"I'm just worried we'll miss the flight. Listen, what if I go through the check-in separately, a little bit ahead of you? That way, if there's a problem with my passport or ticket, you'll still be able to get away."

Shannon thinks for a moment. "Okay. But don't let them lead you off someplace. If there's trouble, I'll slip out and get the car. You try to stall them for a few minutes. Then make a break for it. I'll be in front of the building with the passenger door open and the engine running."

Anderson nods his agreement. He picks up his suitcase and walks toward the check-in area.

The walls and counters in the check-in area are all gray, except for the counter fronts, which are the color of dried blood. There are twenty-four check-in desks, identified by numbers on a black panel running above them. But only a few are in use. Temporary signs on the wall behind announce the airlines, flight numbers, and destinations.

Anderson has no trouble spotting the counter for his flight. There are two men in line ahead of him, obviously traveling together. They hand over their tickets and passports, then hoist their suitcases onto the baggage scale. The man behind the counter consults his computer, processes their tickets, and shifts their luggage to the black rubberized conveyor belt. "Have a nice flight," he says cheerfully, handing the two men their documents and boarding cards.

Finding himself now at the front of the line, Anderson lifts his suitcase onto the scale, then holds out his ticket and passport.

The check-in man takes them with a smile. He types at the computer keyboard and begins to process Anderson's ticket.

Suddenly, there is a loud beep from the computer. The man stops and frowns. He double checks Anderson's passport and ticket. Then he turns back to the computer screen.

Anderson looks anxiously around. He sees Shannon already drifting toward the exit, her suitcase abandoned on the floor.

"We have a package for you, sir," the man announces.

Anderson turns back to the counter.

The check-in man is bent down, extracting something from a cupboard beneath the counter. "This arrived for you by courier this morning," the man says, straightening up. He sets a large padded envelope on the counter. "I just need your signature, acknowledging receipt." He passes a clipboard holding a printed form over to Anderson, pointing to the space where he wants the signature.

Anderson is too surprised to do anything but write his name.

The man withdraws the clipboard. Then he hands Anderson

the padded envelope, along with his ticket, boarding pass, seat assignment, and baggage check. "The plane will be boarding shortly," he says, gesturing toward the corridor that leads to the departure gates. "Enjoy your flight."

Clutching the padded envelope, Anderson walks in the direction the man indicated. When he has covered a dozen yards, he turns back and looks for Shannon.

She is standing just inside the door to the street. When she sees that Anderson hasn't been detained or delayed further, she walks back to her suitcase, picks it up, and gets into line. A couple of minutes later, she is handing over her ticket and passport.

Anderson is too far away to hear what is being said, but the sound of the computer beep carries clear across the terminal. The check-in man bends down and takes out another padded envelope, similar to the one he gave Anderson. Anderson sees Shannon nodding and signing her name. She hands the clipboard back across the counter. Then she accepts the envelope, along with her travel documents.

Anderson walks on to the point where the hand luggage is being inspected. There is more activity here, so Anderson is forced to get into line.

A few seconds later, Shannon gets into line behind him. "What is this?" she asks quietly, holding up her envelope.

"I don't know," Anderson says. "But I think we'd better wait until we're on the plane before we open them."

"It seems to be from some law firm."

Anderson nods. "There's a handwritten note on the outside of mine." He holds up the envelope, so she can see. "Apparently, the law firm was instructed to deliver these the moment they got word of Peterson's death. They've got our names on them, but they're addressed to the airline's check-in desk for international flights."

Shannon looks bewildered. "How did the clerk know he was supposed to hand them over to us?"

"Apparently, the airline put a note in their computer, instructing anyone processing our tickets to make sure we got these packets as well. I suppose it's a service they provide from time to time for businessmen on tight schedules."

"What's going on? This envelope thing gives me the creeps."
Shannon's composure is clearly wearing thin.

"I think I know what's happened."

"Then tell me, for God's sake."

"By using the 'Anderson' identity and presenting these travel
documents *after* the official death of Peterson, we've put the original plan back into action."

"I don't get it."

"It's very simple. We're back on track. We're doing what Peterson intended to do all along. We've picked up the envelopes
he arranged to have sent. We've reactivated the escape route
Peterson set up."

"That you set up."

"Whatever. The point is we've now triggered certain events
which couldn't have been triggered otherwise. We're on our way
out of this mess."

Anderson sees they have now reached the head of the line.
He steps aside, so Shannon can go ahead.

Shannon puts her handbag on the conveyer belt for the X-ray
machine. Then she tries to walk through the metal detector. The
buzzer goes off.

She realizes it must be the padded envelope she is carrying
that is triggering the alarm. For a moment, Shannon looks close
to panic.

Watching her, Anderson realizes for the first time that she is
feeling as much strain as he is.

Then she gets a grip on herself. She steps back and puts the
envelope nervously on the conveyer belt. This time, there is no
alarm as Shannon steps through the metal arch. The padded
envelope passes silently through the X-ray machine. The X-ray
operator makes no comment.

Shannon picks up her purse and the envelope. Glancing casually back to verify that Anderson is following, she strolls on
toward the loading gate.

After observing what happened to Shannon, Anderson puts
his padded envelope on the conveyer belt before walking through
the metal detector. He gets through without incident and picks
up the envelope on the other side.

By the time Anderson catches up with Shannon, her calm seems to have returned.

"What's your seat assignment?" she asks cheerfully.

"Four-C," Anderson replies.

"Mine's Two-A, but I'm sure we'll be able to change seats on the plane."

They walk together toward the departure gate. The plane is already loading, so they weave their way rapidly between the empty rows of waiting room seats. An airline employee glances at their tickets and waves them into line.

When they show their boarding cards inside the plane, the flight attendants lead them off in different directions.

Anderson takes the seat he was assigned. The regular fare section farther down the aisle looks almost full, but first class is largely empty. When the airplane door is closed, Anderson notes that the other seats in his row are vacant, except for one. That one is on the far side and occupied by an elderly lady, who is already falling asleep.

A few moments later, Anderson is joined by Shannon.

She reaches over and holds his hand while they are taxiing and taking off. They both look out the windows as the plane climbs through a layer of clouds.

Then, as the jet levels off, Anderson turns his attention to the padded envelope.

"Go ahead," Shannon says, following the direction of his eyes.

Anderson tears the envelope along the edge where it was sealed with reinforced paper tape. When he has it open, he reaches in and extracts the documents inside. Even at a glance, he can see they are printed on different types of stationery and bear the letterheads of different banks.

Putting the envelope aside, he sorts through the individual documents more carefully. There are five sets of papers, held by five paper clips. The top sheet in each set gives the instructions for accessing a particular bank account. The other sheets list specific transactions.

"What are those?" Shannon asks.

"They're deposit records for bank accounts in the Caribbean and Latin America. They seem to be in dollars."

There is a long silence. Finally, Shannon takes a deep breath. "It's the money, then," she says.

"It looks like it."

Shannon leans over to look more closely at the top sheet in the first set of papers. Then she lifts the paper-clipped corner, to see the top sheet of the next set. "These accounts all seem to be in Anderson's name," she comments. "Does that mean you could withdraw the money using Anderson's passport?"

"I think so," Anderson says. "As long as I have the access numbers that are listed here for each account."

"How much money is there?"

Anderson looks at the last page in each set of documents and does some mental arithmetic. "There seems to be about twenty-three million dollars."

Shannon is again silent. "I didn't realize it would be so much," she says.

Anderson sets the documents on his lap. He picks up the envelope again. He can feel something else inside. He tips the envelope upside down and shakes it slightly. Five keys come tumbling out and land on the other documents.

Anderson picks them up. Each one is stamped with a number. The reverse sides have tiny paper labels with different sets of initials.

"Those must be for safety deposit boxes."

Anderson nods. "There's one for each bank."

"I bet they contain the research notes for the dissertations. It would be good insurance."

"What about your envelope?" Anderson asks.

Shannon weighs it in her hand. It is heavier and thicker than Anderson's. When she shakes it, there are clicking noises as metal bumps against metal.

She tears open the end and pours the contents onto her lap. They include Peterson's watch, his diamond cuff links, and his diamond tie clasp.

A small jackknife tumbles out as well. It has no jewels, but is beautifully crafted and contains a corkscrew.

There is also a slim metal case, about three inches square, apparently made of platinum. It looks like a cigarette case, but it is smaller and much thinner.

Shannon opens it and finds it contains pictures of herself. One is of her head and shoulders. The other shows her posing in a bikini.

Anderson looks over at Shannon and is surprised to see tears running down her face.

"Mementos," she says. She takes out a tissue and blots her eyes, trying to keep her mascara from smearing. "You must really love me," she says.

She picks up the padded envelope and looks inside it. There are papers for her as well. Removing them, she finds they are the records of a dollar account held in the Bahamas. It is in her name.

She turns to the last page. The balance is nearly two million dollars.

"My God, I'm rich!" Her eyes once again overflow with tears. "You wanted to be sure that if I stayed with you, it would never be for financial reasons. That's so sweet." She reaches over and puts her arms around his neck, leaning her head against his shoulder. "Thank you for taking care of me this way."

"I didn't know anything about this."

"Of course you did. And I'm going to find ways of rewarding you that you've never even dreamed about!"

"Peterson arranged it all."

"But *you're* Peterson. You'll gradually come to know that. Your memory will return. In the meantime, I'll take care of you."

The flight attendant comes by carrying a stack of newspapers. "Can I offer you a paper?" she asks. "We've got them from several cities."

"A Minneapolis paper would be fine," Anderson answers.

The attendant hands him a copy of the *Star Tribune,* and he thanks her for it. With trembling hands, he pages through it, looking for Peterson's obituary. He finds it near the end of the first section. The article, obviously inserted at the last minute, is badly written and not very informative. But seeing the words in print brings home the reality of what has happened.

For a long time, Anderson just sits there, clutching the newspaper. Then he realizes he has been dozing. He begins folding up the paper to put it away.

Suddenly, one small part of the obituary catches his attention. It says that Peterson was currently being investigated by the Securities Exchange Commission, because of computer data suggesting the possibility of trades based on inside information.

"What is it?" Shannon asks, suddenly awake, sensing his reaction.

"It's the missing piece," Anderson says. "The motive that started it all. It's why Peterson had wanted to fake his own death. Why everything else happened, why everyone died. Peterson was simply trying to escape the SEC investigators."

"I don't get it."

"It had nothing to do with his clients' response to being blackmailed. You were right about that part. The clients were obviously, on the whole, quite content with the arrangement. In fact, no one had been trying to kill Peterson at all. The only target for premeditated murder, by Peterson or by the doorman, was Anderson!"

"Darling, relax. It's over now. Everything is going to be fine."

"But I'm Anderson, aren't I? Admit it. I'm Anderson!"

"Darling, we'll talk about it later. There'll be lots of time to sort it all out. Right now, you just need to take things one step at a time."

Anderson gradually lets her calm him. There's nothing else he can do on the plane.

The flight attendant brings them a meal of sole meunière and new potatoes, accompanied by Dom Perignon.

Shannon makes small talk about the fashion magazines the plane carries. She is already planning her tropical wardrobe and wants Anderson's reaction to various designs. At first, he is noncommittal. But gradually, as they approach their destination, he begins to catch some of her eagerness.

The captain announces they are starting their descent. The FASTEN SEAT BELT sign goes on.

As the plane comes in for its landing, Anderson and Shannon see the resort area, stretching beyond the airport, like the promised land. The sea in the distance is a deep blue with lighter bands closer to shore. The land is a lush green with curling rows of unexpected colors. There are palm trees and flowering bushes everywhere.

"I knew it would look like this," Shannon says. "Isn't it lovely?"

"Just like your dream," Anderson agrees.

When the airplane stops, Anderson follows Shannon down the aisle. The two of them are among the first off. There is no walkway connecting directly into the airport building, only a metal staircase wheeled across the tarmac to the plane. Their feet clang on the metal treads as they hurry down it.

Over near the terminal, Anderson notices heavily armed soldiers providing airport security. They are standing upright, but look almost asleep. Their presence seems a mere formality.

The tropical air is warm and moist. "Can you smell the flowers?" Shannon asks.

Anderson smiles at her and nods.

They follow the people ahead of them into the terminal. There they find themselves in a line for immigration. Two counters have been set up in a space that is essentially a wide corridor. Behind each is an official checking passports.

The procedure is simple. Each traveler is asked the reason for visiting and the intended length of stay. The answers are always 'vacation' or 'tourism' and 'a few weeks' or less. The name on each passport is compared to the names on the passenger list to be sure they match. Then the official stamps the passport and wishes the traveler a pleasant visit.

Anderson leans toward Shannon, so he can speak to her without being overheard. "If you like, I can go first again. That will warn you what to expect."

Shannon nods. She takes out a makeup mirror and pretends to inspect her flawless face, motioning the people behind her to go on ahead. When four or five have passed her, she tucks the mirror back in her purse and slips back into line.

Anderson is now a half dozen places ahead of her. He gets through immigration fine.

But Shannon is stopped. An officer in an army uniform is summoned from a nearby room.

The officer takes her passport from the immigration official. He holds it up, comparing the picture inside to Shannon's face. "What is your name, please?"

"Shannon Crosno."

"Where are coming from?"

"From Minnesota."

"May I see the envelope you are carrying?"

Shannon tries a look of coy amusement. "I'd rather you didn't. It's personal."

The officer is unbending. "You must show it to me." He takes it from her hand, before she makes any move to hand it over. He opens the end of the envelope and dumps the contents out on the counter. "These are very pretty. But they are *men's* things."

"They were given to me by a gentleman friend. As mementos."

"I am afraid I must inform you that you are being detained at the request of the American authorities."

"May I ask why?"

"It is for the murder of a Mr. Anderson back in Minnesota."

"How could I have murdered Mr. Anderson, when he just went through this line a few places ahead of me?"

The official laughs. "I have traveled widely in America. There are many people from your state of Minnesota who are named Anderson. You evidently killed a different one."

"This is ridiculous," Shannon says.

"You can go back to Minnesota voluntarily this evening. Under escort, of course. Or you can be formally arrested and extradited. It only takes a few days longer."

Shannon is too stunned to reply.

"I think you would prefer to go back this evening. You would not be happy in our jail, even for a few days."

"This isn't right."

"Lieutenant Berglund is seeing to all the arrangements himself."

"But there's no way—"

"The police in Minnesota are also seeking your accomplice. They say he is a private detective. Do you know where he is?"

Shannon looks as though she is the victim of some crazy practical joke and has only just now realized it. For a moment, she seems on the verge of maniacal laughter.

"I've been set up, haven't I? This is all part of Peterson's plan! Like that envelope delivered to me at the airport. I'm right, aren't I? He intended for me to take the fall. Intended it all along! That's why he had me drive to the northern lake. That's why he insisted I help on the night. That's why he told me to keep the drop cloth. The police were never supposed to take the drowning for an accident! They were supposed to blame me!"

"If you would like to dictate a statement, I can arrange to have an English speaking stenographer come here to the airport."

"It doesn't matter what I say! Peterson will have contrived plenty of evidence against me. He's nothing if not thorough! He will have thought of everything! And then there's the matter of the private detective . . ." Her voice trails off as she looks across at Anderson. Her eyes are wild.

Anderson can't tell whether she is accusing him of complicity or hoping he will supply her with a way out. Either way, there is nothing he can think of to do.

Shannon turns back toward the military officer. "I have lots of money," she says.

The officer smiles tolerantly. "Please, don't embarrass yourself. I have turned down offers of money from drug dealers. You could not possibly have as much money as they do."

Shannon looks desperately from side to side. This time what she is thinking is all too apparent. The prospect of being sent back to a Minnesota jail, when she is this close to her dream, is simply too much for her. Shannon starts to run.

"Stop! Halt!" the officer calls.

But Shannon is already dodging through a side door that leads back onto the tarmac.

The officer shouts a command in Spanish. Several soldiers rush to the same exit, hurl the door open, and go pounding through it.

Anderson pushes his way back through the gate and dashes out the door after the soldiers.

Shannon is now running across the runway. The soldiers who serve as airport guards are running after her, shouting in Spanish.

Anderson is behind them, screaming for her to stop, warning that the soldiers will shoot.

There are pools of water at the sides of the runway, left over from a tropical cloudburst. Splashing through them is like running in surf. It slows everyone down, but doesn't stop the chase.

The soldiers fall back, as they see a plane thundering down the runway.

Anderson dashes past them, still running after Shannon.

The plane roars directly toward him.

But Anderson doesn't waver.

Then suddenly the noise is deafening, numbing, blinding, all-enveloping. There is no way to dodge it, because it seems to be everywhere.

From the fact that he can hear it, Anderson knows the plane has missed him. But the blast of its backwash sends him hurtling through the air. He feels himself lifted, twisted sideways, and thrown back.

For a moment, he is upside down. Then his head swings up toward the sky. His foot hits the ground, as though he's skipping, but it seems to be pointed the wrong way.

His shoulders hit as he tucks his head, and he realizes he is somersaulting backward. His knees hit one after another.

Then he is over again and sliding on his upper back. This time, the tumbling is finished.

He lifts his head, before he has even stopped moving.

Shannon is across the runway, but not as far away as Anderson had been expecting. Beyond her is a huge aircraft hangar. Beyond the hangar is a fence. Beyond the fence is a road.

Anderson scrambles to his feet, but he is unsteady and can't run. His limbs are shaky. He has trouble feeling where they are. He has trouble feeling the ground.

As he stares at Shannon, his first impression is that she is heading for the hangar. But then he sees that he is wrong. She is making for the gate that opens onto the road. On the far side of the road are fields of palm trees, stretching apparently forever.

"Don't do it!" he shouts, finally managing to get up some speed.

But Shannon doesn't seem to hear. A moment later, she reaches the gate.

The soldiers call again for her to stop.

Shannon ignores their cries and runs for freedom.

Anderson screams "No!"

A soldier lifts his rifle. He takes aim carefully and shoots.

Shannon is hit before she has made it even halfway across the road.

The soldiers go running over to her, but stop a few feet short.

Anderson catches up to the soldiers. He pushes his way through them and kneels at her side. Shannon is lying on her back. Her eyes are open wide. The bullet has spun her completely around. The exit wound is below her breast. Her blouse is stained with red, and more blood seeps from beneath her.

Anderson gets one hand under her, using it to cover the wound. Then he presses down on the other wound from above. The bleeding is stopped externally. But Anderson can feel her swelling from the bleeding inside.

Shannon is obviously dying. She reaches out for Anderson and murmurs his name.

It is several moments before he realizes that she has called him "Anderson."

Her eyes find his face, and she looks at him questioningly.

Anderson is breathing too hard at first to speak. "I didn't betray you," he finally tells her.

"I know you didn't," she says. "My Anderson wouldn't betray me. And you're my Anderson."

This is the confirmation Anderson needed. But the woman lying on the ground still remains unfathomable to him. "Why did you pretend?" he asks. "I know why you started, but why did you keep it up?"

"I wanted it all to be different. I wanted Peterson to be someone who could love me. I wanted Peterson to be someone like you." Shannon's eyes search his face.

He can see the pain in them, but he can also see that she is unwilling, as yet, to give in. "What is it?" he asks.

"You do love me, don't you?"

Tears come to Anderson's eyes, as he looks at her lying there. He feels more dazzled than ever by the beauty of her face and body. "Yes, I love you," he replies.

"Because I'm rich," she says, managing to smile.

"Because you're rich," Anderson agrees.

Shannon dies as the airport medics arrive with their stretcher.

CHAPTER 22

A huge pyramid rises steeply from the jungle clearing. It is the highest of three that frame a ceremonial plaza ringed with statues. The sun is low in the sky. It illuminates everything with rich golden light.

Gretchen is working near the base of the pyramid. She is standing on a ladder that allows her to reach the head of a large statue. The face of the statue has been partly broken off. Gretchen has a portable wooden platform set up beside the ladder. It holds tools, aluminum foil, cans, instruments, and a notebook. Among the tools is a machete.

Gretchen pries the covers off two of the cans, using the dull edge of the machete. She pours the contents of one can into the other. She stirs the mixture with a wooden stick. Then, using the stick, she spreads it onto a shallow dish made of foil with the edges bent up.

The mixture begins to thicken almost at once. When it has the consistency of modeling clay, Gretchen picks up the whole mass on the foil and presses it against the broken face of the statue.

She works the mixture with her hands, pressing it through the foil, until it has penetrated into the statue's crevices. When she gets it the way she wants it, she stands there holding the mixture in place, waiting for it to set.

Two young men and a slightly older woman emerge from a jungle path onto the plaza. The woman and one of the men carry notebooks and small toolboxes. The other man carries a camera, a tripod, and a measuring stick.

Lagging a little behind these three is a younger girl of Spanish and Mesoamerican extraction. She carries some sort of surveyor's instrument, mounted on another tripod.

"Hey, Gretchen!" the younger girl shouts. "You want to come with us for a drink?"

"Not just now, thanks."

"Miguel has some relatives visiting from Mexico," one of the young men says.

"They're musicians," the other fellow adds.

"There's going to be dancing later," the older woman explains.

Gretchen shakes her head. "I want to make as many of these plastic impressions as I can, before the summer heat gets too intense."

The archaeologists continue on their way, except for the younger girl, who lingers behind. "Gretchen, you should quit that now. You need to socialize more."

"I'm fine, Rosa."

"Too solitary a life is bad for you. You need dancing and music. It will help you get over the sadness you are carrying inside."

"I'm never sad when I can lose myself in my work."

"You must be lonely."

She shakes her head. "When I'm working I never feel alone. I guess it's because I'm so in touch with the past." Gretchen gestures in an arc that takes in the surrounding monuments. "This whole plaza is filled with voices."

"Okay, but you must promise to come around to the cantina later. When the music is playing."

"I promise."

Gretchen returns to her work. After a few minutes, she senses someone watching her. It is a feeling she has had off and on all afternoon. She picks up the machete, but holds it behind her leg, so that it is largely concealed.

She takes a step toward the shadows and stares into them, shading her eyes with her free hand. "You there, show yourself! It is not a manly thing to spy on someone while remaining hidden." She moves toward the edge of the clearing, closer to where the jungle begins. "Step forward or go away! I am ready to talk to you now, even if you are a ghost."

Slowly, a figure emerges from the shadows. It is a man, not a ghost. He walks toward her, his face shaded by a large hat. Then, stepping into a patch of sunlight, he removes the hat, so that she can see his face.

Gretchen realizes it is Anderson.

They look at each other in silence for many seconds.

"I knew you weren't dead," Gretchen says.

"How did you know? I was hoping you would. But how did you?"

"You told me not to believe any news stories I heard about you. The only news stories I heard were the ones saying you were dead."

"I had to leave Minnesota. I couldn't let anyone there know what had happened."

"What are you doing down here?"

"I came to find you. I wanted to find out how your work is going. I wanted to see if there was anything I could do to help."

"Help with what?"

"With your research project. I don't know much about archaeology, but if you tell me which books to read, I'll learn whatever is in them."

"You want to teach yourself archaeology?"

"I know it will take a while. But I discovered last fall that I can pick things up more quickly than I'd thought. And I'm sure I could be helpful in the meantime. At least, with the less technical jobs. I can work long hours. I'm physically strong. I have more money than I know what to do with."

"Why are you telling me all this?"

"I'm sorry. I know I'm saying everything too fast. But I've been thinking about this so much. I've been worried you wouldn't want to see me again. I don't want you to chase me away. It took me months to get up the nerve to approach you."

Gretchen stares at him shaking her head. "I love you, you stupid man."

"If you'd just give me a chance, I'm sure I could show you—"

"I said I love you."

Anderson stops. He can hardly believe he has heard her accurately.

Gretchen drops her machete on the ground. She walks slowly toward him. Her arms go around his neck. Their lips meet.

It is a continuation of their kiss in the natural foods shop all those months before, a continuation of their kiss the night Anderson visited Gretchen's apartment. In some ways, it is as though they have never been apart. In others, it is as though they have been separated for an eternity.

Anderson steps back and looks at her again. His fingers hold hers, but their arms are stretched out as far as they can reach.

His eyes take in the features of Gretchen which had attracted him to her in the first place: her wide, full breasts and her trim legs in short cut-offs.

Somewhere in his changes of identity, all Anderson's feelings of guilt have gotten left behind.

Gretchen sees the way he is eyeing her figure. She breaks into a huge grin. "You know, I think you really *are* sexist!"

"No," Anderson says, "I'm just getting liberated."

A B O U T   T H E   A U T H O R

SCOTT BORG describes himself as "self-educated with some help from the Helmholtz Gymnasium in Frankfurt, the University of Chicago, the London School of Economics, and Yale University." He has worked at various times as a lifeguard, anthropological researcher, commercial photographer's model, university professor, and broadcaster. Although originally from Minnesota, he has spent much of his life in Europe, doing research into cultural history. As a scholar, his major interest has been "that portion of Western thought which was radically new after the Enlightenment." He has lectured in colleges and universities on philosophy of science, art history, psychology, drama, journalism, sociology, comparative literature, and anthropology. In London theater, he served as a playwright, director of actors and writers' workshops, producer's troubleshooter, and as one of eleven judges for the prestigious Olivier Awards. He once spent eighteen months on an anthropological field work expedition, studying ritual activity on the Kerkennah Islands. He has also done extensive work on theoretical problems in molecular genetics. His favorite recreations include skiiing, scuba diving, rock climbing, and wilderness canoeing.